"Ryder ta⸻ ⸻tery."

— *Suspense*

""An acco⸻ ⸻murder mystery, a vivid exploration of the art world, and a meditation on the secrets we keep, Ryder's novel is unlike anything else you will read this summer. . . . *In Malice, Quite Close* is a triumph. Ryder's writing is as gorgeous as the many works of art she describes, and her characters—especially the twisted Tristan and tortured Gisèle—seem to leap right off the page. The novel's many mysteries unfold carefully and beautifully, and readers will be trying to connect the dots until the very last page."

— *BookPage*

"Sophisticates of the contemporary art scene show a lethally sordid side in this superbly crafted murder mystery. . . . Lucid prose, snappy dialogue, and sharp characterization combine to limn a credibly realized world where life imitates art, facades are deceiving, and forgeries cast doubt on seemingly certain truths. The unraveling of the mysteries . . . turns on perfectly prepared surprises and unexpected twists that will have readers guessing, like the characters themselves, until the final paragraphs."

— *Publishers Weekly*

"In her stunning debut, Ryder delivers an assured blend of eros, suspense, abduction, and art. Like a finely aged wine, *In Malice, Quite Close* lingers on the palette with flavors of Fowles, Nabokov, and Ian McEwan, yet it is entirely unique. Ryder sweeps the reader back and forth over two decades and across the continent, from San Francisco to New York and to a remote art colony in the Pacific Northwest in this compulsively readable novel of ideas, intrigue, and mystery."

— J. Sydney Jones, author of *The Empty Mirror* and *Requiem in Vienna*

"What a deft hand newcomer Ryder uses in telling this tale of an innocent muse caught in a web of artistic obsession. No one is wholly innocent, though, and every character has secrets in this extraordinarily well-plotted tale that holds its final revelations for the very last page."

— Cammie McGovern, author of *Eye Contact* and *Neighborhood Watch*

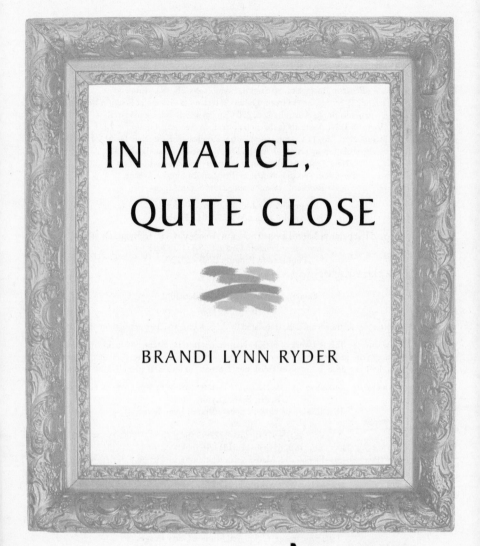

IN MALICE, QUITE CLOSE

BRANDI LYNN RYDER

PENGUIN BOOKS

PENGUIN BOOKS

Published by the Penguin Group

Penguin Group (USA) Inc., 375 Hudson Street, New York, New York 10014, U.S.A.
Penguin Group (Canada), 90 Eglinton Avenue East, Suite 700, Toronto,
Ontario, Canada M4P 2Y3 (a division of Pearson Penguin Canada Inc.)
Penguin Books Ltd, 80 Strand, London WC2R 0RL, England
Penguin Ireland, 25 St. Stephen's Green, Dublin 2, Ireland (a division of Penguin Books Ltd)
Penguin Books Australia Ltd, 250 Camberwell Road, Camberwell,
Victoria 3124, Australia (a division of Pearson Australia Group Pty Ltd)
Penguin Books India Pvt Ltd, 11 Community Centre, Panchsheel Park, New Delhi – 110 017, India
Penguin Group (NZ), 67 Apollo Drive, Rosedale, Auckland 0632,
New Zealand (a division of Pearson New Zealand Ltd)
Penguin Books (South Africa) (Pty) Ltd, 24 Sturdee Avenue,
Rosebank, Johannesburg 2196, South Africa

Penguin Books Ltd, Registered Offices:
80 Strand, London WC2R 0RL, England

First published in the United States of America by Viking Penguin,
a member of Penguin Group (USA) Inc. 2011
Published in Penguin Books 2012

1   3   5   7   9   10   8   6   4   2

"Premiere Soiree" by Arthur Rimbaud, translated by A. S. Kline. Used by permission of A. S. Kline.

PUBLISHER'S NOTE: This is a work of fiction. Names, characters, places, and incidents either are
the product of the author's imagination or are used fictitiously, and any resemblance to actual
persons, living or dead, business establishments, events, or locales is entirely coincidental.

THE LIBRARY OF CONGRESS HAS CATALOGED THE HARDCOVER EDITION AS FOLLOWS:
Ryder, Brandi Lynn.
In malice, quite close : a novel / Brandi Lynn Ryder.
p. cm.
ISBN 978-0-670-02279-3 (hc.)
ISBN 978-0-14-312117-6 (pbk.)
1. Identity (Psychology)—Fiction.   2. Man-woman relationships—Fiction.   3. Art—Collectors
and collecting—Fiction.   4. Rich people—Fiction.   5. Psychological fiction.   I. Title.
PS3618.Y35515 2011
813'.6—dc22   2011004126

Printed in the United States of America
Designed by Nancy Resnick
Title page image: C Squared Studios/Getty Images

ALWAYS LEARNING   PEARSON

For those who first believed in my make-believe:
Mom, Dad, my sister, Charmelle—who taught me to read—
and for my grandfather, my first reader, in loving memory.

FIRST EVENING
(PREMIÈRE SOIRÉE)

She was barely dressed though,
And the great indiscreet trees
Touched the glass with their leaves,
In malice, quite close, quite close.

Sitting in my deep chair,
Half-naked, hands clasped together,
On the floor, little feet, so fine,
So fine, shivered with pleasure.

I watched, the beeswax color
Of a truant ray of sun's glow
Flit about her smile, and over
Her breast—a fly on the rose.

I kissed her delicate ankle.
She gave an abrupt sweet giggle
Chiming in clear trills,
A pretty laugh of crystal.

Her little feet under her slip
Sped away: 'Will you desist!'
Allowing that first bold act,
Her laugh pretended to punish!

Trembling under my lips,
Poor things, I gently kissed her lids.
She threw her vapid head back.
'Oh! That's worse, that is!'

'Sir, I've two words to say to you . . .'
I planted the rest on her breast
In a kiss that made her laugh
With a laugh of readiness. . . .

She was barely dressed though,
And the great indiscreet trees
Touched the glass with their leaves
In malice, quite close, quite close.

—Arthur Rimbaud (Translation by A. S. Kline)

THE COLLECTOR

This is my apology.

There is no other word for it. It is a true account, but it's my truth alone. I tell you this at the start, for while I regret the end, I will no doubt justify the means and this must not move you. I have come to see I'm incapable of drawing clear moral distinctions. For me the question of what can or cannot be done has never been an ethical one. There is no line I cannot smudge with my thumb.

I have always been undone by beautiful things, and it might be said that beauty itself was my quarry. The intangible made flesh. I never set out to "abduct" anyone. I find the very word distasteful, for it establishes so gross an imbalance between subject and object. Beauty and the beholder are complicit in their crimes, you see. And I have been slave to my nature as much as master.

Ah, but what would I be if not for that day? For February, it was tantalizingly warm along the bay, the sun returning with renewed ardor after days of fog and rain. To think that one's fate rests upon the weather—upon a sky so very blue and clouds so starchy white. To think that it rests in the movement of sunlight upon a silken dress.

It was 1979. I was by then thirty-four years of age and found myself in a Ritz-Carlton suite in the city of San Francisco for a short trip that turned quite long. It was her city. I wanted her as soon as I saw her. And I took her.

I should state that I'm as sane as the next man. I bear no traces of the illness that plagued my father. Nor was I unduly traumatized by childhood. Paris was the setting of my formative years, and I inherited its paradoxes as well as those of my parents. My father: staunch Catholic *noblesse ancienne*, my mother a Breton, with bloodlines saturated in magic and druidry. I was their only child. A second son was stillborn—all I remember of him is a tiny, somber coffin—and thus my childhood was both cloistered and wildly indulgent.

From the start I felt a conscious dislocation from the world around me. We were an aristocratic family in a time when aristocracy was meaningless, living in a city made magical by history at a time when history had no following. The Paris into which I was born had been crippled by the war, and the great houses in the quarter of Saint-Germain-des-Prés stood apart like guests who arrive overdressed to a party: silent and self-conscious, the subject of murmuring curiosity but no understanding. In 1945, we were not supposed to exist.

I went to no proper school at all before university but took lessons at home: an opulent, sensual arena in which visitors came and went like audiences to the seasonal programme: artists and poets, musicians and professors, art dealers and collectors. All were in our employ, more or less, jesters eager to please the king. Papa was termed "eccentric"—a man of less privileged birth would have been committed. I found his mania intoxicating, and even his melancholy seemed romantic to a child who did not understand the blackness at its heart.

As a result of his condition and of many a neglectful nanny, I had early access to a variety of mind-altering drugs, so that there are events of my childhood I'm not entirely certain weren't drug-induced visions. I had many intricate dialogues with God that I'd like to believe were real, as they proved quite enlightening—and of course rather flattering—but which I tend to believe were not, as I haven't yet been able to reengage Him.

As I was growing up, my heroes were all madmen of a sort. Madness, my mother said, defined great men, just as fear defined weak ones. It seemed wise to adopt her opinion. My ancestors range from the visionary to the criminal, and I am named for a good many of them (Tristan Leandre Jourdain Mourault III). My surname is a dignified one in my native land, translating roughly to "little dark." I've always thought of this as dusk, just before night and beyond the normalcy of day. It is where we have always existed.

My obsession with beauty began in infancy. I was mesmerized by pictures, by flowers and faces, by the lovely symmetry that even the undiscriminating eye terms beautiful. Though Papa was heir to a fortune in impressionist art, Maman was the true aesthete. I often think of the Mourault Collection as hers alone. She took the paintings like lovers and knew all their stories: the gentle, arthritic Renoir, the tempers of Degas, the humiliations of Lautrec, and the infidelities of Monet. She wove wondrous tales around them, audacious and certainly fictive. Maman knew that the power of a painting, of any beautiful thing, is not in itself but in its afterlife. Not the thing of a moment but a perpetual quest.

My own quests began at the age of five. At my birthday party, I cornered the lovely Yvette Desmarais in the garden. Never was there a more satisfying game of *cache-cache*, or as you say, hide-and-seek. Those wide eyes, the color of ice on a gray day, and the lines of her bow-tie mouth. She began to scream yet in subsequent years took to writing me love letters. The paradox was instructive.

Later I exercised more discretion but found great delight in spying upon one of our maids, Martine, at her bath. I did so guiltlessly; it was not so very different from gazing upon the creamy flesh of Renoir's nudes. Only I preferred my art living.

I hesitate to say I was sex-obsessed. I had not so much an unquenchable appetite as an exacting one, and as a result my cosseted world soon grew confining. I elected to spend summers with relatives in Brussels, Edinburgh, and Munich. My seasons had new names: Jennifer, Adela, Genevieve, Anna. With conscious deliberation I collected them, yet these women were not conquests, they were studies. I soaked in their scent, memorized their outlines, colored them in. Nothing approached the ideal of my vision. And so I sought visions everywhere, following them to their lovely end. And then one came that did not end.

I called her Gisèle.

She was barely fifteen, and she looked it. But I did not think of her age when I saw her. In the bland tourist milieu of Fisherman's Wharf, it was her dress I noticed first: plum-colored and made of silk; the light moved upon it like a shimmering hand. The skirt flared and stopped, and my eyes followed the smooth line of her thigh down to the lovely knee and the childish round of her calf, down further still to the hollow of her ankle where it met her dress shoe. She had soft curls with the sheen of a coffee bean, a pert nose in profile, baby-smooth pale skin, cherry lips moistened with lip gloss. . . .

Into my mind crept lines of Rimbaud, unbidden, memorized long ago:

> *I've been patient so long*
> *I've forgotten even*
> *The terror and suffering*
> *Flown up to heaven,*
> *A sick thirst again*
> *Darkens my veins.*

I stepped in behind her. Embroidered on her shoe was a sunflower.

I reached my own parking lot first and paid, craning my neck to keep her in sight. Navigating the congested lanes, I followed her as she walked to a lot farther down and to a repugnant American car. A Chevrolet Vega, it was. I slowed almost to a stop, as if I desired her space, and slid my window down. An older woman in the driver's seat—her mother, I supposed—called the girl "Karen" in a nasal voice. The name did not suit her. It lacked *l'apesanteur*, a weightlessness, which she possessed. How I longed to cart her back to the bay and it was only then that the obstacle of her youth struck me, like swallowing a mouthful of gravel when one anticipates champagne.

She removed a gift box from the faded fabric seat and slid in, disappearing from view. The back door was open to let in a breeze, and a child lay sprawled there; from my vantage point I could see only the sunlit crown of a dark head and a ragged pair of tennis shoes, laces loose and dangling.

I circled round, and they backed out before me. I followed them onto the Embarcadero. Their destination proved an affluent neighborhood bordering Golden Gate Park. Karen was deposited before a stolid Colonial brick house with a white door, red-shuttered windows, and an American flag. She walked up the narrow brick path, stopping on the third stair to wave. Yet once the car had disappeared, she turned abruptly and descended the stairs again, walking briskly down the path onto the street and toward the park, without a backward glance.

Curiosity piqued, I parked and sauntered along some distance behind her, shielded by the inky shadows of the trees. The brightly wrapped gift went into the trash. She slipped off her shoes and walked barefoot through the grass along the duck pond.

When it was safe to do so, I plucked the box from the bin and ripped it open—anxious to have something she had touched. Inside, I found a battered stuffed bear in tartan hat and scarf, one button eye sagging in a lascivious wink. From the wear, it was clear he'd been loved by her once. Yet it seemed she'd sacrificed him as a decoy—to give the package weight? A made-up gift for an imagined party. It was a fascinating caprice: our first secret shared.

I found Karen in the sunshine, moving with a daydreamer's oblivion past the vast flower beds, the Gothic stone manor and Old Dutch Windmill. She spoke to no one and relished her solitude, an unsettling quality in one so young. I followed as though tugged along by an invisible string.

At the Temple of Music, I watched from behind a great column as she roamed the empty amphitheater, trotting the stage, utterly unaware she performed for a rapt audience.

At last—too soon—we returned to the stately brick Colonial. Had she walked through the neighborhood and imagined being invited to such a house? Watched long enough to know that it was vacant for the weekend, or perhaps the season? Tightness appeared in her posture as the ungainly Chevy materialized at the end of the street. On her face she fixed a bright, buoyant smile. Gone, it seemed, was the autonomy of the park. With a hollow clang of the rickety car door, she disappeared, and the color drained out of the day.

I followed her home but was not to see her again. The car vanished into the single garage of a dilapidated mint-colored Victorian. Her neighborhood was marked by poverty: peeling paint and crooked, half-drawn shades, graffiti on the curb. I shuddered to think of her there.

That night she dominated my dreams with a feverish urgency. I slept restlessly, and when I woke, she was there. An irascible itch, an ache. I was pulled again to the drab Victorian. At a quarter past seven, she emerged—no longer a sprite but a street urchin carting a beaten-up backpack—yet walking with the same wistful, evocative air that was to be my undoing.

I followed her down three blocks and over one, to the school bus. That afternoon I was there to meet it. I followed her to a café and then down to the bay.

Had no one told her she shouldn't be alone on the pier as the sun starts to fall? She was perhaps five feet tall, a waif with a cagey stance. The girlish curves I'd memorized that day in the park were hidden now beneath thrift-store jeans and an oversize hooded jacket. She didn't take up the space entitled to her; she had not been taught how. And who were these people who looked after her? They didn't see the beauty I saw. If I had done nothing, she would not have seen it either. She would be like everyone else, do you understand? She would be only "Karen."

At a newsstand she paused to pick up a magazine—some nonsense about supermodels and movie stars—but the longing on her face as she paged through it was striking. She was at that transcendent age: old enough to sense her power and too innocent to use it. I moved closer. My eyes owned her.

I stepped forward; I would simply walk past her, buy a paper. . . . She was near enough to touch. Cloaked in her hood, she looked up at me, and I looked down at her. Her eyes were a clear aquamarine—free of all variation, without flecks or impurities—and then they were gone, back to her magazine. But it was enough.

Obsession, you see, requires neither audacity nor courage, but only servitude. I became a constant companion to her wanderings. In the mornings I met her school bus, endured the hours in mindless torpor till the clock struck three and I could seek her after school. On the fifth day, I gained the nerve to approach her home, at that time when dusk falls but people do not realize they can be seen in their well-lit kitchens and living rooms.

It was a relatively easy matter to maneuver my way into her dilapidated backyard, though remaining there unseen proved a trickier thing. There was a tiny rusted shed, which offered me refuge on a few uneasy occasions. Yet it was too far from the house to offer an adequate view. I was forced to take cover beneath the elderberry tree. From here a bay window revealed the cramped eat-in kitchen, and a tall, narrow window on the second story gave onto Karen's room. I saw her there, seated at her desk, that first night. There was also a side window into the living room, in which family activity was centered. The window was covered with heavy curtains, but they were haphazardly hung and rarely closed so tightly that they did not provide a crack into Karen's world. It was not without cracks of its own.

I confess it was my first real glimpse of petit bourgeois American life, and I was perhaps overly sensitive to its shabbiness. A dim gloom permeated the house and emanated from her father, who had no apparent occupation beyond watching television. In the window of my observation, he restricted his outings to the corner bar. An attractive man, he was of good height with dark hair and regular, if not strong, features.

La mère de Karen masked her disappointment with industry. Her job occupied her until late in the evening, and when she wasn't working, she was cleaning—dusting while the television droned on around her. She was a petite blonde, with wide eyes that seemed to anticipate doom. It struck me that doom had already arrived.

There was also a sister—the untied tennis shoes I'd glimpsed—who was by all appearances a good sort, laughing and lively and nearly as tall as Karen, though a good deal younger. She was called Mandy and was usually twirling about in the living room or up the stairs.

It all meant for me only one thing: Whilst little Mandy was at ballet, Maman at work, and Papa at the bar, Karen was mine. The more I observed her, the less she belonged to them. And it was a night some ten days into my vigil that gave me the temerity to act.

In Karen's bedroom, the flimsy curtains provided little concealment. I stood below to watch the wisp of her form pass before her window now and then, like a wraith. You mustn't think I was ever so lucky as to see her undress. I satisfied myself with her outline, shivering in my heavy, dark coat and scarf. It was nearly spring, but port cities are cold year-round—the fog worse, I think, than the snows of my childhood, creeping like icy fingers through your clothes to your skin, through skin even to the bone.

I had resolved at last to retreat to my empty hotel room when I saw a strange figure materialize above me. Clearly visible through the sheer linen, the shadow of a man loomed in her window. I jumped from my vantage point below—for a moment I thought him an intruder. Then I recognized the shadow.

Karen passed before her father, shaking her head. He pulled her to him, gripping her shoulders with such violence I thought he intended to strike her. His shadow engulfed hers, a sepia mass, inching her backward. The chair butted against the desk and stopped; I imagined it catching the small of her back, pinning her there. Sweeping her hair aside with a clumsy hand, her father bent drunkenly to kiss her neck.

In a rage I stooped to pick up a stone and threw it at the lit square above, heard the flat ping as it met its mark. He looked up, startled, and Karen eased away. Her father came to the window and peered out. And I hid beneath my elderberry tree, watching helplessly as the lights went out above me.

Up to then my fixation was undefined, without form. I might yet have changed course. But now, perversely, Karen's circumstances justified my voyeurism. I was compelled to act.

I will not lie and tell you I considered a more ethical route—perhaps a rush to the division of social services that handles such "family matters." I wonder, what would they have done? Even in the dark days when one could do just about anything one wished to one's children in one's own home, they would have taken her from her family, I think.

How much better that the task should lie with me.

The choice of our first rendezvous was a simple one: a café called the Daily Grind. Karen went nearly every weekday after school for an olallieberry muffin and a large mug of French roast, into which she deposited two packets of sugar and a watershed of cream. She ate her muffin in highly ritualized style, pulling the top off in pieces with her fingers, then unwrapping the bottom and eating it in a circular fashion with her fork, saving the soft center for last. She made the muffin last exactly as long as the coffee, finishing the final sip with the final bite of muffin. As she went through all this, she read, covering her coffee with the cardboard coaster so it wouldn't get cold during the good parts. I found the whole thing rather charming.

It was only here that she seemed to relax fully. She was so consumed that she seemed not hear the flurry around her: the people who ducked in and out of the rain with a rustle of umbrellas and raincoats, the lively conversations circulating through the air and punctuated only by the sounds of the espresso machine.

I chose a busy time; no tables were vacant. She was alone, reading Hemingway's *The Sun Also Rises*. "*Excusez-moi*," I said lightly. "May I share your table, mademoiselle, until one opens up?"

Her expression told me she preferred I did not, but the hesitation, as I'd hoped, indicated she was too polite to say so. This is a curiously American feminine trait in my experience: too polite to simply say no. Frenchwomen know it is the best answer on all occasions, even when one wishes to say yes.

"All right," she said.

I pulled out the chair, and she dipped her head again to her book, newly self-conscious. I could tell she was reading the same line again and again, for her eyes did not travel the page. Her muffin was midway through the ritual sacrifice: it had been beheaded but not yet defrocked. She would be too embarrassed to eat it in her usual way, I supposed. I was ruining her rite.

Just as the thought passed through my mind, she set down her book, straightened slightly in her chair, lifted the cardboard coaster from her coffee, and eased it discreetly beneath, as it should be. She settled back in her chair and met my eyes. "Excuse me . . . what is your accent?"

"French."

"I thought so." After a moment, "I'm Karen. What's your name?"

I looked at her book and thought of Jake Barnes and the lovely Brett Ashley, then smiled slightly. "Jacques. Jacques Barnard."

"Hello, Jacques. I wanted to take French, but I heard that Spanish is easier. At least in the beginning. And you only have to take a year of it, so . . ."

"So Spanish is the easier year."

"Language isn't my favorite subject."

"Is Hemingway also for a class?"

"Huh?" She glanced down at her book. "Oh, no, we're supposed to be reading *Catcher in the Rye*, but I've already read that, and I thought I should see what's so great about Hemingway." She faltered. "I'd sort of like to write someday."

"You say it like an apology."

"Well, I'm not very good."

I laughed and sipped my cappuccino. "I see. What do you think of Hemingway, then?"

"I miss the adjectives."

"Some would say they merely muddy the waters."

"Maybe." She gave a slight shrug. "But at least you can tell the water's muddy."

I laughed. "*Oui.*" I had hardly allowed myself to expect anything from the conversation. Imagine my elation at finding her so perfectly enchanting.

"What is it you do?" she asked tentatively. "For a living, I mean."

The inevitable American question. "I live for a living."

"But don't you have a job?"

"*Non, non.*"

"Wow." She crinkled her brow, clearly dubious about so well-dressed a bum. "You must have an awful lot of money." She didn't appear to realize the rudeness of this assessment, which I found delightful.

"*Oui,*" I replied easily. "My father's father's father was rather successful at his job."

"But you must do *something.*"

"*Oui, bien sûr.* I do a bit of everything. I paint, write, play piano. . . ."

Her eyes sparked, and she leaned forward across the table. "You mean you're an artist?"

If you wish, I thought.

"That's wonderful." Her eyes took on the wistful expression I loved. "I like to paint." She added ruefully, "I'm better at it than writing. Everyone says so. But I don't like to just copy what I see. It should mean something, shouldn't it? It's finding the meaning of things that's hard, and—" She broke off abruptly, gazed out the window onto the street and back again. "Have you ever heard the saying, Jacques"—It was exquisite, this use of my "name," delivered with such shy hesitation in her self-conscious American accent—"that if you sit long enough in a café on the Champs-Élysées, the whole world will pass by? Do you think it's true?"

"Ah, *oui.* But think how many muffins you would have to consume."

She laughed, a light, lilting sound that made my stomach rise in euphoria. I'd made her laugh.

"But such a thing is true of Paris. I was born there."

"Oh!"

I drank in this exultant exclamation along with my cappuccino and settled back in my chair, determined not to look too pleased with myself. Had I won her already?

"So you were born in Paris and you're an artist." In her voice she gave "artist" a capital A. "What art are you most fond of?" One could tell she was being her most adult; she leaned forward as she spoke and became subtly more vulnerable.

"Like you, I find painting is what I do best. Unlike you, I find it a comfort to be limited to what I see. But to write, to paint pictures with words . . . that is what I love." It was not true, of course, but we were all at once kindred. She smiled at me, resting her lovely chin on her small fist. "Now tell me what you write so badly about."

"Oh, I don't know," she demurred. "People. Tragic things."

"With happy endings?"

"No. Mostly happy beginnings with tragic ends."

"But why is that, *chérie?*"

She evaded me with her laugh. "It's silly to talk about. I haven't written anything much."

"To whom do you show your stories?"

"Well. No one. My little sister . . ."

"Then you will show me."

She stared, started to laugh. "I . . . well, yeah, Jacques, I guess I could show you. If you want me to."

And so we arranged to meet again at the coffeehouse in a few days. But it is a failing of my character that I find it impossible to wait for something I desire. Having met her, I could no longer follow her movements and stay removed from them. And so it was that the next day I followed her to the park, and "happened" upon her sitting on a bench with Hemingway.

"Karen? *Quelle surprise!*"

My hard-won nonchalance was met with a startled jump. "Jacques." She shifted on the slatted wooden seat and bit her lip. "What are you doing here?"

"*Comment?*"

"I just mean . . . well, it's kind of weird the way you pop up every-where." But it was a halfhearted protest; a blush still colored her cheeks and her eyes were bright.

"I'm not sure about everywhere, *chérie*, but I do come here quite often," I replied. "I don't often run into people I know." Smiling my most charming smile, I added, "I am a stranger in a strange city. When I saw you, *naturellement*, I had to say hello."

"Well. Hello." She stared at me a moment and then stood. "You can sit here if you want, but I'm just going to . . . you know, walk."

"I prefer your company to my own, *ma petite*. Perhaps I could . . . you know, walk with you?" My flat American pronunciation produced a slight smile. She had tried to feather her hair but failed. The fog had reduced it to the curled tendrils I longed to touch.

"Don't take this the wrong way, Jacques," she said as we walked. "But you're not some kind of pervert, are you?"

"I don't think so."

We continued to walk.

"Well, what is it you want?" She plunged her fists into her pockets. "I've seen you before, you know. At the café, lots of times. And I saw you on the pier once, watching me—"

She had a marvelous memory. And it seemed I hadn't been as dis-creet as I'd thought.

"Was I? Or perhaps *you* were watching *me*."

She had no reply for this. Her fair cheeks grew flushed again.

"It could be that we simply share the same taste: coffee, the pier, the park."

"Uh-huh." She really was very cagey today. "Maybe. But what is it you want?"

I gazed at her then, wanting nothing more than to do so for hours on end. What did I want? I want to rescue you from your father, your future, your fate. I want to touch you. I want to treasure you and pleasure you and disturb and frighten you. I want to possess you. "Your company," I said lightly. "I just like your company, Karen."

"But you've got to be, what, *thirty*?"

I hesitated to tell her I was even older than that advanced age. "Thirty-four," I said gently. "But you must be, er . . . eighteen, yes?"

She merely laughed.

"*Eh, bien*. Seventeen, then."

It is so tempting for the young to lie about their age. I granted her the opportunity, and she took it, by omission. "That's just it. I could practically be your daughter."

"Practically," I agreed. After a moment, "I had a daughter. Once."

Her suspicions were for a moment forgotten. She echoed, "'Once'?"

"*Oui*. She died in a car accident when she was just three." The words sparked an unexpected tingling in my fingertips, as if the feel of Marie-Gisèle's silken baby skin were encoded there.

A sliver of guilt snuck in with her memory. Had my daughter lived, she would have been Karen's age. With this startling realization came my only hesitation. I had a fleeting impulse to murmur a witticism and a careful good-bye and leave San Francisco forever. But Karen, knowing none of my plans for her, was murmuring appropriate apologies. I could see she hadn't slept well. There were shadows in the hollows of her eyes I longed to smooth away. And as unexpectedly as my conscience crept up to tap me, it tiptoed away.

"You're married, then?" she asked tentatively.

"*Non*. My wife was also in the car. It all happened long ago." The topic irritated me now.

"Oh." She searched my face. "That's awful. I'm really sorry."

"Thank you. It was a very long time ago."

"Did you love her very much?" Her curiosity, it seemed, wasn't to be deterred by propriety.

I sighed. Love Sabina? "Not as much as I should have. We married because she was pregnant. In those days one did the proper thing."

"I don't know why people get married at all. They only end up hating each other."

"You sound as if you speak from experience, but you are too young to be so cynical about love. Is it observation, then?" I paused. "Your parents?"

"No, it's just . . . Well, yes, I guess." A slight melancholy frown. "They got married because of me. They think I don't know, but it's not exactly complicated math."

"You have no hope for love because they are unhappy? But that is foolish, *ma petite*. I have been unhappy, and still I have hope."

I felt her stare but looked casually ahead as if we discussed nothing personal to me, a careless matter. The path turned onto the green. She rushed ahead to a large pond where there were ducks, and, sauntering behind, I watched her go. I learned to do this with her, as in some formal Victorian dance: a quadrille, in which one toys with touching and rarely touches. We walked toward each other and pirouetted away.

After that we planned our meetings: the wharf, City Lights, the Museum of Modern Art and the Planetarium, the gallery on one corner and the bookstore on another. Always we met in the park at three o'clock. It was our safe haven. We spent every afternoon together except Tuesdays. Tuesdays, she explained, belonged to Mandy. Weekends, too, were out. It was never suggested I meet her parents. Perhaps she was ashamed of them or knew that I was not merely after her company. And, too, she was "nearly eighteen." So, you see, we were complicit in it from the beginning. I was her secret, and she was mine.

I knew that even in our short precious moments together we must be wary: the petite young brunette should not be noticed with the well-to-do Frenchman. Do not think me heedless of the risk. When she "disappeared," every clerk at every business she frequented would come forward to say they recognized her, and it was quite crucial that they not recognize me as well. The guilty are prone to paranoia, and I had the sensation many times that we were followed. I'd turn and quiz myself on the crowd. The spare, dark-haired man with the camera—had we seen him the day before? Was the old woman squinting at us for a reason?

I was careful to alter my appearance subtly with a hat or glasses (wire-rimmed with clear glass, though for some time afterward Karen thought I needed them; now, fifteen years later, I find I do). Once I put a dark rinse on my blond hair that washed out after a few days, and I went through various stages of unshaven. But I could never bring myself to dress poorly. I rationalized this bit of snobbery with the fact that a shabbily dressed person would almost certainly be suspected first. I did set aside the showier labels and attempted, chameleon-like, to blend into my surroundings. To Karen I played it all up as a manifestation of my creative nature.

I found, at last, a use for my education. At galleries and museums,

I condensed my years of art history for her and introduced her to real music, albeit not in a concert hall but in the car. We haunted bookstores and libraries, and I bought books for her to read, carefully chosen novels about runaways and rebels, writers on personal odysseys for their craft, romantic tales of Europe and New York and the Orient.

I told her selective stories of my own upbringing and the collection of paintings to which I was heir. She did not believe me at first. She had the quaint notion that such things could not be owned privately—that all the famed pieces in the world were held in public museums, as if there were an international ordinance to enforce such a thing.

I did not tell her that on my annual sojourns to Paris my family home felt very like a museum to me. With Maman and Papa gone, there remained only the paintings to animate the place. And they were tainted by their inaccessibility. A tenet of the family trust held that the paintings could not be removed from France. And so, on my visits to Paris, I sat before them for hours on end, intent as a Sufi monk at meditation, as if the memorization of strokes might make them mine. I knew that my obsession sprang less from the paintings themselves than from the inability to fully possess them. But even that frustration seemed trivial now. The collection served only to entertain my new masterpiece.

For her part, Karen showed me her poems and stories, dismissed with a self-conscious wave of the hand ("The best ones aren't finished yet"). They were as amateurish as one might expect. She possessed a sharp mind and a flair for words, but there was no sign of plot: semiconfessional sketches, they were, and tragic all. She couldn't bear to watch me read them, and so she'd lend them to me for a night. I'd sleep with them on the pillow beside me. I found the poems particularly poignant. Written in feminine cursive on flowery stationery, they staggered under complicated meter and adolescent anguish, in vocabulary clearly palmed from a thesaurus. Yet it was their exposed imperfection I loved, their stumbling.

Having proclaimed my own passion for the written word, I was forced to play the role creditably. In truth, I'd written little of merit and had never taken the trouble to seek validation for what I'd written. But I phoned my apartment in New York and asked Henri to send out some of my stories. My butler and aide, Henri Dupré, was the only reminder of Paris I had in America and well accustomed to strange requests. I received a package the next day. I had a few dark, clever tales à la Poe and de Maupassant, with the dramatic twist at the end that is so appealing at Karen's age. Others were arcane to such a degree that I myself have no idea what they meant or what I meant in writing them. The sound of certain words strung together in certain ways appealed to me, a Joycean collage of ideas without any particular beginning or end.

Yet for the first time in my life, I was an artist. I was creating myself for her.

She had begun to do the same: dressing more and more as she had the day of the fictive party and discarding the habitual sweatshirt and jeans for dresses and sandals. Her makeup was more artfully applied. She ran her hand through her hair frequently as we spoke and was very conscious of me as a man, blushing when I held her eyes too long, when I caught her watching me, when I opened the car door for her. She was terribly curious about me, and so I cultivated mystery.

"How come there are New York plates on your car, Jacques?"

"I had it shipped before I flew out. I can't bear a rental car."

"Oh." A weighted syllable. "So you'll be going back there, huh? To New York?"

"*Oui*, eventually. But for the moment I live here. In a hotel."

"They let people live in hotels?"

"Certainly."

"Do you have a real house in New York?"

"I have several houses, *chérie*. My family estate includes a house in Paris and a country house in Normandy. But I spend little time in France these days. I've lived in New York for years."

"I'd like to see New York City one day. I think it's a good thing for artists to go there."

"Ah, *oui*," I agreed. "Very good."

"All the books are published there. Have you ever noticed that? And lots of artists live there, don't they?" (So earnest, so very charming.) "Not the Hollywood kind, but real artists. In New York you have to struggle to survive."

I glanced down at her, and the worldly air wobbled.

"Anyway, that's what I've heard."

I tried not to smile. "I live on the Upper East Side, so I'm afraid I miss much of the struggle."

"You must have a lot of friends there."

From her tone she meant the female sort. "*Oui.*"

"Are any of them writers?"

"Yes, a few. Mostly they are painters. And French expatriates, like me."

"Hmm. How come you left France?"

"It is good to leave the place one is born, *ma petite.* Otherwise it stays the same for you, and you stay the same with it. When I visit, I find we're both pleasantly changed."

"I like that." She glanced at me wistfully. "I'll leave here one day."

Yes, I thought. *Sooner than you think.*

The next day I brought up the topic of her family. "You never speak of them, Karen. I know only that you have a sister named Mandy who doesn't have dance class on Tuesdays. You never mention your mother. What is your father like?" I let her uneasy silence stretch. I wanted her to tell me about him, you see. Then we could begin to plot her escape.

But she wouldn't meet my eyes and said finally, "Let's not ruin it, Jacques."

"Ruin what, *ma petite?*"

She smiled, a touching smile, entirely unmeasured. "Everything's so easy for you. For me, too, when I'm with you. It's like the rest of the world doesn't even exist."

I touched her beneath her chin, tilting it up to me. "It exists only for us."

And to my immense surprise, she stood on tiptoe to kiss me. It was a very quick, uncertain kiss. Stepping backward to gauge its effect, she had never looked so lovely to me—eyes faintly wild, like a kitten when it's playing. She murmured, "Isn't that what you want?"

I said nothing at all but took her cold fingers in mine, massaging her hands to warm them. I bent forward to kiss the top of her head, the soft curls, and she tipped her face up. I felt her tremble when my lips brushed hers. That was all. A brush of the lips. I didn't trust myself to go further.

As we went back to the car, she kept her hand in mine.

The pivotal day was the first of April, and I remember it still so well, walking through the Japanese gardens in Golden Gate Park, the narrow Victorians like trays of pastels cascading across the steep hills, the bells of cable cars pealing in the distance, and fingers of fog hovering over the pea-soup bay. And at last the cool quiet of the gardens. A wall had come down between us. Karen reached freely for my hand now.

In the stillness it was easy to forget the scrutiny of others, and I decided all at once that it was time. "What if I were to invest in you, Karen? If you were to come with me to New York?"

She stopped before a bed of deep red Japanese azaleas that matched her lips and I savored the surprised pleasure in her eyes. Then she said, softly—at first I did not understand her—"April Fool's."

"*Mais non.* I am not fooling."

She cast me a sideways glance, and caution crept in. A nervous laugh. "I couldn't do that, Jacques. I mean, of course, I'd love to. But my parents would never let me go."

Dear, sweet child. "No. I'm afraid you would have to give up your old life entirely."

"Oh, right. I can't go through life with a ninth-grade edu—" She broke off abruptly. Her eyes focused hard on her shoes, and her cheeks flushed red.

I feigned confusion. "*Pardon*, Karen? Did you say the ninth grade?"

"I'm sorry. Oh . . . God. I was afraid that if I told you, you wouldn't want to see me anymore." There was a tortured silence. "The truth is, I'm not even sixteen yet. I'm fifteen." A pause. "Barely." Her lovely eyes filled with tears. "I should have said so. I meant to. It's just that I feel older inside."

The words were shocking out loud, but I was beyond listening. I paused, conjured up a bit of consternation, then frowned in pretended disapproval. It was an exquisite joy to torment her this way, for it made it clear how important my approval had become. I looked away and back again, watching as various teenage agonies flickered over her features. "Ah."

"You must hate me."

"I could not hate you."

"But you're angry, I can tell—"

I spoke gently. "I'm surprised, Karen. That is all." And played the crucial card. "You seem much older, though age in itself means little. We're all different ages inside." I cleared my throat. "You're no different to me now than you were a few minutes ago. But it does complicate things."

"What was I to you, a few minutes ago?"

It was an adult question.

"You know that, surely."

"No, I don't." Without waiting for a reply, she rushed on. "I think I love you, Jacques—"

I held her eyes. She didn't breathe. How can I explain the sensation? It was as if my pulse rose, I felt my blood beat violently just beneath the skin. She was mine.

"You don't know what you are to me, Karen?" I said softly. "But you are everything."

I could see the horror warring with delight in her eyes. "You could be arrested . . ."

"*Oui*, Karen. I could. Only if we were careless. We would have to trust each other."

"But—"

"We would continue your education, of course. You would be tutored. I was tutored at your age. That way your schedule would be flexible for travel and . . . and that sort of thing."

Doubt crept in. "Would I live with you?"

"Of course." I paused, gauging her expression. "But you would have your own room, *ma petite*. Nothing would happen that you didn't want to happen."

"For all I know, you could be part of an international ring—white slavery or . . ."

"*Merde*," I sneered, contemptuous. "Tales your mother taught you?"

"People do that stuff," she murmured. "It's on the news all the time."

I could barely hear her, but I could hear that she did not believe it.

"There are all kinds of horrible people."

"Then I will protect you from them." I took her by the shoulders and kissed her.

Her lips were so soft, like the petals of a flower—not a rose but a deli-cate flower that needs a greenhouse to survive. They were cold, and I was very gentle with her, so that she responded first, her lips parting so slightly, then the fluttering touch of her tongue to mine. I enfolded her in my arms. She held on to me so tightly and was so slight that I could feel her heart-beat and might literally have crushed her. It filled me with a tenderness I had never known. To feel my power over her, to revel in my restraint.

She whispered into the folds of my jacket, "I can't just run off, Jacques. I can't leave my mom and my little sister—" But the protests no longer mattered. I was sure of her now, and it made it easy to be cruel.

"Perhaps you're right," I said curtly, pulling away. "I should not have men-tioned it. I thought I might . . . I thought we . . ." I sighed. "But you're right, Karen. It would be selfish to take you from the life you know and make you part of mine. It was wrong of me. And I can see I've frightened you."

She watched me with wide eyes and a lip that trembled. "No, it's just—"

"I know what it is. Don't apologize. I'm the one who's sorry." I turned away from her, counted to five. "We will not see each other much more, I'm afraid." How sour the words tasted on my tongue. "My time here is nearly over. I have to return to New York."

"But I thought—"

"We will have a few days more together." When I turned back again, she would not look at me. In a moment, wordlessly, she spun around and ran down the garden path.

I let her go.

That night I went to her house. I had not been there since I'd spied her with her father. It pained me too much. But I saw her upstairs alone, at her desk before the window, writing intently. She paused often, to wipe tears from her eyes, and several times crumpled the paper. Imagine what I felt. I knew she was writing to me.

The next day she came to me at three o'clock in the park. There was no letter. She asked, "Will you take me with you?"

It became almost a joke between us then, getting her away. I'm not cer-tain when Karen realized that the joke was real, when she realized she could not turn back.

We set the date for Friday, the thirteenth of April, 1979. She had a reverse superstition regarding the day, feeling that it would be good luck. I felt we'd need it. She was to leave home that morning as if to catch the school bus and meet me on the corner of Mission and Fourth, taking nothing with her but the backpack she typically carried. My habit of sending my Mercedes ahead when I traveled was a fortuitous idiosyncrasy. An airline ticket could be traced, of course, and even a rental car would present an additional element of risk. This way we'd be across the state line before she was ever missed.

In the morning I checked out after a two-month stay at the Ritz and stopped at her favorite coffee shop one last time. We'd been there together only once since that first afternoon, and I doubted that any of the bedraggled college students—indistinguishable ponytails or pink-haired punks—would recognize me. This is a bit of self-delusion, I see now. I was the child who covers his eyes and so believes he can't be seen.

In the car I dusted the large coffee with sugar and Seconal. She'd be out cold in twenty to thirty minutes, and she'd be out for hours. My greatest fear at that point was that she would not come. It seemed my ribs would crush my heart as I approached the appointed street corner. She could so easily not be there. But there she was, waiting for me.

With an anxious smile, she got into the car. The atmosphere was anticipatory: Grieg's lovely "Morning Mood" from *Peer Gynt* played. Karen didn't recognize it but approved of it with her smile. Possessing none of the sullen pretenses of her age group, she opened herself fully to the experiences I offered her—and they were only beginning. A dark euphoria possessed me, so that I had to force myself to take her hand gently in mine. I wanted her to feel she might easily slip free, if she wished.

We sped down the highway and out of the city. It was only eight o'clock, the fog a picturesque cloak for the battered tenement buildings, warehouses, and billboard signs. Even the fog was on my side, suspending reality, the bridge a gateway to another world.

Karen giggled and turned to me, her eyes wide and feverishly bright. "You're crazy, you know."

I smiled a slight smile, not too sinister.

"Have you ever felt so free?" she asked giddily.

I gazed at her, amused. "*Ma petite*, I have never felt otherwise."

"Well, I've hardly ever left the city. I've never been further than Gey-serville; that's up north a little ways, where my grandparents live. I have an aunt in Seattle, but we never go to visit her. She comes here." Karen held her coffee in her hands. With all the cream and sugar I'd put in it, she wasn't likely to taste anything, not even the coffee. I watched as she sipped cautiously to avoid burning her tongue, then as she swallowed. "Around here we cross the bridges just to cross back again. I think I stopped believing they led anywhere but back to where I started from." She paused, toying with the crude drinking aperture in the lid. The ter-rible things make the coffee taste like plastic, but I'd counted on its hid-ing any residue of the dissolved drug. Another sip. She stared at the cup thoughtfully, and my heart thudded as she met my sideways glance. "You must think I'm crazy, too. Don't you? For going along with this."

"Life's too short to be sane, Karen. We will be crazy together."

She took a larger sip, moving with the lurching of the car to avoid spilling. "Of course, I'll have to write my mother and Mandy eventually. So they won't think I'm dead or something." I flinched inwardly at this. It was, of course, exactly what I intended them to think. I wanted a local hunt for a madman, not an interstate search for an abductor. "I feel worst about leaving Mandy. We're really close."

I managed a slight nod.

"I'll explain things in the letter," she went on tentatively. "Of course, I won't mention you."

I was certain she wouldn't. Just as I was certain there would be no letter.

Another sip. "A lot of people wouldn't understand, but the thing is, I trust you."

"Of course you do." I turned. "You have nothing at all to fear, Karen. I've told you—"

"Yes." She smiled faintly. "You're satisfied just to wait for me."

"That's right."

"Like Elvis and Priscilla." She fished in the bag for her muffin and took a long sip of coffee. "My mother would never understand that. Most of the time she treats me like a kid. Everyone does." She halted, gazing up. "Hey, is this decaf?"

It was. It's not good to mix uppers and downers. "I asked them for regular. Why?"

She shrugged. "Just tastes different." Another absentminded sip and it was forgotten. "Do you know when I first went to school, the bigger girls always wanted to hold my hand to go to the playground at recess? They'd treat me like I was their baby doll or something, because I was small. Even when I got older, it didn't change. People think they can pick me up and set me down again wherever they want to."

"Well, they can't do that anymore."

She paused, biting her lip. "My little sister wants to be like me. We're six years apart. I love her, but I don't want her to be like me."

I couldn't see her eyes, only her downcast lashes; she'd gotten ready quickly today, her eye makeup haphazard. It made her look bruised and vulnerable.

"I hate the idea of leaving her. A letter won't make it okay, but it's easier to write things than to say them . . ."

I nodded, considered safer topics, and discarded them. She sipped her coffee and then yawned, looking out the window at the passing cars. Then I felt her study me again, her appraisal sending a prickling sensation down the side of my neck. She said, "I guess I'm what you've lost, aren't I? A little bit your wife and a little bit your daughter. I can see it, the way you look at me sometimes."

I thought to protest but did not. I answered honestly. "I don't know quite what you are, Karen. I've known many women and left them, been many places and left. But you I cannot imagine leaving."

She gave me a faraway smile. "Well, now I'm like you, Jacques. I've left everything, too." Her voice grew softly slurred. "I wonder what I'll miss."

Heavy-lidded, she laid her head against the back of the seat and let her eyes close. I took the coffee from her hands and set it in the holder. Within seconds she slept.

Sleep was, of course, a euphemism. Karen could have gone through open-heart surgery and not woken. I'd given her well over the normal adult dosage of Seconal, and she wasn't a very large adult—less than a hundred pounds—and unused to drugs. She was quite unconscious. But this was necessary, you see. I needed her blood and a good deal of it.

When I was not yet Karen's age, I was much taken with a popular film in France of the time, called *Pickpocket*, and it amused me for a while to pinch various effects from hapless shoppers in the street markets of Paris. The best method for this, as any reader of *Oliver Twist* will know, is to create a distraction—to divert attention from the intended crime and victim. From an innocent jostling in the crowd to an overturned basket of pears. No one suspected me: the well-dressed, well-mannered youth with pale blond hair and the blue eyes of an angel. This, too, was distraction.

Twenty years later I found I still had the advantage of appearances; I am not the criminal "type." But I was determined to send a pear or two rolling underfoot as I whisked Karen from the marketplace.

As with any plan, there were obstacles to overcome. The Seconal had been no real trouble; I have a number of useful sources when it comes to obtaining drugs. But it is harder than one might think to acquire a hypodermic. So I went to the source, scheduling a physical with a local doctor who sent me to the hospital for lab work. I took careful note of the process as the nurse drew my blood. She was surprised at my interest. "Most people, even grown men, they don't like to watch when they're getting a shot."

I watched very closely.

And then I trailed a harried intern through the halls to learn just how things lay. In the great confused maze of healers and the sick, no one paid me any mind. When questioned, I pretended to be lost. Fluency in another language has its advantages. Less than a week later, I volunteered to donate blood and was given a hospital duffel as a consolation prize. I promptly headed to my staked-out supply closet to fill it. The minor theft would be put down to drug addicts or the ineptitude of the staff. I concealed a few hypodermic needles and several vials inside, as well as a rubber strap to tie off the blood flow. Afterward, I purchased rubbing alcohol, cotton balls, and bandages to add to the mix.

My breath came in shallow spurts as I pulled in to the desolate rest stop I'd selected for the occasion. Karen looked so enticingly vulnerable: rolled over on her side so that she faced me, her legs curled beneath her on the seat. Her lips were slightly parted, and her dark hair curled at her neck. It is impossible to describe the rapture I felt. My fingers trembled as I checked the pulse in her slender wrist. The throbbing was faint but steady. Carefully, I eased her upright so her back was flat against the back of the seat. Unable to resist, I unzipped her jeans and slipped my hand down the front, surprised to feel cool silk beneath my fingers. I suppose I had expected schoolgirl cotton panties. These were too adult for her and most likely purchased for the occasion. I found it quite touching. I slid a finger beneath them, down the slight silken triangle, and it was a keen ache to stop myself. But I withdrew my hand. Pleasure is heightened by restraint. For medical purposes I slipped my hand beneath her blouse and the satiny fabric of her bra. My fingers cupped her breast, a perfect handful, and then felt for the reassuring throb of her heart. I also felt something else. . . . Tucked into her bra was a photograph.

I extracted it and found myself gazing down at Karen and her little sister. They stood on a lawn before a house that had seen better days. Mandy was beaming; Karen was wistful, watching her. Wistful and adoring. On the back was inscribed: *"Karen Louise and Amanda Nicole— Grandma and Grandpa Miller's: 1976."* In spite of myself, I felt a tug of sentiment. What harm could it do? Carefully, I replaced it.

I then turned my mind to more practical matters. Taking blood is more difficult than one might imagine. Now that I was unconcerned about her drugged state, I had cause to resent it. She was unable to stay upright; her head bobbed, and she slumped either to the right or to the left, or forward. Once I barely caught her before her forehead slammed into the dash. And with her inability to clench a fist, a visible vein was hard to find. I plunged the needle in but missed. Twice. I winced and cursed, inhaling sharply at each frustration. I am no sadist. I'd sooner have used my own arm as a pincushion. By the third attempt, the hypodermic wobbled tremulously in my fingers. Yet I found my mark and pierced a good vein, joyously watching as the vial filled with deep red.

At just that triumphant moment, I heard a horrifying sound: the crunch of tires on asphalt and the deep hum of a car engine. I'd chosen an isolated spot to park, beyond the restrooms, and was reasonably certain we could not be seen unless someone deliberately approached us. I quickly extracted the needle and whipped my head around. An RV had parked on the other side of the lot, and three children, four, tore after each other across the pavement, the only buffer between us.

Merde.

Frantically, I capped the vial, wiped the blood from the needle, and hid it in the center console. I covered Karen with a fleece blanket from the backseat and forced myself to relax and recline. I was merely an ordinary traveler, grabbing a few winks.

I closed my eyes, but a tap at my window nearly sent me through the windshield.

I made a show of fluttering lashes, yawned, and turned to glower at a protruding belly beneath a taut T-shirt, jeans that seemed in precarious danger of slipping off. These belonged to a vulgar man with perhaps three strands of hair carefully combed sideways. I lowered the car window.

"Morning," the man said, gazing down with a squint.

I struggled to keep my voice steady. "Yes? What is it?"

He shifted his weight. Paranoia made me think he was angling for a view into the car.

"Sorry to disturb. Wonder if you can tell me how to reach the 580 from here? We're up from Simi Valley, and damned if I can make my way through this city. Think I'd be used to freeways by now—"

"I'm afraid I can be of little help."

"Foreign, are you?"

"French," I contradicted him. "I'm not familiar with the freeways. I would only get you lost." I turned, putting my finger to my lips. "You must forgive me. I don't wish to wake my daughter."

"Sure, sure. I understand. It's the only time they're quiet." But he didn't move. He dropped his voice an octave. "You wouldn't have a map I could just take a peek at, would you? Hoped to avoid gittin' off the wrong exit and havin' the wife think I got us lost." He winked.

I had a map, of course, but it was in the glove compartment in front of Karen. I didn't wish to draw further attention to her, and I longed to be rid of him. "I'm sorry." I forced a commiserative smile.

He turned away, no doubt fuming over the insensitivities of the French.

The children had availed themselves of the toilets and now sent up a great chorus of whines for drinks and candy bars. I heard the long-suffering *clunk-clunk-clunk* of the vending machine and pressed my fingers to my temples to keep my head from flying apart. At last they piled back into the horrid house on wheels and inched away.

With a fresh infusion of adrenaline, I moved quickly, wedging Karen securely into the corner where the passenger door met the seat and letting her arm dangle so the blood flowed downward. I remembered my little rubber strap and tied it around her arm to increase the pressure in her veins. I was rewarded with a promising blue swell. Inhaling sharply, I again inserted the needle and with light-headed glee watched the deep crimson rise. It came fast, and I nearly dropped the first vial trying to attach the next.

But then some instinct took over; I can only say it was greater than me. In a merciful clear-eyed calm, I replaced vial after vial without incident, breathing deeply. Six would be enough, more than enough. I untied the strap, dabbed alcohol on her arm, and held a cotton ball over it to stop the blood. I could not use tape or a Band-Aid. As it was, I was going to have a time passing off the needle marks as insect bites. I positioned Karen's arm upright and applied pressure until the bleeding ceased. At that moment I felt uncommonly proud of her. *Ma petite enfant.* Tenderly, I kissed her cheek.

Pulling on a pair of driving gloves, I quickly riffled through the things in her backpack: a U.S. history textbook and an anthology of English literature. Did she really lug that monstrosity around all the time? There was a lipstick and a compact, a comb and some ponytail bands. Steinbeck's *Of Mice and Men.* Gym clothes. Keys. That was good; her name was engraved on the key chain. There was also a spiral notebook filled with class notes and half-completed homework assignments with her name on them. That was even better. And better still her wallet: complete with student-body and Social Security cards. There was scarcely enough money for a petty thief to bother with, but I emptied it anyway.

I started up the car and turned it around, so that Karen faced forward and I'd be hidden by the open trunk. Were another car to approach, I could simply close it. Thus comforted, I opened a large, sturdy garbage bag and laid it on the carpeted bottom of the trunk. I placed her backpack carefully inside, and with a fish gutter purchased from a sporting-goods store, I ripped a gash in the fabric just high enough to prevent its contents from leaking out. I performed the bloodletting very slowly and methodically. Karen's blood slowly seeped into the blue denim, turning it a deep purple where I concentrated it around the ragged tear in the fabric. At last it was done. I secured the garbage bag closed with twist ties.

As I slipped back into the car, I felt an icy flood of fear. This was the most dangerous part of my plan: a drugged teenager beside me, her blood-soaked backpack in my trunk. If stopped for any reason, I was lost. It's safe to say I drove more conscientiously than I ever have and parked at last along the waterfront. A pungent blend of salt water, seaweed, and rotting fish stung my nostrils as I moved along the edge of the deserted pier. A narrow alley led to the water, and I moved cautiously down its length. It was exactly the sort of place one imagined a brutal rape or stabbing taking place, the victim's body disposed of hastily into the bay.

Soon I was kneeling at the end of the putrid pier. I had staked out the location carefully. From here the currents moved out to sea. I rubbed Karen's backpack along the edge, a trail of smeared blood that led to the gentle green waters of the bay. Beside me a ladder descended from the dock. With my gloved hands, I reached for the great bolt I knew was there. Rust came off on my glove, intermingling with her blood as I positioned a strap of the backpack to look as if it had haphazardly snagged there. It would remain safely above the water even at high tide. I hoped it would eventually be spotted by someone farther down the dock, or from the water. Its discovery was crucial, yet I couldn't chance a more populated place.

At that moment however, all thought of risk receded. All fear. I was quite literally high: a potent brew of endorphins and adrenaline, like a runner's high, but of course not quite so wholesome. It was its very unwholesomeness that intensified the sensation, a giddy surge of omnipotence. Danger was everywhere: in the incessant distant hammering and the empty cranes that loomed above me, quietly watching. Squinting, I could see a great weathered fishing boat out on the water: PACIFIC WATERS COMPANY, it read in stenciled letters on the steel. But I felt invisible. Nothing could touch me. Nothing could take her from me. Nothing.

The final step was to soak the empty garbage bag and leave it to drift, letting the water wash it clean. I watched as the current spirited it gently away. My reflection rippled after it, as if to escape me.

I felt the change in the car when she woke. It was the awful tension before a baby begins to bawl or a dog realizes you're a stranger. Karen watched me through bleary eyes, and I felt the hair stand up on my arms. She said nothing. She pulled the fleece blanket tight around her and burrowed into the soft folds.

"You've been asleep such a long time, *ma petite*. Are you all right?"

"I don't think so," she murmured. "I . . . I feel kind of funny."

"That's natural, *chérie*. It's only nerves."

"No." She sat up quickly. "I feel sick."

I pulled over. She was indeed very sick. "Poor darling." I stroked her forehead; her hair was slick with perspiration and curled in ringlets. "It's all right, it's only carsickness." I spoke in soothing tones, though my heart pounded erratically. "We're across the state line now. We're stopping just ahead."

I'd chosen Oregon over Nevada, having no taste for the desert. I hoped the greater distance from San Francisco would decrease the likelihood of news alerts. We entered Ashland, just beyond the southern border, a charming town famed for its Shakespearean festival. Unfortunately, we wouldn't be taking in any theater.

I'd selected a rambling inn with private cottages. Night was falling as I checked in. I left Karen in the car, safely cloaked in darkness. Inside, I chatted amiably with the clerk but declined the help of the bellboy.

As I switched on the lights in our room, I could see she was still a bit green. I kissed the top of her head. "It is good to be still, *n'est-ce pas?* We won't drive so far tomorrow."

"I just want to take a bath. Where's my bag?"

I frowned, turning. "I'm afraid I had to get rid of your bag, Karen. While you were sleeping."

"What do you mean, you got rid of it?" Her voice rose shrilly.

"You have to understand. If I were pulled over for any reason . . ." I inhaled deeply. "I'm sorry, *chérie*, but you were sleeping and I didn't want to wake you."

Her pupils were dilated, from the drug or from fear I didn't know. "But what if it's found?"

I didn't answer. I wanted it all to dawn on her, what would be thought if her things were found in a dumpster. It would make it easier, eventually, to tell her the truth.

"Well, I don't have anything with me," she said at last. "Not even a toothbrush."

Had I overlooked that? "You didn't put a toothbrush in the bag, did you, Karen?" I asked tersely. "Anything that would imply an overnight stay?"

"No," she said, equally irritable. "You told me not to bring anything, and I didn't. I thought we'd stop somewhere today. But I had gym clothes and makeup—" She stared at the floor. "A few of my stories."

Relieved, I said in a gentle voice, "I didn't know that, *ma petite*. I'm sorry. I'll take you shopping as soon as we're far enough away, I promise. Naturally, I picked you up a few things till then."

"When?"

"Yesterday."

She looked very fragile, very pale, as she contemplated me. "What did you get?"

"Everything." I smiled. "Did you think all this luggage was mine?"

She gazed dazedly at the bags in the corner, and her glassy eyes brightened.

I'd taken great pleasure in shopping for her, and as she opened the suitcase, she let out a cry of delight. I'd purchased clothing from the best department stores, shades that suited her and styles I wished to see her in but that were also suited to her taste. I didn't want her to feel I was trying to make her over too soon. I'd studied her so well that the sizes were correct, down to the shoes. I'd also bought underclothes and silk pajamas sprinkled with tiny yellow daisies. There is something very cheerful about daisies.

Marriage to Sabina had taught me the lengths women went to, and I'd packed all the essential toiletries into a cosmetic case: toothbrush, toothpaste, hairbrush and comb, hairpins, a makeup remover and facial cleanser, a good shampoo and a conditioner made for her curls. Even in the finest hotels, one cannot acquire a decent shampoo. I'd gone so far as to buy her feminine products. How was one to know when the need would arise? I didn't want her discomfited. The makeup, too, was carefully chosen. I'm afraid the saleswoman at the Lancôme counter took great advantage of my zeal. In addition to the usual array of powders and lipsticks, she'd enlightened me as to the need for a tremendous lot of compacts and creams. Even Karen examined several of the items quizzically, but she was utterly enchanted with it all, her semidrugged depression turned to Christmas-morning glee. Money has a wonderful faculty for smoothing things over.

And as Karen took her bath, I took my first easy breath of the day. What a thrill to hear her splashing about behind the door. I had even thought of bath oil, imagining the lavender scent on her skin. She emerged quite relaxed and feeling, by design, very pampered.

I ordered pizza—hardly haute cuisine but her favorite—and we ate a late supper in the room. We had a little wine, which proved charming as she was unused to it and began to giggle a great deal. She had never touched a drop of alcohol before, can you imagine? For a Frenchman such a thing is inconceivable, and even for an American teenager she seemed singularly devoid of vice. To this observation she retorted indignantly that she'd once smoked "an entire cigarette" at summer camp. She paused, wrinkling her nose in distaste. "Yuck."

We avoided all mention of San Francisco, her family, her backpack, her future. We talked about airy things and practical ones: weather, the surrounding area, the long trip ahead. We could stop anywhere she liked on the way to New York, I said. Not only could we, I thought, we must. By the time we reached New York, I had to be very sure of her.

At last we retired to our twin beds (very chaste, you see) to sleep.

Sometime in the night, I awoke to the drumming of rain on the roof and soft, muffled sobs. I fought the urge to comfort her and simply listened, hardly breathing, until her crying at last diminished and stopped. I knew I had to let her leave her way, as well as mine.

The next day I grew more concerned. Karen insisted a little hysterically that we stay in Ashland. "I don't want to drive today, Jacques. Can't we just stay here? Please."

It was impossible, of course. Until her bag was found, it would likely be thought she'd been kidnapped. In my paranoid imagination, the FBI was being called in, the borders alerted, her picture plastered all over the news. Such a furor was rare in 1979, when milk cartons had yet to carry anything to interfere with one's wholesome balanced breakfast, but I couldn't take the chance. "I'm sorry, *ma petite*. We should get back on the road, I think."

Her eyes filled with tears. "Why do you call me that? I don't even know what it means."

I was startled. "I—Oh, well, it's not really translatable, Karen. It's just affectionate. 'My little darling.'" My precious little one. "I will stop if you don't like it." Could I stop? I wondered.

"It's okay," she said grudgingly. "I kind of like it." She turned from me, her gaze raking over the drawn curtains on the windows, a pent-up kitten with aspirations for the outdoors. "There's just a lot I haven't thought about. Like my name. I can't go by my real name anymore, can I?"

"*Oui*, I've thought of that." I tried not to pace. I hadn't thought we'd have to face this particular issue quite yet, but there was nothing to do. "It's a simple process, Karen. It'll be fun to become someone else. That's what you want, isn't it?" I returned her stare with my most charming smile. "Remember I told you I had a daughter who would have been about your age?"

"Yes. She died—"

"*Oui*. She was just three." I fidgeted with the handkerchief in my pocket. A bad habit. I balled it in my hand, clenching and unclenching it. "When were you born, *ma petite*?"

"February twenty-fifth," she said softly, "1964."

"There, you see. My daughter was a little younger; she would have turned fifteen on June third, but I have her birth certificate and her Social Security number—"

Her stare turned stony. "I don't understand. I don't want to be your daughter."

"Listen to me, Karen. You can't apply for a license or an ID or a passport in your name. In France my daughter is dead. She died there. But she was born while I was in college at Princeton. She has dual citizenship, you see, and the records here are *non à jour* . . . er, that is to say, not up to date."

"How do you know the records are '*non à jour*'?" She spoke calmly enough, imitating my accent, but I thought I detected a faint note of hysteria. "Have you tried this before?"

"Of course not." I shrugged. "My American tax attorney wasn't aware of the accident. My taxes are rather complicated, and I wasn't aware he'd continued to declare her. When I became aware, it was a painful matter I never bothered to rectify."

"My dad used to say the tax write-off was the only reason to have children."

"Nice fellow. Do you wish to go back to him?" Her back was to me. I could not read her expression. "I don't want to be your father, Karen. It's a disguise, *ma petite*, like a hat or a mustache. It's a game. Our game. Come."

She didn't turn.

"Come here."

And at last she came to me.

We left the town of Ashland and drove north to the Columbia River, where I distracted her with the wonders of the river gorge. I was nervous, and we scarcely left the car, finally crossing over into Washington. Off Interstate 5 there is a bland town called Centralia, where I found a big bland corporate hotel. We ate a room-service dinner over desultory conversation. Karen's sparkle had gone, and so had her appetite. She picked at her food, pausing often as if listening for something. There was nothing to hear.

Finally we slept. Or rather I slept—for I awoke bleary-eyed to find Karen's bed empty.

Tripping out of bed, I found her fully dressed and a few steps from the door. Was I dreaming? I grabbed her, dragged her through the sitting room, and threw her onto her bed. She squirmed under my weight, her breath coming fast and shallow.

"What the hell are you doing?" I whispered furiously. "You're being a stupid child, Karen. I gave you credit for more guts than this. More brains—"

"If I'm such a child, what are you doing with me?"

The precocious imp. She writhed beneath me, but I pinned her hips firmly between my knees.

"Let me go, Jacques! I'm leaving."

I raised myself above her, supporting myself on my palms. "Oh, no you're not."

"You're a liar," she whispered fiercely. "You gave me something yesterday. That's why I slept so long and got sick." Wriggling, she managed to push up her sleeve. "You injected me with something. Look."

I had expected a few pinpricks, but she was such a tiny thing that her vein was purplish green with bruising.

"I saw it in the bath. I've been pretending since then. I wasn't carsick. I never get carsick." She clenched her hands into small fists and beat them against me. I grabbed her wrists. Her eyes swam with helpless tears. "Why did you do this to me?"

"What did I do to you, *chérie*? What exactly have I done to you?"

She sobbed. "You must've known I'd change my mind or you wouldn't have doped me."

I took a deep breath, rolling over and sitting on the bed beside her. "Listen. *You* haven't committed any crime, Karen, *I* have. Do you understand that? I've invested in you, just as I said I would." I swallowed. "I wanted to do it, and I don't regret it. But now there is only one thing in the world neither of us can do," I said quietly. "I can't change my mind. And neither can you."

"You can't keep me a prisoner here. I want to go."

"Go where?"

"I'll go to my aunt's. I'll take the bus to Se-Seattle," she stammered.

"Will you? With what?"

Her eyes darted to the chair in the corner where I'd laid my slacks, a pocket of which held a money clip. The unconscious gesture told me everything. The little minx.

"Don't make me tell on you, Jacques." She had the temerity to say this. "It's my fault. I shouldn't have led you on—"

"Have you led me on?" I asked. "Have you?"

I held her down and kissed her, not gently as before but hard. I could taste her distrust on my tongue. After some moments, though, she stopped struggling and clung to me. When I pulled away to look at her, her mouth was open and her hair mussed, eyes wide and bewildered. And I knew it wasn't I who bewildered her but herself.

I reached for the robe that lay at the foot of my bed and drew the belt from its loops; she swallowed and sat up. I forced her down again. "What are you going to do?" she murmured.

"Put you to bed."

She squirmed and tried to kick me.

"I'm sorry for this, Karen." I wasn't thinking very clearly. Was this real or only a game? It was, of course, both. I wrapped the belt around her wrists and tied it. She opened her lips to scream. I slapped my hand over her mouth. "If you scream, I'll gag you."

She did scream, naturally.

It was only a muffled sound against my hand. In the end I grew tired and annoyed and did gag her. Then I tied her feet. Her eyes were wide, the pupils so dilated it seemed they'd stay that way permanently. Looking at her bound on the bed, it felt like something someone else had done, not me.

I lay beside her. I explained what I'd done with her bag and with her, while she was drugged. I explained to her that she was "dead." The timing could not have been much worse but was unlikely to get better. I told her she wasn't going back: not now, not ever. Her family would mourn her and recover. She would have a new identity. She would have a new life. She would have me, and the life I wished to give her. My voice grew stronger in the telling, more certain. She remained utterly motionless.

I said at last, "I want us to be as we were, *ma petite*. The trouble is, you haven't learned yet how to be free. But I will teach you. I will teach you everything." She did not seem to blink. "Do you know what would happen if you went back? You'd settle in and within a week be dreaming of escape. You know it as well as I do, *ma chère fille*. You see, I know you. I know you better than you know yourself."

A tear rolled down her cheek. I wiped it tenderly away.

I told her stories then, slanting them to suit my aims. Cupid's abduction of Psyche. Others of that ilk. I spoke endlessly, softly, a perverse lullaby. But her eyes did not close. Finally I said, "I have something to relax you now, Karen, so you can sleep. It won't make you sick, I promise. You'll just slip into a nice sleep. Wouldn't you like to sleep?"

And she closed her eyes, as if to say yes.

I was flooded with relief. I had a number of sedatives that could be taken orally or injected, depending on her mood, but I didn't want to force her. "In the morning things will be different. I'm going to take the gag out now, so you can swallow the pill with water. Can I trust you not to scream?"

She nodded.

The "gag" was merely a clean handkerchief of mine. I removed it and eased her up; she opened her mouth for the pill I offered her and drank when I lifted the water glass to her lips. Her helplessness was touching, so very intimate that I drank it in as she drank, then rested her head back on the pillow. I tucked her in. She closed her eyes gratefully then, as if shutting a door. But I remained beside her, watching until her lashes were still and her breathing rhythmic. I took the spare blanket from the closet and covered her. As I did so, she rolled over, reaching instinctively for the pillow with her bound wrists, her dark hair spread across the starched white. Gently, I untied her.

I woke just after dawn. The sash of my robe lay twisted on the floor like a snake, and my handkerchief was a ball on the bedside table. It was a startling sight in daylight. Karen didn't stir as I gazed down at her. She didn't wake until noon. I had lunch sent up and set about rearranging the furniture, moving a table and chairs by the window. When I turned, she was sitting up straight in bed.

"Are you hungry?"

She swallowed. "My mouth is dry."

"Would you like iced tea? Or there are soft drinks in the minibar—"

"Just water."

I got her water. She gazed at me over the glass as she sipped.

"I ordered sandwiches," I said, making my voice as pleasant as possible. I'd stored away her bindings, placing them at easy reach beneath the bed. I didn't know if she'd be tempted to replay the night before, but, sadly, I could no longer trust her.

Karen yawned and stretched and went into the restroom. When she reemerged, she'd combed her hair. She chose a 7-Up from the minibar, sat down, and said politely, "This looks very good. Thank you." She wore an expression of wary appraisal, regarding me as a rational person might regard a madman. I didn't care for it.

"Typically I prefer to dine out," I said. "We'll do a good deal of that in New York."

She said nothing. And neither, anymore, did I.

Early evening became late evening and then night again. We used the drone of the television to avoid speaking. Oddly, I did not feel caged in. On the contrary, I felt infinitely patient, as Ahab must have been content to stare out to sea. But bedtime presented challenges. I said to her, "Shall we make a plan?"

"What's your plan, Jacques?" Her laugh was harsh and a little off pitch. "To keep feeding me drugs till I turn into a vegetable?"

"If necessary," I said coldly. "You're not exactly living up to your part of the bargain."

"How do you expect me to feel? Seeing as how I've been *murdered*—"

"Don't talk nonsense. I haven't murdered you. I've set you free. Do you think they'd ever stop looking for you otherwise? Do you think they would ever forgive you?"

This was quite cruel, but effective. The silence was poignant. It stretched on and on.

At last she said, "Well, they won't believe it. They won't believe I'm dead."

"Whyever not?"

"I wrote about you."

A diary? I stared. A diary. My mind spun. Could she have been so foolish? But of course she could have. She was fifteen. I kept my voice calm. "Really?"

"It's good for a writer to keep a journal."

I reclined on the bed and studied the popcorn ceiling. "You left it for them to find?"

"Yes."

I scratched my head. "Then it's rather a good thing I didn't tell you my real name."

We sat a moment in silence, on our separate beds, divided by an end table and an overlarge brass lamp that made it impossible to gauge how much the other was lying. I had the advantage. I was telling the truth, and in light of that it didn't matter whether she was or not—whether she'd written about me or not. In a moment she comprehended this. It made her furious.

"I'm not going to be much fun, Jacques. Or whatever your name is." She spit out the words. "I don't want anything to do with you, and you can't keep me drugged all the time. It'll attract attention, don't you think? A middle-aged man carting a stoned teenager through the lobby?"

"We'll stay in."

"The maids—"

"The reason for the sign on the door, *chérie*. I'll get us fresh towels when I pass them in the hall."

Her voice rose. "When *you* pass them?"

"Clearly, you can't be trusted to go out. Yet I do hate a cluttered hotel room. I dislike unmade beds. Perhaps I'll drug you and we'll sit on the terrace while they make up the room. I'll say you're ill."

"Why are you doing this to me?" she screamed. I rose from my bed and stood over her. She dropped her voice to an enraged whisper. "Do you think one day I'll call you 'Daddy'? Do you think I'll fu—"

I slapped her across the face. Not hard. But I'm ashamed to say I enjoyed the effect it had, the rush of red to her cheek, the stunned silence. Tears sprang to her eyes.

"Calm down." I told her sharply. "Do you hear me, Karen? I want you to calm down."

I felt her fear flood through the room and settle there like a low fog, curling at my ankles. She pushed herself back against the flimsy headboard, and gone was all the confidence. She sounded like a little girl. She murmured. "Are you . . . are you going to rape me?"

"No," I replied. "I'm going to give you everything you ever wanted in your life, and I'm going to worship you from afar. If you're good."

"And if I'm not?"

"We'll do this forever."

"I hate you!"

"I don't think you do."

And she didn't hate me, you see. It was obvious all the time in her face. Along with the fear lay attraction. Ours is a marvelously shallow society. Had I looked like Quasimodo or worn dirty clothes and smelled, she would have hated me. As it was, she was growing to love me. Once attracted, we are far more drawn to things the harder a time they give us. By now I was quite overwhelmed with love for her.

"You're a monster."

"You make me a monster, Karen. But I'll tell you a secret." I leaned down, my lips brushing her ear. "You can make me anything you like."

Arms wrapped around her knees, she fixed me with a glassy stare. So I left her alone in the bedroom and went into the sitting room of our suite. I opened the minibar and poured myself a cheap scotch, neat. There was no door she could close, and she would have to pass me to leave. Earlier, as she slept, I'd unplugged the phone beside the bed and removed it. I found a perverse pleasure in keeping her there. Oh, I had all the proper emotions. I was nervous, anxious, even guilty—not for taking her, you understand, but for tormenting her—and yet I would not be honest if I didn't admit also to a very poignant triumph. I had captured what I loved. I would keep her. She was mine.

We spent two weeks in that hotel. I had her drugged nearly all the time, not unconscious but floating in a haze of artificial well-being. You think this cruel, but she was to tell me it was one of the most restful periods of her life. When I asked her why, she replied, "It was nice not to have to think."

In her short life, she'd had more than her share of worries. Can you see that I felt I was doing something almost benevolent? Smudging her leaden memory and leaving her a blank page to write on.

Eventually I trusted her to be quiet as we left the hotel. It was to be a symbolic victory. I would not drug her; she would leave with me willingly. It was the first day of May and, poetically, the very day the discovery of her backpack was reported in the San Francisco papers. I'd been scanning the *Chronicle* each day for news of her. It had been sparse, but enough to make my blood run cold—there had been reported sightings of her and a few contradictory sightings of me. There was discussion of the epidemic of runaways in the city. And then, at last, the discovery of the bloody backpack that brought a tragic end to the search for Karen Miller.

I did not tell her.

As it was, the morning didn't start out well. She refused breakfast, refused my attempts at conversation. She didn't put on makeup or wash her hair; she pulled it back in an unruly ponytail and wore her new clothes in an unfortunate way. I decided that clashing colors were inadequate cause for alarm—half of America is discordant to my eye—and so we left the room at last. I'd already arranged the bill with the front desk. We had only to walk through the lobby to the car. There was no doorman, no valet. I carried our suitcases. Damned heavy they were, too. She toted her cosmetic case. We made it across the expanse of the lobby without mishap. The automatic glass doors slid open wide, and we both inhaled sharply at the shock of fresh air. She had uttered not a single word.

In the car my uneasiness was replaced with a foreign sensation: I glanced at her profile beside me and with a startled pang took in the unwashed hair and the pallor of her skin. Her attempts to appear unalluring troubled me. It was the tactic she'd tried with her father, I recalled: concealing herself in oversize sweatshirts and jeans. In the glare of sunlight, we were awash in reality, and it wasn't glamorous or reassuring. I was flooded with panic, like an actor who has suddenly forgotten his lines.

But I simply drove, and as we drove, something miraculous happened. I don't know if it was the relentless beauty of the Pacific Northwest, with its towering evergreens and raging rivers, or the sudden tangibility of our freedom—but her mood shifted. I stopped at a music store and let her assault my ears with Blondie and the Bee Gees. John Lennon was her favorite, and we listened to "Imagine" more times than I ever care to imagine again.

Snacking on potato chips, she said suddenly, "The thing is, I liked it better when it was my idea, too. Something we were doing together. I don't like it when you try to run everything."

I tried not to laugh. "I can understand that. I'm sorry."

"I'm not a little girl, Jacq—er . . . whatever your name is," she said. "Let's just pretend we're starting over, okay? Let's pretend we're starting now."

"All right." I matched her serious tone. But the incongruity struck me, the touching irony: "I'm not a little girl," followed by, "Let's pretend."

Oui, ma petite. Let's pretend, let's pretend, let's pretend.

She curled up on the car seat, legs curved beneath her. "So what was your daughter's name?"

I cleared my throat. "The truth is, she wasn't my daughter. Not technically. Sabina and I were friends, French students at Princeton, of similar backgrounds. Her family would have disowned her if they knew she was pregnant. She was more Catholic than not—an abortion was out of the question."

"You mean the baby wasn't even yours and you married her anyway?" She blinked. "You must have loved her very much."

"Not really . . . I liked the way she looked."

Karen bit her lip. "Do I remind you of her?"

As the words came out, she seemed to realize she'd gone to great lengths to make herself unattractive today. She smoothed the unruly curls that had escaped her ponytail.

"Not a bit," I replied. "She was blond. Brigitte Bardot–like. While we were married, she made plenty of friends."

"Do you mean . . ." Her voice actually dropped. "Lovers? Didn't that bother you?"

I shook my head. In truth, I'd had Sabina describe her encounters to me, detailed settings and sensations, but I couldn't say so to Karen. "I did not love her, you see? I didn't believe in love then."

She squirmed in her seat to look at me. A flush appeared on her cheek. "I didn't really write about you in my diary. I don't even keep a diary. I tried once, but I wasn't any good at it. It felt so phony, writing to myself. I was just bored in geometry and wrote my name with yours."

"Mrs. Jacques Barnard?"

She made her voice cool. "I don't imagine that's enough to make them look for you. And anyway, it's probably soaked in blood." But she didn't sound sorry suddenly. After a moment, "What name should I have written?"

She was asking me to trust her. I weighed it and said at last, "Tristan. My name is Tristan Mourault."

"Oh!" she exclaimed. "I like that much better than Jacques. Jacques is almost too French for a Frenchman." I laughed as she repeated, "Tristan. And what's my name?"

"Gisèle." Without hesitation. "My daughter's second name. I chose it. Do you like it?"

"Gisèle." She tasted it, tested it like a fine wine on an undeveloped palate.

"It is more charming when you say it."

She turned a little doubtfully. "Do I look like a Gisèle?"

"Exactly like."

And she smiled at me.

HIDE-AND-SEEK

Devon, Washington: fifteen years later

GISÈLE MOURAULT CALLED her daughter's name. The doors to the terrace stood open, and Nicola could hear her mother though she could not see her.

She was hiding. It was August, her parents' twelfth anniversary, and far too beautiful a day for piano lessons. Nicola squinted through the crescent eyehole out at the empty room. The first room off the entry, it was intended for guests to await the arrival of their host. The butler, Henri, called it the "receiving room." Everything in it was old—much older than Nicola. The décor was Louis XV Rococo, which marked the end of the French Baroque period, or so she'd been taught. All the rooms had exotic influences she could name but whose origins existed in the otherworldly haze of history lessons. Rococo meant pale shades: variations on cream. Low-slung settees and wide-legged fauteuils were drawn together by a large Aubusson rug. Books lined one wall; a collection of vintage French dueling pistols was displayed on another. A simply cut crystal chandelier served as centerpiece, highlighting an ornamental plastered ceiling that always reminded her of a wedding cake, with its scallops and scrolls. The pale walls were elaborately carved panels—*boiseries*, they were called in French. Behind one of these panels hid Nicola.

Outwardly, there was nothing to distinguish it from the other panels in the room. The eyehole was concealed by an elaborate design of carved wood. To open the secret panel, one simply pushed the head of a nail in the framed wood at the bottom. Once one was inside, the door fit neatly closed and could even be bolted. She didn't worry that anyone would find her here. It was a perfect way to evade the piano teacher. Nicola had no talent for piano, and Mr. Wilkes took pains to let her know it with theatrical sighs and a withering gaze that turned her fingers to gelatin.

She heard the doorbell ring and watched with malicious glee as Henri showed Mr. Wilkes in to wait. With his black suit, pencil-thin stature and perfect posture, he looked like a piece of wrought-iron from the railing in the garden. The rail drew itself to full height, glanced in annoyance at its watch, and began to pace.

After a moment her mother appeared to apologize for her mysterious absence. "I'm so sorry, Mr. Wilkes. I can't find Nicola anywhere. She must be out playing and forgotten the time." Her tone was distracted, which meant that Nicola would probably even escape the halfhearted lecture on the importance of punctuality and practice.

Mr. Wilkes replied curtly, "Perhaps you should reconsider the piano, Mrs. Mourault, where your daughter's concerned. She won't improve if she doesn't apply herself."

Her mother's brows drew together in a frown, and Nicola felt a flicker of guilt that disappeared along with Mr. Wilkes out the door. She wasn't about to give up such a good hiding place out of sentiment. Once the coast was clear, she'd have the afternoon to do whatever she liked.

But the coast didn't clear. Her mother remained in the room, running her fingers idly along the edge of a console table, lost in her thoughts. From the pocket of her summer dress, she extracted a few photos, lingering over each one an impossibly long time.

Fortunately, Nicola wasn't prone to claustrophobia.

Falconer's Point was full of secrets. Practically every room in the house had something to hide: a hearth that lifted or a hollow window seat, a spring on a bookcase or a removable stair. Many of the spaces were no bigger than drawers; a few, like this, were tiny rooms. Outside, the house was surrounded by gardens with mazelike hedges and crisscrossed by curving walkways. There was a vast pool house and a courtyard beneath Nicola's room that held her favorite climbing tree, a wide-limbed English oak with leaves that brushed her window. The house had been built in the 1940s but seemed much older, with its sprawling staircases and long halls, creaking doors and quietly rusting cornices. But it didn't frighten Nicola, even at night. She'd been born here, and the house was a familiar friend.

She had little opportunity to make others. She was an only child and didn't attend regular school but was tutored at home. Once in a while, she met a girl her own age, but living as she did—across the lake from the village, atop a long, winding mountain road—the friendships quickly withered. Her disappointment was usually short-lived; she emulated her mother in all things and Gisèle Mourault was fond of solitude. They were happiest in each other's company. Her mother had a way of making everyday things magical—shopping in the village, elaborate picnics or tromps through the snow, and acting out plays on rainy days.

Into these idyllic romps her grandfather figured prominently. It had been Grand-père who'd shown her the secret passages. No one else knew about them. It was only in August, when he went away to France, that she could use them to get out of piano lessons and dental appointments. Strangers often mistook Grand-père for her father, less out of physical resemblance than emotional attachment. She was more often with him than with her father. Happier with him. A quixotic soul, at forty-nine years old Tristan Mourault was slim, with blond hair going gray in a distinguished way, at the temples and in his slight sideburns. His face was tanned, emphasizing the pale blue eyes behind his elegant wire-framed glasses. With his French clothes and fragrant pipe, he looked as though he ought to be sailing a yacht on the Mediterranean.

Though he'd lived for years in America, he retained the accent of his birthplace and had a habit of quoting obscure French poets and speckling his English with interesting phrases, so that among Nicola's first words were *"mon chaton"*—my kitten—which he had always called her. He let her have sips of his wine and had good ideas, like spading the garden at night to find earthworms or climbing out on the roof to watch the eclipse. He'd taught her to paint and to ski, and he even made a game of geography. She'd close her eyes and point at a map of the world, and he'd tell her stories of the region, so that it wasn't just a pink or green or orange blob, but a real place, like book places.

Her father, on the other hand, possessed a flair for making easy things difficult. Tall and distant, he often eyed his daughter with embarrassment, as if he himself were not sure of his role. The condition was contagious, and when left alone with him Nicola was often seized with qualms of shyness. She found herself resorting to strange but true bits of trivia: *Did you know a leech has thirty-two brains? Bats always turn left when exiting a cave. A hummingbird weighs less than a penny, Dad. Can you believe that?* If he noticed this was in any way odd, he never let on. Her father's affection was unpredictable and arbitrary. It came and went. And so did he.

Her mother was the center of Nicola's world. She taught her all the important things: how to wear one's hair, how to dress, how to hold oneself. Nicola loved to watch her get ready for the day. The feminine ritual held tremendous power for her. Mysterious bottles extracted from mysterious drawers, powders and brushes, hair gels and sprays—all the sacred items that magically transformed you into anything you wished to be. Yet her mother was beautiful without all this. Gisèle Mourault wasn't like other mothers. At eleven and a half, Nicola was nearly as tall as she, and sometimes Gisèle seemed to Nicola like an older sister, with her youthful, lilting voice and luminous eyes. Her hair was a lustrous dark chocolate, her skin even and fair, and she smelled like springtime. When Gisèle walked into a room, it was as though someone had opened a window and let in a breeze.

Yet there was also something fragile about her—a quality Nicola recognized but could never pin down—a sadness laughed away. It tugged at the corners of her mouth, played in the shadows of her eyes, and was both captivating and disquieting to her daughter. When Nicola fell off her bike or had the flu, it was the housekeeper, Maggie, to whom she ran. It wasn't that her mother wouldn't or couldn't care for her, it was that she cared *too* much. She suffered more than the one suffering. And absolutely everything worried her where Nicola was concerned. She was worst about the water. In the Pacific Northwest, lakes and streams abounded, but Gisèle couldn't swim and had a terrible fear of water. Though Nicola swam like a fish, her mother insisted she be accompanied by an adult at the lake—and even in their own swimming pool.

Nicola peeked out again. Her mother had turned toward the door, eyes glistening with tears. Nicola's stomach tightened. What had happened? Gisèle moved to greet someone beyond Nicola's view, speaking so softly that it was hard to hear. Nicola strained to detect her words and caught a name. "Marc . . ."

That would be Marc Kreicek, a family friend who was often at Falconer's Point.

". . . my message," her mother went on. "Thank you."

They moved farther into the room, so that Nicola could see their quick embrace.

"You're the only one I can tell," her mother murmured.

"Haven't I always been here for you?" His words were always a bit difficult to make out, because his accent was so strong.

"Yes. You're very good to me. I'm afraid I haven't been as good to you."

"Sshh."

Her mother spoke quickly in an urgent, agitated tone that was utterly foreign to Nicola. "No one else can know about this. I want to know everything, Marc. Anything you can find out for me. Tell me what she's like. All I know is her name."

Nicola could not see Marc's face. He spoke too softly to hear, ending with, ". . . more photographs?"

"Yes, but don't let her see you."

"Trust me, Gisèle. Come here. It will be all right." He reached out his hand, and she went to him. And then there was only a soft murmuring in masculine, comforting tones and the brush of clothing. Was her mother crying? Nicola fidgeted in frustration. From an early age, her mother's moods had been a preoccupation for her. They were so close it was as if they shared the same thoughts. Why was she so upset?

At last Gisèle came back into view. She smoothed her hair and wiped her cheek with the back of her hand, stepped out onto the terrace, and disappeared. Nicola waited a few minutes, listening carefully, but the room sounded empty. Marc must have gone, too. She reached for the latch. She'd find her mother in the garden and try to learn what was wrong. But just as she was about to step from her hiding place, Nicola heard new voices in the hall. Quickly, with a frustrated sigh, she darted back behind the panel.

She recognized Robin Dresden, her godfather, laughing with Henri but he strode into the room alone. Darkly handsome, Robin had eyes the color of charcoal and nearly black hair, a lock of which fell roguishly onto his brow. It was rumored he slept only four hours a night, and he very often looked it, yet a palpable energy surrounded him. Hollow-cheeked and unpredictable, he was prone to unexpected visits; he'd sweep in with gifts for Nicola, make her mother smile and her father angry, speak French with her grandfather, and sweep back out again.

Robin had works in museums and galleries all over the world, sculpture ranging from figurative to abstract and paintings of a style no one seemed able to define, though she'd heard her father call them "the work of a troubled mind." Robin simply called them experiences. Nicola thought they were wonderful. Some made her think of a tornado—shapes and figures seemed to whirl through the canvas coming into focus suddenly and inexplicably, when you least expected it. Others were complex stacked images, in which the sum equaled something remarkably different from its parts. One she was particularly fond of he called the inside of a raindrop. In describing Robin, Grand-père had once quoted Picasso, and Nicola had remembered it ever since: *Some painters transform the sun into a yellow spot. Others transform a yellow spot into the sun.*

Having such a glamorous personage as her godfather, Nicola knew, made her unique. She was flattered by his attention and flustered by it, and quite under his spell—which was not, of course, the same as feeling at ease. She had the eerie sense Robin could see through the walls. In the silence her breath was suddenly deafening. She waited.

It was not her mother who appeared to greet him but again Marc Kreicek.

Nicola couldn't see him much better this time. Marc had his back to her and pulled from his pocket a rag streaked with blues and grays, like the sky after a rain, and began to wipe his hands. Yet he hadn't been painting a moment ago; he'd been here with her mother. Maybe he did it out of habit. He was a very good painter, though not as good as Robin.

"K." Robin stepped forward to greet him. He'd called Marc that for as long as Nicola could remember, because of a character in a Kafka novel she was too young to read. Marc told her she could call him that as well, but it seemed too informal. Something about Marc invited formality. He was from Czechoslovakia, and though Nicola was used to accents, his was sometimes hard to decipher. He and Robin often spoke together in his language with baffling ease. Even when they stuck to English, Nicola found them hard to understand; they spoke of things far beyond her. She'd learned to assemble bits of their conversations like puzzle pieces.

"It's nearly finished," Marc said to Robin. "*L'Ingénue* is my best yet. It is perfect." He often spoke like this. He'd never learned that it was more polite to let others compliment him first.

"Glad to hear it," said Robin, unfazed. "Because I'm afraid it's the last, K. I've just heard from Tristan. Getting past the new security system is like dancing on land mines, apparently. He claims it's impossible to bring us *Déjeuner.*" He waved a dismissive hand. "It isn't impossible, of course, but he's paranoid. With the recent thefts in Paris, he's under pressure to have the paintings reappraised. He's panicking, and if he panics, he'll be caught. For the time being, we'll have to be satisfied with what we have."

"And what exactly do *we* have, Rob? I have shit." Nicola savored the epithet.

"You've been paid well, no?"

Marc scoffed. "Pennies of what they're worth—"

"They're worth twenty to twenty-five years."

"*To kravina . . .*" The words trailed off in disgust, and Nicola couldn't be sure, but she thought he'd cussed again. "*Co byste udělal na mém místě?*"

Robin laughed then. "You wouldn't be in this position at all if not for me. And we've had a good run of it. Tristan wanted to stop long ago."

"Ironic, is it not? To find he's the principled one among us."

"Principles have nothing to do with it. He's had to turn his family home into an amusement-park attraction. Tourists tromping in and out for a few lousy quid. That's the real fucking crime."

Marc spoke urgently. "But surely you can see the possibilities. The sale of just *one*—"

"We didn't do it to sell them."

"You don't see. I'm suggesting we sell one of mine."

"I *do* see. You've suggested it often enough." Robin paused. "If it were simple greed, you wouldn't be such a loose cannon, but it's ego and spite. You want to put one over on the collectors, eh?"

"If they can't recognize a fake, they deserve to be cheated. Buyer, beware."

"Do you think any copy can go undetected forever? Even you're not that good."

"Not good enough for the black market, but good enough to pawn off on our dear friend."

"Shut up," Robin said, sharply. "For Christ's sake, the walls have ears around here."

He didn't know how true that was, Nicola thought. *But what was it all about?*

Something about Grand-père's collection. Her grandfather returned from Paris each year with one or two paintings. He told Nicola they were only copies of pieces from his family collection. The Mourault Collection was renowned, a splendid array of the greatest artists of the impressionist age. But the originals were held in trust and couldn't be taken out of France.

It was his legacy, and Nicola knew how important it was to him. Just as she knew that the paintings Grand-père brought to Devon couldn't be copies. She could tell by the way he looked at them, the way Robin looked. They did not seem to breathe. And Marc Kreicek was a cat eyeing a plump bird—his eyes narrowed and fairly glittered.

Besides, why would Marc spend so much time copying copies? Nicola thought it far more likely that her grandfather was bringing the originals *here* and taking copies to France. But she never said anything. It's a benefit of childhood that adults feel so much is over one's head.

Marc was saying tersely, "What are you doing here anyway?"

"Offering my moral support."

"You've become very moral all of a sudden."

Robin laughed. "Cheer up, K. I can't bear to see you so dispirited. We'll find new laws for you to break. In any case, the support's not for you, it's for Gisèle. Today's her anniversary."

"Yes, I know."

Robin frowned. "One too many, it seems."

Nicola blinked. Her godfather dropped his voice, and though she leaned forward and strained to hear, she missed his next words.

Marc's tone was derisive. "What a fool he is. Will she divorce him?"

"Don't bet on it. Anyway, you had your chance years ago."

"She didn't know what she was doing. She regrets it."

Robin gazed at him thoughtfully. "Someone sent her photographs. Anonymously. You wouldn't know anything about that, would you?"

Marc gave a shrug. "Do you think I take an interest in such things?"

"I do, yes. And I don't think she's this upset over one of Luke's affairs—"

"No?" Marc laughed, but there was an edge to it. "Well. Perhaps this one is different." He smirked down at the dirty rag and began once more to wipe his fingers. "I do know one thing—she'll never be happy, our Gisèle. Her feelings are not important enough to her."

"Still practicing psychology, I see." Robin rose impatiently. "Where is she anyway?"

Another shrug. "Perhaps you misunderstood her. Nothing's out of the ordinary here. No hysterical scenes. I've just seen Luke on his way to the wine cellar. For champagne, he said."

"And Nico?"

"Not at the piano, thank God. Come, look at my painting." Marc moved to the door. "It is absolutely perfect. We must convince Tristan it's lunacy to stop now."

Nicola stared out at the empty room. Their indistinct voices faded to nothingness in the hall, and she slid the wooden bolt upright and stepped from the passage. Frowning, she pushed the hidden door tightly closed behind her.

✍

Chill air rose to meet Luke as he descended the stairs.

To come down to the wine cellar was to enter a private club. It was Tristan's wine, of course—he and Robin, the connoisseurs. Luke spent considerable time on the consumption end, yet still couldn't tell the good years from the bad and privately preferred beer. But it was safe to say that everything here was from a good year. He liked to come down when he could be alone and not worry about betraying a total ignorance of viticulture.

Today he was particularly grateful to escape into the cool quiet. Something was definitely out of kilter around here. He'd expected a tedious night of anniversary make-believe, but Gisèle wasn't playing her usual part. Something had upset her, and he had no idea what it was. Luke tended to think it had little to do with him—little in her life did these days—but the timing was suspect. She didn't come down for breakfast and had avoided him all day. He had no idea what to expect of the evening.

He traveled along an aisle of champagne bottles, allowing the festive multicolored foils to buoy his spirits with their promise of celebratory things. From one row he chose a predictably good Dom Pérignon and carried it with him.

Gisèle typically preferred to spend this occasion at home: a candlelit dinner outside and, over dessert, gifts. Thoughtful, not too intimate. She would give him a watch or a robe, a sweater or a new long coat. From him, jewelry. The cards would be the carefully worded kind.

How had all his ardent fantasies come to that?

But that was the trouble with marriage, Luke thought, you don't marry another person—you marry a mirage. And Gisèle had beguiled him from the start. The strange girl with an air of enchantment about her and her distinguished father, whose refined manners spoke of worlds Luke had never known.

His first glimpse of them was in downtown Devon, strolling through the park. A nymph in a pale summer dress, the breeze stirring the dark hair around her shoulders. He could still hear her laughing, a lovely lilting sound carried to him on the wind. Even from a distance, you could tell that her father was European. There was no brashness in his movements, no impatience. He walked with a kind of Old World let-them-eat-cake attitude Luke wanted to disapprove of but instead envied. An equally poised little Yorkshire terrier matched his pace perfectly to theirs. They moved in the dappled shade of the trees, and Luke could not stop watching.

He was that unfortunate combination, a young man filled with romantic yearnings yet faced with distinctly unromantic prospects. He liked to tell people he was from the Isle of Wight, which invariably brought a smile on account of his slight southern drawl, but it was actually the county in Virginia where he was born, nestled along the James River. He was from the town of Smithfield, home of ham. "Isle of Wight" just had a better ring to it. In the summer of 1982, he was long-haired and a pothead, a man without a future. The last was a matter of opinion, of course, and his father's to be exact. As if to prove him right, Luke managed to get himself fired from his summer job on the first day and so wound up in Devon, Washington, renewing strained relations with his wealthy Aunt Eleanor.

She was given to throwing lavish parties on her lakefront estate, charitable events that evolved more out of loneliness than philanthropy. To Luke they were dull affairs. But on an occasion in June, Tristan Mourault was in attendance. And with him his beautiful daughter, Gisèle.

They were never formally introduced and so settled for the usual foreplay between strangers: lingering erotic glances across the room. Her long-lashed eyes met his rather than demurely dipping after a moment or two. With his tennis player's build and Scandinavian good looks, Luke was used to attracting women and less certain of what to do once they'd been won. In adolescence he'd been prone to puppy-dog adulation. Lately he ran to boredom in all things: school, work, conversation, and even, after a month or two, sex. Once the intoxicating cloud of curiosity dissipated, he was left with a hollow, impatient feeling, viewing with puzzlement and faint disdain the object he'd desired only yesterday. But it was different with Gisèle.

She wore a peach-colored dress and a summer hat, when no one wore hats; her shoulders were bare, and her necklace held a single pearl, poised like a raindrop above her breasts. There was no attempt at modernity. Her beauty was the classic kind: high cheekbones and wide eyes, accented by a mischievous smile and belied by her diminutive size (she was just five foot three and did little to disguise it with her ballet-style dress shoes). Luke looked at her and was bewitched.

As the stodgy three-piece band launched into "Summertime," he watched the hem of Gisèle's full skirt disappear through the French doors to the terrace. He followed.

She met him with a smile and no feminine attempt at surprise. "Hello."

His brilliant opening line? "Hey there."

"I'm Gisèle." She held out her dainty hand.

Was he meant to kiss it or shake it? Luke decided on the former, at which she laughed, probably because he did so clumsily. How gauche he'd felt next to her. Her skin was porcelain, cool to the touch, and when she withdrew her hand, it was like water flowing through his fingers, the movement was so graceful and smooth.

"I'm Luke Farrell," he managed. "This is my aunt's little shindig." Virginia had loomed large in his vocabulary then.

"Your aunt is Eleanor Halvorson?"

"Yeah." He pulled a face.

"It can't be *that* bad. She must be thoughtful, giving to families of the terminally ill."

"If people want to give their money away, they don't need a party to do it. Why not donate the money it takes to throw the party? No one would see her do it, that's why."

"Well, you might want to keep that to yourself while you're staying with her."

So she had asked about him. Luke grinned. "I guess I don't believe much in lying."

"Hmm." She raised a dubious brow. "A liar would say the same thing. Robin and Tristan tell me lying's one of the first skills we learn."

That is how she was. Bright as a diamond that catches your eye in a window full of other jewels. He laughed. "I suppose that's true."

She traced a flagstone with the toe of her shoe. "But I think that when you lie, you tell a sort of truth. Like, if you lie about your age, you say you're afraid of growing old."

"You're a philosophical one, aren't you?"

"An unattractive quality in a girl." She was teasing him.

"Nah, it's rare, is all." Luke straightened. "I'm a humanities major." His father was fond of saying he'd majored in indecision. "I study philosophy." Rubbing his stubbled chin, he added, "Who are Robin and Kristen anyway? Your girlfriends?"

"Oh, no." She laughed as though this were quite funny indeed. "No. It's Tristan: T-R-I-S-T-A-N. It's French. Breton, actually. You know, like the story, Tristan and Isolde?"

Luke didn't know, but he nodded.

"He's my father," she said.

"But neither of you like that term?"

"Oh. Well, no, it's not really that." She flushed faintly. "It's just he's not like a regular father. He and my mother split when I was small. I didn't live with him till I was fifteen—"

"And Robin?"

She gazed down. A flutter of long lashes. "Robin Dresden, the artist. Do you know him?"

"In a roundabout way. Robin, spelled M-O-N-E-Y?"

Gisèle looked up, smiled. "How old are you?"

"Twenty-one. How old are you?"

"Eighteen, last week." Then, "You're just in Devon for the summer?"

"Yep. Till the end of August."

She turned away and back again, gazing at him with the slightest hint of a smile, as if at a private secret. "Well, since we're being honest, Luke, hadn't you better kiss me now? Tristan will be looking for me, and you might not get another chance."

And so he had. Her lips parted for his instantly, and he remembered still the cool, sweet-tart taste of her tongue that was not the punch but just naturally Gisèle.

The wedding was less than two months later. It was a simple ceremony, intimate and outdoors, along the lake, no groomsmen, no bridesmaids, not even a church. Tristan gave Gisèle away; Robin Dresden and Aunt Eleanor witnessed it. One of Gisèle's most attractive qualities was her lack of pretense. "It's our wedding," she said. "Why clutter it up?" Luke was grateful for the minimalism; he couldn't have provided a lot of clutter if it had been called for. His mama had died when he was ten, his college friends couldn't afford airfare, and in a letter—the coward's way out—he'd told his father not to bother making the trip.

Luke still got a lump in his throat when he thought of the ceremony and wondered if it was from real emotion or idealized expectation, the way as a child he had most eagerly awaited the least fulfilling experiences. The lump was for the fragile bubble of fantasy. Gisèle's veil blew on the gentle breeze, tendrils of her dark hair escaping a chignon. He knew how it flowed over her shoulders, and this made it more desirable up—a gambit, however clichéd, a promise of what was to come. The white gown was form-fitting, flaring at the bottom, and she looked like a bejeweled mermaid, sparkling in the sunlight. Her eyes were the color of the lake in shallow places, translucent and bottomless at the same time.

The reception had been a grand affair held at the Devon Country Club. Everyone had been there, or so it seemed to Luke. Devon was full of colorful personalities with provocative backstories. There was Tristan's friend Kreicek, a painter who had escaped then-communist Prague. Rather a shady sort, wiry and hungry-looking beneath his designer clothes, his only real source of income appeared to be his life-long friendship with Robin Dresden.

Dresden, as Tristan often said, was good to his friends. And he could well afford to be. His arcane paintings were the toast of the art world, and by the age of twenty-eight he'd already inherited the whole of his uncle's estate, which amounted to most of the land in Devon. And Devon was an apt place for Robin Dresden: a mecca of art, it was a far cry now from its humble beginnings as a slapdash artists' colony. The town—or "village," as it was often pretentiously called—had prospered under each of Dresden's forebears, most notably the last. Robin's uncle, Bryan Prescott, was the architect who had turned charm into a building code. The quaint English hamlet of old was meticulously recreated, and in recent years Devon had become a tourist haven, Washington's version of Carmel-by-the-Sea.

Robin had met Tristan and Gisèle in New York and was responsible for their move to Devon. He'd even made available to them Bryan Prescott's secluded old hilltop estate, the austerely named Falconer's Point, where Luke was to live once he and Gisèle married. Tristan had insisted. "Think nothing of it, *mon fils*. Let me invest in you." (Though Luke had little in the way of talent, he'd decided he would be an artist. In Devon there were few other acceptable choices.) "You need time to develop your craft. And I could not part with *ma chère* Gisèle. . . ."

And so Luke had been flattered, relieved, indebted. Indebted forever thereafter. Gisèle kept her name, Mourault. Tristan's name. Their bank accounts were regularly funded by Tristan. Luke preferred to assume that it was really Gisèle's money held in trust, yet he now suspected the trust to be the intangible kind. It was never discussed. Luke might have been uncouth enough to live off his father-in-law, but not enough to query him about money.

There were few awkward moments in his new world. Everything operated with choreographed precision yet little emotion. It had begun with the wedding day itself. Strangers murmured compliments to Luke on his lovely bride, yet no one seemed to know anything intimate about her; there were no rambling toasts filled with nostalgic witticisms, no tears. Luke remembered Gisèle sipping from her champagne goblet all night, yet she never lost her poise. Once he caught her gracefully pouring her champagne down the back of a shrub.

For his part, Luke swallowed a good deal. He'd literally drowned in his joy, too drunk to carry her over the threshold or to consummate the marriage by much more than legal definition. Afterward, he blamed himself for her rapid withdrawal, though through the years he'd gone to great lengths to redeem himself.

That night she'd simply murmured, "Luke, it's all right. Really." Naked and heart-stoppingly lovely, Gisèle lay on her side, cool and clear-headed, quietly watchful. "I don't mind."

He would always remember her strange, abstract gaze. The sadness in it. But then her eyes had crinkled into a reassuring smile. She'd run her fingertips over his face, softly over his forehead, gently rubbing his temples until his eyes closed. Her touch, so light and cool, quieted the buzz in his ears and all the whirring rush of the day.

But when she thought he was asleep, she'd rolled over, away from him. And he had heard, faint but distinct, her sigh of relief.

Less than seven months later, little Nicola was born. "Premature," Gisèle claimed and the obstetrician dutifully agreed. After that, sex became a mere physical release that involved little eye contact, and never intercourse. "It's not your fault, Luke," she'd said at last. "I've just never been able to like it much." Then, meaningfully, "I don't expect you to be celibate."

And so he hadn't been. But he *had* been discreet, carrying on his affairs in Seattle, where he often stayed for weeks at a time, enrolled in art seminars at the University of Washington. He gave these women—

mostly young co-eds—his mother's maiden name, Halvorson. There was no way to link any of it back to his life here. In Devon, Luke was pure. And the truth was, he'd never stopped loving Gisèle.

He kicked around the cellar aimlessly. A red wine with dinner . . . no, two. Gisèle wouldn't drink much—she never did—but Luke had a feeling he would. The bottles got dustier the farther back he traveled. The ones in the last rack were dustiest of all, and he knew these to be Tristan's most prized vintages. He didn't dare drink one, but there was no harm in gawking. Idly, he set his champagne on the floor and reached for a bottle: Château Margaux 1945. And another: Latour '47. They had to be vinegar by now, merely a pretentious form of investment. He knelt down and pulled out a 1939 Haut-Brion. Making wine while the war raged. Seen in that light, it was impressive, he supposed. A bit of bottled resistance.

Gently, Luke replaced the bottle on the rack, only to rise and kick his Dom Pérignon, shattering it. Tiny bubbles spread over the limestone and beneath the prized bottles. *Shit.* Shards of green glass winked up at him insolently.

He cursed again. Tristan would have sent a maid down. But Luke swept up the glass on his hands and knees, dabbing gingerly beneath the rack of precious wine, sopping up the spilled champagne with an old rag from a utility closet and trying not to find it all symbolic. When he felt the sharp sting of glass enter his palm, he plopped down on the cold limestone floor in resignation and began to remove the bottom row of bottles so he could see what he was doing.

The second bottle from the end felt impossibly light, and it rattled when he extracted it. It wasn't terribly old, an '84, and held far more fingerprints than dust. Luke peered through the tinted glass to a dark object at the bottom. The foil was intact but loose and slid easily off the bottle in one piece. There was no cork. He turned the bottle upside down, and a single key fell into his bleeding palm.

It was too large for a trunk key or a diary. Forgetting the spilled champagne, Luke rose and walked to the rear of the cellar, to a series of doors there. The first was the utility closet; the second held boxes, rolled-up carpets, paint cans. But the final door accepted the key, and he heard a decided click as the lock gave.

Luke had barely cracked the door when he caught sight of her. Gisèle. Staring back at him.

She was not flesh and blood, of course, but oil on canvas. The room was a makeshift artist's studio, with all its expected sights and pungent smells. He stepped inside, and his mouth fell open, a single unintelligible syllable spilling out. A worktable held palettes and paints, rags and paint thinner, brushes and turpentine; there were stretched canvases stacked against the wall, rolled canvases in a corner, canvases on two different easels. Each of them shared the same subject. His chaste, almost celibate wife. Nude.

Canvases literally filled the room. Luke examined them one at a time but could find no signature. Nothing at all to betray the artist. However, the paintings were relentless in their scrutiny of their subject: Gisèle, from the fine carpal bones of her feet to the hollow of her throat, the curve of her hips, her buttocks, her navel; the detail was extraordinary yet erotic all the same. Beautiful. But who knew her so well as to capture every freckle and mole, tendon and vein? Who had she *let* know her so well?

Ironically, this is how Luke aspired to paint his wife, the subject he yearned for. But in his attempts, Gisèle had always come out looking like a Baroque cover girl. Here, she was three-dimensional and vital.

By the time Luke reached the last of the canvases, his eyes felt unfocused, battered and numb. Jealousy coursed through him like a dark poison. Many of the paintings were not even full nudes, but pieces of her, and these were worse somehow—the intimacy that lay in the simple abstraction of her body. For the first time, he realized that abstraction was possible only for one intensely familiar with reality, familiar enough to play with flesh and bone, breath and skin.

Someone had painted her. It was suddenly painfully obvious to Luke that Gisèle could be having an affair, and the notion hit him like ice water in the face. He stood, frozen, fixating on the empty space in the corner where the artist's signature ought to be: his invisible rival.

"Dad?"

Startled out of his reverie, Luke spun around. His little girl was not so little anymore. It seemed Nicola had grown up overnight; there was no more giveaway pounding of footsteps.

"I'm sorry. The door was open." She frowned. Luke realized she must be alarmed by his expression, but he couldn't seem to alter it. "Marc said you'd come down here. . . ." Nicola's voice trailed away, her eyes widening as they traveled over the canvases around him. Embarrassed, she dropped her gaze but said in her matter-of-fact, perceptive way, "No one knows you paint down here, do they?"

Luke's thoughts were spinning. "Oh, no. Nic, *I* didn't—" But of course she would think he had. It would be natural. If anyone were going to paint Gisèle, it should have been he.

"Not even Mom knows, does she?" A sympathetic pause. "Does she?"

Did she? Of course Gisèle must know about the paintings. "Nicola, I—" The words hung there, broken. He gazed into his daughter's innocent, perplexed face. How could he tell her someone else had painted her mother nude? It was impossible. "You shouldn't be in here."

"It's *okay*, Dad." Her tone was precocious, yet her eyes flitted around the room like a butterfly, without resting. "Robin lets me check out art books at the college. Nudity isn't anything to be ashamed of. I'm not a kid anymore, you know." But she was. She bit her lip. "When are you going to show Mom?"

Show Gisèle? Luke was silent, dumb.

"Oh, but you *have* to, Dad. It could be . . . you know, an anniversary present." She frowned. "If she knew you'd been painting her, she, well . . ." Well. "You *have* to tell her."

And he supposed he did. Someone did. "Why don't you run up and tell her, Nicky," he said at last. "Tell her to come down here and see."

After she'd raced upstairs, Luke regretted it, of course. What a pathetic bastard he was. But it gave him a few more moments to think.

If Gisèle was having an affair—who was it? Robin Dresden? Luke had always been jealous of him for all the usual reasons, not the least of which was his easy intimacy with Gisèle. Yet Robin was practically one of the family and always dating different women. And these paintings weren't his style at all. One could never tell what the hell he was painting, but he never stooped to realism.

Marc Kreicek? He was the kind of man whom women find attractive and men despise: slippery, cunning. He was on the thin side and two inches shorter than Luke but impeccably stylish, with a cold, precise manner and that strange indifference to almost everything that attracted some women. In spite of this veneer, Luke knew that Marc had long had a thing for his wife, and Gisèle had even admitted to a brief infatuation. "Before I met you," she'd assured him. But now Luke wondered.

The only person to whom Kreicek showed any deference was Robin. He rather suspected that Marc wanted to *be* Robin. With everyone else it was as if he were in on a private joke he had no intention of sharing. Maybe it was one he shared with Gisèle? Marc's knowledge of Luke's own infidelities gave him little solace. He may have felt that turnabout was fair play.

But was he capable of painting these? Marc was a damned good painter, but he painted only copies, and he copied only the impressionists.

Luke groaned aloud. There was certainly no shortage of artists in Devon. *It could be anyone.* But then, that wasn't quite true. And it brought Luke to the fundamental question. Why paint her *here*? Obviously, the paintings were secret, done in secret, celebrating a secret relationship. But why hide the secret *here*?

His next thought stopped him short. *Tristan?*

Tristan painted. It was his house, his wine cellar, his *style*. He was a real-ist, at least in the artistic sense, and possessed of far greater skill than Luke.

But Gisèle's *father*? Surely not.

And yet there had always been an odd energy between the two of them. In the beginning Luke thought their relationship refined and pro-gressive, but it struck him very quickly that Tristan and Gisèle didn't really act like father and daughter. For one, she always called him by his first name. Luke was reminded of her words at their first meeting: *I didn't live with him till I was fifteen; he's not really like a father to me.* And Gisèle was different when Tristan wasn't around; she was more affectionate, more open to intimacy—less Tristan's daughter and more Luke's wife. When Luke moved to Devon, he'd been jokingly told there were only two seasons in the Pacific Northwest: winter and August. His marriage had been much the same. And he'd often wondered why Tristan chose the month of their anniversary to go to France.

Dizzied by pity and disgust, Luke gazed helplessly around him. Surely not his Gisèle and Tristan . . .

And that's when she came, as if timed for maximum effect, her cheeks flushed as though she'd rushed down. Gisèle's first expression was one of horror. There was no disguising it. It was darker than surprise. She stood in the doorway, taking in the kaleidoscopic array of nudes before her. Her eyes settled on his and didn't leave. "Nicola said . . . She told me you'd been painting?"

It was a question. Luke opened his mouth to speak but heard voices behind her: Nicola's, exuberant and excited, and, to his dismay, Robin's clipped English accent came in reply, and then Marc's cynical laugh. An odd little posse coming to lynch him.

"Ella, I—"

Robin appeared then, looming over Gisèle in the doorway. For a moment even he was uncharacteristically dazed. But when he spoke, his tone was reassuringly dry, if derisive. "These don't seem quite your style, Luke. Not a deer or a meadow in sight."

Gisèle turned to him, her tone reproachful. "Rob—"

"They're very precise," said Marc. "Did you work from photographs?"

Photographs. Of course. Luke shifted his weight. He looked at his wife.

"There were those few," Gisèle offered. "When we were first married."

Robin gave her an odd look. His expression was frankly incredulous.

Gisèle seemed to notice Nicola's presence for the first time and murmured without much conviction that she ought to go back upstairs.

"All these from a few photographs taken twelve years ago?" Robin said dubiously. "Come, come. What's the story?"

Luke had been rendered incapable of speech. Robin knew his stuff; he'd never believe that Luke was capable of painting these. From photographs or paint-by-numbers. He had always thought, quite rightly, that Luke wasn't capable of painting much more than a wall.

Nicola, sensing tension, piped up. "Aren't they good, Robin?"

"They're very good indeed, Nico."

"Good enough for the gallery? You could exhibit them, and Dad will be famous."

Robin raised a brow. "Mum, too." Behind him Marc snickered, but Robin continued with a concerned frown. "I'm not sure your mother wants that kind of exposure."

"Nicky, run along upstairs. We'll be up soon." Gisèle swallowed hard, turning. Nicola remained where she was. "They *should* be exhibited, Luke. Not hidden away down here. Did you think I wouldn't like them?"

"No, I—"

"Why else have you kept them to yourself?" Marc peered through the sliver of space in the doorway not filled by Robin and Gisèle and Nicola. He added cattily, "It certainly seems all the art seminars have paid off."

"For Christ's sake these aren't—" But something stopped Luke from saying "mine." He finished, "Meant for anyone to see."

Robin scoffed. "Well, now I've heard everything."

"My friend, they are far too beautiful not to be shown," Marc agreed emphatically.

Luke gazed back at his wife. This was his last opportunity to laugh outright and confess. But for a moment Gisèle's expression was heartbreaking, complicit and imploring. "I think they're beautiful, Luke." Then she laughed, shattering the spell. "What are we all doing huddling in the doorway?"

She stepped into the room determinedly and began to examine the paintings. She held them at arm's length like strangers.

Robin frowned, opening his mouth as if to speak but seeming to think better of it. He entered the studio after her, followed by Marc. Only Nicola hung back.

In the midst of the crowd, Luke waged an internal argument. Either Gisèle knew nothing of the paintings or she had her own reasons for behaving as if she did not. He couldn't fathom why.

But then all at once, like magic, the solution was clear. Luke would sell the paintings and take Gisèle away from here. Tristan couldn't do a thing to stop him. At Falconer's Point they had always been under Tristan's thumb, but somewhere else things could be the way Luke had always envisioned. He floated giddily on a sea of fuzzy logic. Gisèle would love him. She wasn't cheating on him after all. The looming threat of losing her dissipated like a deflating balloon; it swirled around the room with a high-pitched hiss and landed harmless at his feet. For the very first time, Luke felt superior to Tristan Mourault.

～

Seattle, Washington

Amanda Miller was dreaming.

The streets were inky-edged and the scene a stained haze, as though someone had spilled coffee on the film. She felt, rather than recognized, San Francisco—the city of her childhood. Drunken laughter rose through the fingers of fog; she could make out a warehouse of corrugated steel along a darkening wharf, a ghostly green marked with rust and faded stenciled lettering.

Inside, the air was heavy and smelled of loamy earth, of mildew and must. A janitor worked alone in a long, dark hall. Whistling cheerfully, he pushed a broad industrial broom. As she moved closer, she could see the object of his work: teeth, fingernails, and tufts of dark hair were methodically gathered in a mound. Blood smeared the floor like streaks of oil.

Screaming, she vaulted past him to a door at the end of the hall and entered a white cinder-block room. Her sister sat perched on a stool in a gown stained with blood, her head pale and shaved. Her knees were drawn to her chest, and she was rocking.

"Karen!" Amanda cried. Relief welled up in her so that she could hardly speak. "Thank God I've found you . . ." But the face she met was not her sister's. The azure eyes were hollow and void.

The creature tipped its head and spoke in a voice without inflection. "Poor Mandy, it's too late. Can't you see that I'm already dead? They're taking me apart now—"

Amanda gasped, choking. She wrestled with the dark until she could hear her own moans and was shuttled forward, funneled through time. Her eyes darted around the small, still apartment, but Karen wasn't there. *Of course she isn't here. . . . She can't be here.* This wasn't San Francisco, and Amanda wasn't nine years old; she'd never be nine again. Her heart was the last to believe; it thudded painfully against her rib cage, unable to distinguish this world from the other.

Amanda was a psychology major, but it didn't take one to explain why the nightmares had started again, why her nice, bright apartment suddenly carried a sickly air of déjà vu.

A single sheet of stationery lay open on her nightstand. It had arrived this morning, in an innocuous envelope without a return address. It was signed "Karen."

She'd contacted Lieutenant Mitchell of the SFPD as soon as the letter arrived. His promotions had correlated oddly with their sporadic contact over the years: he'd been a young detective on her sister's case and a sergeant when it went cold. Now that he'd made lieutenant, he delivered the same disclaimers without any halting hems and haws and with a decided air of preoccupation. Yet he told her to send the letter to him personally and he'd rush the preliminary forensics. "But I wouldn't get my hopes up."

Amanda had been through this too many times to believe in hope. Hadn't she? Switching on her bedside lamp, she reread the words.

The letter *sounded* like Karen somehow. It was addressed to "Mandy," which is what Karen had always called Amanda. But then that was the obvious diminutive. And while the words were heartfelt, they were also deliberately vague, raising far more questions than they answered. There were no inside jokes, no references only the two of them would know, no address, no phone number. Only a blurred postmark Amanda had gone half blind trying to decipher. The last paragraph said it all:

> *I wish you could write to me here, but that's impossible for now. Please don't share this with anyone. There are no fingerprints, no identifying clues to trace, no point in trying to find me. Please let it be enough that I've found you. I never meant to hurt you, Mandy, and I've missed you more than you'll ever know. It's as if I were walking through a dream that was beautiful and terrible and absurd by turns, but now I've woken up. Things are finally coming clear to me, and I have to believe one day you'll understand. I love you more than life. . . .*

Amanda set the letter down. She went to the window, feeling the chill night air on her skin and simply breathing in and out. In the year after her sister's murder, there had been many anonymous letters. One had contained nothing but a heart-shaped locket, identical to the one Karen wore in the school photo that ran in the papers. Only the real locket was discovered in her jewelry box. There were people who did these things. And there were people, like Amanda, who believed every time.

Her earliest memories were dominated by Karen, the big sister who'd told her stories and taught her to read them, taught her how to tell time and how to multiply. When Amanda started school, Karen had defended her against the teasing of older boys and the scornful glances of girlfriends who didn't want the kid sister tagging along. She'd let her play handball with the big kids and pushed her on the swings, let her in on jokes with a wink and a secretive smile that was theirs alone.

But after grammar school, the smiles grew rare, as did the teasing boys and girlfriends. Karen stopped having friends over at all. She was supposed to look after Mandy, but was rarely home when she was dropped off after ballet. For a year Amanda lied for her. Payment was in ice cream and Tuesdays, the one day a week when things were the way they used to be.

And then one evening Karen didn't come home at all. Five o'clock came and six went. Seven. Her father got angry, her mother made frantic phone calls, and Amanda walked through the days that followed in a sort of heat haze. The air trembled, and the world was drawn in sluggish, wavy lines. Through it there were "MISSING!" bulletins and candlelight vigils. Newspaper people and school psychologists and volunteers gathered around the dining-room table. Dad blamed Mom, and Mom blamed Dad, and Amanda blamed herself.

Detective Mitchell quizzed her about Karen's friends, her home life, her habits. Amanda had remarkably little to tell him about these things, but she was able to report that a photograph had been taken from Karen's scrapbook. *If Karen had been kidnapped, why had she taken it?*

It was a question the detectives answered for her. Had Karen told her she was planning to run away? No, Amanda insisted over and over. Absolutely, no. She wouldn't have done that.

And then Karen's backpack was discovered, gashed with a knife and soaked with her blood. Dumped off the edge of the pier, it had snagged on a ladder descending to the water below. Amanda still saw it in nightmares, though she'd never seen it in life.

Details of Karen's death could only be sketched in broad strokes. The presence of the book bag implied a timeline. (Karen had most likely been killed the same day she skipped school.) She had probably been the victim of a mugging. No money was found in her wallet and the extent of blood loss made it clear she'd been killed violently, using the bag to shield herself from her assailant—perhaps after refusing to hand it over. Smears of blood were found on the edge of the pier, indicating that Karen had been disposed of along with the bag, into the bay. The currents from that point would have carried her out to sea. Her body was never discovered, yet there was little doubt she was dead.

After that, everything had fallen apart. The day of Karen's funeral her mother told Amanda quietly that she was leaving her father. A few months later, she'd heard her mother arguing with him on the phone in an urgent whisper. Amanda was whisked off to a friend's house for the night and awakened to a new nightmare. The accident was all over the news: a Chevy Vega had crossed two lanes and crashed into a truck carrying flammable gas. The car was charred, yet Amanda knew before the investigators did that her parents were inside.

Amanda went to live in Seattle with an aunt and uncle she barely knew, had a nervous breakdown, and wasn't treated for it. She hid it well; she didn't want to be treated, to be studied and scrutinized by strangers. She comforted herself with books and a rich fantasy world, suppressing her memory of the pinched Victorian on the corner in San Francisco until she'd forgotten how it smelled, how it felt beneath her feet and her fingers.

Funny how a few words could bring it all back.

She'd asked Detective Mitchell to return the letter to her once it went through Forensics. Otherwise it would end up in Karen's file along with all the other letters. Amanda couldn't explain the impulse—even to herself—except that in the fragile moments of her first reading, her sister had been alive.

≈

It was Tristan's habit to phone a few times a week while in Paris. Luke heard Nicola answer the phone, followed by a buoyant, "Grand-père!" Lately her voice rose an octave when she spoke to her grandfather; it was an unconscious regression Luke found poignant, this awareness that growing up would change things. She had no idea just how *much* growing up changed things.

He picked up the extension in the hall and listened as Nicola brought Tristan up to date, enthusiastically detailing her discovery of "his" cellar studio. "I still don't know why Dad hid them down there," she finished. "You'd think it'd be too cold to paint."

Tristan had been silent throughout; now Luke listened intently for his reaction.

"*Oui,* it is very curious, indeed." His voice didn't sound quite right, but then it wasn't a very good connection. "*Eh bien,* you know the temperament of the artist, *mon chaton.* You must promise me you will grow to be something more sensible."

Nicola only laughed. "Do you want to talk to Mom, Grand-père?"

Luke flinched. What would Tristan say to Gisèle? What *could* he say?

"No, don't trouble her. We'll make it a surprise. I am coming home earlier than planned."

"Oh, *cool*! But, how come? Is everything okay?"

"*Oui, chérie.* Only I'm getting too old to be away for so long from the people I love. My business here is done. And I'm rather interested in these paintings of your father's. . . ." The line crackled. "There is just one problem."

"What's that?"

"I have too many gifts for you to bring back on the plane." Tristan's tone was normal again, even light, and Nicola was delighted. She resented the long August without her grandfather and could hardly wait till he was back in Devon again. For his part, Luke had never felt so much dread.

True to his word, Tristan arrived home just two days later. It was early evening, and Gisèle and Nicola were in the village, shopping. As much as he wanted to, Luke knew he couldn't avoid him forever. This was his chance to speak to his father-in-law alone.

Tristan had gone up to his room. Luke heard the shower start and stop as he paced in the hall, playing out the conversation in his mind. At last he went to the door, rapping with more assurance than he felt.

"Come in." Crisp and clean, the words. Very like Tristan.

Luke went in.

"Ah. Luke. *Comment vas-tu?*" There was a little more silver in Tristan's blond hair, or maybe it was only that the tan he'd brought back from Paris accentuated it. His pale blue eyes were paler. He looked well. Luke stepped into the vast, opulent room and shut the door behind him. The builder, prompted presumably by the reclusive Bryan Prescott, had made the doors and walls heavy enough to keep out invading armies. A small comfort when the enemy was in the same room.

Tristan smiled warmly. "I hear I am to congratulate you, *mon fils*. You must show me these paintings of yours. Then we will go into town and celebrate."

Luke stared. He wasn't sure what he had expected, but it wasn't a celebratory dinner.

Tristan went on, "You've chosen an eccentric place to paint, *n'est-ce pas?* In the cellar?"

Luke braced himself by studying his father-in-law's dress socks in detail. Paisley print, monochromatic gray. He cleared his throat. "Why don't you tell *me*, Tristan?"

Tristan simply gazed at Luke in his aristocratic, unruffled way, but the eyes behind the wire rims receded. "Excuse me?"

"The room in the wine cellar. It's *your* art studio, not mine."

Tristan's voice remained cool. "Well, I suppose the room is technically mine, *mon fils*, but you've never concerned yourself before with such things." Funny, the way he said it, it didn't even seem an insult. "You might have taken any number of rooms for a studio, Luke. We would have respected your privacy. I am a firm believer in privacy."

The evasion was so perfectly executed that Luke was taken aback. Tristan must have rehearsed it on the plane. "Nicola found me in there. Otherwise I'd never—" He floundered. "She just assumed I'd done them and was set on telling Gisèle." An expression crossed Tristan's face that Luke couldn't decipher. Shrewd. Something more. "Ella believes it, too. And it's better for everyone if she doesn't find out that your concern isn't exactly fatherly—"

"Luke. I'm afraid I don't understand. Perhaps it is my jet lag." Tristan slipped off his glasses and rubbed the bridge of his nose. He did look weary, suddenly. Straightening, he slipped them on again, like armor against Luke's scrutiny. "Where is my Gisèle? And little Nicola?"

My Gisèle. "She didn't expect you back. They're out shopping."

"Ah. Well, let me understand you, then. You seem to think I *knew* about all of this? But I assure you I did not. I can't imagine a setting less suitable for art. I prefer to paint *en plein air.*" The careless arch of a brow. "Did the room appear intended for a studio? Perhaps the formidable Mr. Prescott did his drafting down there. I understand he was a rather eccentric man." Turning, he rifled through a drawer in the bureau. "I sense you're uneasy sharing the paintings with me, Luke, and I know why. I was led to believe they're nudes?"

The innocent act was very good. But then, what other defense did he have? Luke said testily, "You know they are, Tristan."

"I know only what Nicola told me on the phone."

"And it was enough to make you rush home?"

"I was curious, yes. Forgive me, but it's rather a surprise to find you've begun to paint."

"Begun? There are nearly forty canvases—"

"Yes. I'm sorry. I see now you've been quite busy. Unusually prolific, in fact. And I've misjudged you. But you should not have kept them hidden from us."

"*I* didn't."

But Luke's words were met only with an expression of guileless incomprehension. After a moment Tristan sighed, an elegant, superior French sigh, and in frustration said, "Well, if *you* didn't hide your paintings, *mon fils,* whoever did?"

Mon fils: my son. His father-in-law had called him that so often before. And a sickening chill ran through Luke. Could he have been wrong? Tristan focused on tying his tie, a thing he accomplished perfectly the first time. If that wasn't proof of an untroubled mind, Luke didn't know what was.

"Robin tells me they're quite good." Tristan regarded Luke's reflection in the mirror. "Really, Luke. Did you think I would disapprove?"

"Well, not exactly—"

"The nude body is a beauty to behold." Tristan fastened a cuff link; it glinted in the mirror.

"Even your own *daughter's*?"

"*Eh bien*, that will give me pause, to be sure." Tristan's reflection held Luke's eyes steadily. "But art is art, Luke, and I am French. We do not share the American phobia toward nudity. Gisèle is not a child anymore. Do not concern yourself."

It was surreal. Tristan seemed very like he always did. Amiable, charming. Was it only Luke's imagination that they fenced with their evasions? Either way, he was outmatched.

Tristan tipped his head, frowning in concern. "Are you quite all right, *mon fils*?"

Luke wasn't all right. Had the paintings painted themselves? He gazed into his father-in-law's worried face. "I'm fine, Tristan. Yes, I'm fine. I'll just go . . . change." And he turned gratefully to the door and its ephemeral offering of escape.

III

THE INGÉNUE

I shall never forget the day we arrived in New York. It was late May, trees shimmying in the spring breeze, full and verdant, the flower boxes brilliant with color. And outshining them all, my beautiful Gisèle as she raced up the steps of my brownstone. Her floral dress danced at her knees, and I watched the rounded backs of her calves and the soles of her shoes disappearing up, up. At the landing she paused between the lion's-head pillars; she turned to smile at me. In that instant the dream coalesced.

My influence over her had grown with our distance from San Francisco, and by the time we reached New York, she was a very different girl from the lonely thing who'd roamed Fisherman's Wharf with no one to look after her. My approval and disapproval became the poles of her existence. By this I do not mean that we'd ironed out the kinks in our relationship but simply that there was no reality beyond them. The relationship was our world.

We lived very well in New York. The only early difficulties arose from the duality of our public and private personae. In public she had to be my daughter; in private she was most certainly not. I understood that these father-daughter connotations would be painful for her. And for my part, I wasn't at all fond of having my perversions aligned with her father's. We agreed very early on that she would never call me "Dad" or any

reasonable facsimile; she called me, always, Tristan. But there were pro-
prieties to be observed, a role to be played. Gisèle particularly resented
playing it at home among the servants.

There was a Puerto Rican maid, Nora, who came and went each afternoon and spoke little English in between. And the indispensable Henri.
He was an ex-schoolteacher and my favorite tutor when I was a boy. He
later became my aide, valet, chauffeur, and confidant. *Eh bien*, perhaps
"confidant" is too strong a word; suffice to say there was much I did not
tell him and, in his wisdom, much that he did not ask.

To explain Gisèle's presence, I told him a story of a tryst during my
time at Princeton. Her mother had since died, I claimed: death, the most
decisive—and for me the most familiar—explanation for absence. I told
him I'd gone to California for the purpose of meeting my daughter; she
had no one else to care for her. Naturally, she was unaccustomed to me,
to my life, to New York. We must be protective of her. He agreed to this,
and we never spoke of it otherwise. Henri was valued most for his discretion, and he knew this. He had his rooms on the bottom floor—a far
better accommodation than he could otherwise afford—and thus was
happily on call, but not on watch.

The third floor had become a kind of glorified attic for my things:
mirrors, chests, desks, rugs, fauteuil, sculpture and paintings. Rare finds,
all. I admit to haunting auction houses and antique stores like an addict,
and I was fond of altering my surroundings. The décor was in constant
flux. I amused Gisèle with the stories behind each acquisition but found
that these lesser passions fell away: she was my prize.

Our living was confined largely to rooms on the second floor. In the
beginning she was rarely out of my sight. To the neighbors a simple,
"Have you met my daughter, Gisèle?" was adequate explanation. I was
close to none of them. Even the obstinately sociable Mr. Mulligan from
next door, who seemed perpetually to be walking his pugs (a sight that
bore a queer sadistic edge, as the poor things were strangling on the
leash all the while he made his pleasantries), seemed to know better than
to pry too deeply into a delicate family matter.

As time wore on, I would occasionally leave Gisèle with Henri,
who became her tutor as he had been mine. Her lessons took place
from twelve to three as Nora cleaned. I was always near enough to

overhear and enjoyed watching Gisèle playact for me; it was a continued expression of my power over her. Each day she didn't confess, didn't race down quiet, pristine East Seventy-fifth Street screaming, "I've been kidnapped and kept by a madman!" was a psychological victory and filled me with the buoyancy of a sculptor who has triumphed over a stubborn lump of clay.

Yet there were adjustments to be made. I'd been a bachelor for years and had little experience living with anyone. Sabina was a capricious creature to be sure, but in our three-and-a-half-year marriage we lived mostly separate lives in separate wings of the house. I'm not at all certain of her more private idiosyncrasies; we shared the public ones when we met for dinner or the theater or posed for parties.

And so it was with some wonder that I discovered Gisèle.

She quickly showed herself to be a person of singularly meticulous personal habits, given to lengthy showers and an elaborate toilette. I had corrupted her with the early gifts from the Lancôme counter, it seemed. She soon found the point of all those creams and powders, toners and cleansers, moisturizers and brushes, and they ever afterward became an indispensable part of her "look." Once a routine was established, she clung to it as if it were a talisman. I see now that she was suspended in a new world and rootless. All she had were her routines.

And though I was often kept waiting, I found it rather endearing as I presumed it to be done for me. While the process rarely varied, the styles invariably did. In those early days, Gisèle was in a state of constant metamorphosis. Most of her incarnations pleased me: the daily shade of lipstick, the new coiffure. She'd pull her hair back in a French braid one day, up in a twist the next, and occasionally she even worked out the curls by some feminine alchemy. I preferred it tousled and free yet found her attempts to harness it quite a spectator sport. She also liked to change her scent. Before settling upon Yves Saint Laurent's Paris (in homage to me), she collected perfumes for the bottles. Often this backfired: a fifteen-year-old girl in Gucci? I was also disturbed by her experiments with blue eye shadow and a troubling phase of aqua mascara.

Ah, but I had a wonderful time dressing her. Such exquisite pleasure it was to see her turn for me, the flare of her skirt or the line of her pants, the faint line of panties beneath and an anxious expression upon her face. It was for me to decide yes or no, like a Roman emperor in the Colosseum.

Gisèle loved the energy of New York, the immensity, and each afternoon after her lessons we roamed the city. We explored the parks and the endless galleries, block after block of shops. I saw everything again for the first time. Times Square and the Flatiron Building, the Empire State Building and St. Patrick's—one of the loveliest cathedrals in the world pocketed so neatly among the Fifth Avenue skyscrapers and boutiques. It is not the same in Paris, where things seem to have always existed in relation to each other, a subtle tapestry. And it was a very far cry from San Francisco. I made sure the contrast was a pleasant one. Once led down the yellow brick road, I intended to ensure that Dorothy would never wish to leave Oz.

We enjoyed traveling vicariously through food and ate out nearly every night. Otherwise, her eating habits appalled me: at breakfast she spurned the omelets or crepes that I enjoyed for questionable items like Pop-Tarts. She didn't eat lunch but instead grazed through an exhaustive list of snack food, which I tried in vain to infuse with cheeses, breads, and fruit.

I gave her no money of her own, apart from pocket change, but she had no need of it; I denied her very little. And she was so illuminated by the simplest of things that it was a joy to spoil her. She adored the gaudy Art Deco grandeur of Tavern on the Green and delighted in the topiary. Afterward we took a carriage ride through the park, and she fed the horse peanut M&M's she'd stashed in her evening bag. I was utterly charmed by her naïveté. She puzzled over the attendant one must tip in the ladies' room, insisted we ride the subway as a sort of "wild safari," and believed all the stories taxi drivers told. The city, it seemed, was alive with former KGB agents. She was taken in by the street hawkers and the glitz of Times Square, so that it was requisite to stand in line at the ticket box at fifteen below zero when I could easily have obtained tickets to *Peter Pan* and *A Chorus Line* through more seasonable channels. Afterward—seemingly immune to frostbite—she asked to have her picture taken with the Planter's Peanut Man. I purchased a Polaroid for the occasion and finally realized their true value, a thing completely untapped by Madison Avenue. Polaroid: the choice of the paranoid.

One lovely day we went to the Met in the snow, the tires of the car fishtailing all the way. After taking in the impressionists, we watched through the windows as giant flakes blanketed Central Park and, like participants in a peculiar performance art, urbanites donned cross-country skis and had snowball fights. Later we joined them, writing our names in the windshields of snow-buried cars.

With time I grew comfortable, even lax. New York is a vast city; it lulls one into a false sense of security. One night I took Gisèle to '21' and we were careful to keep to our roles. I was merely an indulgent father taking my daughter to dinner and the theater. She was delighted by a private tour of the room hidden behind the kitchen, left over from the days of Prohibition when the club had operated as a speakeasy. Inside, there was a table once reserved for the mayor and racks of dusty wine bottles laid down for the likes of Cary Grant and Elizabeth Taylor. Afterward, in the restaurant above, we met rather unavoidably the Pools from Iowa: "Ed and Edith from Edna." They had come because the club is mentioned in *Rear Window*. I should thus have been warned, for they were soon to play voyeur.

The next day we were on the viewing deck at the top of the Empire State Building, blending chameleon-like into a group of disparate tourists. Gisèle was teasing me at the edge. I suffer a bit from vertigo, but she distracted me so that I went to her and imprisoned her between my arms, placing my hands on the cold rails. She looked so lovely, with her windblown hair and laughing eyes, I could not resist a kiss. Turning, we were confronted by the Pools, whom we had rendered entirely incapable of speech.

They were too near to avoid; we pushed past each other with incoherent mumbles and moved rapidly in opposite directions. Horrified of being trapped in an elevator with them, Gisèle and I took refuge in the restrooms.

The door opened almost immediately after me, and there was Ed. I was thus forced to make use of the facilities. He took a urinal two down; naturally, neither of us looked at the other.

"Don't mean to pry, but the wife and I couldn't help noticin'—"

"She's not really my daughter," I said hastily.

"Like 'em young, do you?"

"She's eighteen."

"Sure she is."

"She's small; people think she's younger."

"Masqueradin' as your daughter . . ."

"It's a game she likes to play. She has a kink that way."

"I'll say. Mighty strange."

"It's not so uncommon." I forced myself to add, "In France."

He cleared his throat and zipped his pants. "Well, my advice is play it in private; people don't like seeing that sort of thing right under their noses. Got my wife all upset." Then he grunted something vulgar about the French and left without washing his hands.

And so the cloak went back on, for good this time. This involved, for me, duplicity to old friends and associates, as well as to new acquaintances. But in a strange way, the role made more poignant our hours offstage. I treasured our "secret life." There was the play, and there was the sweet refuge of the wings.

And yet the details of our private life may also surprise you.

Gisèle was very naïve about male sexuality, and in the beginning we did little more than kiss. She believed I could resist an erection through sheer will, and this suited me. Slowly, I gained her trust. There was no rush. These early moments of discovery were precious to me.

In light of what I knew of her past, her genuine terror of the finer parts of my anatomy was less than surprising, and at last she confessed to me her father's drunken forays into her bedroom. In the sordid spectrum of incest, it wasn't as bad as I'd thought, but quite bad enough—a matter of clumsy fumbling about the breasts and buttocks, under bras and down panties, wet beery kisses, and "I love you, angel. You know that, don't you? You know I love you." But she claimed he stopped at masturbating in front of her.

Privately, I suspect this wasn't so.

One night she'd had too much champagne. As I was talking her through the bed-spinning stage, she began to cry in great pitiful sobs, murmuring something about being taken "out on the boat" by her father. What boat and what her father did there, I don't know. I could get nothing more intelligible out of her, and later she pretended not to remember. But it perhaps explained her morbid dread of the water, which was equal only to her morbid dread of the penis.

I felt very protective toward her, and for a long time we merely slept together, side by side, surprised by the ease of our intimacy. Do not think me so chaste I didn't wish for more. All it took was a glimpse of her, even the scent of her (I could write a volume upon this alone: the honey-sweet scent of her hair, the salt of her skin, the sharp scent of the soap she used at night to wash her face, her light floral perfume, the tart newness of panties left on the bathroom floor). Any part of the whole was enough for me to become so aroused that it seemed my entire body throbbed. As time wore on, I explored her, of course. To touch her was a sort of converse thumbscrew, so acute was the torture of being on the outside. She touched me "everywhere but." And yet I enjoyed this dance: my self-denial and her innate mystery. She had her secrets, and I had mine. She was the Chinese box I had not yet learned to open.

IV

CHASING BUTTERFLIES

MARC KREICEK SAUNTERED down the hall toward Luke. In the dim light his pale green eyes shone luminous against his olive skin, like a cat's. When he smiled it did not touch them.

"Ah, Luke. Exactly who I wished to see. I have just spoken to Robin. He's set up some meetings for you in Seattle—a few select previews of the paintings to build excitement for the exhibition. We will leave tomorrow."

"Tomorrow?" Luke stared. "That's a bit sudden, isn't it? Why didn't Robin mention this to me?"

"Oh, I often handle these things for him. He's quite busy just now. But he's made the right introductions to the right people. The rest is very simple. We will go together."

"Sure, Marc. Uh, thanks. Thank Robin for me."

Marc appraised him. "It will be good for you to get away. Things have been a little tense since Tristan came back from the motherland, have they not?"

Luke faltered. "Things are all right."

"Yes." A measured pause. Marc's expression grew conspiratorial, and he motioned Luke farther down the hall. "I do hate to put a damper on things, my friend."

Luke's heart hammered erratically in his chest.

"But I'm afraid you're being set up for a fall. I think Tristan may be behind it all. Or perhaps it is Gisèle herself. She knows of your affair, Luke. The charming young woman in Seattle?" Marc hesitated. "I admit I feel somewhat responsible, having introduced you to her. Naturally, I could have no idea Gisèle would be so upset. . . . You led me to believe there was an understanding between the two of you."

It came from left field. Luke simply repeated, dumbly, "My affair?"

"There seem to be photos."

Luke stared at the floor. It rose up to meet him.

A laugh. "*I'm* not judging you, Luke, believe me. I don't share the American hysteria for fidelity. I'm simply telling you, Gisèle knows about it. She's had you followed. Or Tristan has. There are whispers, you know. Divorce has been mentioned."

"Divorce?" Luke choked on the word. And why was Marc privy to the whispers in this house? "But Gisèle and I . . . we *do* have an understanding. We did. And now, with the paintings—"

"Now, with the paintings," Marc echoed, "you have a business arrangement. And you had better cling to it for dear life, my friend, because everything here belongs to Tristan. Gisèle has no real property at all. It would be a shame to have to earn an honest living, would it not?" A self-deprecating laugh. "God forbid any of us should have to do that. Art is so very much better."

Luke's mind reeled. "Why are you telling me this?"

"So that you can be prepared, that is all. Say good-bye to your lovely girlfriend while we're in Seattle. Make up something to pacify her. It wouldn't do to have that come out. Not at all. The draw of the paintings is obsession, Luke. Robin and I have discussed it."

Had they? Why hadn't they discussed it with him?

"Critics, collectors—they all want an obsession to mirror their own," Marc went on amiably. "They will bite if they swallow the story. An obsessive love story. Endless attempts to tackle the feminine enigma. Gisèle must remain in the shadows, a mystery." An indecipherable expression crossed his face. "That will not be hard for her. But you are going to receive a fair amount of scrutiny, and you must be up to it, my friend."

"Gisèle's said nothing about any affair—"

"Well, it isn't her style, is it?" A shrug. "Confrontation? And it would be a mistake to mention it to her. But take it from me, your run here is nearing an end. Gisèle has her own reasons, and God knows what those may be." Yet from the way he gazed off down the hall, Luke suspected both God *and* Marc knew much more about Gisèle than he did. "Take my advice and look to the future. You have one thing in your favor."

Luke tried to process his words. "And what's that?"

"She wants the paintings to be a success as much as you do."

"And how do you know that?"

Marc's mouth turned down in exasperation. "Have you heard *nothing* I've said? Gisèle has no property of her own. Robin's offered her the gallery cut from the paintings. That is more than you will see, my friend. Sixty percent. These paintings are all she owns in the world."

"But why does Gisèle need money? Tristan gives her everything she wants."

Marc stared at Luke as if waiting for a dim-witted child to get the joke.

Luke stared back. Then, at last, "You mean she's thinking of leaving Tristan?"

"Given the evidence, it seems very clear. She's going to leave both of you."

And so it was hardly a pleasure trip to Seattle. Luke made his way through his meetings—perhaps it helped that his mind was weighted with other things. He had met Amanda Miller while attending an art seminar that summer. She was certainly not his first liaison, nor one of so many as to defuse the masochistic cycle of sex and remorse. Only this time it had been more than sex. Amanda had something—how else to put it?— something more that he was lacking. She saw Luke for who he was. What a wonder this was to the ego; to be accepted and wanted *anyhow*. She had a candid, shockingly frank way of looking at things, as if she didn't see the point of pretense. And Luke's life, long before the paintings, had been simply one pretense after another. With Amanda, for the first time, he'd asked himself what made him think he could do no better?

But she was just twenty-four, a grad student at the university barely getting by on grants and a work-study job. He had nothing to offer her. The baser truth was that she had nothing to offer him. As peripheral as he was to his world, he could not leave it behind.

Now, in the cab, on his way to her place, he told himself he'd come clean: he had a wife, a daughter. Yet when he emerged, he knew he wouldn't go through with it. She opened the door and he was lost again in her spell—the long, silky hair and the adorable dimple in her left cheek, eye contact so direct he'd always been the one to break it. Like Gisèle somehow. Only real.

They hadn't seen each other in weeks, yet Amanda gave no sign of reproach, only curiosity, then concern. The softness in her eyes was deeper than a touch. He could talk to her.

I'm lost . . .

Luke told her half-truths: family troubles. As he always had, he found old surrogates for new emotions. Her sympathetic ear and gentle touch soothed his jangled nerves. She was something special. Lovely and light—but with dimension. She absorbed all his darkness, yet it scarcely dimmed her. He had the sense that even the truth wouldn't shock her. The truth of his wife, his father-in-law, "his" paintings . . . It was so tempting to confide in her, to confide in *someone*.

Instead, Luke told her he loved her. There was magic in those words; they were an incantation. *I love you. . . .* When he'd said it, it had been true. He'd made love to her as if it were the only honest thing he had ever done in his life.

Afterward he regretted it, of course. He panicked. How could he have been so careless? He saw Gisèle reflected in Amanda's eyes, heard her echo in Amanda's voice, saw the specter of her profile as she turned. Felt his future drain away with his afterglow. What if he *were* being watched? He slunk back to his hotel room and flew home with Marc just a few hours later.

Sitting on the plane, Luke felt as blank as the sky around them. Empty inside. When they landed, he called it relief. Amanda had no reality in Devon. He didn't owe her anything. She didn't expect anything. He was free.

⁓

Amanda parked in a permit lot at the University of Washington and stepped from the car. She was early for her shift at the library. Traffic hadn't been bad, which in Seattle was so rare as to give one alarm. Unfortunately, it was the only pleasant surprise of the day.

Early that morning Detective Mitchell called to report that, true to its claim, the letter sported no trace of its sender: No fingerprints, no DNA; the envelope was sealed with plain H_2O. He confessed he'd never considered the possibility that the letter might be authentic. "But it's unusual for someone to follow such an old crime, Miss Miller, let alone follow *you* to a different city. We may be dealing with someone seriously unstable. Keep your eyes open, hmm?"

And so Amanda couldn't help the sweeping, paranoid glance as the automatic doors parted and she entered Odegaard Library—her second home for the last six years. It was more common for grad students to TA for a professor, but Amanda knew that if she didn't get out of the psych department once in a while, she'd end up in a psych ward.

It was this that had prompted her decision last spring, after a grueling research project, to request on-leave status for the fall semester. Her adviser reassured her it was normal to suffer burnout from time to time. Except that school wasn't all she was burned out on.

Jay Quinn was an esteemed professor and psychologist, well liked and admired by everyone. Including his wife. When they met, he'd told Amanda he was recently separated. It was not for some time that she realized he meant separated "emotionally," that it was hardly recent—and that he'd failed to let his wife in on the fact.

Jay had the capacity to make everyone blind to his faults—colleagues, students and advisees, of which Amanda was one. It worked for two tumultuous years. But June saw him with an infatuated undergrad, while Amanda became involved with another emotionally inaccessible older man.

Luke Halvorson hadn't even been her type. If she had one. He was certainly not at all professorial, and perhaps it was this that appealed to her. Ironically, they'd met through Jay—or rather an acquaintance of his named Marc Kreicek.

Marc made Amanda uncomfortable from the moment she met him. Attractive in a slinky, feline, untrustworthy way, his dark hair was rumpled and shoulder-length, and there was a starved quality to his foam-green eyes. He wore a showy medallion around his neck and had a showy sort of sexuality. The first time they met, he'd crossed Jay's office with a quick, agile step, and Amanda had the irrational feeling he might spring.

He and Jay were collaborating on a book about Kreicek's father. Marc himself had studied but no longer practiced psychology. He "painted," Jay said. Not houses. Whatever the case, he creeped her out. Amanda treated him with kid gloves and tried to avoid him altogether. But one day in June, while she and her adviser were muddling through an awkward post-breakup lunch, Kreicek arrived with his friend, Luke Halvorson. As Marc sat and talked shop with Jay, Amanda had turned gratefully to Luke.

He had dirty-blond hair and a sheepish sort of charm. A slight southern drawl accentuated a naughty-little-boy quality she found endearing. He was enrolled in an art seminar at the university, not an academic, and the relationship they developed was unstudied and uncomplicated— walks in the park and on the wharf, dinners and movies. It was oddly innocent. But in early August his seminar ended, and so had the budding romance.

He claimed he was visiting relatives and planned to return to Seattle "soon." By September, Amanda began to write it off, but then he'd returned dramatically, showing up at her door with long-stemmed roses and heartfelt apologies. He hadn't shaved, and his clothes were rumpled. It seemed to startle even him that he was there. And there was a look in his eyes—raw, but sweet and almost frightened underneath. As though he'd never been loved and never expected to be.

The innocence flew out the window. There was a reckless abandon to the sex; they were like two alcoholics on a bender. She didn't know what Luke was escaping, but she was escaping Jay and more than that—her own ghosts. Luke's touch was reassuringly solid. Early the next morning, he'd tucked her in sweetly, kissed her, and told her he had to go. That had been two weeks ago. He hadn't called since.

This morning, after speaking with Detective Mitchell, she'd been flooded by disappointment. It seemed to fill her small apartment. She'd paced and at last picked up the phone. On a whim, she broke her cardinal rule.

"Hello, Luke. It's Amanda."

"Oh. Hi there."

"Is . . . everything all right?"

"Fine." His voice was brusque. "Look, I just can't do this, okay?"

"Excuse me?"

"I can't explain. It's . . . well, obviously, I've changed my mind."

Obviously. His voice sounded so squirmy and scared: scared of being caught. And suddenly it was clear to her what sort of relatives he'd been "visiting." Undoubtedly, his wife. Horrified and embarrassed, she had simply hung up.

She had fifteen minutes to kill, and so Amanda roamed the main floor of the library, taking in the usual academic clutter on the tabletops—notebooks and book bags, geometric proofs, the entire opus of Steinbeck in a precarious stack. She paused to collect Janson's hefty *History of Art,* open to Vermeer, from a recently deserted table. A lone magazine and a battered school newspaper had also been left behind. The magazine was a regional art review called *Reflex,* and her eyes caught on a caption in the corner: "The Latest Wizard from Oz: Devon's Luke Farrell."

Luke. The name should have made her flinch, but there was a picture with the caption. Amanda flipped through the pages until she located the article, The pleasant hum around her died, worries mercifully fled; her skin began to tingle, her ears to ring. Images of a woman accompanied the words, and it was a woman she recognized.

It couldn't be . . . These were paintings, not photographs. Many women had hair that shade of brown, high cheekbones and wide eyes.

Still, she began to read.

MAKE ME A VOYEUR

What is the artistic relevance of the nude? In art school, one studies the human form for only one reason: nowhere is the topography more profoundly varied. The body is composed of every possible geometric angle and shape. One is taught to study it abstractly, to segment it into triangles and circles, rectangles and squares. This is thought to subtract the sexual element.

The obsessive focus of Luke Farrell's work is his wife's body. It is presented in ways that can be described only as unapologetic objectification. She is bare and covered, beauti-

ful and flawed, by turns shamed and obscene, vital and free.
The works are viscerally erotic. Not many, I venture to guess,
would dare to know their wives so well.

Yet in my preview sampling of six (there are rumored to
be some forty more), I was struck by the level of engagement
Farrell manages to achieve—not only between viewer and
subject but between the seen and unseen. A fetishist focus on
parts rather than the whole as well as a very deft use of negative space create a running commentary on sexual dynamics, in which each piece questions what it appears to know.
By the end I felt almost redeemed, in guiltless dialogue again
with the feminine form. The subject of these paintings, the
beguiling "Gisèle," knows she's being looked at. She looks
back. Together we shrugged off our mutual ignominy, easily embracing our roles of voyeur and exhibitionist. Even, in
some strange way, exchanging them.

Make no mistake, these are challenging paintings. One
camp will label them feminist, another will find them misog-
ynistic; they are too erotic, too harsh . . . too *real*. Their contradiction is their strength. Love them or hate them, buckle
up or be unfastened: this is not the neutered, defamed nude
we've grown accustomed to. Luke Farrell single-handedly
delivers a shock of Eros to a vulgarized art world and, better
yet, makes Eros a damned interesting raconteur. And nothing
in recent years has struck this reviewer as quite so relevant.

The Artist and the Exhibition

Luke Farrell hails from Devon and is fortunate in his bene-
factor: the renowned Robin Dresden. In Farrell, he proves his
vision as keen as ever. The exhibition (titled simply, the Gisèle
Paintings) will be held through October at Dresden Galleries, 1212 Front St., Devon, WA. A reception will be held Saturday, October 1, at 7 p.m. for those who like cocktails with
their oeuvres. As for me, I will be happily peering through
the window.

Amanda let her eyes travel the page, wryly titling the works as she went: *Before the Bath, In the Bath, After the Bath,* for they weren't titled but numbered. Yet they transcended the derivative theme, even poked fun at it. There was a poignant, searching quality to Gisèle. *I know you're watching me; what are you looking for?* And despite her beauty, there was an honest imperfection to the way she was portrayed. In most paintings Amanda sensed the distance between artist and subject, an analytical remove, yet here there was no distance. To look at Gisèle was to know her.

Three more pieces were pictured on the facing page. The model's face appeared in none of these; she'd been divided into disembodied parts. In the first, shapely calves were curved neatly beneath her thighs. Robbed of color, only shadow and light, the legs ceased to be legs and became more universal: a play on yin and yang in the calf and thigh, while her feet were arched and parted—curved pale shapes enveloping the phallic shadows. If one looked at the whole piece, the opposite occurred: her legs became phallic and the background, the encompassing shadow, was feminine. When Amanda refocused her eyes, the effect receded; the legs were simply legs again.

The next image was no more than a midsection, the woman's torso turning so that one could see the flare of hip and buttock, the twist of her waist and the curve of her breast. It was erotic, but almost painfully so. Her skin was faintly blue, as if under the harshest fluorescent light, and the depiction was equally severe: a road map of plotted moles and freckles. Down to the pore, it seemed.

The final painting was on a background of pure red. Gisèle's skin was fragile porcelain, like a doll's. Her head was turned to the left, but her body faced forward, so that one could see the bones of her clavicle, a yoke beneath the skin—and, at the top, the line of her jaw. Around her neck she wore a black silk choker. A large pearl hung from it, like the teardrop of a mime.

Amanda's fingers traveled up to her own throat; she loosened her scarf and breathed in sharply. It wasn't a decision at all, simply the knowledge that she would go to Devon, as if glimpsed from the future gazing back.

❧

Overnight, it seemed, Luke had been thrust into a haze of illusory power: the paintings had gained Robin's patronage, Marc's envy, and even Tristan's sanction. The last of the three discouraged their exhibition out of concern for the "overexposure" of his darling Gisèle, but Gisèle herself disagreed, and so it was. The paintings were previewed by select critics during the trip to Seattle, and their reviews had appeared today—just in time to promote the exhibition. It would open at Dresden Galleries in two weeks.

Luke had officially been launched.

And today of all days, Amanda had chosen to call him. The sound of her girlish, uncertain voice made his blood run cold.

His fear made him cruel, and in the end he'd said something about having changed his mind about her. Amanda was better off, Luke knew, but he thought of the gentle awareness in those eyes and hated himself for it.

He resolutely shrugged this off as he dressed for dinner. Another dollop of guilt—it got lost in the sauce. Things were going too well to be derailed by a romantic whim. None of Marc's dire warnings in the hall showed any signs of coming to pass. Gisèle mentioned nothing of the affair, life at Falconer's Point continued as it always had.

Luke's arm was around his wife as they entered a swanky restaurant in the village, called the Moors. Tristan was with them, and Marc Kreicek was meeting them there. Luke saw him sitting at the bar and thought of how many times in the past he had entered this or similar restaurants and felt like a third wheel. Though he aspired to be one of them, he'd always felt out of place with the cliquish art set. They were of two types: reclusive and uncommunicative with little or no social sense, or among Robin Dresden's elite and more or less like Marc—sleek, sure-footed, elegant, speaking many tongues even when they stuck to English. They never grew familiar with increased acquaintance. Anyway, not to Luke. He could hear himself as they heard him—eager to impress, pointing out the obvious, wavering between cocky and obsequious. The dull-witted student.

But all that had changed.

Surrounded by a small crowd, Marc waved them over to the bar, smiling his close-lipped, secretive smile over his martini glass. For once Luke didn't look to Tristan or Gisèle to navigate him through the social labyrinth. Marc rose to embrace him, with a hearty, "Congratulations, my friend!" Other voices, who had never uttered his name aloud, belonging to people who had perhaps never known it, were offering up congratulations, too. Marc ordered a round of drinks, and the conversation that buzzed was surreal.

Luke took a perverse, almost sadistic, pleasure in the farce. Gisèle and Marc spoke excitedly of the reviews and the exhibition, and Tristan listened quietly to it all, a cat on a crowded mantelpiece, stepping gingerly yet somehow managing to break nothing.

And how was Luke able to sit there drinking with him? It was surprisingly simple. He had separated the paintings from their suspected painter. Sometimes he questioned whether or not the paintings even *had* a painter. Gisèle believed they were his; to all intents and purposes, they *were* his.

As if to ice the cake—or haze the new initiate—Robin Dresden arrived. The awed, interested gazes that always followed him led directly to Luke. There was casual talk of introductions in San Francisco and New York. Gallery owners. Critics. Collectors. Robin spoke of it in a mundane way, but Luke knew that with every well-placed word from him the paintings would double in value. No exaggeration. This was the inner circle. And for the first time, Luke felt a slippery sense of belonging.

The young woman to whom he'd declared everlasting love only weeks before could not compete with this mirage. And in that moment, Luke rejoiced in his escape from her. Amanda stirred up emotions in him that were unsettlingly real, but he was an artist now, and artists dealt in illusion.

Another round of drinks and Robin was toasting them all: *To artists and muses and immortality . . .*

It was everything Luke had ever wanted.

❧

Amanda gazed from the tiny window of the puddle jumper as the chiseled white tips of the Cascade Mountains appeared below, glaciated peaks that gave way to rolls of pine-laden hills and meadows blanketed in green. Finally Lake Devon came into view. Jagged granite cliffs plummeted to waters of deep indigo blue. On the northwestern edge, the raging Bastille River sliced through the mountains and emptied into the lake so forcefully that it created a whirlpool at its mouth. Amanda had often heard reports of drownings on Seattle news stations, accompanied by footage of searchers scaling the cliffsides and too-familiar tales of bodies never found.

The "upper" lake was actually one of a pair in the alpine resort area. They were conjointly labeled "Devon Lakes" on the map, yet in practice the upper lake was called "Lake Devon" and its lesser twin simply "the lower lake." Even from the air, it seemed benign by comparison, a great pale sapphire on the valley floor. A popular, affordable retreat for college kids and families, the town of Lakewood on its western shore possessed the sole public airport in the area. Amanda would have to rent a car and drive up to Devon. It was reachable only by a single ribbon of road that was often closed in winter due to heavy snows. Fabulous, if one could afford to be cozily snowbound—otherwise it meant chartering a seaplane or a helicopter. Many of the residents had private hangars, which was indicative of the average local income. For her part, Amanda could only hope it didn't snow.

The plane curved in a great arc over the shimmering water. She yawned to pop her ears, and as they touched down, she felt a rush of anticipation. Wild-goose chase or not, it had the air of an adventure. Amanda collected her suitcase and trailed to the Avis counter to rent the requisite SUV for the mountain roads. Squinting down at her map in the slanted autumn sunshine, she soon found the road to Devon.

The drive was breathtaking: forty minutes of evergreens and granite and a climbing road that inspired vertigo. A flimsy guardrail to her right was meant to prevent her from plunging down to the Bastille, which rushed along indifferently below. At last the vista widened, and the rolling hills of a private golf club were the first signs of civilization. Deer strolled across the green like members in good standing. Amanda reached a gate shortly thereafter and was charged six dollars for the privilege of entering and being overcharged for everything inside.

Oh, well. Amanda had a small savings account—the result of an insurance policy that had been her only legacy from her parents. She'd never wanted to touch it, but it seemed poetic to do so now, in search of her sister.

The Cascades loomed dizzyingly overhead as she crossed a scenic bridge to pass beside the gauzy veil of Clannad Falls tumbling hundreds of feet down to meet the lake. It sparkled darkly in the dappled afternoon sunshine. As Amanda drove along the water, sprawling mansions and cottages began to appear, peeking shyly from behind evergreens that lined the surrounding hills. The town of Devon lay at the west end and was like something from a storybook. All the shops were thatch-roofed, with shuttered windows and Dutch doors, or tall Tudor style. The inns and B&Bs were English country homes or tightly corseted Victorians, scalloped and turreted and infallibly charming. In the historic section, the streets were cobblestone, the streetlights lit by gas. There were gourmet markets and bakeries, cheese shops and chocolatiers, myriad canopied boutiques and fine restaurants, spas and salons. And over fifty art galleries.

Though Amanda had been unable to find out anything substantive about the artist Luke Farrell or his muse, Gisèle, there was plenty to be learned about the Dresden galleries. The local consensus was that Dresden himself was a "genius." He'd earned a doctorate from Oxford at an obscenely young age, though not in art but philosophy. Yet his personal philosophy was hard to pin down; he was labeled both philanthropist and elitist, Svengali and guru, fearless artistic innovator and opportunistic charlatan. None of it seemed to hurt business. One of his works, *Desecration,* had recently sold for $3 million at auction.

It all painted a very colorful picture, but one that seemed less and less likely to include Karen. She'd somehow escaped death to run with the artistic elite? It was a stretch, even to one who wanted to believe. But Amanda was on a quest, if only for her sanity's sake.

She found a parking spot and set off at once for the gallery. Around her an upscale throng of tourists ducked in and out of shops, and the aroma of something divine floated from a restaurant above. It mingled with crisp air already piquant with pine, anise, and the smoky scent of dry leaves. She made her way to Front Street, which meandered along the lakeshore. Shimmering water stretched as far as the eye could see, an astonishing shade of cobalt blue, and a lone sailboat bobbed like a giant dorsal fin on the surface. Lake Devon lapped hungrily at a smooth swath of sand where children played just out of reach among the driftwood. One balanced precariously on a low stone wall like a miniature tightrope walker.

The outpost of Dresden galleries at number 1212 was an impressive building in the thatch-roofed style. Broad bay windows held the muted still lifes of a Russian artist and a trio of lush Mediterranean scenes by a French one, the paint applied so thickly with a palette knife that it looked more like bas-relief.

The upper portion of the Dutch door was open, and Amanda peered in to find the gallery director on the phone. He acknowledged her from his wide marble desk with an encouraging smile. Chiding herself for needing the encouragement, Amanda depressed the door handle firmly. The exhibition wouldn't open for another ten days, yet she'd been unable to wait. She'd glean what facts she could about the artist and his model, and that would most likely be that.

Inside, the gallery was an architectural feat of soaring coved ceilings, glazed walls, and distressed wood floors. She roamed down the gently sloping walkways. Angled walls created the illusion of separate rooms, each holding an exquisite array of art and sculpture. Idly, Amanda browsed until she heard the director end his call, and then she returned to the front of the gallery.

His nameplate read ROLF VAN DUREN, which sounded like something out of *The Sound of Music*. And indeed he looked like Rolfe all grown up, with his pale blond hair, perfectly coifed goatee, and tailored silk suit. The cost went into the price of the paintings, she imagined. He rose to greet her. Could he be of help?

"Well, yes. I'm interested in an artist named Luke Farrell. I understand there's to be an exhibition of his work in October?"

"Ah, yes. The Gisèle Paintings. Exquisite." A solicitous smile. "Will you be attending?"

"I hope to, yes. But actually, I'm interested in speaking with the artist and his wife before the exhibition." Rolf's expression grew veiled, and Amanda realized this was an odd, even intrusive, request. "You see, I write for *Reflex*." She swallowed. Her mouth always went dry when she lied.

"I see." A hesitation. "And did you have an interview arranged?"

"Well, no. It was a rather last-minute assignment."

"I'm afraid Mr. Farrell and his wife are both very private people. If I may take your contact information, I'll pass it on to Mr. Dresden."

Amanda rattled off her name and hotel, but her heart was sinking. "I'm only in town for a short time. Might I arrange to speak with Mr. Dresden today?"

Surprisingly, it was agreed to. Could she meet him in an hour at Devon College? She assured Rolf she could.

The institution was known to Amanda by reputation, one of those rarified progressive schools in which grades were thought to damage the delicate psyches of the students. With a tiny student body and a vast, distinguished faculty, it was renowned for its art programs, particularly an unusual interdisciplinary arts degree that encouraged students to cross-pollinate among sculpture and painting, music, theater, and writing. One of the less favorable articles she'd read on Dresden concerned his involvement with a group of students he mentored within the degree, in a major called art philosophy. The program was limited to just six, one of whom was his son, Joshua. Not only had the article been critical of this perceived nepotism, but Dresden's influence over his students had been characterized as "cultish."

If the students in question were indeed being brainwashed, Amanda couldn't imagine a lovelier setting for it. The campus was an arboretum, and pale sandstone buildings spread luxuriously over a thousand gorgeous acres. It was the official start of fall, and many of the trees were already in the throes of their early-autumn transformation; brilliant shades of yellow and orange carpeted the walkways and punctuated the endless expanse of green. Leaves blew on the breeze and crackled underfoot, scratching out a lonely melody. Familiar strains of a Pearl Jam song emanated from a dorm window above, and two boys tossed a Frisbee on her right. To her left, a flock of girls lay on blankets in the grass, alternately giggling, studying the boys, and gazing up in boredom at a sky that was impossibly blue, pale rays of sunshine illuminating the puffy cotton-ball clouds.

At last Amanda reached the tower at the center of campus. Impressively Gothic, it had once been part of a monastery, Rolf had told her, a relic around which the school was built. "One can't miss it."

One certainly could not. Ivy clung darkly to the stone exterior in a death grip, and it was a dizzying view to the top, where sunlight glared off leaded-glass windows, blinding her and leaving the landscape alive with wraiths as she blinked. A high gate entwined with rose vines surrounded the base of the tower, isolating it from the flow of students traipsing to and from class. There was a romantic, forbidden appeal to it all that filled Amanda with a childish desire to trespass and explore.

She found the gate locked. Through the wrought-iron bars, Amanda glimpsed a garden and called loudly, "Hello? Anyone?" With a start she noticed a tall man leaning against the wall of the tower, completely in shadow and staring directly at her.

"You really mustn't yell," he said as he started toward her with a pained expression. "There's a buzzer, as you'll see, to your right." His accent was a surprise: upper-class British and tremendously resonant, like an actor's. "It rings inside, and generally someone will emerge to let you in." He pushed a lock of hair from his forehead and gave her a wry smile through the bars. "Like magic."

"I'm sorry, I didn't see."

He reached to unfasten the gate. She recognized Robin Dresden from his photos, but his presence overwhelmed them. His attraction wasn't the healthy kind. His dark clothes accentuated his nearly black hair and the dark smudges beneath his eyes, and the eyes themselves were such a strange color—a clear, deep gray as dark as charcoal, with pale flecks in them like ice. Or ashes. Yes. Pale, iridescent ashes and black soot. And then there was his mouth. It turned down slightly at the corners, giving him a demanding, restless expression. Amanda found that these quirks were his appeal, for otherwise his face was a study in symmetry: dark hair, dark lashes, dark brows, sculpted cheekbones and lips. They twitched now, amused by her scrutiny.

Was he a part of her sister's world?

Hastily, Amanda introduced herself. "Thank you for agreeing to see me, Dr. Dresden."

"Please. 'Doctor' brings to mind white coats and antiseptic. It's Robin." Yet while Robin had opened the gate, he didn't step aside to let her in. Instead he peered down at her, clearly unwilling to commit himself to the interview. "Rolf tells me you write for *Reflex,* but they've already previewed the paintings. And reviewed them." *So what are you doing here?*

"Well, yes. My story is more personal. I'd like to focus on the relationship between the artist and his muse."

"Ah. You mean between the husband and his wife?" Robin shook his head and gazed past her. "I can't help you there. I rarely grant interviews when I'm the subject. And never with regard to the private lives of friends."

"Well, no." She flushed in spite of herself. "But surely you can give me some background information on the paintings and the painter. You *are* the force behind the exhibition. I mean, it's your gallery?"

Robin Dresden closed his eyes momentarily and reopened them, too long for a blink—more as if he were garnering patience, or resurfacing from a deep meditation—and either way, Amanda thought, rather rude. But then his expression softened. "Yes. Yes, I suppose I can spare you a few moments." He stepped aside and, with a motion of his long fingers, ushered her in. Turning, he led the way down the garden path, leaving the heavy gate to swing shut behind her with a clang.

And yet for a moment, Amanda hesitated. She felt as if she'd entered another world—one that, in spite of its beauty, wasn't at all benign. Karen didn't belong to this world any more than she. Not *her* Karen. And for one absurd moment, She felt an overwhelming urge to retreat and head back to the familiar gray miasma of Seattle, with its traffic and smog and urban solidity.

But Robin turned back with an impatient glance. "Ms. Miller?"

And she followed.

V

THE FALSE START

Our first year together was so lovely and euphoric a time for me that perhaps I underestimated the strain of it upon her. Every so often Gisèle would fall into states of melancholia: sullen, accusatory silences I liked to think had to do with feminine vagaries I could hardly be expected to comprehend.

One night, inexplicably, in the midst of watching *Three's Company*, she ran crying from the room.

I found her lying on her stomach on the bed and sat beside her, stroking her hair, until at last she confided, "Today is Mandy's birthday, Tristan. My little sister. She's ten."

And so, curled up against me, she told me about Mandy: her favorite ice cream (strawberry), favorite color (red), favorite television show (*The Dukes of Hazzard*—I was dubious at this, but Gisèle assured me it was so)—favorite author (Beverly Cleary). And it seemed they both shared an enormous crush on the pretty pop idol Shaun Cassidy. On the debit side, Mandy had a habit of borrowing Gisèle's things without asking and had eaten half of her chocolate Santa the previous Christmas, attempting to cover up the crime by smoothing the foil wrapping over the empty part of his belly. But she wasn't a tattletale or a crybaby, and the day Amanda was born had been the best day of Gisèle's old life. Her first word had been a bastardized version of her big sister's name: "Kow-en." Tears filled her eyes. "And I just left her there, Tristan."

Well, what was one to do?

I thought of buying a cake with Mandy's name scrolled in frosting and ten candles placed on it, so Gisèle might close her eyes and send her sister a birthday wish. This might easily snowball into a confectionary remembrance of all her relatives, of course. But there were worse fates, I supposed, than the consumption of a great lot of cake.

As I pondered these frivolous concerns, she gazed at me and frowned, as if she'd read my thoughts.

"You don't understand, do you, Tristan? I left her there with my father." Gisèle dropped her eyes and swallowed. "Listen, you're going to find out when the phone bill comes anyway, so I may as well just tell you."

She hardly needed to say the rest. My heart had stopped.

She continued unsteadily. "While you were in the shower, I tried to call her. Mandy likes to answer the phone, and I just wanted to hear her voice, Tristan. She has such a cheerful hello. I wanted to make sure it hadn't changed." Glancing at me, she rushed on. "Don't look like that. I . . . I didn't even get through." A worried V formed between her brows. "I don't know what could have happened. The number's been the same forever. I even tried dialing information for Patrick Miller, and nothing. We've *never* been unlisted. It costs an extra dollar a month." Tears shone again in her eyes. "I don't know what's happened, Tristan."

And it was my turn to feel apprehensive then, for I knew exactly what had happened.

I still read the *San Francisco Chronicle* as habitually as *Le Monde*. Earlier in the month, I'd scanned a report of a fatal car accident. Scrolling down idly, I'd caught the driver's name: Patrick Miller.

He was drunk and his driving more than reckless, it seemed—it was suicidal. The car had been burned, the bodies inside initially unidentifiable. In the first report, it was thought his wife and daughter had died with him. Later reports would clarify: Gisèle's mother was the only passenger. Mandy was later located and placed in the custody of an aunt.

In the last weeks, I'd found myself haunted by the little ballerina: she of the dangling shoelaces and my lost Tuesdays. I even wrestled with the notion of telling Gisèle. But it was impossible, of course. She could hardly fail to contact her sister under such a circumstance.

Unless she believed there was no sister to contact.

Staring then into her perplexed, tortured face, I saw a chance to snip the last tie to her past, and I took it. Gently, I told her of the accident. I told her that her entire family was dead.

She would not believe me. At her urging I sent for a copy of the paper, making certain it was the date of the initial false report. Her response frightened me, for at first there was no outward response at all. For days she refused to speak of it. And then with a frightening abandon, in the middle of the night, her sobs cut my heart from my chest with razor blades. I have never seen someone so distraught.

Her anguish was very nearly unbearable. Very nearly.

I banned Henri and Nora from the apartment. I bathed her, fed her, held her; my conscience pricked me keenly all the while. But common sense prevailed. Fate had handed this to me, you see. What else could bind her to me so completely?

At last, days later, red-eyed and hoarse from crying, she confessed to me "the whole truth." I could feel no anger. I simply listened to her broken voice.

It seemed she'd spoken to her mother; she'd spoken to her the very day of the accident. This is why she had called again and been so puzzled to find the number disconnected.

A phone call seemed safest, Gisèle said. She'd taken precautions. It had been made from a phone booth, near the restrooms, while we were out dining one evening. She hadn't told her mother about me or where she was, just that she was all right now and not to worry about her. She'd told her to worry about Mandy.

"It just came out, Tristan. What he did to me. And then I was so horrified I hung up. I never even told her I loved her. . . ."

And with those soft, choked words went the last of her childish wonder.

Afterward my most extravagant diversions were met with a delight that never quite reached her eyes. There was a restlessness and a sorrow that would never leave her, as much as she tried to suppress it. In her mind Gisèle hadn't merely abandoned her family but had single-handedly destroyed it. In her attempt to save her sister, she had killed her.

And I committed perhaps my gravest crime. I let her believe it.

VI

THE START OF THE HUNT

ROBIN DRESDEN LED AMANDA up a stairway unlike any she had ever seen; it spiraled dizzyingly, and art lined the curving walls—a quick study of artistic periods from the Renaissance onward. They were only reproductions, of course. Even with Amanda's limited knowledge of art, she was aware that the *Mona Lisa* was in the Louvre. But they were fine copies, printed on canvas and framed, delicately lit by savage iron sconces. By contrast, the stairs were formal and refined: highly polished dark cherry with a fine Persian runner. They went up three floors. At each landing, burnished wooden doors led off to the right and left: "My students' rooms," Robin said.

She wondered what it was like to be a student of his.

Another flight up. The room into which he led her was too luxuriously appointed to be called an office, though there was a kidney-shaped mahogany desk in such a state of disarray that she glimpsed only a corner of its leather inlaid top. The room itself was a wide semicircle and possessed none of the sterile asceticism of an academic workspace. Here the paintings were profuse, covering the walls like wallpaper, and these didn't appear to be reproductions—a daunting collage of figurative and abstract, classical and modern. Books covered any remaining wall space and stood in stacks upon the floor. She felt rather like a novice stumbling upon the sacristy.

Robin swept the disorder on his desk into one neat pile and motioned her to one of the seats before him. A mismatched yet complementary set, one was a leather club chair and the other an overstuffed wing chair. Amanda chose the former. She didn't like having her peripheral vision hindered and imagined that Robin Dresden was overaccustomed to an audience perched on the edge of its seat.

He had gone to a bar in the corner of the room, selecting from an array of crystal decanters and glasses. Another corner held a sculpture of a female nude, which along with a lush hanging plant lent a sensual quality to the space.

Beside her was an antique table of inlaid wood in a geometric design. An old-fashioned kaleidoscope stood upright beside a leather-bound tome of great size. It lay open, its language foreign. She caught the musty scent of yellowed pages but doubted, given his irreverent air, that it was the Bible.

And then all at once she understood. It was in the analytical way he was studying her now, like a shrink. She recognized the room as a stage with props, designed to trigger a response from the humble trespasser. In Robin Dresden's codex, each piece probably possessed revelatory power. Yes, now she saw the shapes: the masculine elements, the feminine, the empty spaces, the claustrophobic ones, metamorphosing images like a room of Rorschach inkblots.

She had chosen the masculine chair. She met his eyes. "This room says a lot about you."

"And you." An ironic half smile. "Would you care for a drink, Amanda?"

"Thanks. Some water would be nice."

He turned back to the bar. "I prefer scotch in mine. Are you similarly inclined?"

"Oh. Er, no. Just ice."

She heard the clink of ice against crystal. He handed her a tumbler and sat behind the desk with his scotch.

"Now. To your story, Amanda. I'd be very interested to hear it." He thumbed through the papers on his desk as he spoke. "You see, I know the editor at *Reflex* quite well, and he has no writer called Amanda Miller on his staff." She was again startled by the intensity of his gaze. He was accustomed to controlling the conversation.

She wasn't going to give him the satisfaction. "Well, that's right. I'm not a staff writer. I'm only freelance. I should have said so at the gallery." She gave him her most ingenuous smile, ignoring the fact that her mouth felt like cotton.

Robin sipped his scotch. "I see."

Amanda cleared her throat and opened the notebook she'd brought along, a prop to suit the room. After years of college, she at least knew how to take notes convincingly. "Well, to start, can you tell me a bit about the artist? Luke Farrell burst onto the scene very suddenly."

Amusement played on Robin's lips, as if he knew she knew nothing of the "scene." A shrug. "He's thirty-three years old, with an indifferent education. A few years at the University of Virginia, no degree. A great many aspirant art seminars in Seattle. Apparently a natural talent."

"You sound doubtful."

"I'm in very little doubt as to the quality of the paintings."

"Well, how did you become aware of them?" Awful. She sounded like a halfwit.

"I'm close to the family. He sought my opinion, and it was favorable."

"And he paints only his wife?"

An indecipherable expression. "That's all he seems to paint well."

This is going nowhere fast. "Have they been married long?" A pause. "I mean, to paint her over and over again. It must be a passionate relationship."

"Must it?" Robin turned in his chair, gazing out the window. "Do you think Monet had a passionate relationship with his water lilies? He studied them in different light; he was seeking to know them in all their guises."

Amanda forced herself to focus on her notebook. To write. "Does she have many guises, Gisèle?"

"More than most." There was a note of sorrow in his voice.

"She is thirty years old, is that right?" Karen would be thirty.

Robin gave a curt nod.

Her heart quickened. "Born in February?"

"No." Again his gaze was unnerving. She avoided it. "June."

But birthdays, like names, can be changed.

"You are considerably more interested in the model than the artist, Amanda."

"But she's more than that—" She swallowed. "From what I've seen of the paintings."

"How would you characterize them?"

Amanda shifted in the leather seat. "Well, technically, they're—"

"Not technically. How do they make you feel?"

"Uncomfortable." *A little like now.*

"Why?"

"I don't know. They're . . . *she* is very compelling. I think it's that she doesn't know how beautiful she is. But the way she's depicted. In pieces." Amanda gave a small shudder. "I wouldn't like anyone to study me so closely, so unkindly."

"Unkindly?"

"The reviewer for *Reflex* found them erotic. Maybe that's the male perspective. I found them critical. Claustrophobic." She swallowed. "I had the feeling Gisèle lived in a fishbowl."

"And yet it was a passionate relationship?"

"No. No, I guess not," she admitted. "A smothering one."

"Of course, the two aren't mutually exclusive. Is that why she interests you?"

Amanda didn't know how to answer and had begun to expect him to do it for her. *Who's conducting this interview?* Gulping down the last of her water, she straightened. "I'd always intended Gisèle to be the focus of the article, Robin. I promise you I'll deal with the relationship in a respectful way. But in order to give any depth to my story—"

"You'll have to come out with it." He scratched his head, idly. "Really, now. You're no journalist, Amanda, freelance or otherwise. Start at the start, build to the middle, arrive at the end." He made a conductor's motion with his hands. "You have a rapt audience."

"I don't know what you mean."

"I instructed Rolf to send you over in an hour, so that I'd have time to research you."

She flushed. She'd liked him better as a prop. "Why research *me*?"

A smile. "To see why you should wish to interview *me*. Don't look so mortified. I research everyone I grant an interview. It dictates the tone. Saves time. And so I've just finished your fascinating article in *Psychology*

Today. 'The Empathetic Effect'? A very impressive publication for a graduate student. Though I am not entirely convinced of your results."

She bristled. "Excuse me?"

Robin rolled a pen back and forth across the blotter beneath his long fingers. "Oh, I'm not questioning the validity of your process, Amanda. Simply the outcome."

"That's no small thing."

"According to your research, experience did not foster empathy. Subjects with a history of trauma were *less* affected by violent imagery, correct? Scar tissue of the mind, you concluded. But the mind scars in one area only to increase awareness in another. It's the thing of a moment to be horrified and quite another to be haunted." She focused on the pen. Back and forth, back and forth. "Can empathy be measured in the same way as trauma? I think not. I'd be more interested in the aftereffects of your study. Take your Group A: the fucked-up set. And Group B: the boring—"

"Those weren't quite the technical terms."

A shrug. "My guess is that Group B, those happy, well-adjusted subjects who displayed such great stress in the short window of your analysis, washed their hands of it immediately afterward. That's called healthy in our society, but true empathy can only be born of experience. I'd be very interested in the dreams of the traumatized group. In their emotional states after such an experiment." The pen went still; he gazed up at her. "How was *your* state of mind after the study?"

It went on leave. "Are you asking whether I'm fucked up or boring?"

"No, no." A pause. "I only wonder, have the nightmares stopped?"

She stared. He was manipulating her, she knew, a magician dazzling her with his tricks. But for a moment she held his gaze and there was a strange kind of comfort in it. Too much.

"I'm sorry about the reporter bit," Amanda murmured at last. "I'm not a very good liar."

"You mustn't write yourself off so quickly." He stood the pen upright, tapped it. "It was merely a bad lie."

"Well, I don't get much practice."

"Personally, I prefer it when people lie to me. It's far more revealing than the truth."

She studied him. "How did you come to read people so well? You're not a student of psychology."

"You needn't attain a degree in order to study, Amanda. As with any unusual knowledge, it merely requires natural interest. Placed under duress." Robin swept a lock of hair from his brow and gave her an enigmatic smile. "A bit more water? Or would you prefer something stronger? You look as though you could use it."

He really was very unsettling. "No, I can't— I mean, I don't often drink."

"I see." Robin gazed at her a moment. He turned to replenish her water and handed it across the desk to her. "Now, shall we come to the reason for the psychologist's sudden interest in art?"

And so it was that she told him. Everything. The pain of her sister's disappearance, the mysterious letter, her first glimpse of the Gisèle paintings . . . As she spoke, Amanda felt her fears slip away, her long unease with confiding in strangers. It was dwarfed suddenly by a single-mindedness that surprised even her. She had come for Karen, for the hope rekindled by the mysterious "Gisèle," and she would not leave without knowing the truth. Appearing foolish was a small price to pay. The eccentric Robin Dresden was thoughtful and fidgety, his pen flipping now in rapid circles through his fingers. Yet he listened attentively, actively. When she'd finished, Amanda reached for her purse and extracted a photo of Karen she always kept with her. It was only as Robin studied it that the full force of what she was asking him struck her.

The photo had been taken the fall before Karen disappeared; she was fourteen years old. It was a smiling face, not a happy one, and she wore the expression she'd often worn then: wistful, self-conscious. It adhered to all the noble traditions of stock school photography—a backdrop of static, impenetrable gray; garish light; the predictable tilt to her head. But beneath the seventies feathered haircut and diamond-patterned gold sweater, there was Karen: the odd combination of lovely, cagey eyes and shining lip gloss that accented a smile full of secrets.

"Well," Amanda said at last. "She does *look* like Gisèle, doesn't she?"

"*You* look like her." His voice was clipped, but she was beginning to recognize this as emotion. He sighed. "It's impossible to tell, Amanda. This is a child. Did Karen have any scars, any distinguishing marks I might recognize?"

"Nothing I . . . well, no, nothing distinctive—"

"A behavioral quirk?"

"Not really. I mean, that wasn't my specialty then. I was nine when she disappeared." In frustration, Amanda rubbed her temple and racked her brain. Surely there was something. "She had a phobia. An overwhelming fear of water. Not the kind of thing you get over."

Robin hesitated, staring at her. "Gisèle doesn't swim, but that's hardly conclusive."

Amanda sighed. There was something he wasn't telling her. She sensed it. "But the photograph, Robin. For a moment you seemed to recognize her—"

"I like her, that's all. Your Karen." He handed the photo back to her and plucked a cigarette from a drawer, not bothering to ask if Amanda wanted one, if she minded. She didn't smoke, and she did mind. For a long time, she hardly breathed, but when she did inhale, she decided that the sharp, musky scent of exotic tobacco suited him, suited the room. And, strangely, it suited her, too. He took a sip of scotch. Amanda envied him his vices, the comforting numbness they must provide.

Finally he spoke. "You don't quite understand the position I'm in. I've known Tristan Mourault for nearly fourteen years."

"Sorry. Who is Tristan Mourault?"

"Gisèle's *father*." A pause. "And my dear friend."

Her father? As the meaning of the words settled upon her, Amanda's heart sank. But her mind calculated. "But if you met fourteen years ago, she would have been only—"

"Elle was sixteen when I met her."

"Then she wasn't much older than that picture."

"I'll grant you the resemblance is very great, but it's hardly definitive. Change the hairstyle, the clothing, the context and it could be nothing more than coincidence. Many people have similar features." He took a long drag off his cigarette and released a whirling white wraith into the room. "But you've been refreshingly frank with me, Amanda. So I'll be frank with you."

And in spite of herself, she slid to the edge of her seat.

"When I met them in New York, Tristan claimed that Gisèle had only recently come to live with him." Robin shifted restlessly. "He was

French, she was *very* American. He explained she was a 'love child,' quaintly enough, from his years at Princeton. But I happen to know he had married another woman there. And *she'd* had a child the same year. They both died a few years later in a car accident. . . . But it seemed one daughter too many, if you know what I mean. It's not impossible, of course, but on top of this, Gisèle looked nothing at all like him. And her accent was not New Jersey but California."

Amanda's stomach began to churn. "Californians have accents?"

"You do."

"I've lived in Seattle for years."

"Your accent is the place you were born. You can leave it, but you can never be rid of it."

Amanda didn't like to consider this; every part of her rejected it, a thing she knew meant it contained some truth. In her nightmares she was always back in San Francisco, stalking her past through alleyways and warehouses, disappearing up the steep stairs of the old Victorian.

"It wasn't just the accent, but the climate between them." Robin took another long drag. "To be honest, I took her for a runaway."

The room began to hum. So she had been right about slipping into the sacristy.

Robin ran a hand through his hair and rationalized. "It was New York. Runaways are like stray cats." He shrugged. "If he wanted to take her in, who was I to stop him? Tristan's a kind man, Amanda. Cultured, wealthy. He gave her everything she wanted. She was happy." Robin stared at the rising smoke. "In later years he certainly *acted* the father. He gave her away at her wedding, for Christ's sake. She's been married for twelve years."

Twelve years of the fifteen she's been dead. It was habit to think it, and the reverse was inconceivable. That Karen had been alive all these years and never contacted her? That she'd lived *here*, within driving distance of Seattle? And there had been so much blood at the scene. . . . Could it all have been orchestrated? *Planned* somehow?

Her thoughts must have played across her face like a silent film, for Robin interceded gently, "Have you considered yet whether or not you *want* Gisèle to be Karen?"

For the first time, Amanda considered this. To say no was unthinkable. To deny Karen fifteen more years of life and love and experience? And to say yes reopened painful volumes that had been tightly closed for years. It wrote new ones, in which she had no part. Gisèle, unlike Karen, had left her by choice. She focused on the ash of Robin's cigarette—the burned edge hovered dangerously near the tips of his fingers—and said only, "Would you recognize her handwriting?"

"I would, yes." He stubbed out the cigarette between his forefinger and thumb, dropped it in the silver tray. His manner was brusque. "You have the letter with you?"

She hesitated. "No, but I will. I've requested it back. I sent it to San Francisco—to the detective in charge of her case—for forensics tests. Turned up nothing. He thinks it's a hoax."

"Perhaps it is."

"Either way, I need to know."

Robin sighed, swiveling restlessly in his chair. "Gisèle's a dear friend. Whether your story is true or not, I can't force a confrontation between you."

A confrontation? Is that what it would be? *To see Karen again . . .* Part of her recoiled at the idea of meeting "Gisèle," a stranger. Or was it the idea of finding her sister a stranger?

Amanda sat dumbly, and he read her mind in his disquieting way. "You came to Devon to convince yourself Gisèle *wasn't* your sister. Of course you did. So shall we approach it from that perspective?"

She managed a nod. Again she was struck by the kindness in his eyes, the concern there. Why should he be concerned for her?

"I could, for instance, arrange for you to meet Tristan. He's a reclusive man, but he has many interests—wine, books, music. I can put you in the same place at the same time. The rest is up to you."

"But he's hardly going to *confess* to me, Robin. Why would he tell me anything at all?"

"Come, now. You're a student of psychology. People tell you all manner of things without trying. You needn't say anything directly to challenge him. Your very existence is a challenge to him. How will he handle it? Observe. Study his body language. Read between the lines."

"But he's your friend," she said softly. "Why would you help me?"

Robin finished the last of his scotch and frowned at the glass.

"Because Gisèle is also my friend. And *if* she wrote to you, she wants to put the two halves of her life together again. She will need our help to do it, Amanda. It's not only her own illusions at stake." He gazed up and past her, unseeing. "She has a daughter. My goddaughter, Nicola. A beautiful, lonely little girl whose entire world is built on lies."

❧

Nicola and her mother sat in their favorite café, a place called André's, in the village. The air outside carried an autumn chill, and a fire raged before their usual table in the corner. Two art magazines sat on the table between them. In the car there were many more, to be on hand for the party. Nicola's father's reviews had been "glowing," and since then she and her mother had been secretly preparing a party for him—a private pre-party to take place this Saturday: exactly one week before the gallery opening of the Gisèle Paintings.

Her mother phoned each guest personally, apologizing for the short notice, but everyone loved a surprise and most had cleared their calendars. Things should have been perfect, Nicola mused, but somehow they weren't. Everyone had been acting strangely lately. Her father was dazed and nervy, talking too fast and dropping things at dinner; her mother was increasingly remote. Today, instead of being relieved that plans for the party were nearly complete, Gisèle seemed abstracted and worried—as if she were dreading the whole thing.

Something was going on, and it infuriated Nicola not to understand. Marc Kreicek was involved in it, somehow. It was more than the scene she'd witnessed on her parents' anniversary. Her mother and Marc always seemed to be huddled together, whispering. If her father had really had an affair, maybe her mother had, too? Nicola couldn't see it, though. Her mother wasn't in love with Marc Kreicek. This much she knew. So what was the big secret? Even her grandfather was behaving peculiarly. Nicola could tell he didn't really like the paintings, so why was he *pretending* to like them?

And then there was the argument Nicola had overheard yesterday between her mother and Robin. Somehow this was most troubling of all, because it was so unprecedented. To her knowledge they'd never argued before. Robin had always seemed the one person—the one person other than Nicola—with whom her mother was truly relaxed, truly happy.

Suddenly it seemed everyone in Nicola's life had taken on unsettling new dimensions. It was like walking into a familiar room at night and bumping into all the furniture.

To distract herself from these thoughts, Nicola picked up a magazine and thumbed to the article on her father, scanning the words while they waited for their food to come. "What's 'objectification,' Mom?"

Her mother had opened the other magazine. She glanced up. "You really shouldn't be reading that, Nicky. It won't make sense to you."

Nicola gritted her teeth. "I'm almost twelve. It makes sense to me—I just don't understand why he used that word. It's a bad thing, isn't it? To objectify someone?"

"Well, it's easy to think of nudity as objectifying, because it focuses on the body rather than on the person inside. But that isn't what the paintings are about. The article goes on to say that."

"Oh." Nicola was silent a moment. "Well, what does 'voyeur' mean, then?"

"Darling, I . . . It's difficult to explain. When you're older, you'll understand."

Nicola gazed at her mother reproachfully. She never said things like that.

Gisèle laid her magazine down and bit her lip apologetically. "I'm sorry, Nicky. I just have a lot on my mind." She cast a glance around, taking in the hustle and bustle of the Saturday lunch crowd as if searching for something, or someone. With a slight frown, she returned to Nicola. "It's just difficult to explain. The article is . . . well, it's a bit tongue-in-cheek. By definition a voyeur is someone who watches someone else without that person's knowledge."

"So it's not a good thing either. But it *is* a good review?"

Gisèle laughed ruefully. "Doesn't make much sense, does it? But in the context of the review, it is meant to be a good thing. I guess it's simply honest. We're all voyeurs and exhibitionists both. Watching and being watched. Do you understand?"

"Uh-huh. It's like when Grand-père tells me that life is just a spectacle.

A sort of parade. He says everything is the act of seeing and being seen."

Gisèle frowned. "Well, yes, I suppose he looks at life that way."

"Do you?"

"No." She gazed down at the tablecloth but shook her head sharply. "No, sweetheart. The most important things can't be seen at all."

The food came. Gisèle had ordered a croque-madame and Nicola a croque-monsieur, because she didn't see the point of putting a fried egg on *top* of a sandwich. Inside was one thing, but on top it just seemed to stare at her. And what was the point of a sandwich you couldn't pick up?

Her mother pierced her egg delicately, and yellow goo flooded her sandwich.

Nicola gave a small shudder.

Gisèle cut a demure bite with her knife and fork. "How would you like to go shopping after lunch? We'll buy you a new dress for the party."

Nicola nodded enthusiastically. "Everything I have makes me look too young and unsophisticated."

Her mother arched a brow. "Well, it might be hard to find something sophisticated in your size, but we'll try."

For a moment they ate in contented silence.

"Robin's coming to the party, isn't he?" Nicola asked. "You didn't call to invite him."

"I didn't need to. He already knows about it. Of course he's coming."

"Will he bring Josh?"

"I don't know, hon. Josh is at that age. Consumed with his college friends, you know."

Nicola knew. Suddenly, over the summer, she'd noticed that Robin's son was at that *perfect* age and perfect in every other way, too. Sun-streaked hair in a ponytail and heavy-lidded hazel eyes that changed color with what he wore. With effort she turned her thoughts back to her mother and Robin. "Did you two have a fight?"

"Josh and me? Heavens no."

"No. You and Robin." Nicola took a bite of her sandwich, chewed and swallowed, but her mother still hadn't replied. "I know you argued about something, Mom. I heard you."

Gisèle looked up, startled. "Nicola, it's not polite to listen—"

"I wasn't listening," Nicola said quickly. "I didn't hear what you said, just that you both sounded mad when you said it." The double doors to the sitting room had been closed, their voices urgent and low like the wind in the chimney, coming in spurts too faint to decipher. "What's it all about? Everyone's been acting weird lately." Robin was behind the exhibition, yet it seemed to Nicola that he didn't want anything to do with the paintings at all.

"I don't want you to worry about it. Robin and I are very old friends." Realizing that this wasn't an answer, she continued. "He was encouraging me to do something I just can't do."

"What?"

Gisèle gave a slight, sad smile. "Be honest."

"But you're honest," Nicola said defensively.

"There are different types of honesty. . . . Rob believes in being true to yourself no matter what. It's something I admire about him. It's daring to live that way."

"Aren't you *supposed* to live that way?"

Her mother nodded. "Yes, but sometimes pursuing your personal truth can cause a lot of pain to others, those whom you care about even more than yourself." She swallowed. "Sometimes their illusions can be more important to you than your truth."

"I don't understand."

"I know you don't." Her mother said it with a finality that let Nicola know it was futile to push her further. Gisèle reached forward to smooth a strand of her daughter's hair. Almost to herself she murmured, "I don't ever want you to."

❧

Amanda awoke with a sense of the surreal that only escalated over the course of the day.

A torrential downpour that morning discouraged pleasant distractions like window-shopping, but late afternoon brought a break in the storm, and Amanda put her pacing to some use. Devon's cobblestones glistened wet and reflected the glow of the gas lanterns, already lit due to the darkness of the day. The boutiques and galleries lost none of their charm in the rain; smoke spiraled from chimneys, and cottages clustered cozily together in the cold. She stopped at a café for a late lunch, watching the elegant passersby swaddled in scarves and overcoats, their multicolored umbrellas reminding her of sails on the sound.

None of it seemed quite real. Neither did her plans for the evening.

Robin was taking her to a rarefied cellar in downtown Devon that required membership. Not to mention knowledge of things like tannins and legs and the Brix scale, the difference between American oak, French oak, and stainless steel, all of which were utterly foreign to her.

And there she would meet Tristan Mourault.

They would be doing a vertical tasting of wines from the Bordeaux region in France. Three first-growth châteaux: Margaux, Haut-Brion, and Latour from 1970, 1982, and 1989. The wines had been decanted and sat on a long zinc bar. The interior of the cellar was rustic, with stone walls and a wood-beamed ceiling, just as Amanda imagined tasting rooms in the real châteaux to be. The atmosphere was very cool. Baskets of bread and French cheeses were laid; the wine was served by sommeliers.

The room was bustling with well-heeled food-and-wine types. Robin was greeted by several other members and Amanda made her way through the cursory introductions, feeling as though she'd stepped into a play for which she had no script. Tristan Mourault had already arrived, and Robin pointed him out to her discreetly.

On the surface there was certainly no cause for alarm. His was the picture next to "urbane" in the dictionary: slim and reasonably tall, with dark blond hair going salty gray at the temples and pale blue eyes as cold and clear as diamonds. His face fell into natural lines, slight weathered grooves in skin that had the patina of perpetual tan. He wore a white linen suit and looked as though he might have just flown in from the Cannes Film Festival.

They moved closer. Amanda had learned from Robin that he was French, and so she was prepared for the accent as he spoke animatedly with a few friends in the corner. Still, she was struck by the mesmerizing cadence of his voice. His English managed to maintain the melodious vowel-consonant-vowel rhythm of French, and it was easy to stop listening to what he said in favor of how he said it. But there was something dichotomous in his air; it was both engaging and distancing at once. He wore his refinement like camouflage.

Tristan glanced up then and saw Robin. They were perhaps ten years apart in age and as different in looks as night and day, yet bound by a European air. The two greeted each other with the embrace of old friends. Yet as Robin introduced Amanda, Tristan's warm smile faded; his eyes narrowed on hers and undermined the dulcet tones of his *"Enchanté."*

She greeted him warmly, meeting his critical gaze and trying not to look as self-conscious as she felt. Could he be seeing Gisèle in her? Had he recognized her name? She reined these thoughts in. More likely, she'd simply broken some unspoken code of the wine club.

He gave her a smile that didn't reach his eyes and then turned abruptly, moving past them to greet another member.

"Well, well," said Robin under his breath.

"He doesn't seem very interested in talking to me."

"Give it time. I will give you space."

As the wine was poured, Tristan did not move to rejoin them but simply stared at Amanda from the other end of the long bar. She tried to imagine this distinguished man taking her sister, a runaway, in off the streets. Giving her away at her wedding. Did that make him a sexual predator or father figure? And how had Karen ever made it all the way to New York in the first place? The improbabilities piled up until Amanda could barely breathe.

As Robin chatted to a club member, she looked up to find Tristan standing before her. He'd slipped on a pair of wire-rimmed glasses, and in the dim light she could not read his eyes, but the ice had thawed, it seemed. His expression was surprisingly warm.

"Bonjour again, Amanda. How are you finding the wines?"

"Oh, they're lovely."

"Which do you prefer?"

Unconsciously, Amanda's eyes traveled to Robin, who had been beside her only a moment before. Now she saw him in a far corner of the room, talking quietly into his cell phone. Purposefully out of reach. "They're all very good. . . . I'm afraid I'm no connoisseur."

Tristan gave a sophisticated shrug. "In matters of taste, you mustn't let others influence your choice, Amanda. You must simply choose. How else will I know you?"

How else indeed?

"If I had to choose one, it would be the Château Margaux. The second one. The '82?"

"Ah, an excellent choice. Dark fruit. Graceful and silky, but with great depth. A very feminine wine." And he smiled at her, a playful smile, that translated not to shock or surprise or an instructive flash of guilt but, to Amanda's dismay, flirtation.

For a moment words fled. "And you?" she managed.

"We share the same sound judgment. The '82 Margaux was my favorite as well." His eyes went to Robin and returned to her. "May I ask a rather impertinent question?"

"I won't know unless you ask it."

Tristan gave a light, amused laugh, yet his gaze was anything but light. It was searching. Cloying. "Robin introduced you as a colleague. I'll take him at his word and hope I'm not trespassing. Will you have dinner with me one evening, soon?"

She tried to cover her surprise. She was here to assess Tristan Mourault's character, strike up conversation, observe him. But a date? Her eyes skipped around the bustling cellar, the noise level elevated with the consumption of wine. She drew in a breath. *In for a penny, in for a pound.* "Yes, Tristan. That would be nice."

"Tomorrow?"

Amanda hesitated. "Well, yes. I suppose tomorrow is all right."

"*Bon.* And where shall I pick you up?"

She gave him the name of her hotel, and then Tristan took her hand in his, a gentle, warm touch. "Until tomorrow, then. *Bonne nuit*, Amanda."

And she was released.

The next evening, over cocktails, Amanda found she had more in common with Tristan Mourault than she'd ever imagined possible. Her experiences were limited and his were vast, yet it seemed they shared the same taste in movies (old), cars (not quite as old, but old), architecture (very, very old), food (Italian), wine (not Italian), music (classical), art (impressionist), and literature (all of it). There was something almost *too* agreeable about him. Was it chemistry by design?

"Tell me what you do at the college," Tristan said over an hors d'oeuvre of Willapa Bay oysters and champagne. "You are very young to be a professor."

The lies would begin and keep growing. Amanda decided to keep them as honest as she could. "Oh, I'm not a professor. Robin was being generous with the term 'colleague.' I'm only a grad student visiting for the semester. I go to the University of Washington in Seattle, but . . . I don't know. I guess I needed a change of scenery. I'm here working on a research project."

"And what is the topic?"

"The psychological basis of empathy."

Over his champagne flute, Tristan studied her. "Ah, empathy. Literally 'passion,' yes?"

She nodded, surprised. "Yes. The etymology is Greek, from *empatheia*."

"To understand why another acts, feel how another feels, even when it defies one's natural scope of understanding . . ."

Amanda spoke carefully. "It plays a particular part in our treatment of those on the fringes of society. The humane treatment of criminals, for example. Clearly, it often falls short. Many feel that to understand criminal behavior is to excuse it."

"You do not think so?"

"Well." She paused. Her breathing felt shallow. "It's one thing to understand and another to forgive. I aspire to . . . understanding."

For a moment he scarcely seemed to blink. And then he busied himself with spooning a bit of mignonette onto an oyster. "I must confess I find you very mysterious, Amanda."

"How flattering. But I can't imagine why."

"*Eh bien,* I shall lay my case before you." The teasing tone didn't quite conceal his inquisitiveness. She glanced up to find his gaze glacial, despite the smile that played on his lips. "You're in town for only a short time, and yet you've already managed to make the acquaintance of our most esteemed local celebrity."

"Oh, you mean Robin? I don't really follow art."

"*Oui, bien sûr.* And you are visiting for the semester—a student—yet you live not on campus but in a hotel? It is curious, *n'est-ce pas?*" Amanda felt her cheeks grow warm. "And you have managed, very charmingly, to tell me very little of substance about yourself. Nothing of your family and friends. Your life in Seattle. Or what it was that prompted you to leave it."

"Do most people get to all that before the entrée?" Amanda laughed nervously. "In any case, I was thinking the very same about you, Tristan. You don't talk about yourself at all." *You talk about taste . . . about things.*

"Ah, but that is deliberate, *chérie*. I have too many skeletons."

He was just teasing. Of course he was.

The waiter came and whisked away her only distraction. "Well, I hate to ruin the mystery, but I'm twenty-four years old. I've lived alone for years. I honestly can't imagine returning to dorm life." She gave a short laugh. "And one semester's too brief a time to deal with an apartment and furnishings, all of that." She traced a finger up and down the stem of her glass. "I left Seattle for a change of pace. To be perfectly frank, to escape a dead-end relationship."

This seemed to please him.

"As far as Robin goes, I met him by chance in the library. I guess the chance is decreased when you consider how much time I actually *spend* in the library. He took pity on me, sitting alone with my stacks of psych journals. It can be difficult to make friends in a new place."

"That is true." Tristan sat back. "Well, I am pleased to be counted among your new friends. I hope I haven't offended you with my curiosity. It's a flaw in my character."

"Of course not."

He had very kindly opened the door for her. Why was she so hesitant to go through it?

"As far as my family goes, I'm afraid it's not terribly good dinner conversation. When I was ten, both my parents were killed in a car accident." With effort she met his eyes. "My only sister, Karen, was murdered eight months before."

"*Mon Dieu*, I am sorry." A wave of genuine empathy, even shock, crossed Tristan's face. "Please forgive my intrusion."

"You couldn't possibly have known." Amanda gave weight to the words.

He didn't seem to feel it. "I must say, from such tragedy you have emerged remarkably poised and sane."

"Well," she said dryly. "Don't give me too much credit too soon."

The waiter arrived with the entrées, and over the feast of local rainbow trout Tristan managed to draw out Amanda's personal history without even seeming to try. She hadn't anticipated the intensity of his interest and found it disarmingly morbid. By dessert she was showing him Karen's school photo. If she'd hoped it would prompt a heartfelt confession, she was disappointed. His reaction was more disturbing still. He held the photo gingerly, utterly enraptured.

"What a beautiful girl she was." He cleared his throat and seemed to remember Amanda. His cool blue eyes met hers. "It seems only yesterday that my daughter, Gisèle, was that age."

"Your daughter?" She tried not to pounce on the words. "Yes, Robin mentioned her."

"Did he?" It was not quite a question.

"Well, he mentioned the exhibition. The Gisèle Paintings? They're getting a lot of attention, I understand."

"Oh, yes. It will be quite a spectacle." He made no attempt to hide his disapproval. "I'm afraid the opening is already filled, but the paintings will be on display through October. You'll have plenty of opportunity to tell me what you think of them."

"What do *you* think?"

He looked reflective. "I think that were they the paintings of someone else's daughter, I would like them very much."

It was such a fatherly sentiment, Amanda had to smile. "I would like to meet Gisèle."

"I'm sure that can be arranged." His tone was blithe, no hint of guilt, no awkward pause.

The only awkwardness arrived with the check. Amanda insisted on splitting. Amused, Tristan insisted she would not.

"Please don't be offended, Tristan. It's just something I like to do."

"When you're uncertain of the man across the table?"

"It's not an uncommon practice nowadays." And then, uncomfortably, "I don't want to lead you on—"

"This notion of leading one on, I wonder, is it a feminine invention or an American one? It is foreign to me. I'm not a child, Amanda. But then I imagine you've already recognized that." A self-deprecating smile; it was hard not to be charmed by him. "I'm far too old for you, it is true. However, with age comes a lovely ebbing away of expectations. I have none at all. I only want to spend time with you, and you are indulging me with your company."

"But—"

"What does any of it have to do with the cost of dinner? I am more than fit to pay; the price means nothing at all to me. And so it would be a petty sort of symbol in which to seek equality, would it not?"

Amanda laughed apprehensively. "Well, how do you suggest I seek it?"

Tristan seemed entertained by the very notion. He gave a faint shrug. "You are terribly concerned with rules, *chérie*. With boundaries. Do I make you feel unsafe?"

It seemed ludicrous put like that; seated in La Dolce Vita and surrounded by it in force. And yet Amanda did feel unsafe in this elegant game of cat and mouse, in which she was decidedly the rodent in the equation. He had given away exactly nothing; she had revealed a great deal. Probably too much. And there was something almost predatory in his attentiveness. She forced a smile. "No, Tristan. I feel perfectly safe."

"You mentioned a desire to meet my daughter." The words were casual.

"Yes."

"She is downtown tonight, as it happens. At an art show just up the street."

Amanda turned to him, trying not to show her eagerness. It overwhelmed her. She didn't hear the name of the gallery or the artist; she heard nothing but the rush of blood in her ears.

". . . open to the public. We might stop in, if you wish."

"Yes." She felt utterly unprepared. Flushed. "Yes, Tristan. I'd like that."

The gallery was in fact barely up the street. It gave Amanda no time at all to organize her thoughts. What would she say to Gisèle? What *could* she say? Tristan's very willingness to allow the meeting seemed to negate all possibility of his guilt. So why was her heart pounding?

As they entered, she saw a few dozen patrons sipping champagne and perusing the work of a modern artist. Amanda's eyes skipped over the canvases—cold, static blocks of color—in favor of the faces. All were strange to her. She was being offered champagne. *Yes.* She already felt intoxicated, cheeks warm and pulse racing. This was what hope felt like, she realized.

And there she was.

Gisèle walked from the back of the gallery toward them, moving with quick, graceful steps. She was very petite, as Karen had been, and everything about her—dress, makeup, hair—was meticulous and precise. Yet there was an appealingly unpracticed air about her that softened it. As she neared them, long-lashed azure eyes the color of Karen's curved into a warm smile and seemed to dance in the soft spotlights.

Gisèle arched on tiptoe to hug her father.

They looked nothing alike yet shared an ease of manner. Wealth. Breeding. An undercurrent of something else Amanda couldn't place. Gisèle turned to her inquisitively as Tristan introduced them.

"I'm sorry, it's Amanda *Miller?*" She leaned forward. "It's terribly loud in here. Everyone's had too much champagne."

"Yes, Miller. Amanda." Her own voice sounded foreign. The resemblance was haunting. It ran through her like a ghost touch. "Mandy," she added. She had always been Mandy to Karen.

Gisèle paused perhaps a moment too long, but there was no recognition at all in her friendly smile; she extended a finely manicured hand. "It's very nice to meet you, Mandy."

Amanda took the other woman's hand in hers. Surely she would know Karen's touch. But in spite of the warm room, she found Gisèle's hand ice cold and clammy. From a champagne glass?

Gisèle gazed through the front windows beyond them. She bit her lip, and there was something determined in her next words. "Ah, there's Marc with the car. He was so eager to come to this show and then had his fill of it in ten minutes." She held Amanda's eyes a moment. Again a moment too long. "It was truly a pleasure to meet you, Mandy." Abruptly, she turned to her father. "Don't stay out too late." Her tone was light, teasing. She apologized for rushing off and then did so, with one last backward glance, a toss of coffee-colored curls. A wave.

Amanda looked after her a long time. When she turned, she found Tristan frowning down at her. "Is everything all right, Amanda? Are you unwell?"

"I'd like to go," she murmured.

"*Oui.*"

They stepped outside. As if in a chorus of agreement, the skies opened and it began to pour.

VII

THE PHILOSOPHER

In autumn of 1980, the blackmail began.

An envelope arrived one innocuous morning, postmarked New York and containing nothing but a single photo. It was Gisèle and I, standing on a street corner—a street corner in San Francisco.

We were doing nothing compromising. She was smiling. We were not touching. Yet I flew around the room, absurdly closing shades.

Gisèle gazed at me placidly. "What's the matter, Tristan?"

"Nothing. Nothing at all." The illusion perforce must be maintained. I fought to maintain it in my own mind. Nothing could harm us. Not after so long. Not now.

There were others in the photo surrounding us; it might have been shot by a tourist. The street sign was famous: Lombard Street. The crooked road.

For the next three weeks, we did not leave the house. I feigned illness and holed up in my bunker, living for the post to arrive each day. Henri ran all my errands; we ate takeout, or Gisèle made a game of cooking for me, dreadfully complicated concoctions from *Bon Appétit* magazine that were mostly inedible but terribly chic. I kept my worries from her, though the phone call to her mother weighed heavily on my mind. Had Mrs. Miller confronted Mr. Miller with his depravity at once, or had she first phoned the police? Had she confided in a friend—or even little Mandy— that Karen was alive? Had that someone tracked her here, to me?

My mind presented a series of similar non sequiturs, but the photograph itself was proof against them. It had clearly not been taken *here*, but in San Francisco, long ago. Before we'd gone. But who would do such a thing and then wait so long to act?

It was a conundrum. And yet after a month of no more photos and no demands for money, I began to wonder if I'd imagined it all. I allowed a blissful cloud of denial to surround me, for this is my natural state, and, as all substances do, I reverted back to it as soon as environmental factors allowed.

Gisèle's natural state these days was one of restlessness. Her blue period had passed, and she chafed at her incubation. It was true, we were too much alone. My reticent blackmailer was in New York. If he wouldn't come to me, I decided, perhaps I might go to him.

And so, after a year of solitude and refused invitations, I reentered "society." For me this consisted of a group of artists and writers I knew in the Village and SoHo. They were an idiosyncratic, amoral group, interested in pursuing their own pleasures and thus not critical of those who did likewise. Those I knew had not missed me, but they welcomed me back with open arms.

Among the new faces, only one stands out in sharp relief. In art circles he was called "The Philosopher," for he had read not art but philosophy at university. I'd heard a good deal about him before we met. Robin Dresden had a rather iniquitous reputation; he was a genius, an elitist, a hedonist—even a hypnotist, or so I had heard. A "head tripper."

Overnight he seemed to be everywhere, yet was that rarity in the art world: an artist who lived up to his hype. All the rage in London, by the age of twenty-six he was just beginning to break into New York art circles. It was clear he had a strategy. He was exhibited at few galleries, yet they were the right galleries. He was showcased in the right art magazines. He was saved from his ambition by his talent and from arrogance only by his wit. He seemed to like to cut it fine, but even my most cynical artist friends followed his rise and admired it. He had interesting things to say. I've kept many relics of those years; I insert here a page of an old interview in *ArtLine:*

Does it bother you that critics seek meaning in your work?

No. I hope they find it.

That's rather glib.

Not at all. The very idea of meaning is an artistic one; our attraction to art is the longing for meaning, for epiphany. To "seek" epiphany is the proper occupation for critics and spectators. Artists *create* epiphany. I like to give critics multiple epiphanies.

Ha! But what does that mean, exactly—to create epiphany?

Everyone but the artist is too specialized to move through the world and understand its secrets; the shaman's sleeping, and Sisyphus reigns. For the most part, human beings are ants, but with less clarified purpose: performing our menial tasks and living for the weekend. Politics and religion try to soothe the chafing, offering up notions of the "betterment of society" so they can collect their tax and tithe. The artist reminds you you're alive. Art is *why*.

Working for the betterment of society isn't a noble aim in your view?

Society—like religion and politics—is an artificial construct. A healthy society consists of healthy individuals; the notion of "society" smothers individuals. Man's forgotten his own magic, and even most art is no more than mindless distraction. True art reenacts the moment of creation. We recognize it unconsciously and respond.

But that seems a religious sentiment.

(laughs) Hardly. Religion claims a monopoly on creation while at the same time stifling the creative impulse. It's hypocrisy. No, no. Mine is a philosophical sentiment. If we know why we create, we know why we exist. That is where the riddle lies; all else exists only to distract one from it. Either you live within the riddle or you are the distraction.

And so I was intrigued when one evening he materialized at the party of a friend in SoHo. I had time to choose my distractions, why not with elitist riddles? But he was exactly the sort from whom I steered Gisèle wide. It was more than his looks. It was his certainty. At that first party, I saw him mesmerize a girl to such a degree that I wondered if she wasn't, in fact, hypnotized.

She was the most beautiful woman in the room. I say "woman" for she showed my Gisèle to be just a girl. To me Gisèle—whose very appeal was elfin, gamine—was made more beloved by this woman's voluptuousness, which had about it so blatant a fecundity, an insistent sexuality we men typically find impossible to resist. She reminded me of Sabina, and she was, unsurprisingly, an artist's model. I watched for sport as she took stock of the room and gravitated to Dresden in a practiced way that betrayed no outward sign of doing so. She was confident and cool. They didn't appear to have met before and engaged in what looked to be casual conversation. He stared at her, she at him; it was a predictable game made interesting only by the brevity with which it was played. I saw him merely touch her hand, not as a lover touches a hand but as a sculptor does, and look at her not as a lover does but as an artist does, as if to memorize the minutest detail of what is before him. He murmured a few intent words, and she went from flippant flirtation to the most ardent devotion.

I saw it in her posture: her teasing inaccessibility turned to acute vulnerability in the space of a few minutes. A rather pathetic spectacle. Yet some men have that power over women. It was said Robin shared a flat off Central Park West with two of them: ménage à trois as lifestyle choice—a thing one imagined limited to Anaïs, Henry, and June, and to *Penthouse* forums.

When I looked again, the woman had gone down the hall, glancing at him anxiously as she waited for the bathroom. Robin looked at me, as though aware I'd been watching. He smiled.

I went protectively back to Gisèle. She was with Henri, who was acting as chaperone precisely to protect her from the Robin Dresdens of the world. I murmured to Gisèle that I thought we ought to leave.

"But we just got here—" Her protest broke off suddenly, and I turned.

"*Bonne nuit,*" Robin said, addressing me formally as "Monsieur

Mourault," which made me feel old. He introduced himself and extended his hand.

I took it. "Please, call me Tristan." With a slight inquiring arch of his brow, he rather forced me to introduce Henri and Gisèle. "This is my friend and associate Henri Dupré. And my daughter, Gisèle."

"A great pleasure." Robin greeted them in an easy, elegant way that spoke of good European upbringing. Then he said with the slight twitch of lips that was his smile, "Are you all coming to the wake?"

"Pardon?"

"Tomorrow. The wake for Lennon." Oh, Christ. John Lennon, whom some religious madman had shot just days prior. A tragedy, of course, but one I personally resented, as it had swallowed up all of Gisèle's attention. She'd been wearing black the entire week. She was wearing black now. So was Robin, though I doubted it to be for the same reason.

He went on to give us the wake's time and locale, making oblique mention of his having known Lennon slightly. Gisèle had been gazing at him quite obviously besotted (and trying to conceal it), but here she could take no more. "You knew him?" she echoed, awed. "You knew John Lennon?"

"Not well. He and Yoko came to a show I had in London. He bought a few pieces; we had dinner sometime after that. Quite an extraordinary person."

"In what way?" she asked. "I mean, apart from his music."

Dresden studied her, his dark, perceptive eyes missing little. "He didn't say anything unnecessary, Gisèle. In our entire conversation, he never relied on the usual things to fill up space. You would have liked him."

She nodded, rather infuriatingly starry-eyed. I placed my hand at the small of her back, and she cast a quick, almost apologetic glance at me. I winked at Henri and with a touch of her chin said, "You should eat something, *chérie*."

Before she could say anything more, the priceless Henri was whisking her away.

Once they were out of earshot, Dresden said, "She's about the same size as Lolita, is she not?" And, to my horror, he began to quote, "'Wanted, wanted: Dolores Haze. Her dream-gray gaze never flinches. Ninety pounds is all she weighs . . . With a height of sixty inches.'" And again he smiled his unwholesome ghost of a smile. "Or is it sixty-two?"

I gave a pious frown. "I've never thought about it, to be sure."

"Her height?"

"Her resemblance, or lack thereof, to Lolita."

"Come now, Tristan." Robin stroked his chin. "She's clearly not your daughter. Is she a runaway?"

A chill ran down my spine. I confess I had no words available to me.

"No half-observant person will swallow it," Dresden was continuing amiably. "Despite her name, she has all the mannerisms of an American of middle class, born and raised. And she doesn't look a bit—"

I interrupted. "She was raised here, of course. Her mother was an American."

"Yes," he agreed equably. "That works better." As if I'd been offering a suggestion, not a fact.

"From my days at Princeton, if you must know. An American," I repeated feebly.

"I see."

Did he? I attempted to steer the conversation to easier terrain. "I should congratulate you on your recent exhibition. I've just read an interview in *ArtLine* and another piece in *Le Monde*."

"Thank you." Robin's smile lost its irony and was appealingly open. "I never read my interviews. I always sound like a prick in them."

"Not at all," I lied. "But I do find it hard to believe you've had no formal training in art."

He didn't reply, as Moira—that was the name of the voluptuous blonde—returned then, having scavenged some scotch. He took it from her, opening her palm as he did so and running his fingers over the icy wetness from the glass. She giggled, and I turned gratefully to go.

"Tristan," (I suppose I should insert that the conversation that followed was carried on entirely in French. To exclude the lovely Moira.) "You needn't go. Please, let's talk a little longer. You interest me."

"I can't imagine why," I replied. It was a keen pleasure to speak French again.

"I find your present situation quite intriguing." But then, instead of elaborating, as I feared, he went on, "As it happens, you've interested me for some time. Like every serious collector, I've heard of the Mourault Collection. The impressionists are favorites of mine." A slight reverent pause, during which I nodded jerkily. "It's rumored you have a van Gogh that has never been shown. Along with *Butterflies and Poppies?*—painted two months before his suicide." He paused. "How the butterflies will go after the poppies, eh?"

Oui. As collectors will go after another's collection. I gazed away to deflect him.

"You also have his notes, I believe, on *The Potato Eaters* and *Starry Night?*" Robin proceeded to catalog the high points of the collection. "And Manet. My, my. *Luncheon in the Grass*, as well as his preliminary sketches of *Gare Saint-Lazare*. One of the largest private collections of Morisot. And Degas. *The Rape? The Collector?*" He glanced heavenward. "And a Renoir of which I'm particularly fond."

"Oh?"

"*The Ingénue?*"

I smiled. I, too, loved the piece.

He gave a gesture to encompass the collection, too many others to mention. "It's quite well known."

I hadn't realized *how* well known, it seemed. "Thank you, we are fortunate."

"You are fabulously fortunate. How can you bear to leave them?" Robin seemed to expect an answer, but I could think of none. "We have mutual acquaintances as well," he went on. "Eve Duvalier?"

His eyes had the most discomfiting prismatic effect; one wished to look away but somehow could not. I squinted at him to diffuse it. "Duvalier, you say?"

"Yes. Your daughter, as you prefer to call her, reminds me a bit of her. Eve knew your wife, Sabina. At least, the families were close. Perhaps you remember her? She would have been just a child then, playing at having tea while the women gossiped. As a result she knew a good deal more about Sabina than she ought to have."

My heart pounded. It would not do to discuss Sabina. And Sabina and gossip paired . . . ? I felt as if I were inside a house of cards that was rapidly collapsing. I forced myself to speak. "I . . . er . . . Ah, yes. Eve. The little dancer?"

"She is not so little anymore. She is the mother of my son."

An odd way to say it. In French *"la mère de mon fils."* Of course it's more typical to say "my wife" or "my mistress." "I remember only an enchanting little girl with a long ponytail, who danced." I'd danced with her while she stood on my shoes, many years before. She would, of course, be near to Dresden's age now.

"It is very sad about Sabina. And your daughter, of course. A tragedy." His expression was shrewd. "She would have been about sixteen." A measured pause. "She was called Marie-Gisèle, wasn't she?"

I could think only, *This is it; this must be him.* I was face-to-face with my blackmailer. But why should Robin Dresden wish to blackmail *me*? But, of course, my family's collection. At last I said feebly, "I don't like to speak of it." Paranoia circled round and round me. Its hum filled my ears. How had I been so ignorant as to believe that no one would know? That no one would put two and two together? You will also consider me naïve, perhaps, to think no one would know of Sabina, or my daughter's full name. But I'd led a very solitary life; my family had led a sequestered one. I was close to no one.

"Have I said something wrong?" Knowing full well that he had, Dresden wore a quizzical expression that I would later come to recognize as ironic.

"I feel I should explain, Robin," I began brusquely, then faltered. The truth was out of the question, and lies could be checked. But the game, with him, was up. I said quietly, "It's not at all what you think."

"That's too bad. She's lovely."

The man was perverse. Even I had the decency to feel ashamed of myself. "The ethical implications. They don't concern you?"

He gazed at me very directly. "Is there reason to be concerned?"

"No, no. I assure you—"

He held my eyes. "You misunderstand, Tristan. Moral judgments don't interest me; I only mean to warn you. The world is small. Especially the art world. I'm concerned not with implications but with facts. She appears very well taken care of and rather taken with you—that's the biggest giveaway—she's far too interested in pleasing you to be a teenage daughter." He gave a shrug. "She is rather young, of course, but I don't share the American need to prolong infancy. Better to be with you than on the street."

He believed she was a runaway I'd rescued. Close enough. I conceded, "She had nowhere to go."

"Do not trouble yourself, my friend. Whatever she chooses to call herself, she's charming and, one can tell, quite bright. There's more energy between you than between the rest of the couples in this room put together. It's unnecessary to detail your relationship. Let people guess. It'll explain her uncertainty. You've dressed her nicely, but she acts as if she's trotting out of a dressing room when she walks into a room. I happen to like it, but—"

"So do I." And I stared at him meaningfully, before shifting my gaze to Moira, who stood beside him, utterly enraptured by this lengthy conversation (or his side of it, at any rate) carried out before her in a foreign tongue. All the while he held her hand with his free one, running his fingers over her wrist and down her palm, but otherwise paid her little attention. I looked to Gisèle, who was talking charmingly to Henri but gazing uncertainly past him to me.

Yes, she had a few bad habits: When bored she tended to fidget. When intrigued, as now, she liked to rest on her ankle, twisting it to an extreme angle that made one flinch to watch. She gagged on caviar and would eat a very fine Camembert with saltine crackers. She could stomach Lafite-Rothschild only when mixed with 7-Up. "I don't want to change her," I said.

"Ah." Robin's eyes flickered with an odd, unhealthy light. "Don't you, really?"

"No."

"How extraordinary. That seems to me the benefit of her youth and inexperience."

"Yes, well." I cleared my throat. "I should go back to her now. Everyone here is strange to her." And he, I had concluded, was the strangest. "I can trust you to—"

"Of course." He flashed a disarming smile. "Forgive my intrusion. It's inevitable that I should offend you, but I wouldn't like to think I've done so quite yet."

"Of course not. No. It's been, well . . . revelatory. We'll see each other again, I'm sure."

I sincerely hoped not. Turning away, I was plunged into a panic rather like the vertigo I'd suffered as a child. I felt dizzy; the walls compressed around me. Staring at me, Gisèle swallowed her protest. I took her hand, and with Henri following we pushed toward the door. Dresden did not glance in our direction. He leaned down to kiss Moira, and they were beset by a boisterous crowd. Somewhere a champagne cork popped. Nobody seemed to pay us any mind. But for the first time, I knew better.

VIII

IN THE GARDEN

AN IMPATIENT BREEZE rustled through the trees. To Nicola the air smelled of restlessness, of approaching rain, dry leaves, and chimney smoke. It was the day of the party.

The kitchen was alive with activity. Three courses for fifty guests, and Mrs. Pengilly, the cook, was at her wits' end, barking an outraged rebuke to one of the hired help, who was using her pastry marble as a cutting board. A deliveryman entered with the cake: a frosted *Mona Lisa* atop which CONGRATULATIONS, LUKE! had been inscribed in calligraphic script. It would sit upon a great chocolate easel.

Nicola raced up the stairs to her mother's room, where they would get ready together. Normally it was a ritual she relished, but she couldn't help feeling anxious about tonight. Her mother had been confined to her room for the last two days with a migraine. She'd never had a migraine before. Apart from Maggie, who acted as nurse, she refused to see anyone but Nicola. Not even her father or Grand-père, and Robin had been conspicuously absent since their argument. Nicola was allowed in only for a short time. Her mother held on to her hand in the darkened room. The pain pills made her speak in a slow voice, but she insisted that plans for the party proceed, reassuring Nicola she would be "just fine."

Sure enough, she had come down to breakfast this morning, but Nicola could tell she wasn't fine. Beneath a false cheerfulness, she was pale and shaken. She wasn't terribly fond of parties even when she was well, and Nicola worried that she wasn't up to tonight.

She found her mother's room empty but could hear her rummaging around in the closet and wandered in. "The cake just came, Mom."

Startled, Gisèle jumped, and something dropped from her hands to the floor.

It was a stuffed toy: a little black bear wearing a tartan scarf and a derby hat. One of his button eyes drooped. Nicola stooped to pick it up.

"Darling, no! Don't touch that—"

Nicola dropped the bear as if burned. "What's wrong?"

"I'm sorry, Nicky." Gisèle pressed a hand to her head, as though it still ached. "I didn't mean to snap at you. It's just that he's filthy. He's been . . . outside."

He didn't look filthy. Nicola frowned and studied her mother; she knew her well enough to know she wasn't upset about a teddy bear. "Are you feeling all right, Mom?"

"I'm fine."

Just fine. "Well, he's not mine," Nicola said carefully. "He probably belongs to Sara." Maggie's niece, Sara, was six and always "borrowing" Nicola's things. "You know, I think she took one of mine. Remember Baxter? She liked his glasses."

Her mother's expression was strange. She reached up and pulled Baxter down from a shelf. In his collegiate sweater and preppy glasses, he looked prosperous next to the worn little thing on the floor. "They were together."

"Oh!" Nicola snatched Baxter up and gave him a satisfying squeeze. She'd outgrown teddy bears, really, but nothing else was quite as comforting when things got confusing. "I've looked all over for him."

Gisèle gazed at her a moment and hesitated, "Sweetheart . . ." Even her voice sounded strange. Not the softened slur of the pain pills, but constricted and strained. "Do you know of any reason your grandfather would have these?"

Nicola shrugged absently. "He could have found them, I guess. I bet Sara just left them out somewhere. I'm going to start locking my room."

Gisèle gave a slight shake of her head, as if clearing away something unpleasant. She reached for Nicola's hand, gripping it so tightly it hurt. "You would tell me if anything was wrong, wouldn't you?"

Nicola paused, uncertain. "Nothing's wrong, Mom. The cake just came—"

"Did it?" Her mother replied vaguely, the worried frown still between her eyes. "How does it look?" She gathered their dresses as she spoke and headed out of the closet.

Nicola retrieved the discarded bear from the floor and set him on a cedar shelf. He wasn't dirty, just old. A hand-me-down. He looked like he was winking at her. Nicola winked back.

She trailed after her mother, twirling carelessly across the bedroom carpet and stopping to make a face at herself in the vanity mirror. "It looks good, but what if the easel melts?"

"That would be apt," Gisèle said dryly. Then, "How should we do your hair tonight?"

Nicola shrugged. As the only child, she'd always been the center of attention, but puberty had begun to wreck everything. Overnight, it seemed, she'd grown two and a half inches and gone from full-cheeked and "adorable" to angular and blank. All arms and legs and cheekbones. And when was she going to get curves anyway? Her training bra was a brash display of optimism. She twisted a strand of hair around her finger; it was thick and dark and had honey highlights from summer, but lately it seemed too long, just like the rest of her.

Her mother understood without words, as she often did. "Why don't we do it up?"

Nicola brightened. "Okay."

Gisèle disappeared into the bathroom for hairpins. Reaching down, Nicola grabbed some Kleenex from the vanity table and stuffed her bra with it, and this cheered her considerably.

Predictably, though, her mother resisted her pleas to wear makeup, apart from a little blush and tinted lip gloss. "You're so lucky, Nicky; you'll never need mascara. When I was your age, I used Vaseline to make my eyelashes show, but yours don't need a thing." Gisèle smiled. "When you were born, everyone said your eyes would change. They were such a beautiful deep blue, almost gray, and the nurses all talked about how wise you looked with those dark, solemn eyes. I knew they wouldn't change."

Nicola smiled, too. It was nice to be talked about as a baby, and it made her mother happy.

Gisèle turned back to the mirror. Nicola watched her put on eye shadow, expertly wielding the tiny brush to smudge a rich taupe into the crease, and a pale neutral tone beneath the brow. Gisèle looked up to meet her daughter's reflection. "I used to think makeup was glamorous, too. I'd try to do it like the models in the fashion magazines. But do you want to know the truth, Nicky? I don't use it to have others look at me; I use it to hide. Appearances can be a kind of trap. Once you start, you have to keep up the illusion . . ." She dropped a lipstick into her evening bag and met Nicola's eyes directly. "You don't have anything to hide. You're beautiful just as you are. Never, ever forget that. Promise me?"

Nicola noticed only then the slight shadows beneath her mother's eyes and the redness at the corners, as if she'd been crying. "Mom—"

Her mother noticed it, too. She reached into a drawer and, applied eyedrops, fluttering her lashes so her mascara wouldn't run. Her eyes glistened, as if with tears. "Got shampoo in them," she murmured.

Nicola's stomach tightened. She knew it wasn't shampoo. But with a few more blinks, her mother's eyes cleared, and like magic they'd whitened. She looked just . . . fine.

By seven-thirty, guests had begun to arrive. Nicola stood beside her mother and grandfather to greet them as they were led into the vast hall. Mostly there were painters, of course, but there was also a director of plays at the repertory theater, a balding German sculptor and his boyfriend, a pointillist from Oregon, a skeletal multimedia artist from California, and a plump poet who wrote haiku. Marc Kreicek arrived, and Nicola watched him as he greeted her mother, but there was no conspiratorial whispering. He'd brought a date, an attractive woman named Elyse, and greeted Nicola with mock formality, kissing her hand.

Turning, she saw her mother speaking animatedly with the next guest, and in the soft light she glowed. Distracted from her worries, Nicola focused on the new faces and clothes. She studied the evening dresses that swished past, the lines of the suits.

Robin was among the last to arrive, entering with a cold gust of wind and without his son. Nicola planned to marry Joshua Dresden once the age difference no longer mattered, but for now Josh called her "kid" and tousled her hair; the last time she saw him, he'd tossed her into the pool. It was probably better he hadn't come.

For his part, Robin looked very handsome in a black trench coat with a white silk scarf, which he handed off to Henri, revealing a charcoal silk suit that matched his eyes. Nicola came to meet him, and he swept her into a dizzying hug. The distinctive scent of his cologne washed over her—spice, musk, and something else. Sharp but lingering and, like his paintings, impossible to pin down. She liked it a lot.

"I haven't seen you in a whole *week*," she said, leveling an accusing glance at him.

"I know. I'm sorry, Nico," he said gently. "I won't let it happen again." He rose to kiss her mother and gave her a warm hug, whispering something in her ear that made her smile. He embraced her grandfather, too, and introduced them all to his date, a stunning young brunette named Chelsea Delaney. Her perfection depressed Nicola so terribly that she was glad to turn and find Great-Aunt Eleanor, arriving last as if to provide contrast. Distinguished by her flaming red hair, purple eye shadow and multicolored caftans, she had no children of her own and was only moderately fond of her nephew—but did, at seventy-four, enjoy a good party.

At last Henri motioned that Luke's car had arrived.

"He's coming!" Gisèle announced and conversation abruptly ceased. There was only the swish of fabric and a few random whispers of *Shhh!!* as the lights went out. Nicola could still see the outline of the cake prominently displayed on its easel—which showed no signs of melting—at the center of the wide hall. Stacks of *Reflex* and *ARTnews* were spread on the table beside it. They heard the door open and close as Luke greeted Henri and then the *click-clack* of his footsteps on the tile floor.

"Why are all the lights—"

They flew on all at once: "Sur-*prise!*"

Nicola's father stumbled backward, bewildered, breaking into a wide grin as her mother stepped forward to kiss him. "Congratulations, Dad!" Nicola whispered, standing on tiptoe to kiss him, too. The music began, and waiters navigated through the guests with trays of drinks and hors d'oeuvres.

As the room hummed to life, Nicola stood back and surveyed the crowd. So much for wearing her hair up to look older. There wasn't anyone young enough to notice. She reconciled herself to being a voyeur of the spectacle around her. When dinner was served, she chose to eat in the kitchen with Mrs. Pengilly and Maggie, preferring their gossip to the more cryptic kind at the long table assembled for the others. But afterward curiosity got the better of her, and she ventured out again into the music and laughter.

As she stepped into the great hall, her grandfather caught sight of her and said, "*Mon chaton,* how lovely you are." She liked the way he put things. Not how lovely you look, but how lovely you *are.* One glance at her face and he understood. With a slight brush of his fingers beneath her chin, "Ah, but you're bored with the grown-ups, *n'est-ce pas?*"

"A little."

"Truth be told, so am I." He raised a finger to his lips, then bowed before her formally. "Will you do me the honor of a dance, *ma belle* Nicola?"

"I'd like to, Grand-père, but my shoes . . ." She winced. "They felt fine in the store—"

"*Eh bien, chérie.* They always do. Let's set the shoes aside then, hmm?"

Nicola kicked them off gladly, and he whisked her into an old-fashioned waltz. She enjoyed the amused smiles of those they swished past. There was no need to count steps with Grand-père. He whirled her around most of the time, so that she was dizzy by the end of the song and quite cheered.

Then her mother brought her punch and reintroduced her to the sort of people who never remembered her name the first time. Her father rescued her, bringing them slices of cake; she and her mother shared Mona Lisa's smile. But the highlight of the evening was cards. Her grandfather and Robin escaped to one of the side rooms and got a game going.

For as long as Nicola could remember, they'd played pinochle and she had partnered with Robin. "It gives me a clear advantage," he claimed now, going on to tell Chelsea about the double run Nicola had gotten the first time she'd played. "Barely tall enough to see over the table, pink curlers in her hair, and she proceeded to win the game with a single hand."

Perched on his knee, Chelsea sipped champagne and offered Nicola an indulgent, languorous smile. Nicola bet she didn't even know what a double run was.

As if reading her mind, Robin caught her eye and gave her a wink.

Her grandfather partnered with Marc, who was explaining the rudiments of the game to Elyse; Grand-père lit his pipe and shuffled the cards in his funny French way, and all was right with the world. That night Nicola's lucky streak continued, and she enjoyed Chelsea's faintly startled expression when she announced she was going to shoot the moon. They played it out, though she could have laid it down; Robin knew it was fun to take all the tricks. Afterward he gave her a celebratory sip of his scotch that tasted bad and made her throat burn but also made her feel quite grown up and as though she belonged.

But at midnight the party was over for Nicola. They were going to show some of her father's paintings and toast the upcoming exhibition. At the pool house that afternoon, she'd watched as a lighting crew assembled festive torches and placed ground lights at the base of at least a dozen easels. It would be beautiful at night, with light reflecting off the windows and the stars visible through skylights above—the pool acting as jeweled centerpiece, a cool, glimmering aquamarine.

Maggie came to collect her at fifteen minutes before the hour. Nicola could hear the music drift tantalizingly up the stairs from below but faked a yawn for Maggie's benefit, brushed her teeth, and hugged her good night. She waited till she heard the housekeeper's footsteps fade away in the hall and then took the back stairs down again. She was still buoyed by the win at cards and knew that the party would continue well into the night. They were far from town, and many of the guests would stay over. Secreting a glass of champagne from a discarded tray on a tabletop in the hall, she stole out into the garden.

Before long the music died, voices faded. Nicola wandered through the cool garden in her slippers, wondering what it must feel like for her mother to be the object of so much attention. Everyone was calling the paintings "the Gisèle Paintings." Part of her cringed at the idea, but it was romantic, too, in a way. She hoped that one day someone would want to paint her.

The outer terraces were warmed by heat lamps, and the doors had been flung wide for the guests to move in and out, but the walled inner garden was private. Nicola could see through a darkened sitting room into the hall and watched as the three-piece band started up again. Guests were drifting back in. She envisioned the elegant couples entwined and gliding across the floor. Now and then their shadowed silhouettes passed the arched doorway.

Nicola danced outside by herself. It was funny how naturally the steps came when no one was watching. She sipped more of the champagne. The first sip had tasted like toothpaste, and the second made her pucker, but the rest was fizzy and pleasantly forbidden and made everything seem all at once . . . lighter. She giggled, and in her mind she danced with Josh Dresden in a great ballroom, no longer eleven-year-old Nicola Farrell but a world-class designer of Paris and Milan, her body not awkward and underdeveloped but lovely and lithe like a fashion model's. Fashion models didn't need to pad their bras. They were chic anyway.

At last she sank down onto a bench in the far corner of the courtyard, her head still light but her eyelids heavy. From here she could see only a sliver of the glow from inside; it spilled along the trunk of the ancient English oak whose limbs formed a canopy beneath the night sky. Her favorite tree rose from the exact center of the garden and had been there long before she was born. Long before the house was even built, her grandfather said. The inner courtyard had been built around *it*. The outline of its trunk was thick and black and immutable, even as it softened at the edges and grew hazy. Nicola watched, lulled to sleep by the ballad that floated out to her on the cool night air. For a moment she was strangely weightless, and then all at once she was dreaming.

With a start she heard her mother's voice. It was thick with emotion or with wine. The words floated in and out of clarity. "Please, just leave me alone. . . . You've gotten what you wanted. Just leave me alone." A murmur came in reply, lower than the rustle of leaves. And then the tone of her mother's voice brought Nicola fully conscious. "I chose it because I didn't feel I *had* a choice." Silence. Then, again, a voice responded: gentle, masculine, indiscernible. "Yes. I know all of your arguments—" There was desperation in the words, and Nicola sat straight up, blinking in the dark. She began to rise from the bench but something stopped her.

The man's answer was still too low to distinguish, but this time she caught random words: "barely dressed" . . . "indiscreet." Was he talking about the paintings? Nicola squinted hard, but he was hidden by the tree trunk. She could see only her mother's silhouette beside the gnarled oak, her dress glistening like the sliver of moon above. She said something too quiet to hear, but it came in a rhythm like poetry. Nicola tried to make herself small so she wouldn't be seen. She didn't want her mother to know about the champagne.

Gisèle spoke again. "I don't know why. I've never known." And the man's hand reached out to wipe her cheek. *Was she crying?* Nicola sat motionless, her fingers gripping the arm of the bench. There was an intimacy in the simple gesture that she couldn't interrupt. Could it be Marc Kreicek? Why else were they always whispering in corners? Maybe her mother *was* having an affair with him.

Gisèle's lips moved, and Nicola heard only her last words. "Yes, I love you—" She sighed, deeply. "Of course I do." And then, in a slow graceful movement, Gisèle stepped forward. She stood on tiptoe, and a hand appeared at her waist. Nicola knew what was going to happen next. It was always that way in the movies before the kiss.

Beyond her, across the garden, a figure materialized on the terrace like a ghost, and Nicola jumped in surprise, kicking the crystal flute with her slipper. It shot out from beneath the bench, and the sound of shattering glass filled the courtyard. It wasn't a ghost on the terrace. It was her father. And for a moment, just a moment, she caught a glimpse of the man behind the tree. She knew him in an instant. She'd known him all her life. His black silhouette disappeared almost at once, but she understood now why his voice was indistinguishable, its low melodic accent lost in the rustle of leaves in the wind. It was her grandfather.

Gisèle was frozen, uncomprehending; her eyes shifted from her daughter to her husband and back again. Luke stared, his hands limp at his sides. His face could be seen in the moonlight, and he looked like Nicola felt. Utterly horrified.

"Nicola, go in." Gisèle did not turn, but her voice was so sharp, so unfamiliar, that Nicola's body responded automatically, rising from the bench. Hesitating, she turned back again. Her father had vanished.

"Go to your room." Her mother didn't exactly yell. It was something

worse than that, something awful, like the sound of a teapot screeching. It made the hair rise on Nicola's arms.

She ran as fast as she could from the garden, pushed open the French doors, and raced up the stairs without turning back. Once in her room, though, she ran to the window. The leaves of her broad oak stretched forward to touch the glass, but no one was visible beneath its branches; the night was empty and black. The moon, too, had disappeared.

∽

Luke stepped in from the terrace. *Escape. Escape.* It beat in his brain, sounded in his ears. But there was nowhere to hide here. Walking quickly through the darkened sitting room, he felt his head spin, awash with half-formed thoughts and undefined sensations that told a single story, like how the scent of jasmine made him think all at once of the river in Virginia where he'd lived as a child, and his father's brooding frown, and his mother dying, and his first kiss, and a dirty novel he'd read when he was twelve and hid in a hollow tree trunk covered with moss: longing, loss, and loneliness like a cloud of mosquitoes buzzing at once.

Luke could smell jasmine in the dimmed light of the hall.

He gazed through the thinning crowd of couples, no more than oblivious props now, well-dressed puppets on a string. It was a party thrown for the benefit of others, a masque, but one he'd almost begun to believe. It was all a blind. Gisèle had posed for Tristan. He had painted her. She'd *kissed* him. The joke was on Luke, and the whole time Gisèle had been in on it.

Robin Dresden stood across the hall from him, in the doorway of the drawing room, contemplating him over a snifter of brandy. Again, Luke glanced around for some means of escape. He was in no condition to speak to anyone. Especially not Robin. And who, he wondered, was going to speak to Nicola? *Had she seen Tristan?* Surely not. It was his only comfort. The oak tree was in the way. It was dark. She had merely witnessed her mother kiss "someone" who wasn't him. A wave of nausea made him close his eyes, but in his mind he saw their silhouettes joined, Gisèle's fingers caressing her father's neck.

"Luke?" There was a sharp glint in Robin's dark eyes that made Luke feel he'd read the story of his life in that one unguarded moment. "You look knackered. Too much champagne?"

He managed some sort of wordless reply.

"Where have Tristan and Gisèle gotten off to?"

To his jaded mind, it seemed a double entendre. "Not sure," he replied acidly. "Bed?"

Robin put his hand in his pocket and raised a shrewd brow. "Had a falling-out with Tristan, have you?" When Luke only stared, he went on, "The two of you can barely stand to be in the same room these days. It's no surprise, really."

"No?"

"You're coming into your own." Robin swirled his brandy, and Luke's head felt as if it was spinning round and round with the amber liquid. "The paintings show every sign of success. I know the signs. You must think it's time you were independent of Tristan."

Luke hesitated. "Somehow I don't think Gisèle will leave him."

"Ah. Well, there is that." A weighted pause. "Perhaps it's time *you* were independent, then. Theirs is a complex relationship. You see it more often between mothers and sons, this sort of dependency. I see its effects on Nicola, too. It troubles me." He frowned. "It often happens in wealthy families. One would think their world limitless, but it's often perversely small."

It's often simply perverse, thought Luke. He swallowed. "Listen, I need to ask you—"

But Robin's date, a lovely thing half his age, had floated down the stairs and tugged now on his arm. He turned. Her green eyes sparkled with youth and champagne and utter infatuation. "We've switched rooms with Marc and Elyse," she murmured. "She liked our view better." With a flirtatious dip of her lashes and a giggle, Luke could barely hear, ". . . has a bigger bed."

Robin slipped a hand around her waist. "We'll talk in the morning, eh? Get a bit of rest."

But Luke had a feeling neither of them would get much rest that night.

❧

There had been no yelling, as Nicola expected. Her mother's voice and her father's. Slammed doors and angry words she couldn't make out.

Then she remembered that the house would be full tonight. It was a tradition: brunch the day after for an intimate, bleary-eyed group, those closest to the family. And so there had been no yelling. There had been no noise at all.

She must have fallen asleep, because very late, or rather very early, there came a knock on her door, a soft knock, her mother's. "Nicola? Please let me in—"

Nicola sat up, the bed springs giving her away with a slight squeak that screamed in the stillness. She watched as the knob twitched under her mother's fingers but did not yield. She had locked it.

"Darling, can you hear me? Please let me explain."

She said nothing.

"Nicola . . . I—Please forgive me, darling. Please forgive me." Gisèle's voice broke, and still Nicola sat perched on her bed, staring at the door. She opened her mouth to answer, but no sound came. Her mother's voice had made it real. The kiss in the garden hadn't been a dream or a figment of her imagination. It had all been real.

And at last she heard her mother's soft steps receding down the hall.

Luke liked to think he was capable of understanding, of empathy. It was this that drove him to Gisèle's bedroom at half past two that morning. Her door was locked, yet he could see a tiny crack of light at the bottom. He rapped hard on the wood. In the silence it sounded bullying. But she knew his knock.

"Please, Luke." Her voice, so weary. "I'm sorry, but I can't talk. Not now."

Luke's pride was too far gone for that; it was as if there were a sinking ship at the center of his soul. "I'll stand out here till morning if you don't open the door." And then, *"Please, Ella."*

And at last she appeared. Gisèle had undressed and was softer in her silk robe, her hair in waves down her back and shiny from brushing. But her face was drawn, her eyes cold and stricken. She turned away from him when she spoke, and her voice was ragged. "You must despise me."

And he couldn't then. The way she said it, she crept under his skin. He followed her into the room. "I don't despise you. . . . I don't understand you. You . . . your own *father*." No, he couldn't go that route. "Listen. It's Tristan's fault, for God's sake, not yours."

If only she'd agreed, collapsed into tears, asked his forgiveness, told him how horrible it had been and begged him to take her away, asked him anything but what she asked. "How long have you been seeing Amanda Miller?"

He doubted his ears. It was like complaining of sniffles during a holocaust. What was an affair to incest? But Gisèle went to her writing desk and retrieved a photograph. Turning, she held it out to him. "How long have you known her, Luke? When did it start? *How?*"

He didn't need to see the photograph, but he took it robotically. To do something with his hands. He and Amanda were walking together—up Pike Street, from the look of it. He was laughing; so was she. For a moment Luke was overwhelmed with the desire to be there with her, to be anywhere but here. It made him see red. "Is this a contest? Which of us is the bigger sinner?" His voice sounded like a stranger's, a stranger he couldn't control. "Incest trumps adultery, I think."

Gisèle flinched; she didn't want to talk about that. And so they wouldn't? Luke felt the rage building inside, waves of heat that consumed him.

"What is she like?" Her voice broke on the words. "Amanda? Or does she go by 'Mandy'?"

"I don't want to talk about her. It's not fucking *about* her."

She flinched; the word was too coarse for her. The act. "I'm not angry with you, Luke."

"That's big of you."

This hurt her. He wanted to hurt her. She said softly, "She's so beautiful. . . ."

"Is she? She reminded me of you."

And for a moment the light in her eyes gave him hope. Even then, the anger ebbed away. That was the power Gisèle had over him, even when he hated her. She was his redemption. In an instant she could wash him clean. Or not.

"How did you meet?" Her voice was barely a whisper.

"Marc introduced us through a mutual friend at the university. Her professor, if you must know. What does it matter? It doesn't fucking matter. He was in the city, we met up."

"Marc?" She closed her eyes; her breathing was uneven. "I see. Did Robin know about her, too?" Her voice wavered. "Please tell me he didn't know."

"No, Gisèle. I haven't done anything to embarrass you in front of your precious Robin, if that's what you're worried about. Nobody knows except Marc, and he said he wouldn't tell anyone. She's never been to Devon. She doesn't even know my real name. It was all very discreet." He laughed. "Look who I'm talking to about discreet? All these years, right under my nose, and I never suspected a *goddamned* thing—"

Gisèle frowned. She spoke very quietly, and something in her restraint enraged Luke even more. "You have the paintings, Luke. Take them and go away. Please. Sell them, do whatever you like with them. But if you see Mandy again, I'll come out with the truth about them. You can't see her again. Promise me." Her voice softened. "It's not jealousy. I know it's been over between us for a long time. It's just . . . her. I can't explain." She bit her lip. "I'm sorry."

But it wasn't sorry for the garden, for the kiss, for all the lies. It was, *Sorry, I don't love you.* Luke would forever remember her expression: reflective, full of pity and sorrow.

And then he knew she must actually be in *love* with Tristan. She didn't even try to apologize for it. Luke saw it all so clearly: he had been nothing more than a façade of respectability, a red herring, a prop for the audience. Is that why she was so worried about this affair? People might begin to see that he'd only played husband to Gisèle and father to Nicola, when *all* this time—

Gisèle stood very still before him, inviolate as a sculpture, her washed face an unblemished ivory and her robe wrapped tightly around her, so chaste. Luke wanted the woman in the cellar, the woman of the paintings. He wanted Tristan's Gisèle. He wanted in.

❧

Late the next morning, consciousness penetrated the hazy residue of Nicola's dreams in a single slash. Her eyes fluttered open, and light splashed through the window onto her bedspread, bathing her in its glare and making the night before the stuff of nightmares. Dimly, she remembered locking her mother out, then getting out of bed to go to her. But they hadn't been able to talk. Through the door she'd heard her parents arguing in voices too low to make out and she'd retreated back to bed. At three-thirty, unable to sleep, she'd risen again and from her bathroom window had seen her father's tall, lanky form striding through the glass corridor back from the pool house. He must have gone out to his paintings.

She blinked now, and the images receded. Everything would be all right. It had been stupid to lock the door last night. Without even pausing to brush her hair, Nicola slid out of bed and padded down the hall to her mother's room, rapping softly on the heavy wooden door. "Mom?"

There was no answer, but the door was ajar. Nicola pushed it gently inward and sniffed. There was a strange, too-sweet scent in the air. The window was shut, and outside it was autumn cool, yet inside there was the fragrance of honeysuckle on a still summer day, cloying fruit . . . flowers. It was perfume, her mother's favorite: Paris. Yves Saint Laurent. She saw the bottle lying on its side on the carpet, the lid off and an oblong stain beneath it, the color of apricots.

"Mom?" Nicola walked through the room to the bathroom, but it, too, stood dark. There were traces of water around the drain in the bathtub, nothing more. Funny, her mother never took a bath in the morning. A towel was folded on the marble ledge, but it was hardly damp. A mug sat beside it, empty.

Nicola went back to the bedroom. Everything was perfectly ordered, the down comforter in plump square tufts beneath the duvet, the cherry sleigh bed polished and gleaming in the clean morning sun; the stone fireplace stood in the corner, its iron grate cold and dark. Her eyes traveled over the huge armoire and the sturdy chest of drawers, writing desk, and bureau, all dusted and tidy and beyond reproach. Even the vanity table was pristine, holding none of the clutter of the night before. But something was wrong.

The vanity mirror was a triptych, its wide central portion bolted securely to the wall and flanked by two narrow mirrored panels. Nicola had never realized these could be closed. They covered the mirror neatly, revealing an intricate carving in cherrywood: three bouquets tied loosely with ribbon.

Her mother had never closed them before, and there was something eerie about it, something final. The room felt utterly vacant. Alarms went off in Nicola's mind. Had her mother gone away without her?

She ran to her father's room. When he came to the door, rumpled and grumpy, she could not tell him why she was crying.

Nicola pulled him down the hall to her mother's empty bedroom, pointing out the perfume-soaked carpet and the covered mirror. "She *never* closes it."

"Maybe she couldn't stand her own reflection."

She stared at him, but he avoided her eyes. "Her bed's not even slept in," she said. "I think she's gone away."

Her father's voice was hoarse. "For God's sake, Nic, your mother wouldn't go away without you. There's nothing to get so upset about. A little spilled perfume . . ."

"Well, where is she, then? It doesn't look like she's been here since last night. And something happened last night—" She broke off and stared at her father, begging him to contradict her, to make it better. "Didn't it?" *You were in the garden, too,* her eyes said. *You saw. Too.*

Luke looked peaked and haggard, his hair sticking up at awkward angles. He hesitated. "What do you *think* happened, Nicky?"

"I . . . I don't know. I didn't see anything, really," she lied. "Only Mom was so upset, and you looked angry." She stared at her father. "And I thought I saw her . . . kiss someone."

Her father inhaled sharply. "It wasn't that kind of a kiss. It was only your grandfather she was talking to. It was just a fatherly kiss. In the dark you couldn't see."

"But Mom yelled at me, and she never yells—" Fresh tears stung her eyes.

"You weren't supposed to be up."

"Is that all?" *I don't believe you.* "What's wrong with everyone lately?"

Luke rubbed his eyes hard with his forefinger and thumb. "We had a sort of argument last night, Nic. That's all. It didn't have anything to do with what happened in the garden."

"Are you going to get a divorce?"

He sighed heavily. "I don't know. But I don't want you to worry about it."

The more he told her not to worry, the more worried she became. "We have to find her, Dad. She tried to talk to me last night, and I . . . I just have to talk to her." *She has to tell me.* She *has to tell me it was a fatherly kiss, not you.*

Her father said gently, "Well, we can't go beating on doors. She may be downstairs. We'll go see, huh?" He reached for her hand. "Did you have a bad dream or something?"

Nicola simply nodded, wiping the tears from her cheeks. She was ashamed of them. She never cried anymore.

Downstairs, Maggie was disposing of the last remnants of the party. She hadn't seen Gisèle all morning. "She'll be sleeping in, hon, surely . . ." But she's *not.* A sensible shrug. "I don't know then, dear." Henri hadn't seen or heard her since the night before. Mrs. Pengilly had set up the breakfast buffet and then left to run errands in town. The kitchen was empty, spotlessly gleaming. The buffet was untouched. None of the cars were missing except Mrs. Pengilly's.

Grand-père came down in his robe. He looked a little sleepy, but otherwise the same as always. Nicola gazed at him, and her tongue turned to mush. In daylight it was hard to imagine him as he'd seemed last night. It was *impossible* to imagine. He smiled his normal smile, and she tried to return it. *"Mon chaton,"* he said, peering down at her. "Have you been crying?"

"Have you seen Mom, Grand-père? She didn't sleep in her room last night."

Tristan's expression was not terribly concerned. "Well, she'll be in the cabana, I imagine, by the pool. That's the only place she could go. The other rooms are full."

"Well," Luke said darkly, "We should have known to come to you first."

"Mais oui." Tristan turned and plucked a grape from a fruit platter on the sideboard. His voice sounded strangely distant. "The house must have gotten too cramped for her."

But Nicola hardly heard. Flooded with relief, she ran to the door, was outside. The morning air was chill on her skin, a reminder that she was wearing only pajamas and slippers. Dew soaked her feet, and she slipped on the wet grass as she ran across the lawn to the pool house. Behind her she heard her name but kept running until she reached the French doors. Through the glass she could see that the paintings were still set up, a ghostly audience of draped easels gathered around the spectacle of the pool. Nicola was surprised. She'd thought her father had come out to put them away. Humidity wasn't good for paintings.

She stepped inside. The door to the cabana was open to her right, and the vast pool lay sparkling before her. Sunlight shone through the sky-lights above, and the smooth, clear water was gently rippling. And then she stopped short.

From here the edge of her mother's scarlet robe looked like a dropped handkerchief in the water, the belt a great streak of blood. Nicola's stomach clenched into a tight coil, twisting tighter and tighter. "Mom?!" Her voice rose, but it was still a question: *Mom?* Behind her she heard steps. Her father, her grandfather.

"Mon Dieu—"

"Nicola, stop!"

But she'd flown mindlessly across the flagstones to the pool. A deafening roar rose in her ears. The world tilted, and then she was wet in the water, struggling with her mother's slight weight; Gisèle's dark hair spread and covered her face. Nicola tried to lift her, but she slipped in her arms; she was so very heavy. Her head fell back, and her eyes—her mother's warm, familiar, dancing eyes—were fixed and staring, horribly still.

Nicola came up screaming. Her father and grandfather were in the water, pulling her back, forcing her out of the pool. She couldn't fight them, and her throat constricted so that her cries were no more than a sobbing hiccup, an absence of sound, her thoughts black and still, an endless downward tumult.

IX

TWO ROSES ON A TABLECLOTH

I have always had that faculty of ignoring that which I don't care to see. Yet in the inexplicable way one runs across a word repeatedly after hearing it the first time, I was doomed to run into Dresden. One had the irrational sense he did it on purpose. I spotted him in restaurants and bars, and once inside a questionable shop in SoHo, where Gisèle and I were merely sightseeing. The place sold corsets, Victorian erotica, and various "antique" sex toys. He was with two lovely young women I took to be his flatmates. I quickly hurried out.

He was in the magazines. I would happen upon Gisèle reading them. There was an exhibition coming up at the MoMA, his first, and he was interviewed in *Face* regarding it. There had also been some controversy over a piece he was commissioned to do for a traditionalist art academy, called Clerestory, in Connecticut. They must have been misled by a few of his more mainstream sculptures of the human form, for there was some outcry when what he sculpted was not the human form but an abstract piece in granite: sexually graphic bas-relief amid the message "Nothing is written in stone" in several languages.

Naturally, all that this earned Dresden was a backlash from the conservatives of the art world who would never have bought his work in the first place and increased his following among the remainder. A following that could no longer be classified as "cult." He had, as they say, made it.

And I could see that somehow, under my nose, Gisèle had grown enamored of him. I was less threatened by this than I might otherwise have been, for I could see that it was more awe than affection—as she might behave were she sitting across from John Lennon. It made her seem very young to me.

And then came a cozy evening in late winter. She was in the kitchen, and I sat watching her at the small table in the breakfast nook, which is where we preferred to eat when we ate in. Gisèle had already set it for two, with two pastel-colored roses lying between us as centerpiece.

"Robin came to visit you today," she said.

I was sipping a lovely Côtes du Rhône whose loveliness abruptly vanished.

How had he known where to find me? Mutual friends. Had he come in? Had she wanted him to? Of course, yes. Had they talked? What had they talked about? What had happened to Henri?

"Did he?" I asked mildly. "What about?"

"He never said." She wrinkled up her nose adorably. "What do you think of him, Tristan?"

"I don't."

"Well, personally, I think he's a little odd. He doesn't do things people ought to do. And he has a funny way of turning conversations around."

"You talked to him for some time, then?"

"You see, it's like that. We didn't. Not really."

"No?" I waited.

"We talked about nothing, really, and then suddenly he tells me I mustn't be afraid of him." She swallowed. "I mean, really." She always says "really" when she's nervous. Americans do.

"And were you?" I cleared my throat. "Afraid of him?"

"Not till he said that."

"You don't find him attractive?"

Her response was immediate and vague. "Hmm. Well, anyone would. He is very." (As if "very" were a noun.) She focused on chopping her already chopped vegetables. "But he's not really my type." A glance up, a winning smile. "You're my type."

Methinks she doth protest too much.

She turned back to the stove. "You're not jealous, are you?" She glanced at me sideways, and I noticed something in Gisèle then that I had never noticed before, something manipulative. She was growing up.

"*Non, non, ma petite.* Of course not." I stared down at the roses on the tablecloth, their delicate velvet petals so fine, and I wanted nothing more than to crush them. "Did he . . . Do you . . ." I stumbled over it, dreadfully. "He didn't do anything to make you uncomfortable?"

"No."

"Where was Henri? I've told you about answering the door when I'm not here." A pause. "I worry about you."

"Uh-huh."

"Gisèle?"

"Yes?"

"Promise me."

"All right." So easy. All right.

I held her eyes. "I'd kill him if he took you from me. You know I'd kill anyone who tried."

She gazed at me a long time, her countenance as sweet as it had ever been, but newly wise. And then she dropped her eyes, staring in an unfocused way at the sizzling substance on the stove, which seemed to be burning.

"Yes, Tristan," she murmured at last. "Yes, I know."

X

THE WATER'S EDGE

GISÈLE'S FUNERAL WAS a painting drained of color but for one bright umbrella among the black. No blue broke through the marbled sky, and no light shone on the somber party in the cemetery on the hill. Even the vast gray pearl of Lake Devon was subdued, emptied of sailboats, its shimmering surface pitted with raindrops.

Nicola would remember the sound most of all: alternately blaring and diffuse, as though the normal threshold had arced wildly out of control. One moment, she was deafened by the brush of Great-Aunt Eleanor's black silk taffeta and the swish of men's trousers. The next, there was no more than a low-frequency murmur all around her, the minister's mouth moving up and down without making any intelligible sound. His words seemed to emanate from inside her head: *From dust we are made, to dust we shall return.*

Dimly, Nicola heard the minister ask if anyone had last words to offer. Her godfather, Robin, stepped forward: the one bright umbrella, his. He wore black because he typically wore black, but he didn't feel death was to be mourned. Even the minister eyed him skeptically, Nicola thought. Coat and scarf billowing with a flurry of autumn leaves, he began to recite:

Death is nothing at all
I have only slipped into the next room

I am I and you are you
Whatever we were to each other, we are still.

The raindrops stung.

Wear no forced air of solemnity or sorrow
Laugh as we have always laughed
At the little jokes that we enjoyed together
Play, smile, think of me, pray for me
Let my name be ever the household word that it always was.
I am waiting for you, just around the corner.
All is well.

It was as if he spoke to Nicola alone, his voice resonant and strong, the sharp dark eyes landing on hers, concerned. All is not well, she wanted to scream.

The small assembly on the hill represented the only family Nicola had ever known. These were the people who loved her mother most. *And they all know it's a lie.* The house knew and she heard its whispers everywhere. Whispers of sleeping pills and suicide. She gazed around her. Robin's son, Josh, stood beside his father, his dark hair pulled into a more refined ponytail. Even his beauty failed to distract her. Slight, dark, and elegant, Marc Kreicek was busy examining the cuff of his coat, expressionless and inscrutable as always. Henri stood just beyond, stolid and frowning, and Maggie and Mrs. Pengilly were beside him in tears, holding handkerchiefs to their eyes. Rounding out the circle was Great-Aunt Eleanor, in a theatrical hat with black veil, looking like something from an old movie.

Nicola turned to look at her grandfather, who stood motionless beneath an oak tree, as far from the small party as he could be. The tree trunk was blackened with rain and he pressed a palm against it as if for support. Seeing him there made her shudder, made her think of their own English oak in the garden and the night her mother died. *It was just a fatherly kiss.* She could not think of it. As Nicola watched, wind drove rain under his umbrella, into his eyes, like tears.

Nicola clutched her father's hand. She couldn't remember when she'd last done that, but he was for her like Grand-père's tree: If she let go, she would fall. He looked down with an anxious frown, pulling her close. His blue eyes shone with tears that did not fall. The minister was speaking again in his somnolent drone. Nicola clenched her eyes shut.

In the hours after she found her mother, she'd been buffered by shock. The doctor's sedatives made her feel flattened like a creature on the ocean bottom, weighted by miles of water above. All the noise in her head was forced down, down, like the sound under water—tinny and distorted. Dreams under sedation are eerie, sluggish things: spurts of luminosity punctuated by deep black holes. Yet in them her mother was not dead. For a time, she was protected by her incomprehension and she had not wanted to wake.

It was over. The pallbearers began to lower the coffin inch by inch and Nicola knew she couldn't let them; she couldn't leave her mother *here*. She didn't belong here. Her father stepped forward, crying silently as he tossed handfuls of dirt into the grave. Nicola tried to tell them, but the words got mangled in her throat and she began to sob, knowing she couldn't do anything to stop it. She couldn't do anything at all. And it was her godfather, murmuring words she couldn't hear, who gently led her away. Her grandfather, still motionless beneath his oak, did not seem to see them as they passed.

For Luke it had been a grueling week. The goodwill, the well-intentioned phone calls, it was all beginning to wane. But not Gisèle. At one time he thought he'd grow to hate her, but the chance for that was gone. She was gone forever, and his punishment was to love her still.

It would be a gross understatement to say his relationship with Tristan was strained. They lived in the same house and rarely ran into each other. When they did, by tacit agreement, they confined themselves to brief, inane pleasantries. There were no open accusations.

The only overt confrontation came when Luke told Tristan he was enrolling Nicola in school. "She needs to get away from this house," he'd said. "To make normal friends and have a normal life." In other words a life that Tristan had little part in.

"*Tu fais l'imbécile.*" A thing Luke didn't need French to comprehend. "What nonsense."

"Then I'll take Nicola and go."

Tristan scoffed. "Go where? You have no money, and you're unlikely to earn any. Your only talent is being the kind who can make others earn your living for you."

"I have the paintings."

"You can't possibly expect to continue with that charade."

There it was at last: an admission that the paintings were his—his denial abandoned along with the pretense of "*mon fils.*"

"I'm enrolling Nicola in school, Tristan, whether you like it or not. Even Robin agrees she's alone too damned much. It's my decision to make. Public school's free."

Tristan flinched at this, as if in physical pain. "Public school? Without telling her?"

"I've told her."

"And she agreed?" He was incredulous.

"Yes." Unhappily. Because Nicola was, of course, deeply unhappy. When her eyes weren't red from crying, they were glassy and disillusioned, fixed on something no one else could see. She needed to be with kids her age and *laugh.* "Yes, she did."

Tristan frowned at this, and Luke could see the wheels turning; he saw doubt creep in. Self-doubt.

Tristan spoke in short, assured sentences to hide it. "Well. Public school is unthinkable. She's far too bright for that. There's a private school, Prescott Primary. You must have driven past it. Fine grounds. *Eh bien,* she will go there." Agitated, he began to pace. "She'll be advanced far beyond her level." A disdainful shrug. "But if you insist upon it, she will go there. I will pay her tuition. Of course."

Of course. Luke only shrugged. "Fine."

"It's natural she should want to meet new people," Tristan said, as if to himself.

He was hurt, Luke realized. And he saw then that Nicola was his continued hold on Tristan. On life as he knew it. On the new life he wanted.

He didn't voice his concern that Nicola hadn't been quite satisfied with his explanation of what she'd seen in the garden. Tristan did not bring it up either. To do so would be to acknowledge that it had happened at all.

Tristan paid the tuition (an ungodly sum), and there had been no other change in financial arrangements. Luke's bank account was replenished on the first of October, as it would be the first of November—as it had always been. The only difference was that now it felt uncomfortably like just what it was. Blackmail.

❧

Nicola turned, and her mother was there. She could see her sometimes for whole seconds before she disappeared. Her hair was sometimes up and sometimes down. Her outfits changed. The word "Mom" still escaped Nicola's lips, and her thoughts betrayed her: *What would Mom do? What would Mom say? Maybe Mom will come, will like, want . . . wear . . . wish . . . know. Wait'll I tell Mom.*

But even while her mind tricked her into thinking of her mother as though she were alive, Nicola found she could think of little but her death. Everyone else was careful not to mention her, and she hated this most of all. *Were they trying to erase her?* Her mother couldn't be erased any more than you could erase every other note of a song. There was no melody without her. Nothing made sense.

This time tomorrow Nicola would be in "normal" school, but now she walked determinedly across the lawn from the house to the pool. She hadn't been there since that terrible morning, but a question plagued her, and she had to put it to rest.

It was colder today. The dew had turned to frost that crunched beneath her feet like fine eggshells. When she reached the pool house, she shuddered uncontrollably all over. Her hand shook as she depressed the handle of one of the French doors and pushed it gently inward. Taking a sharp breath, she stepped in.

She'd had such fun here once. The sounds of splashing water and laughter still echoed faintly off the flagstones, a hollow sound that seemed to belong to another lifetime. Pale sunlight penetrated the skylights and shone wanly on the cerulean surface of the pool. It was too blue, Nicola thought now, and smelled too strongly of unnatural things. Chlorine. Death.

Sunlight painted the floor before her with long outlines of the doors and windows. The wide wall across the pool was a mirror image of this one but lay in darkness. Tall French doors with divided windows on each side were flanked by broad picture windows that gave onto the gardens. Despite this, the immense room appeared dim at this hour. The reflection off the skylights obscured the water, just as they had the morning she'd found her mother. It was why Nicola hadn't seen her at first, only the edge of her familiar scarlet robe.

Moving down the wall, she flipped on the overhead lights. The reflection of the skylights on the surface of the water practically disappeared as the room was flooded with light. She had been right. The lights hadn't been on that morning. Yet her mother would have needed light to view the paintings at night; she would have needed them to move around the pool house at all. The runner lights inside the pool wouldn't have been enough to see by in the dark. No one seemed to have thought about it, but it bothered Nicola.

She gazed at the southern wall where a door led to the cabana. Nicola had often changed clothes there or showered after swimming, taken a nap or read. But she'd never known her mother to spend any time there at all, let alone spend the night. At the opposite end of the pool room was a glass corridor that connected the pool to the house. In bad weather one could reach the heated pool without ever stepping outdoors. Nicola hadn't told anyone she'd seen her father use it that morning. Why hadn't *he* told? And why had he come out here at three-thirty in the morning? Had he spoken to her mother? Had they had another argument?

Nicola's fingernails bit into her palms, and tears blurred the scene before her. She stood in the vast room and stared at the water, crying silently. Nothing made sense. She didn't believe that her mother could have drowned herself, even if she'd wanted to. She was terrified of water in daylight. She would never have gone near it in the dark. Why hadn't the lights been on?

※

Luke was losing it. He saw Gisèle everywhere: she lingered in every shadow; she haunted his dreams. He couldn't look at his daughter without envisioning his wife and Tristan together, their bodies entwined and imagined ecstasy on Gisèle's face. It was driving him mad, yet he could not stop picturing it. He even fancied he could see Tristan's features in

Nicola's. He couldn't close his eyes and escape Gisèle; he could not keep them open.

It was this that drove him, mere days after the funeral, to the office of a private investigator. Disguised under the demure description "Personal Inquiries," it wasn't the smoky digs of a Philip Marlowe or the seedy backstreet Mike Hammer variety, but a dainty-curtained Victorian that looked more like a tearoom.

Preston Murphy was suited to his surroundings, failing in every respect to live up to the burly job description. A fastidious-looking man of slight build with glasses and flyaway hair, he resembled a butterfly collector more than a detective. He rose. "You must be Luke Farrell."

Luke nodded; they shook hands. There was an awkward silence. At last he blurted out, "What guarantee do I have of your confidentiality?"

"My desire to continue my thriving practice in Devon." A reproving smile. "Please, sit."

Luke sat. "Well, it's a matter of paternity," he said brusquely. "I have reason to believe that my daughter's not mine." Where he was raised, it was ill-mannered to get to the point so quickly, particularly this sort of point, but Luke couldn't come up with a polite way to get to it.

Preston Murphy only blinked, waiting.

"I know there are tests for this sort of thing. Blood tests, but that's no good. She has my blood type, but so do a lot of people; I'm A-positive. My wife, she was A-negative. So's my daughter. I hear there are DNA tests—"

"Yes, there are several companies I work with that will do the testing."

"I understand you can use hair, but it has to be pulled out by the root, isn't that right?" Luke went on uncomfortably. "That's possible for my daughter." He'd tried to braid Nicola's hair that morning. "And of course it's possible for me. But there's another party involved, and I don't want him to know anything about this."

"And your wife?"

"My wife is dead."

Hurriedly, Luke opened the leather satchel he'd brought with him and extracted several Ziploc bags. "I've labeled these. This one here, A is hair from my daughter, and B, that's me. For C, I have three bags. I wasn't sure . . . well, anyhow, I have two cigarette stubs and his coffee cup. And this is his wineglass from last night—" Luke broke off abruptly.

The detective's mild eyes sparked. "He is a member of your household?"

"Does it make a difference?"

"Not to the DNA. It's of personal interest only."

Luke turned and gazed through the gauzy curtains without seeing. "Well. C is a member of the household, yes." He cleared his throat and steeled his voice. "C is my father-in-law."

He left the detective's office and headed downtown, honking at a lunatic on a moped going the wrong way up a one-way street. *Damned tourists.* There was no parking on Front Street, as usual, but he knew of a permit-only lot that never checked permits. He found a space and walked over to the gallery, swinging the Dutch door wide and giving a nod to Rolf as he moved past the marble desk. The man was always on the phone.

It was the first time Luke had been to the gallery since Gisèle's death, and though she'd never graced the walls, he imagined her everywhere. Spotlights trained on her face, on every inch of her body. It was ironic and a little sad. He'd never known anyone who liked being naked less than Gisèle had. Now it was the only way he could ever seem to think of her.

He wiped beads of sweat from his brow and inhaled deeply. *You can do this.* Surely fate had willed it. At the rear of the gallery, Luke rapped on the office door with a reasonable facsimile of confidence. He would simply demand a timeline from Robin. The exhibition had been postponed, of course—for a "decent interval" of indefinite duration. Like so much else, it would not be up to Luke. But his name was on the damned canvases; he had a right to know.

"Ah, Luke." Rolf's effete voice came from behind him; he floated across the room and extended his hand. "Are you looking for Robin?"

Luke turned warily. He could barely tolerate Rolf's obsequious air, but the man had an unerring eye when it came to distinguishing buyers from browsers, and as Robin had once said, "He makes buying art feel like basic hygiene."

"Yep."

"Ah. You've missed him, I'm afraid. He's rarely in these days." Rolf knit his brow in concern and spoke in soft, empathetic tones. "And how are you? You're looking so well." (A lie, Luke knew.) "I do hope we'll be able to organize something soon. You have no idea how many inquiries I receive about your paintings. And a reporter was asking after you recently—"

"Oh, Christ." Luke grimaced. "You didn't give her my number, did you?"

"Naturally not. I took *her* contact information." And before Luke could protest, Rolf had fluttered off to his desk and Luke was being handed the same, written on a sheet of elegant office stationery.

He stuffed it blindly into his pocket.

"She writes for *Reflex*," Rolf continued. "Didn't Robin mention it? He agreed to talk to her. But of course that was before . . ." The sentence tapered off discreetly.

Luke cleared his throat. "Has he indicated any kind of timeline to you for the exhibition?"

"No." Rolf frowned. "But Gisèle was *so* supportive of your work, my personal feeling is that she would want it to go on." Luke's personal feeling was that Rolf wanted his commission. "It is a celebration of her memory."

Luke managed a nod. "Well. We'll see what Rob says. Do you have his private number?"

"His mobile?" A discerning arch of the brow. "You don't have it?"

"Gisèle did." Luke extracted the crumpled stationery from his pocket, ignoring Rolf's frown of distaste as he took it and gracefully scribbled a number.

Luke gazed down as he left the gallery. Beside Robin's number he read in Rolf's concise hand, *"Reporter/Reflex: Amanda Miller. The Dorrington—Room No. 301."*

Luke stared at the name until the letters blurred. She was *here*. Somehow she had found him.

❧

"Nicola . . . ?"

She jumped; ink derailed the line. "Grand-père, you scared me." He'd been sitting there all the time she wrote in her notebook, blending into the granite and the tree trunks and the shade, like the twig that had once curled round her finger. Nicola had never been able to look at twigs quite the same since. She squinted at him, closing the cover of her notebook a little too quickly. "Why didn't you say hello?"

His voice was low, blending into the rush of the creek beside them. "I didn't wish to disturb you, *mon chaton*. What are you so immersed in writing?"

"Just . . . you know, homework." She tried to be casual as she slid her pen into the spiral. In fact, she had been writing out all of her questions and doubts about her mother's death.

"So soon? You've only just started school."

She shrugged.

Tristan frowned fleetingly. "And how do you find it?"

"It's fine, I guess." Nicola traced squiggles in the dirt with the toe of her sneaker. "I don't really know anybody yet." So far she'd written off both genders. The boys teased her about her height—it seemed to Nicola that they were simply short—and the girls were worse. A popular one named Kelly had called her "Ricola," after the commercials for the Swiss cough drops. Normally she'd have laughed it off, but now it seemed that small talk eluded her; quick comebacks crawled into her consciousness too late. It was as if she'd forgotten how to *be* with people, and they sensed it.

"But you'll make friends easily, *chérie*." Tristan cleared his throat. "I know you will. It's why your father felt it so important that you go. I am more selfish. I miss our days together."

"So do I, Grand-père." But Nicola focused on the mossy rock, sweeping away fallen leaves and tracing a picture with her finger. She'd never had this trouble with her grandfather before. They'd always been able to talk about anything. "Can I ask you something?"

"Of course, you may." From his pinched frown, she knew he had guessed the subject.

"It's just that . . . the morning I found Mom, the lights in the pool house weren't on. The only light was from the skylights. I remember the reflections on the water."

"Well, *mais oui*, that is true."

"But everyone said she went out to look at the paintings. How could she have seen them in the dark? And if she *could* see, how did she fall in? You know how she hated the water. She'd never have gone near the edge—"

"You've given this a good deal of thought." Tristan caught her eyes. "But of course you have. The truth is, no one knows exactly what happened, *mon enfant*. She had a change of clothes in the cabana and her cosmetic case. It's clear she'd gone there for the night. She'd changed into her dressing gown and taken her sleeping pills. . . ." Tristan's voice trailed away. All at once he looked very weary.

Nicola felt a pang of regret for making him talk about it but couldn't help herself. She had to talk to someone. "That's why they told us it was an accident," she said slowly. "But—"

"Yes." The interruption seemed deliberate, as if he didn't want to hear her doubts. "Even with the pills, she couldn't sleep, it seems. Instead of staying safely in her room, she went out to the paintings. She wouldn't have needed to turn on the overhead lights in the pool house, *mon chaton*. We had special lights set up for the party, don't you remember? Uplights around the easels? *Eh bien*, it's not the best light for paintings, too many shadows." A frown. "But the lights were timed, you see, to come on at midnight and shut off at three. If she was out there when they went off, she could easily have become disoriented in the dark."

Nicola bit her lip. It was too awful to think about. Her mother, stumbling in blackness, falling. All alone.

Tristan rose and came to sit beside her. Nicola scooted over, onto her notebook. The wire spiral bit into her hip. He gazed down at her and said gently, "You mustn't think of it."

"I can't help it, Grand-père. I can't stop. It doesn't make any sense that she would be out there at all." Nicola swallowed, hard. "How did *you* know she'd be there?"

He hesitated. "I didn't know, but the house was full. There was nowhere else."

"I just can't believe she could drown." Nicola said miserably. "I feel like I'm going to wake up and it'll all have been a bad dream. I still feel like she's . . . here."

Her grandfather put his arm around her and pulled her close. "I know, I know."

For a moment they sat saying nothing, side by side, comforted by their shared grief. There weren't words to hold it. It could only be contained by the vast outdoors. Even in the sprawling house, it smothered her. Nicola wondered if that was what had drawn Grand-père here.

He called this place his *chutes cachées*, or "hidden falls." A stream emptied into three natural pools linked in a series of small waterfalls—it was serene and isolated, a good place to think, encircled by the trees that towered protectively overhead. The air was bittersweet with withered leaves and pine, the gentle rush of water blotting out the rest of the world. Water was everywhere lately.

At last Nicola spoke. "Why was Mom so afraid of the water?"

"Ah. The worst fears have no rational cause, *mon chaton*. It was simply always with her. I did try to teach her to swim once." His eyes were fixed on a point beyond her, on a picture from a past she could not share. He gave a short, sad laugh. "She was like a cat in the bathwater. Within two minutes she was out again. Phobias are strange, crippling things. Like obsessions, I suppose. Addictions. There are things that choose *you;* they are not chosen, and not so easily abandoned. I know this from experience, Nicola." His pale eyes were no more than slashes of blue as he squinted into the stark sunlight. "To live here, the land of lakes and streams and waterfalls and want no part of them . . . And yet she loved Devon. We had many happy times when we first came here. Everything was magical then, unspoiled."

What spoiled it? Nicola wanted to ask. "You said you know 'from experience'?"

The frown in Tristan's forehead deepened. "*Oui.* I had a fear of heights as a child, a tendency toward vertigo I've battled all my life. I willed it away, and over time elevators ceased to trouble me, I was at ease upon balconies. I thought I had conquered it." Nicola waited, watching. Her grandfather had always been able to order everything, to explain it all. He swung his leg as he spoke, striking the heel of his shoe against the granite shelf on which they sat. "Some years ago I was walking with Robin along some old railroad tracks, and we came to a trestle. *Eh bien,* it was sturdy enough; we were discussing some project or another, and I was halfway across when it struck me. There I was, gazing down through the slats, and the canyon below rushed up to meet me. I was sick with fear, Nicola. Paralyzed. The narrow gaps seemed too wide to cross. It was irrational, of course, but I was so certain I'd fall that there is little doubt I should have."

Nicola leaned forward. He had never told her this. "How did you get across?"

"Robin talked me through it somehow. He has ways of dealing with fear. It was not a dignified crossing, I'm afraid. Fear—simple, irrational fear—is the most terrifying enemy one can face. I am lucky I had help. No one was there to help your mother."

Tears welled in Nicola's eyes. She ought to be out of tears by now, but they were always there, waiting. And then she knew she had to try to confide in him again. If she lost him, too, there would be no one. The words spilled out. "She came to my room that night, Grand-père. She wanted to talk to me—to explain what I'd seen in the garden, I guess." Nicola did not meet his eyes; she wiped her cheeks and stared at her knees. "But I didn't let her in. I don't know why. I didn't understand. She was crying that night and then she yelled at me. And she never yells—"

"Ah, c'est ça. . . ."

Nicola forced herself to meet his face; the kind familiar face she'd always adored.

He spoke intently. "You mustn't feel guilty, Nicola. Listen to me. She was upset, but not at *you*. It was your father and these paintings. That's why she was crying. That's why she yelled at you. She didn't mean it, *ma chère*. You should have told me this at the start."

"But she seemed to like the paintings at first. The day we found them." Nicola swallowed. "Was it because she and Dad weren't really in love? They were only pretending?"

Tristan raised his eyebrows. "You are not such a little girl anymore, and we have hurt you in trying to protect you. *Eh bien,* I will tell you the truth. Your mother was unhappy. She worried about the effects of a divorce on you. But that night she had decided to leave your father."

Nicola gazed at him. "That's why she was crying? And why Dad looked so angry when he saw her in the garden? And you—" But she couldn't say the words.

"She was upset, and she'd had too much champagne." For a moment his eyes regained their characteristic twinkle as he teased her. "I understand you indulged a bit yourself." But, like his smiles these days, the twinkle soon faded. "You will find as you get older, Nicola, that people drink to become happy, but it often has the opposite effect. Emotion and alcohol fogged your mother's judgment. Having to pretend for all the guests at the party, having to watch while they ogled her . . ." He gazed away, his voice steely and full of contempt. Nicola had sensed he'd disapproved of the paintings, yet she realized only now how well her grandfather hid his emotions. She'd never heard this tone in his voice; she'd rarely ever seen him angry. He turned back, remembering her. "I learned from your father that you thought she was having a romantic tryst in the garden." His faintly outraged, amused tone made what she had thought seem absurd. "But of course it was only me, Nicola. *I* was behind the tree. I was trying to comfort her. I don't understand why you thought otherwise." His brow furrowed, and all at once it was impossible not to believe him. "It's like judging a painting by looking at only a piece of it, *chérie;* it's easy to misinterpret what you see."

Nicola nodded, feeling very foolish. Usually she took pride in understanding adult matters. How could she have thought something so awful about her mother? Her grandfather? The people she loved most in the world.

"Then you don't think she could have done it on purpose?"

Tristan gazed at her blankly. "On purpose?"

"Yes." Nicola met his eyes. "You don't think she could have meant to . . . to drown?"

"*C'est de la merde!*" he exclaimed. "Where have you heard these lies?"

Mrs. Pengilly. Maggie. "I just heard some people talking in town." Her mother's death was "news," a thing for strangers to peruse on the front page of the paper. Funny how this had never before struck her as cruel, the objective detailing of the death of someone else's loved one.

"God save us from the scourge of a small town. It's a malicious lie. She would never have done it that way. Take it from me, a person with vertigo doesn't climb up on the roof, Nicola. Not even to jump. An aquaphobe doesn't choose to drown." Tristan's tone was withering, but his gaze softened as he reached out to smooth Nicola's hair. "No wonder you've been acting so strangely. To keep all these doubts to yourself. Why didn't you come to me at once?"

"I don't know."

"Listen to me. The investigators declared your mother's death an accident. That's what it was. But death is always inexplicable—accidental deaths, natural deaths. . . . One is never satisfied. You must remember that we *knew* her, you and I. *We* are the reasons she wouldn't have killed herself. She wouldn't have left us." Nicola nodded, blinking back tears. "And we still have each other, *mon chaton*. We mustn't ever lose that."

With a crunch of dead leaves, Nicola turned to hug her grandfather. The sun had disappeared behind a cloud and she shivered. Tristan slipped his sweater over her shoulders, and they started home.

"There is to be an eclipse tonight, I understand," he remarked as they walked. "Do we have a date on the rooftop? I will bring the hot chocolate."

She nodded, smiling, but then remembered she had real homework and school tomorrow. "I don't like the kids at my new school very much Grand-père," she confessed. "I don't fit in at all."

"Ah, but you needn't fit in, *ma chère*." Tristan looked down at her affectionately. "That is an American conspiracy. I've never fit in anywhere. Simply be yourself, and they will fit in with you."

If only it were that easy. Nicola hugged her notebook to her chest, as if to keep it closed would erase all the vagaries of that night. She looked up at her grandfather wistfully. As much as she wanted to believe him, she'd begun to suspect that things weren't quite as simple as Grand-père made them seem.

❧

Amanda paced the small room, both startled to find herself in Devon again and feeling as though she'd never left it. Her real life in Seattle was fading into obscurity. Here she was, back at the Dorrington, chasing ghosts old and new.

The walls pressed in on her. The inn was the cheapest in town, and her room consisted of a large four-poster bed and very little else. Dainty lace curtains were flimsy armor against the encroaching darkness outside, but lowering the shades only made the room more claustrophobic.

Amanda had read in the Seattle papers of Gisèle's drowning, and the news had shocked her, devastated her beyond reason. They'd had one brief, unsatisfactory meeting, yet it haunted her. Had Amanda only imagined Gisèle's discomfiture or was she hiding something beneath the polished façade? When she learned of Gisèle's death, the lines blurred once more—it was like losing Karen all over again. Amanda read every news item in the *Times* and the *Post-Intelligencer* and the folksy Devon weekly, but details were frustratingly spare. Officially, the death was ruled an accident, though there had been some speculation of suicide. Amanda attempted to reach both Tristan and Robin, but neither had returned her calls. Until yesterday when, unable to shake her unease, she'd come back to Devon.

Robin then returned her call promptly and arranged to meet her tonight. Tristan had taken longer. Instinctively, she'd kept to her former cover story and hadn't let on to him that she'd ever left. Tristan apologized. It had been a harrowing two weeks, he said, but he'd like nothing more than to see her again.

Robin had been characteristically mysterious on the phone, insisting they discuss it all in person. He was late.

Amanda flopped onto the bed. A cherrywood credenza had been wedged into a tight corner and held an offering: a half bottle of cabernet and two glasses. Welcoming the idea of well-being, however artificially induced, she rose and popped the cork. She poured a glass of wine, and a knock on the door startled her so that she nearly spilled it.

Amanda peered through the peephole and was met with a beautifully cut charcoal suit and a flash of beautiful charcoal eyes. She opened the door. "Robin—"

"Good evening, Amanda. You're looking well." With a glance down the hall, he swept in. His gaze flitted over the room critically. It seemed to grow smaller, the bed larger. "More than I can say for your surroundings. This hotel's in need of renovation."

"I like it."

He frowned. "You need a sitting room, at least. The inn down the lane is in much better condition. More private, no wallpaper. I'll see that you're moved."

"That's not necessary." *I can't afford it.* "Please. This is fine."

Robin went on smoothly, "There's no question of cost. I realize Devon is pricey for a student. You are my guest." She opened her mouth to protest, but he said firmly, "I insist." And his expression dismissed the subject.

"Well, now that I'm here, can we—"

But he was rather presumptuously lowering the shades. Then he paused to straighten a picture frame and stepped back to study it. "This is crap, isn't it? Why do hotels hang such crap?"

At last he turned, as if taking her in for the first time.

His smile, when genuine, lit up the room. "It is good to have you in Devon again, Amanda. And I see you've overcome your aversion. Did I corrupt you with your first wine tasting?"

Her eyes dropped to the glass in her hand. "Oh. Yes. Well, would you care to join me?"

"Thank you. I'd suggest going out, but it's not wise to be seen together. I don't want us to seem to be conspiring."

She took the three steps to the credenza and poured another glass. "That's very cloak-and-dagger. *Are* we conspiring?" But he didn't answer.

"Shall we drink to Gisèle?" He lifted his glass and met her eyes. Only then could she see the depth of sorrow there. As with the smile, Amanda felt it genuine. She heard it in the inflection of his voice as it gently touched her name.

"Of course. To Gisèle," Amanda murmured, and they clinked.

"And now . . . tell me why you've come."

"I don't know, exactly. There's no reason for me to be here. I met Gisèle, and she didn't recognize me at all. Yet I've been mourning her as if I knew her." She felt her throat constrict with emotion.

Robin spoke gently. "Tell me about your evening with Tristan."

She swallowed. "I told him a lot and learned absolutely nothing. We have frivolous things in common. Food, movies, literature. We both have a passion for Guy de Maupassant's short stories, though it seems I've always mispronounced 'Guy.'"

He waited.

She sank onto the edge of the bed and waved him to the sole chair. "Can I be honest with you, Robin?"

"Lying doesn't appear to be your strong point." He made himself at home, crossing his legs at the ankles and reclining, so that the chair looked almost comfortable.

"The truth is, I have absolutely no reason to believe that Tristan's anything other than what he claims to be. He hardly seems the sort to take in underage runaways off the street. His accent, his clothes. Half his allusions escaped me. His experience is worlds away from mine. Karen and I were born middle-class, if that, educated in public schools. I've never been out of the country. Karen had never even been out of *California*. Surely Tristan's known many, many women. *Why* would he do this thing? He's the sort of person to whom things come easily. Like you are." Amanda paused, biting her lip. "I . . . well, I just don't belong here." *And neither did Karen.*

Robin's dark eyes narrowed. "And yet I'm here with you, Amanda, and I think you belong perfectly. It may be precisely because things *haven't* come easily to you." A pause. "So you let yourself be intimidated by Tristan. Tell me about your meeting with Gisèle."

Amanda forced down a sip of wine. "Gisèle was . . . well, I had the feeling she was performing. That everything about her was a performance. There was something familiar in her eyes, something of *my* world, not Tristan's. I saw Karen there." She gazed at him. "The trouble is, I needed to see her there. I know that. Nothing else seems to have any meaning suddenly. . . . I came back because I can't live with any doubt. I've brought her letter with me. You said you'd recognize her handwriting. I just need to know, Robin. I don't feel like I can trust myself anymore."

Robin said quietly, "Ah, well. Doubt all else, Amanda, but trust yourself."

She stared. Her heart lurched painfully. "What do you mean?"

"I mean I don't need your handwriting sample. I have a great deal to tell you, and I'm not sure how to prepare you for it. . . . It probably isn't possible to prepare you. But your sister did only what she felt she had to do."

Her hand gripped the bedspread convulsively. "My sister . . ."

"I believe Tristan insisted on the performance that night and Gisèle complied out of a desire to protect her daughter from the truth. She tried to preserve little Nicola's world. That is the only thing that could keep her from you, Amanda. I think it was the most difficult thing she's ever had to do—to choose between those she loved most."

Amanda continued to stare. "You're telling me it's all true? That it was my *sister* who drowned, that it was Karen who died . . . Again?"

Her voice broke on the words, but tears would not come. She'd cried when she read of Gisèle's death. The emotion had surprised her. But no tears would come now. Angrily, "You 'believe' this and 'think' that. You *know* far more than you're telling me, Robin. And you have from the beginning—"

"Yes, I have," he said calmly.

She had no words. She waited.

"Gisèle and I were very close. I knew that Tristan was not her natural father. That didn't necessarily make her your sister. I spoke to her after you came to see me. And she told me the truth . . ."

Numbly, "And what is the truth?"

He leaned forward, speaking gently. "She thought you were dead. She thought you died in the car accident with your parents. As soon as she learned you were alive, she wrote to you. She didn't think it through. Afterward she questioned what such a thing would do to you now. What it would do to her daughter—"

Her daughter. Her *sister's* daughter. The wineglass slipped from Amanda's hand, and its contents splattered across the bedspread. She didn't feel or notice. She spoke with a quiet fury. "She took my hand and said my name like it was a foreign word. I don't . . ." She gazed around her without seeing. "You . . . you buried her, and you *knew*." Tears came then. They blurred the room. "I wasn't even at the funeral. I could have . . ."

But what could she have done?

"I couldn't tell you, Amanda. I'm sorry. It's vitally important that no one know who you really are. Or exactly what you know. Not yet." Robin spoke softly but with determination. "The person responsible feels safe now, and that is how we will catch him."

"The person responsible?" she echoed in a hollow voice.

"Yes. There's much more at stake than even you realize. You see, I don't believe that Gisèle died by accident. And I don't believe it was suicide." He steeled his voice. "I believe Elle was murdered."

XI

THE ARTIST'S STUDIO

The second blackmail envelope arrived that spring. It was postmarked April 13, 1981—two years to the day since Karen's disappearance.

It had been months since the first letter, and I had by then convinced myself no more would come. Yet when I saw the plain white business envelope with no return address, it seemed, of course, inevitable.

The contents rather settled matters. There we were, Gisèle and I, in all our burgeoning glory, emerging from a bookstore, holding hands in the park. It was absurd. I'd so often had the sense in those days of being followed, and here, *years* later, was my shadow. It had been preternaturally patient. And still made no demand for money, no threats.

But I knew they would come.

And when, not a week later, I learned from Henri that Robin Dresden meant to "sketch" Gisèle, it seemed I could rule out a single bad apple and expect a bushel of them.

"A surprise for you, sir, but I thought perhaps you'd prefer to know." Henri possesses a great flair for understatement.

"Yes, Henri, thank you. When and where is this to take place?"

"On Friday. Mr. Dresden has a loft, it seems, in SoHo. She has given me the address."

I'd happily believed Robin's primary residence to be on the Continent and his living arrangements here rather crowded. Had he tired of his ménage in Central Park West? "Gisèle asked you not to tell me?"

He apologized for her with a pensive frown. "It's a surprise, you see. I was made to promise."

"I'm afraid I'm not terribly surprised, Henri."

"Nor I, sir. You will wish to prevent her going."

"No." No, I did not wish to prevent her going; I wished to ascertain her purpose in going. I thought I could pretty well ascertain his. "No, no. I imagine that would only worsen things."

"You're quite sure?"

"Quite. But I will take the address."

It seemed Robin was to pick her up at two and return her by five. It was my habit to be out on Friday afternoons, and I was particularly anxious to be out on this one, breaking into Robin's loft.

I wished only to be a fly on the wall, but the clever fly must determine his entrance and exit strategies. In spite of my skills as a pickpocket, I'm under no particular illusions that I would make a good cat burglar; I cannot pick locks, and the scaling of walls is not one of my strong points. But I have never lacked nerve, and nerve is all one needs. I had no time to observe Robin's habits as I'd once observed Gisèle's, yet I did investigate flats across the way from his. None were conveniently vacant. I thought of concocting a distraction that would inspire a rush downstairs while I rushed up, but any suitable diversions were along the lines of fire and flood, bomb threats, or a shooting on the street below—all of which held for me very little appeal.

At last I settled upon a plan. Gaining access to the building itself was a trifle. I simply used the intercom to buzz apartments until one had the geniality to buzz back. It may not have been so simple a matter in my neighborhood, but SoHo in those days was delightfully slack about such things. Robin's building was old and picturesque and came with a fire escape. These do not extend to the ground, of course, and in any case my vertigo would scarcely allow me to make the entire ascent to the top. And so I approached his downstairs neighbors.

On the floor directly below the loft, I found four doors. My first three attempts produced no answer. On the fourth I was met with a distrustful fragment of a face through the cracked door. My polite request for access to the fire escape (as I'd carelessly mislaid my house key . . .) was met with a snicker, and the door was promptly slammed shut. Down another floor the apartments were smaller and there were many doors to try. The first was opened by a promising-looking young woman with a pixie haircut and an open smile. In such situations it pays to be French; she was only too pleased to find a hapless Yves Montand in the hall. Her neighborliness extended itself to fire-escape access as well as an invitation to a disco.

My first crisis of nerve came on the fire escape. The wind is less than polite at great heights, and the abstract spinning of the earth is corporeally felt. My vertigo returned *en force*, and for a moment I stood outside, immobilized. I can only say that my anxiety at leaving Gisèle alone with Robin Dresden exceeded that of plummeting to my death, though it was a near thing. I climbed the two floors in fits and starts, and to anyone watching I appeared either a very foolish thief or one wrestling with waves of scruples.

I found Robin's window open, as expected; it was springtime and lovely. But it was stuck halfway and required a good deal of coaxing and cajoling and cursing before at last it gave. It all took much longer than I'd planned, and I half expected Robin and Gisèle to burst through the door as I stepped in. But I found the loft silent and empty. It was a vast space, a thing emphasized by sparse furnishings. The scent of paint and turpentine stung my nostrils. Paintings covered the walls, were propped against them, and sat on easels draped like ghosts. Clerestory lighting fell in exaggerated oblong arches onto a cherrywood floor, the sunlight revealing nicks and dings in the finish. Rounding out the scene were a great many books and a bed rather conspicuously unmade.

I had just enough time to steady my nerves (the room had ceased to sway) and decide on my hiding place when I heard voices from the hall. There came a fumbling at the door, the fingernails-on-chalkboard grating as it was slid open, and I scarcely breathed. I'd taken refuge behind a massive antique Italian sideboard, a lovely Tuscan piece, solid and sturdy and large enough to conceal me yet leave vantage points to either side of the immense room. I could easily peer over the top or hide behind the stacked plates and bowls. I could only hope he did not intend to feed her.

They came through the door together, Gisèle in a pretty floral dress (which had better remain on) and Robin uncharacteristically rumpled and unshaven after what looked to be a rough night. The phone rang almost at once, and he spoke shortly to someone, then excused himself and stepped out the door. I was overcome with panic. Had I been observed by a friend across the way?

I broke into a cold sweat as Gisèle roamed the room without a care. She scanned the vast wall of bookshelves, kneeling to eye titles on the third row; she extracted one and fanned through its pages. After a moment she gave a guilty glance over her shoulder and then furtively pulled out another. This engaged her to such a degree that she jumped when she heard the door, shoving the book hurriedly back into place.

Robin went to the kitchen. He offered her a ginger ale, which she declined, and took a bottle of beer for himself. Impatiently, he posed her in the corner of the settee, chin up, head tilted. He brought a lock of hair forward to sprawl across her right shoulder, curled her fingers under her chin, and positioned her elbow on the padded arm. Her legs were curved beneath her. He took up his sketch pad and sat in the chair opposite.

"Should I look at you or past you?" Gisèle asked, in the tentative tone I had nearly forgotten. In the beginning, when she'd looked to me for approval . . . It had gone so gradually that I had not felt the loss.

"At me," said Robin. "Just so. Good."

For long moments I could hear no more than the scratch of charcoal on paper. Her eyes wandered.

"Gisèle." Sharply. "I said, focus on me."

She blushed, protesting, "But I feel like I'm staring at you."

"Stare."

She inhaled deeply. Silence.

"You're not comfortable being alone with me. Why is that?"

"I'm fine."

"No you're not. I can tell by your breathing."

"What's wrong with it?"

"You're not doing it. Your fingers are clenched, and from the rate of your blinks you're either wearing contacts, suffering from an allergy, or nervous about being here. I'm convinced it's the last. You needn't lie."

"I guess I'm just not used to being sketched." She swallowed. "And . . . I've heard stories about you. That you killed someone in Prague." A question mark in her brows. "That you live with two women. That you're a hypnotist, a sadist, a drug smuggler, an art thief, and a spy. And no one knows your real identity at all."

From my hiding place, I frowned. Where had she heard these things? What was said about me?

Robin only laughed. "It's a wonder I find time to paint. Which one is your favorite?"

"Which ones are true?" she countered.

He scratched his unshaven chin. "Taking them in order: Not that I know of . . . yes, until recently . . . yes . . . I hardly think so . . . no, occasionally, perhaps, and what's a 'real' identity?" The last was the one that offended him. "I don't think I believe in that; it sounds very dull."

Gisèle, I thought, ought not to believe in a real identity either by now. But she asked, "Is it something you can 'not' believe in?"

"Everything is." He gazed up from his sketch and smiled at her puzzled face. "Even as a child, I knew I was not who I appeared to be. My parents were blond and blue-eyed and by all outward appearances respectable. I rather suspected I was not their real son. . . ." He flashed an irreverent grin. "And I no longer go by the name they gave me. What does it matter in the end?"

"I guess it doesn't." She cleared her throat. "You're a wonderful artist. I paint, too, a little. With Tristan." I smiled, thinking of this. She was quite good; she took direction very well. "The great thing about painting is you can't do it and think normal thoughts. It's like your brain floats on the surface of a thing. It doesn't matter what it's there for, what it means. . . ."

"Of course, one can come to the meaning of a thing by searching the surface. Or one can create it." A slight smile. "Take these walls. How I paint them gives them meaning. Are they to keep one in or others out? Is the room a closed box or an open space? Is the view in or out? Surfaces are no more static than identity. Surfaces tell a story; they are possibilities."

She smiled, but then it faded. "It must be nice to look at things that way."

"Things *are* that way, whether you look at them or not. We create everything we see."

"How old are *you?*" she asked.

"Twenty-six."

"That's young to be so sure of everything. Is it your way of not letting people know you?"

"Absolutely." He laughed with gusto. "Thank you for the character assessment. Very astute. How old are you?"

"Seventeen." He'd slipped it in so nimbly that she'd answered without thinking. Karen's birthday had been in February, but "Gisèle Mourault" would not be seventeen for several months. Though Robin had guessed our secret, I had asked her not to confide in him. "I was going to be a writer," she mused. "Once."

"When you were young?"

She rolled her eyes but smiled. "It's just that I'm not sure now. Things come to a meaningful end in books, but in life things are just things. Disconnected things. And everyone pretends to have control."

He raised that damned articulate brow. "And you?"

"I pretend, too."

Robin took a sip of beer and frowned. "What is it you want to control?"

She shrugged. "I don't know. Everything. *Anything.*"

I didn't care for the way he watched her, as if he could see beneath her skin. "I used to pretend all the time," he said evenly. "I pretended my whole life—walk, talk, dress, history, different accents. I didn't go to art school; I pretended I was an artist. And then I found something wonderful. Everyone began to believe in my make-believe. Go figure. The key to acquiring anything is to imagine you already have it."

Her smile was slight and wistful, but her almond eyes shone. "Is that true?"

I thought of her, my first glimpse of her, and realized it *was* true. Almost.

"If you have no control, perhaps it's how you're pretending."

Gisèle laughed nervously, gazed away and back again. "Can we talk about something else?"

"Probably. You start."

"I'm not sure I followed you before. Is it really true you live with two women?"

"I did. I do, sometimes. When I'm not elsewhere."

"And they don't mind? I mean, they don't get jealous?"

"No."

She looked as skeptical as I felt.

"They're more in love with each other, Ana and Marie. And I . . ." Robin scratched his head. "Well, occasionally I enjoy being the hyphen between their names."

Nice little euphemism, that.

"They're in love with each other? Don't you think that's kind of . . . well, gross?"

He laughed outright. I had to suppress my own. "Um, let me think. No."

Her eyes darted around the room. "Have you really read all these books?"

"Yes. Stop fidgeting."

"I was looking through them earlier." A pause. "Er, the third row . . . from the bottom."

"Ah." There was something in his tone; she heard it, too. "You shouldn't have done that, Gisèle."

"I'm sorry. I would have asked, but—"

"It's not that." The scratch of charcoal. "It's just that it's not my job to corrupt you."

"Whose job is it?"

Scratch-scratch-smudge. He gazed at her a moment. "I see, now. All this talk of pretending and control. It's about sex." An amused smile. "What is it you want to know?"

"I want to know if I'm normal."

"That pretty much proves you are."

She laughed, but her voice was eager. "When you came to see Tristan, you asked me about California. . . ." He had? "And . . . um, Tristan says you already know about us, so I guess I can tell you. He's not my father, of course. He's *nothing* like my father, and . . . well, I'm in love with him." She said it carefully, gauging its effect. It affected me the greater, I think. All at once I felt quite well.

"Glad to hear it. What's with all the playacting, then? The father-daughter bit. I've told him he ought to give it up. It's perverse. No wonder you feel trapped."

"He does it to protect me. You know—driver's license, insurance, all that. I've got to be someone."

"I see." Benignly, "There are people looking for you?"

She was silent, hesitant to face the answer. "No. No, I don't think so. Not anymore. I feel bad about leaving, but I had to go. I had to. And— Well, I was in love with Tristan."

"Then you knew him before you left home?" Artless, casual, but I stopped breathing.

She dropped her eyes. "I would have left anyway."

"I see." Robin studied her closely. "Well. The cops don't bother much with runaways once they've crossed state lines. And in another year you'll be legal."

She gave him a hard look. "I've just realized what's so strange about you. Nothing bothers you. . . . It's like you're from another planet." Wistfully, "I wish I could be that way. Tristan can't believe you won't tell, but I know you won't." She held herself very still as she spoke, but a frown appeared between her eyes. "I hope he'll like this for a present. He'd freak out if he found out I was here alone with you. He's very jealous, you know."

Robin frowned. "Do you never venture out by yourself?"

Damn the man. She squirmed a little and said nothing.

"Stay still. All right, so let me see if I have this straight. You're in love with a man you have to pretend is your father, who's so jealous he barely lets you out of his sight, but you're sexually frustrated—"

"I'm not frustrated."

Robin sighed. "You're a virgin, Gisèle. By definition you're frustrated."

"How did you know I was— I mean . . ." She straightened. "Did you think I *wasn't* a virgin?"

"No. It was quite clear to me that you were. How long have you been with him anyway?"

"Tristan? A while."

"A long while, I think."

"So?"

"It puts you pretty young when you ran away." Robin set down his charcoal and reached for his beer, tapping the bottle with his forefinger. "I'm guessing your situation was bad and he's a very patient fellow. The problem's not with you, Gisèle. He's just a swell guy."

"The thing is," dropping her eyes, "the problem *is* with me, Robin. I told him I was scared of it."

"It sounds like you are."

Indignantly, Gisèle retorted, "I am not. I *want* to do it. I'm not afraid it'll hurt. I know it does. I just . . ." her voice trailed miserably away. "I just want to get it over with."

His gaze was appraising. "That's understandable. Virginity's best gotten over with and forgotten. Sort of like the chicken pox. You probably won't like it much the first time, but there are ways to make you forget. And afterward it gets infinitely better, I promise."

She was back to holding her breath. On the exhale, "Make me forget how?"

"Surely you and Tristan haven't been entirely idle. Haven't you ever come with him?"

"Come where?"

Ma petite . . .

Robin rolled his eyes disparagingly.

She flushed red. "Oh, that. Right." But she just continued to blush and didn't answer.

I shifted my weight, and the floorboards let out a deafening creak.

"So that's a no," Robin continued carelessly. "How about with anyone before him? Ever go a little far playing doctor? Spin the bottle? No precocious little boyfriend or girlfriend in childhood?"

But she simply shook her head no. "Just kissing and not with *girls*."

"How gross!" Robin mimicked her flat Californian outrage. He scratched his head with charcoal-smudged fingers and went on pragmatically, "You must have come by yourself, then."

"That's none of your—"

"So that's another no. Right. Well, this is going to be harder than I thought."

"It is *not* a no. I've had a . . . you know."

"Orgasm? The word doesn't bite, Elle."

How dare he abbreviate her name! And why didn't she correct him?

"I have, but not *with* anyone. Not yet. I told you, I'm a virgin," she murmured.

"Well, the two aren't mutually exclusive, love."

"Well, they are for me. I've never had one with anyone. But I know I will when we go all the way."

He frowned at the utter illogicality of this. I frowned at the fact that it came as an utter surprise. I'd been encouraged and rather proud of the ease with which she . . . faked it. I thought she'd had many. And I am French. I was truly very shaken.

"What a lot of rubbish," Robin said.

"Well, it's just that with Tristan I get worried about not having the right reaction, so I pretend. But it doesn't work for me, pretending." She twisted a curl around her finger. "I can't seem to pretend it into being."

Imagine what I felt? To hear her say this to my rival. I was dazed, deflated. Betrayed.

"Oh, my." Robin groaned and shook his head. He rose to get another beer and turned on the stereo. Music filled the silence. The Stones. "Sympathy for the Devil." It was horribly apt. Quite firmly, he said, "You must certainly promise not to do that again."

Gisèle grimaced at the idea. "I can't do that. He's used to it now."

"I really must make you promise, Elle. It's hardly fair to Tristan, and it's worse for you. Do you want someone to think you're having a great time, or do you want to *have* a great time? Really, love. All you're pretending into being is the quote, unquote 'right response.' I assure you a real one is better."

"I know. It's just that nothing was happening. It felt nice, but then I started to worry I was taking too long."

"Classic feminine response."

She dropped her fist. "You mean it's normal?"

"You are sweet. Of course it is. Especially when you're just starting out. Remember, Elle." (Damn him.) "It's not a chore for the fellow you're with; it's not a race. No one's holding a stopwatch."

"I just didn't want to hurt him. In the movies it always happens fast. And anyway, what if I *can't* have one with him, or with anyone? Maybe I'm not normal. I mean . . . then he'd feel awful. He's nice; he's not like you."

Merde. Since when had I been relegated to "nice"?

"At least I'm well mannered," he said dryly, "*Your* manners are appalling. Not nice indeed."

She was unfazed. "So I've had a . . . you know . . . by myself. That counts, doesn't it?"

"Well, yes, under the circumstances I think we'd better count it."

"Why is it so much harder with someone else?"

"Because you're worried about pleasing him more than yourself. And he's only touching you, while you're touching yourself and feeling at the same time."

I shifted my weight. I was growing increasingly uncomfortable with the entire situation. Robin was quite at ease, sketching again. He'd switched to a new page, and she was more animated now. He'd stopped restricting her pose.

"Tell me about the first time," he said.

"I was thirteen."

"And where were you?"

"In bed, in my room, at night. And it was kind of funny, because—" She gave a slight girlish giggle that tore at me. I wanted so badly to swoop in and cart her off. And yet I was a voyeur now in the truest sense of the word. I was on the outside looking in. And, sadly, we were past the stage of my carting her off.

"Funny because . . . ?"

"You'll only laugh at me," she demurred.

"Quite possibly."

"All right, but don't tell anyone." Her voice dropped. "You know how women in the movies moan and scream, like they're being murdered or something? I thought it was something you couldn't help, so if I— if it happened, I'd start to scream uncontrollably and wake the whole house."

As predicted, Robin laughed. But—worse—there was affection in it. "Charming."

She blushed, and he tilted his head, lifting the charcoal and bringing it down in quick, sure strokes. He flipped the page again, capturing her from different angles, I imagined. I longed to see the image of her as it was coaxed from the paper—the curls, the fleeting smile replaced with a pensive expression as she waited. "And what did you think as it was happening?" he asked.

"I couldn't breathe. I was shocked."

"Yes, it is shocking the first time."

"That my body could do that and I never knew."

"Amazing, isn't it?" His voice was very gentle, as if to contradict the rapid motions of the charcoal in his hand. "And what were you thinking about?"

"Oh." She bit her lip, blushing deeper.

"You were thinking of something."

"Just a story I read in a magazine. A friend of mine found a *Hustler* in her brother's room."

"What did you feel afterward?"

"Guilty. I didn't really do anything after that. Well, there was one other time. In the tub."

"One other time?" He dropped his charcoal and stared. "Please tell me you're joking."

She dropped her eyes. "I always thought I'd wait till I was married or something. I don't know. You're supposed to make love with someone. I don't want to go to hell."

Robin let out a groan. "Then choose to go elsewhere."

"You're so weird. It's not a choice."

"Everything's a choice. I don't *believe* in hell. It's a made-up place, and as *I* didn't make it up, I'm not required to go there. That's a choice."

"You're just weird."

"All right, but we're discussing you. Tell me about the story in the magazine. What was it about?"

"A guy and a girl."

"How inventive."

"They were . . ." she hesitated. "Brother and sister."

"Ah."

"Well, yeah. That's the thing. That doesn't turn me on at all. I mean, ick—"

"Your body didn't think so."

"It should have."

He rolled his eyes. "Who says?"

"You wouldn't understand." She squinted. "You don't even believe in God."

"Not the same one you do, I guess. Mine is a wonderful artist. He made your body and invented the frightful O-word. He—she, it—is much more fun than people seem to think."

She smiled. Then frowned. "It doesn't explain why I was excited by the story."

"Oh, please. You liked the dirty words."

She blushed.

"Anyway, did you sleep with your brother?"

"I don't have a brother."

"I rest my case."

She laughed uneasily. "That doesn't prove anything. For all you know, I'm some depraved pervert."

"I'm betting you're not. Anyway, far more perversions arise from repression than from expression."

"That's why people go to psychiatrists to talk about sex?"

"That, and notions like you'll automatically get off if you do it missionary style on your wedding night. If all your illusions are built around that, you're going to be very disappointed."

Her face fell. She dropped her eyes.

"On the other hand, you're still young. You're not too far gone. There's a chance for you yet. It's more a matter of the man you're with not giving your body a choice."

Her lips had parted slightly. She tried to tease. "I thought everything was a choice."

"Hmm." His gaze was too direct. "Suppose Tristan were to say to you, 'Gisèle, I'm going to make you come, very hard, no matter how long it takes and whether you like it or not.' Do you think you'd race from the room?"

She blushed very red and squirmed pleasantly. I wanted to beat the crap out of him.

"No," she murmured. "But I can't imagine him saying that."

I couldn't really imagine myself saying it either. It seemed a little . . . well. Presumptuous. Sure of oneself. Of course, I *could* say it. Perhaps I would. A variation thereof.

He'd said nothing. She didn't seem to know what to do with her eyes. "Can we talk about something else?" she asked, for the second time.

"Probably," he replied in kind. "But you're not afraid of sex, Elle. You're afraid of guilt."

Softly, "Maybe I don't deserve to enjoy it. I've done a lot of bad things."

"Have you? Like what?" She didn't answer. "Here's what I think. I think a lot of bad things have been done to you, and you've let them stick. But whatever happened before this moment is null and void. You decide whether you carry it with you from here."

She straightened. "Just because you don't have a conscience—"

"Isn't the point of a conscience to prevent one from doing something one would feel guilty about? The act of feeling guilty seems a *failure* of conscience, then, wouldn't you agree?"

She gazed at him thoughtfully. "I guess so."

"Don't guess. You have nothing to feel guilty for. It's your body. It's yours to touch. Where's the guilt in that? Guilt's a cage, Elle. Believe me. It will keep you where you are forever. And in that case, you don't really need to worry about hell. You're already in it." Robin looked at her intently and made a gesture with his hands, of release. "If you let it go, you are free. Do you see?"

She didn't say a thing. She bit her lip. But she did see. All at once, light crept into her eyes.

"There. That's lovely." Robin flipped the page. "Look at me. Just like that."

She resolutely bit her lip and so could not speak. Robin didn't speak either. His hand flew across the page. And she grew older before my eyes. She took him in, it in. The room, the feeling, the fact of being sketched. She liked it.

At last he said. "Good. All right, relax. We're done."

And I let out my breath.

Gisèle gazed at him. "Thank you."

His eyes flickered with amusement, and with a very definite affection. "For sketching you?"

"No."

He smiled but then said sternly, "No more guilt and no more faking. Agreed? We'll discuss it when I sketch you again."

Again? But she only nodded. "I'll try."

"Don't try, do it. You have fantasies. Let yourself have them. Look at your body in a sexual way. Be conscious of the way it feels in your clothes, in bed, in the shower. You have a beautiful body, Elle."

Elle. "She" in French. Her. The fathomless feminine.

"When you touch yourself, focus on the feeling, but also your fingertips. You'll know you're doing it, because they'll tingle. Feel the air around you. Take time to notice the shapes of things, the colors, the textures." Robin smudged here and there with his thumb and forefinger and closed the sketch pad. "And for the next two weeks, you're to think of nothing but sex."

She laughed. Even I had to smile.

"It's an order, you understand." Robin rose, rubbing his neck. "I'll know if you don't do it."

"Oh, really." Saucily, "How will you know?"

"It'll show up in your sketch."

She gazed at him, twisting her ankle to its awkward thoughtful angle, painfully inward. "Can I see it?" With a toss of her head, she indicated the sketchbook.

"No." Robin pushed the lock of hair from his brow. "Right now it's just the way you look. I add things later, as I re-create you in my mind. I sketch in what you leave me with. Those are the essential things, the things you leave behind in a room."

"I did all right, then?"

"You did exactly right. Tristan will be pleased."

Tristan doubted it.

"You won't tell him we talked about all this stuff, will you?"

"What stuff?"

Gisèle smiled. "You know, I actually think you're very sweet."

Robin rolled his eyes. "Let's not have that one get out. I rather fancy myself a degenerate spy." He touched her chin; she let him. Then he turned, impatient and preoccupied again. "And now a little light reading to help your homework along."

She giggled, a lovely lilting sound, as he pulled selections from his infamous third row. I was consumed with yearning, loss, jealousy. . . . It should have been me discussing these things with her. Me handing her these books. But the greater pang was that they spelled for me not a beginning but an end.

Robin was not, it seemed, able to escort her home as I had planned. Fortunately for me, he did go down to hail her a cab. ("Don't tell me you're frightened of those, too?" he scolded. "Very well. I shall have to teach you to whistle.") I made my way out after them, avoiding the lift for the stairs.

It was a long, long way down. I could not see them, though at one point I thought I heard their whistles echo up from the street below. I descended another level down the Inferno. I didn't want Gisèle to learn to whistle for cabs. To go by "Elle." To ever lose her virginity. I wanted her to remain scared and unready, fragile and naïve. I did not want her to grow up.

But in the space of an afternoon, using only words, I felt Robin *had* corrupted her. And that he'd meant to do so.

XII

TWO SISTERS

NICOLA WAS READING a very dull account of the roots of democracy in ancient Greece when she heard the sound of shattering glass. It wasn't loud, like a window breaking, more like a trinket falling to the floor. She rose from her desk and went to the door to look out, but the hall was quiet and empty.

Nicola's room was at the corner, off the stairs. Her mother's room was farther down the long hall on the other side, and at the farthest end was her grandfather's. In between were guest rooms and sitting rooms. Intuitively, Nicola felt that the sound had come from her mother's bedroom. Every time she walked past it, she had to fight the urge to go in. It was so easy to picture her mother there . . . in the window seat reading, in the chair before her vanity, lying in bed. As long as the door was kept closed, Nicola could imagine her going through the various steps of her day.

Now Nicola hesitated before the door, the way she had as a child after a nightmare. She took a deep breath, trying to fight the voice that told her she'd find her mother inside, waking at a whisper, rising to comfort her and tell her it had all been a bad dream.

She turned the handle and entered. The room was cool, too cool to contain her mother. Eerily, the closet light glowed. Maggie must have left it on. She must come in here to clean, to dust her mother's things.

Once she was in, Nicola was strangely reluctant to go. She went to her mother's writing desk and sat in her chair. There was her mother's favorite pen lying on the blotter, and several small books of poems, held upright and spaced with small sculptures of the Muses that Robin had done for her. Nicola slid open the top drawer and found more pens and odds and ends. She tugged open the side drawer. There should be stationery there. She used to love writing on her mother's stationery; it was a pale, mottled ivory with a ragged tear along the bottom of each page instead of a straight edge. She ran her fingers over the top sheet and could feel tiny impressions from the last letter her mother had written. She savored the impressions of her mother's thoughts, the pressure of her hand.

Rising, she turned and went to the dresser. A lace runner covered the top, and in the center was a mirrored tray of perfumes. Their existence was something of an enigma, since Gisèle never wore any of them. They were just for looks—like the fancy bath towels you weren't supposed to use. They were beautiful bottles, though. A kind of collection her mother had begun as a girl. Nicola often made a game of arranging the decorative bottles in different patterns, by shape and size. She went to the tray now and located the source of the shattering sound. She knew all the bottles by heart and recognized the Eau de Givenchy. It had been toppled and lay on its side. Or rather it had been dropped, for a crack ran through the mirror in an ugly scrawl, beneath the beautiful bottles.

Who could have done it? Not Maggie, surely. It was too late for her to be dusting, and she would have set the bottle upright again. Maybe it had been Nicola's father, or her grandfather . . . coming here, like her, to be near her mother. To feel her in her things.

Nicola forced her eyes from the broken mirror. Beside the tray was a vase of flowers she and her mother had dried together last spring and, on the other side, three framed photos. The first was a snapshot of Nicola and her father at the lake, their faces dappled beneath a canopy of trees. Her father looked much younger, she thought, though the picture had been taken only last year.

She picked up the frame and studied her father's face. In spite of their troubles, he must have loved her mother once—to paint her again and again. Thinking of this and looking at his smile, Nicola felt a flicker of guilt. She had finally confided in someone that she'd seen her father that morning—his tall form walking determinedly through the glass corridor, to the pool house. A small part of her regretted it. She knew there must be some innocent explanation.

She picked up the next picture. It was of her grandfather and Robin in New York and had been taken before Nicola was born. There was no gray in Grand-père's blond hair and no crinkles around his eyes. She felt a pang to see him like that. Since her mother had died, he'd lost weight and there was sorrow in his step. She often caught him standing in doorways, with a glassy-eyed, nostalgic expression on his face, like some Ghost of Christmas Past gazing fondly on a familial scene from long ago.

Robin was much younger than her grandfather, and though the photo was nearly fifteen years old, he looked much the same then as now. Very handsome. His hair was longer then, but his smile just as cocky. He looked as though he were teasing the person taking the picture.

Had that been her mother?

Robin had always encouraged Nicola to call him if she needed to talk about things. About "anything at all." Godfathers were special, he said. They weren't for practical things, like fathers were, but for sharing confidences and games, wishes and magic. They were there to call on when you needed them most. And it was this way with godmothers in stories. Nicola had often wondered why there were never any godfathers in fairy tales. . . . When she was younger, Robin had told her it was because she had the only one.

Since her mother died, he'd been particularly concerned and attentive. There was something intimidating about him at times, but he'd always been very kind and patient with her. She trusted him. He was very smart about things, especially people, and never offended by anything she said. So she'd decided to confide in him. She told him what Grand-père had said about the lights and the timers set to go off at three. And he was the only one she'd told about her father—that she'd seen him go to the pool house at three-thirty.

It didn't make any sense, and Nicola liked to make sense of things. So did Robin. Her father would have had to turn on the overhead lights, wouldn't he? Robin agreed that he would. And if her mother had already slipped and fallen, he'd have seen her in the pool. But then why wouldn't he tell anyone? And if her mother *hadn't* died before three, then the timers meant nothing and Nicola was back to her original question: Why had Gisèle been so near the water, walking around the pool house in the dark?

Sharing her concerns had lightened them. Robin reassured her he would find the answers, and she believed him. It helped to have an ally, and a formidable ally at that.

Turning from these thoughts, she picked up the last frame. In it she was just a baby and her mother was holding her. Gisèle was so young, just nineteen, with a mischievous glint in her eyes, as though thinking of a secret. Her chin was lifted, and the smile on her lips was secretive, too, but also exultant. Triumphant. Nicola was in a pretty pink dress, white lacy socks, and shiny patent-leather shoes; her mouth was open, and she was laughing. Her hair was very dark but curled behind her ear, just like her mother's, and she clutched a teddy bear tight with tiny hands. It was hard to imagine ever being so tiny.

Nicola decided she would take the picture with her and put it on the dresser in her room. Her mother would have wanted her to have it, she knew. She still had the little bear she held in the photo. Maybe she'd put them together. Then she remembered the teddy bear from the day of the party: the battered one in Scottish tartans. She'd rescue him, too.

Wandering to the closet, Nicola inhaled the familiar scent of cedar. The light was already on, welcoming her, but her mother's clothes lined the walls like colorful ghosts, hanging formless and empty. Her shoes were lined up on racks and her sweaters neatly bundled on the shelves. Sudden emotion choked Nicola; it was as if remnants of her mother were woven into the fabric of her clothing. The little bear was missing from the shelf, and somehow this worsened things. Why should he disappear? It was, like everything else, inexplicable.

The lump in her throat grew as she backed out of the closet. It was so utterly empty here. Nicola switched off the light, and shadows seemed to rush at her. Clutching her baby picture tightly, she decided to take the other photos, too. They were meant to be looked at, as her mother had looked at them. They shouldn't be left here in the dark. Quickly, she slipped out of the room and into the warmth of the hall.

Her own room was smaller and bright; there were no shadows here to reach for her. She twisted the stays on the back of one of the frames; the one that held the photo of her grandfather and Robin. She wanted to see if her mother had written anything on the back. She had. It said simply, *"New York. Spring, 1981."* But what a keen pleasure it was to see her mother's handwriting. The one of her and her father said, *"Luke and Nicky at the lake, 1993."* But as Nicola lifted away the backing of her baby picture, a small loose snapshot tumbled out and landed facedown on her bedspread. It was old, with creases that had been carefully smoothed and an inscription in an unfamiliar hand: *Karen Louise and Amanda Nicole— Grandma and Grandpa Miller's: 1976.*

Nicola frowned quizzically. She didn't recognize the names. Turning it over, she was met with her mother's face.

❧

Rain pattered on the rooftop, but the silence in the room was palpable. Despite the drawn shades, Amanda could feel the black night press against the windows of the narrow room, sidling up to eavesdrop. She lowered her eyes and noticed her spilled wine for the first time. It splattered the white bedspread like blood. Robin rose and returned from the bathroom with a towel. He covered the stain. His previous words filtered like molasses through her brain. *"Murdered?"* She repeated the word twice more in varying inflections. "I don't understand. The papers—"

"Printed the sanitized version." He sat once more in the chair opposite her.

Amanda felt a rush of anger. "But if you suspect *murder*, Robin, where are the police? For Christ's sake, what about an autopsy?"

He spoke calmly. "They were called in. Naturally, one was done. There were no defensive wounds and no sign of foul play. She had no marks on her. There was some discussion as to whether she jumped, but in the end they couldn't resolve to call it suicide. I had to agree. Quite apart from her fear of the water, I simply don't believe that Gisèle would have left her daughter. She was trying desperately to keep her world *together*, not shatter it." His eyes roved the room restlessly. "And the dose of sleeping pills was too high, but not lethal. Three times the usual dose. She'd also had a lot of champagne, impaired judgment. . . . Officially: an accident."

"Well, *unofficially*, where do you get murder? What proof do you have?"

"Nothing tangible. But two people appear to have known she was at the pool house that night and failed to include this fact in the investigation. And a good many facts that *were* included aren't what they appear to be on the surface." He appraised her. "And then there is simple psychology. That is your forte. Think about it a moment, Amanda. You know the facts."

But Amanda couldn't seem to wade through the fog in her mind. It was all too much to assimilate. She still wrestled with the underlying notion: Karen was Gisèle and Gisèle, Karen? The process of naming things was the way the mind ordered reality, but her sister's names were entirely separate entities to her.

She took a deep breath and forced herself to make sense of what little she knew. "Well, I can't believe it was suicide. She was . . . she was far too vital for that. And I can't imagine Karen doing it that way." How foreign her name felt in the present tense. *Not present. Recent past.* "She was terrified of the water. Her phobia was real, Robin; I saw it firsthand. She'd never choose to *drown*. Why not just take an overdose of the pills, if that's what she wanted to do?"

"Precisely."

"But then an accident seems equally unlikely. I can't imagine Karen getting close enough to the water to fall in. And if she *had* slipped and fallen, there would be marks—scrapes or bruises. You said there were none. Even if you push those things aside, an accident seems unlikely precisely *because* of the sleeping pills."

"Tell me what you mean."

"Well, Gisèle often took them, you said. She'd been drinking. . . . Maybe, in confusion, she doubled the dose, but three times? That seems significant." She stared at him and saw on his face an expression she was beginning to recognize. The arrow hitting the bull's-eye. She had reached his conclusions. It was an unhealthy triumph—as if he were playing a game but deriving little pleasure from it. "You suspect that someone drugged her, don't you? They would have to, in order to get her into the water."

"Bravo." Robin clasped his hands together, and his eyes flickered with a dark light. "A victory for the public-school system."

"But then it's *Tristan*, Robin—"

"Why?"

"She . . . she was a threat to him. I was."

"Why? He'd gotten what he wanted. She'd denied you in order to protect Nicola. Why should that threaten him?"

Amanda pressed her fingers to her throbbing temples and tried to order her thoughts. "But he's still worried about *me*. He called me. . . . Or, I should say, he returned my call. He wants to see me again. Tomorrow."

"Of course he does. You're *more* of a threat to him now that she's dead. Alive, she could refute your suspicions. Now there's no one to deflect you. He'll want to know exactly how much you know. How much you suspect."

"And you don't find that disturbing?"

"Of course I do. That's why it's worth following through."

"But—" She paused, forced herself to breathe. "But you said two people were aware she'd gone out to the pool house that night, Robin. One of them *was* Tristan?"

He frowned, hesitated. "It appears so, yes. The next morning, when she couldn't be found in her room, he suggested she may have stayed out there. But I don't believe it was Tristan that killed her, Amanda. I can't rule him out, but he was devoted to Gisèle. I don't believe he'd harm a hair on her head. And, too, the very fact that he *mentioned* the pool house seems to negate his guilt."

She regarded him dubiously. How much was friendship clouding his judgment? "Sorry I can't share your confidence, Robin. He took my sister, a fifteen-year-old child, off the streets, changed her name, and kept her hidden from her family for years." Rage flooded through her. "Did God-knows-*what* to her—"

Robin spoke quietly. "Your sister wanted to escape her life, Amanda. Whatever the nature of their relationship, it was hardly nonconsensual."

She scoffed. "Do you think a fifteen-year-old girl can give consent?"

"Not all significant relationships are sexual." A pause. "Are they?"

Was he *trying* to rile her? "Of course not, but do you really think that at the age of—thirty-five?—Tristan was looking for a teenage daughter?"

Robin ran a hand through his hair and sighed. "No, I don't."

"But then . . ."

"I don't know," he said. "I've never quite known." He rose and wandered around the tiny room, making Amanda feel even more caged. "He certainly never raped her. I know for a fact that it wasn't sexual—at least not in the traditional sense—for a long time. She once complained to me about it."

Amanda was at a loss for words. *Who had Karen been, really?*

Robin went on, "He *was* obsessed with her, I'll grant you that. But in a way they were piecing together an illusory ideal. An idyllic life, built on lies. How else could she marry? Have a child? I don't imagine we'll ever know what held the two of them together."

"Stockholm syndrome?"

"Or a kind of love. Who are we to say?"

"Well, I don't want to guess. She was my sister. I want to *know* what happened to her—"

"And that's why you agreed to have dinner with Tristan." A pause. "Even before you knew the truth."

"How did you— Oh, what's the use? Yes, Robin. I said I'd go."

"Of course you did. In a way you're as drawn to him as he is to you."

"I don't want to *date* him, if that's what you mean."

"No." His expression was shrewd. "You want inside his head."

Amanda didn't like the compulsion, but it was true. She hadn't been able to turn away from it earlier. Now she was lost to it. "Well, who do you suspect, if not Tristan?"

"Her husband, Luke Farrell."

Amanda looked up, startled.

"He was entirely financially dependent on her. He was also having an affair. Not a terribly wise combination. Gisèle wanted out of the marriage. He was seen walking to the pool house in the wee hours, which he mentioned to no one. And there are a few other reasons I'm unable to share just now, that I'm partial to him as a suspect."

"You're 'unable to share'? I feel like I'm totally in the dark."

Robin spoke steadily. "Let me take care of Luke. I need you to concentrate on Tristan. Draw him out. Talk about your history and your sister. Get him to open up. Pretend he's a future patient."

She gave him a withering glance. "I think I'm giving up psychology." *Physician, heal thyself.* "You honestly think Tristan will confess to me that Gisèle wasn't his daughter?"

"I think that *if* he will, it will be to you. He will wish to win you over to his point of view. To vindicate himself in your eyes." Robin dropped back into his chair. "We have to regard him as a suspect, but I'm too close to Tristan to see him clearly. And you deserve that much. You deserve clarity. I want a bit more, I'm afraid."

"What more?"

"Blood." His voice was ice. "His, whoever did this to her. His for hers."

"You think I don't? If my sister was *murdered*—"

"I think you'll have to understand why. And, in understanding, forgive."

"How do you know that? You don't know me."

"I recognize empathy. And you, my dear Amanda, are empathy incarnate."

"But not you."

He only laughed.

Yet there was something about Robin she trusted, implicitly. She wasn't quite sure why. Studying him, she remembered his own words of warning: *Doubt all else, Amanda, but trust yourself.* "The papers said the house was full that night, with guests who stayed on after the party. You were there, weren't you?"

"Yes." He looked at her and laughed. "Ah. You want my alibi?"

She held his eyes.

"Good for you. As it happens, I had company that night." In a tone that implied they had not been sleeping.

"Were you in love with Gisèle, Robin?"

"I loved her."

"That's a different thing."

There was a silence. "It is indeed."

"Was she in love with you?"

He said not a word, but his eyes told her. The lack of delineation between the dark iris and the pupil; it was mesmerizing, a little inhuman. It was as if he had infinite energy at his disposal, to focus or diffuse. When he focused, she felt it inside and out; when he did not, she felt oddly invisible. What, she wondered, had Gisèle felt?

"It has nothing to do with this," he said at last.

"Well, what if we're wrong? What if there's no one to blame for her death but a very cruel twist of fate? For all our theories, suicide is the decision of a moment. And no one ever understands why accidents happen." She paused, appraising him. "I think you believe—just a little bit—that she killed herself and maybe it was because of you. And for my part, I didn't know 'Gisèle' at all. I don't know how Karen could have left me to begin with, so maybe I never even knew *her*." This was a chilling sorrow unlike the others she'd known. Amanda dropped her eyes. "Maybe she'd gotten over her phobia. Maybe it *was* an accident. Or maybe . . . she killed herself rather than explain it all to her daughter. And to me."

"Ah, you see? That is empathy. We are all guilty and no one is." Robin picked up his wineglass and twirled it between his fingers, gazing at the dregs in the bottom. "But I would be willing to bet that *someone* is very guilty indeed. I felt it the moment I saw her in that swimming pool." He inhaled sharply, as if he were seeing her there now. "We both need the truth, Amanda. And we will have it."

❧

It had started to rain, and the soles of Luke's shoes squelched on the wet pavement as he walked up the street to the Dorrington Inn. He'd actually stayed there once, long before his marriage, in order to avoid his aunt after a night of underage bingeing. Set atop a hill, it was a Victorian relic filled with the kitschy sort of things they refer to in advertisements as "Old World charm": narrow, rickety stairs, cramped rooms, and ancient plumbing—the joys of which included separate faucets for hot and cold water and thus the delightful choice of either freezing or scalding one's hands.

Ancient plumbing, Luke thought, had a lot in common with modern life.

As he opened the gate, he heard the clatter of a loose shutter above being battered by the wind, and the long narrow sash windows glowed like yellow eyes. Kids probably thought the place was haunted. For Luke it was.

Amanda would have chosen it for the rates. She didn't have the money to be here, hunting him down. What he felt was guilt, pure and simple, a guilt that stopped his breath short and ran like ice through his veins, because it was compounded by so many others. What exactly was he going to say to her?

To pose as a writer for *Reflex*, she would have to have seen his face in connection with the paintings. Yet none of the art magazines had run his photo. There was nothing concrete to connect Luke Farrell to Luke Halvorson. He'd been a prick to her on the phone, and he could only guess she'd come to make him squirm. But Amanda didn't seem the type to seek revenge.

He would know soon enough.

As he mounted the last of the sagging stairs, a familiar figure met his eyes. It wasn't hers. Luke could see into the small lobby with its brothel-like décor of ornate red velvet couches and fringed lamps to a tall figure with his back to him, collecting his black trench coat and scarf from a coatrack. *Robin Dresden?* He'd hardly bring a woman *here*. By Devon standards, and particularly his, this was slumming.

Luke squinted. Quickly, he moved away from the entrance, treading lightly on the outer edges of his squelching shoes. He had no intention of explaining his presence here. Fortunately, the porch was a wraparound; he'd simply wait around the corner till Robin had gone. Through a crack in the window, he heard the impatient ringing of the bell at the front desk, and the beleaguered clerk appeared at last, fixing a smile on her face. "What can I do for you, sir?"

"Amanda Miller will be checking out tomorrow," Robin said in a clipped voice. "I'd like to take care of her bill tonight." He handed her a credit card.

"Of course, Mr. Dresden."

Luke backed away from the window; he skipped down the side steps and jogged through a maze of streets, as if pursued. The rain began to pour in torrents. At last, drenched, he took shelter beneath an awning; he leaned against a damp, darkened building and tried to quiet the thumping of his heart. But he could not quiet his mind. *What in hell was Robin Dresden doing paying Amanda's hotel bills?*

❧

Morning shone clear and bright. After a rain everything sparkled: the puddles turned to long mirrors, and sunlight danced in the drops that still clung to Nicola's oak tree, casting rainbows. Stretching, she gave a protracted yawn. She'd barely slept, but when she had, she'd entered the world of her mother's photograph—her only window into the mystery of her mother's life before her.

Nicola had never seen a single photo of her mother as a child. Gisèle never spoke of her childhood. Grand-père often talked of having grown up like Nicola, an only child surrounded by art and artists; he detailed the architecture of their homes and his mother's love for painting, for music and books. Yet he never spoke of Gisèle's mother, and Gisèle didn't either. It was almost as if she'd never had one.

Nicola's father's side of the family wasn't much better. Luke didn't even speak to his father, and his mother had died when he was Nicola's age. But at least there were photographs. There was also Great-Aunt Eleanor, though she viewed children as one might a problematic strain of alien plant life.

And so the tattered snapshot opened intriguing new doors. Could her mother have been adopted? It was romantic to cast her in the role of Sara in *A Little Princess*, orphaned and rescued by a kindly man after a long string of misfortunes. But it didn't seem likely. Why would her mother have kept such a secret?

That morning before school (even the sixth grade was rendered less abysmal by her new treasure), Nicola went to visit her grandfather's paintings. Over the years she had come to regard the art collection as a kind of family album, for there was no other. She named all the subjects in the paintings and assigned them familial relationships: aunts, uncles, cousins. And the gallery was a good place to think. It was very still, cool, and quiet, with a dark cherrywood floor and whitewashed walls. Spotlights were trained on each of the paintings, and it had the hushed air of a museum. Beside the door was a keypad. The secret code was Nicola's birthday. Inside, the room was temperature-controlled, the door specially fitted to keep the air within from mingling with the outside air. Nicola always had the sense she was stepping into a refrigerator.

She wasn't in the refrigerator alone. Marc Kreicek startled her, though he was a familiar sight, seated with his easel before a sketch by Degas, his hair sticking out at angles because he had a habit of running his hand through it as he worked. Nicola always thought she'd spot a streak of cadmium red or titanium white there. Today's medium, charcoal, wouldn't show in his dark hair, but his fingers were black with it and there was a streak on his cheek.

"Good morning, Marc."

"Ah, *malý květina*." This meant "little flower," and he called her that because Robin did, when they spoke in his language. He often did things Robin did. "Good morning."

Marc sipped coffee from a large mug and regarded the sketch with a critical eye. All the while he jiggled his knee impatiently. He was not a morning person, Nicola knew, and could go great periods of time without speaking at all. It was best not to intrude on this fragile pre-breakfast state. But she grew tired of watching his knee jiggle. She drew up beside him. "That's very good. Almost as good as the real thing."

"Almost? You wound me."

"Well, it's not done. I bet it'll look better than the original when it's done."

Marc gave a nod of appreciation. He was always more formal with her than anyone else. Nicola supposed it was simply that he didn't know how to talk to kids. His eyes returned to his sketch. The original was called *Lying Nude*. The prostrate model's face was turned away from her viewer, and Nicola was reminded uneasily of her father's paintings.

"How come women in art never wear any clothes, Marc?"

His hand froze in midair and managed to express annoyance. "Sometimes they do. But the female body is one of the loveliest things in nature."

"Well, that sketch is my least favorite," Nicola said. "I mean, nothing against yours, but the woman looks uncomfortable and sort of ashamed."

"Perhaps she is."

"It's a little like some of Dad's, don't you think? You know, of Mom."

"It is very like."

"I thought the paintings meant Dad loved her."

Marc shrugged noncommittally.

"I suppose it's possible to love someone *too* much. . . ." Nicola pressed.

"It is very possible, I should think. Especially if that someone doesn't love you."

"I guess that's what I mean. That's why people have affairs, isn't it?"

To her surprise, he laughed. "Nicola, *malý květina*, these are not questions you should be asking me. I don't know why people *marry*."

But she persisted. "Was Dad having an affair, do you think?"

"You are too young to concern yourself with such things."

"That means yes, doesn't it?" His expression told her it did. "I've been wondering if Mom had affairs, too. Do you think so?"

"Why on earth do you wish to dwell on such things now?"

Nicola bit her lip. "I just feel like there was a lot I didn't know about her. And I thought I knew everything." She scratched her head. "Were *you* in love with her, Marc?"

He gave a great hollow laugh. "Love is life's greatest hoax, my sweet. There is no love between men and women, because there is no understanding. There is only delusion."

She stared. "That's a terrible way to look at things."

"Ah, well. Yes. That's why we all prefer the delusion."

Nicola wasn't sure exactly what he meant and didn't want to ask. She took it that Marc's delusion involved loving her mother and that she hadn't loved him back. With effort, Nicola changed the subject. "What do you do with all your copies?"

"Nothing," he said. "It is merely a hobby of mine."

"You don't sell them?"

"It wouldn't be worth the trouble." His tone was cross. "Copies do not sell for much."

She gazed around her. "But what's the point of copying copies?"

A spark flickered in his eyes. "There is very little point, but these are very fine copies."

She hesitated. "Well, between you and me, I don't think these are copies at all."

"No?"

"No." Nicola stood before the withering gaze of the man she had christened "Pierre," in a painting by Degas called *The Collector:* a collector like her grandfather and Robin, she supposed. "I know we all have to pretend, because Grand-père could get in trouble if anyone knew. Even though the paintings are his. It doesn't seem fair. But if he wanted to bring the paintings here, I figure he'd have to replace them with something."

"Well, yes. They would be missed, I think."

"That's just it. You go to Paris a lot and stay at his house there. My idea is that *your* copies end up there and these are the originals."

He stared at her. "Indeed?"

"You're a very good painter. No one would ever know."

Marc's index finger tapped his bony knee and left smudges on his faded jeans. His expression grew amused. "I'm flattered. But then why am I making more copies here?"

"Grand-père says you're a perfectionist. Maybe you're trying to do a better one. Or maybe it just makes you happy to paint." She shrugged, frowning. "I don't really expect you to tell me the truth. Everyone lies to me. They think I'm too young to understand."

"I think you understand a good deal more than you should, *malý květina*." But it wasn't really a reprimand. His clear green eyes glinted with an unhealthy light. "Shall I tell you a secret?"

Nicola nodded. Why did people ask that? Did anyone ever say no?

"If my copies are as good as you say, then all of *these* might be copies as well. Who would know? I might have replaced every one of them." He smirked. "Collectors are only interested in possessing a thing no one else can possess. But in the end it's all just strokes of a brush, Nicola. With the right provenance, a copy would not even be questioned. People can't tell the real thing from an illusion. *That* is true art."

Nicola gazed around her. "But doesn't Grand-père know which is which?"

"I'm afraid he knows least of all."

"But they belong to him."

"Art doesn't belong to anyone." Marc picked up his mug of coffee from the floor and sipped from it, appraising her over the rim. After a moment the flicker in his eyes died and his usual heavy-lidded, bored expression returned. "Come, now. Do not look so disapproving. It's best not to believe anything I say." She already knew that. "I am only teasing you."

"How do you live if you don't sell your paintings?"

"I have other work."

"What do you do?"

"Well. I work for Robin."

"I didn't know that. What do you do for him?"

"A bit of everything." An indecipherable expression. "Things he doesn't wish to do."

"Does he pay you a lot?"

Marc laughed. He had a big laugh; it echoed in the barren room. "You could say so, yes."

Nicola shifted her weight, debating with herself. She wanted to talk to *someone* about the photograph, and suddenly Marc seemed perfect. He wouldn't care enough about anything she said to repeat it. "Marc? Could Mom have been adopted, do you think?"

The question took him aback. "What's given you that idea?"

"I found a picture of her as a kid. She's with another girl, and they look like sisters." Nicola extracted the photo from the deep pocket of her sweater and handed it to him. "See? Only . . . the names on the back are all wrong."

Marc gazed down, flipped it over, and gazed up again. "I should forget it, my sweet. These must be old friends of your mother."

"No, it's her."

"The bones of her face are different, her cheekbones."

"No, no. See, that's just the shadow from the tree. Anyway, people change—"

"Yes, people do. Not their bones." His clear eyes were fixed on her; they were unsettling. "What is it you believe? That your mother had another name? And a sister? That's very unlikely." He ran his blackened fingers through his hair and frowned. "You should forget this, Nicola. It can only lead to unhappiness for you. The photograph can't bring your mother back. And she had no secret life, I promise you."

"Well," Nicola said stubbornly, "I thought I'd ask Grand-père. He'll know for sure."

A flicker of pity crossed Marc's face. "Yes, yes. He would certainly know. But I would not ask him."

"Why not?"

"He may find the question insulting. Think of it. To imply that his daughter was not his?"

"But—"

"Forget it." Marc said firmly. He returned his attention to his sketch.

"Well, I'll let you go back to . . . to your hobby. I'm sorry I bothered you."

"You bother me less than most people do." This seemed to surprise him. "Run along and play, *malý květina*. You need fresh air and sunshine. The air is too still in here. It is for paintings."

❧

The moment Luke both anticipated and dreaded had at last arrived.

"Mr. Dresden called while you were out, Mr. Farrell." Henri spoke in a clipped voice. "To discuss the Gisèle Paintings." He was good, old Henri. No sign of disapproval in his expression, no emotion in his eyes. The only giveaway was the avoidance of first names, compounded by the use of the formal "Gisèle Paintings." Rather than the member of the family he was, Henri sounded like a paragon of butlery.

Luke knew it was only his way of putting distance between himself and the sale and distribution of Gisèle. That's how he would see it. And deep down, Luke had to agree with him.

Still further down, he feared that what Robin really wished to speak with him about was Amanda Miller. The more Luke thought about it, the more convinced he was that Robin had paid her off to keep quiet about the affair. He'd backed the paintings personally; his reputation was on the line. More than this, he would wish to protect Gisèle. He'd always been oddly protective of her.

He was *not* protective of Luke. What would he want from him in return?

He steeled himself and called. Robin spoke in a remote, business-like tone. They would begin with an intimate exhibit in just three weeks, he said, and invite select critics and press, escalating interest by offering only a few of the paintings for sale at a time. It would be delicately handled, not a zoo. He had set up a few interviews by phone, but they should meet to discuss how these would be best handled. They scheduled a meeting that Friday over lunch, and Robin quickly rang off.

Somehow Robin's silence was more ominous than open accusations. Why was he keeping his knowledge of Amanda a secret? Could it be that he simply felt the subject beneath him? Beside the point? Something dealt with and swept under the rug? He was very shrewd about the art world, while Luke was befuddled by it. At times he wondered whether the art world paid any attention to art at all.

He did know that Gisèle's death had only fueled interest in the paintings, like tossing kindling onto the fire. Rumors were rife that her accident was anything but—collectors and critics alike were champing at the bit to examine the crime scene, even if it were only in oil on canvas. And Luke had to admit, he was afraid of what they might find there.

XIII

THE RAPE

Gisèle read the books. I found them beneath the bed in her room. (A prop, this—both the room and the bed. We made a show of making it look slept in for Nora.) They were bookmarked.

The apartment hummed with her sexual awakening, and the weather grew warmer as if in accompaniment. She sunbathed on the balcony, the black bikini she'd chosen gathering the heat of the sun to her in a sort of foreplay. I watched as she lay on her back, her knees bent and thighs slightly parted. Occasionally she would arch her back as if to meet an invisible lover. She made believe she was stretching, but I was not fooled. She glowed, and her skin was warm to the touch. Ah, my beautiful Gisèle.

I began to observe her baths, for they had grown suspiciously long and frequent. I cracked the door to observe her in the tub. As ever, I reveled in the strange delight of observing her unseen, but now it made me see how much she put on for me. I saw her caress herself, raising her legs and spreading them beneath the cascading stream of water until she choked back her moans, her eyes narrowing feverishly as she came. One night I walked in at the pivotal moment, which is not during but just before. I sat beside her. Her eyes opened. She saw me there and jumped, her legs crashing down into the water, splashing me. She gathered her arms around her knees, her mouth open and a guilty expression on her face.

I placed my finger on her lips so she would not speak. When I bent forward to kiss her open mouth, I could taste the heat of her, and her lips were newly languorous, her tongue not the timid fish darting from its cave but brazen, lingering and exploring. She wanted to touch me, spreading her palms to my chest, her fingers traveling up and down my neck, over my shoulders and down, down. She'd never done that before.

I helped her from the tub and wrapped her in a towel. I carried her to the bed, and she lay there, just as she had when sunbathing, her knees bent and thighs parted so I could see the glistening there. The lights were on, but she did not try to hide from me. I caressed her gently and then dipped my head, using my tongue to arouse her again; I had to force my gentleness. I could have consumed her.

I teased her and toyed with her, plucking at her tiny hardened bud, sucking it and then releasing it, the pressure of my lips and my tongue direct and then indirect, leisurely. It made her writhe beneath me and brought her breath in quick gasps. How had I ever been fooled before? Was I so out of practice? I felt her hands on my shoulders and did not stop, her fingers through my hair and did not stop, and at last she was lost, giving in to me, her moans incoherent and uncontrolled. Her hips arched to meet me, as violent as my tongue, on her, inside her, part of her.

I looked up at her face caught in the glow of the lamplight like an angel, a shocked, surprised angel, her hair lying in damp ringlets around her face, lips swollen from our kissing and deep red, her skin moist and eyes dewy and hazed in the fringe of dark lashes: a blue-green slash of light. All the light I needed.

She reached her hand to me, and I raised myself on one arm; my other hand ran over her breasts and between her legs, as if I might take her then, and it was as if I had, swimming in the infinite softness of her.

"Please, Tristan," she murmured. Her hand slid down my chest. I caught it in mine and lowered myself on top of her.

"Please, what?" And though I spoke in a whisper, I felt suddenly fierce, to be denied the act but not the words. Not the words. "What do you want me to do, Gisèle?"

It embarrassed her, so foreign was it to *have* the desire, let alone artic- ulate it—but I was relentless, waiting just for the words. At last, her voice heartbreakingly soft, "Make love to me, Tristan. I want you to. I want . . . you."

The emotion made her voice tremble and break and made the romance-novel script real. A throbbing pulsed through my body. I had the feeling that were she to beg, all that hunger in her eyes, begging me, I would experience a climax as a boy does in wet dreams, never needing so much as a touch. It would be my sort of climax, of course, an internal shuddering, so very little to show for it.

But I could not. I could not have her see me diminished. And so I pressed my eyes closed and eased beside her; I ran my fingers lightly over her nude body. "Just rest now, *ma petite*. There's no rush." The tight skin, the taut little handful of breast and pert upturned nipple, the hollow of her throat, rise of her chest, the slope of her abdomen. I will never forget the way she looked then: more child still than woman. She would never again be quite so open, for at that moment I had both her naïveté and her belief. The two were symbiotic, host and parasite, and the truth would abolish it all.

For here at last is the rub. In our strange way, we were quite perfect for each other. The erection she'd always found so abhorrent, I could not maintain.

It was not always so. As I've noted, I began very early, losing my virginity at the age of thirteen, and was a happily promiscuous young man afterward—until the ripe old age of nineteen and a half: coitus interruptus, quite literally.

Alas, now you find sympathy for poor Sabina! She knew the grim realities, as it happens; we each got what we wanted—she a legitimate last name for her child and me a (however illegitimate) marriage entitling me to my inheritance. Her pregnancy allowed me the illusion of virility; I allowed her the illusion of respectability. We played a rousing game of gin rummy on our wedding night.

There is no medical reason for my impotence, and no known cure. I've tried herbal remedies, Western medication, Eastern meditation, acupressure and acupuncture (not quite the painful image that rushes to mind; the needles are not placed *there*). And still nothing. An aftereffect of my drug-addled childhood, perhaps, or a recessive family gene. I sometimes wonder if it wasn't this that drove my father mad.

Ah, yes. How very apt the novel Gisèle was reading at the time of our first meeting—*The Sun Also Rises*—and the poetic choice of my early pseudonym. It was all very poignantly apt. Perhaps you suspected from the start, for it explains my restraint. A pity it is not such a noble thing.

Yet our relationship was more than mere masochism on my part, for I am better off than poor Jake Barnes. When I found Gisèle, I felt a stirring I hadn't felt in fifteen years. Not enough for penetration, intercourse, coitus—all the lovely mechanistic terms for the act of love—but enough for release. I had been a halfhearted priest, my chastity forced on me, but at last I was delivered. She had come to release me.

And for that one transcendent moment, I had released her. Gisèle lay curled against me, her silken hair on my chest, her body tingling against my skin as if enchanted. She murmured against me. My sweet, innocent darling. She felt I'd made her new; I'd brought her to life. But I thought of Dresden's words, the effect of his words and his books on her. And in my heart I knew it was not I who had done so.

I didn't have long to wait before I saw Dresden's sketch. I should say sketches—for in plural they were. Gisèle gave them to me for my thirty-seventh birthday. I could tell them by their size, of course, eleven by fourteen. How had they come to be? I'd made certain she did not meet him two weeks later, or three, that she wasn't alone with him again.

Privately, I seethed as I gently removed the bow and ran my finger beneath the carefully taped folds. The aplomb upon which I so prided myself gave way once again to the basest jealousy. Yet how exigent the surface smile I directed toward her eager upturned face. And the light tone: "Whatever could this be?"

There were three. The first was a chaste scene. They had somehow bypassed Henri and me both, for the setting was my apartment, no less. Gisèle perched self-consciously on a stool at the breakfast bar. It was brilliantly done, for one could feel her self-consciousness rise from the page, her youth and inexperience. He had captured it all. She sat on her hands (a child's attention span), her lips parted anxiously (eager to please), but her eyes were buoyant, alive, exultant. (He's sketching *me*!)

It hadn't been a real sketch, she confessed. Not at first. It was no more than a doodle done quite quickly, she said, on a napkin the day he'd asked her about California and come to see "me." That's what had given her the gift idea. Privately, I wondered how much of the idea had been hers.

The second sketch was abundantly familiar. Gisèle was curled up in the corner of the sofa, a thoughtful V between her eyebrows, light climbing into the pensive eyes and her mouth slightly parted, the full lower lip indented where she bit it. Yet in the loose waves of her hair and the legs curved beneath her, the shadowed neckline of her floral dress, and the Y fold of fabric between her thighs, it was quite erotic. She was on the brink.

In the third she became a woman before my eyes.

She was nude. Her curls fell to her bare shoulders, her arms wrapped around her knees to hide her breasts and crossed at her ankles to hide the rest. But it was . . . so very sensual. The stab of it ran through me. *Mon enfant, ma petite.* You have grown up.

Tentatively, "Do you like them, Tristan?"

I could only manage a nod. My fingers shook, and mad thoughts coursed through my brain: How dare he? It was the worst kind of betrayal, a kind of artistic adultery. And he claimed to be my friend.

She must have read my expression. "For the last one, Rob wasn't even in the room with me." Rob? "It was from a photograph. He told me on the phone to do it. I took it in the mirror in the bedroom—you know, the oval floor mirror that tilts? I posed myself. He didn't see anything."

It quite broke my heart. I pulled her into my arms and kissed her salty-sweet skin. "*Ma petite.* They're beautiful. I am speechless."

And I was. My mind was flooded with horrors. Robin had managed to speak to her on the phone, exchange film and God knows what else behind my back. . . . Surely this had not been the only photograph. What had become of the others? The questions kept me awake all night. The answer was always the same: If I did not do something, I would lose her.

I attempted to contact Robin the next day. His number, like mine, was unlisted, but with a few discreet inquiries I learned he was still in the city. I'd nearly resolved to swallow my pride and arrive at his loft unannounced when I happened upon him in the Oak Bar at the Plaza.

Gisèle was home doing her studies with Henri; I'd stopped in with a friend for a drink. And there was Dresden, beneath one of Everett Shinn's muted murals of nineteenth-century Manhattan, sharing a bottle of wine with two other men in a cloud of wispy gray smoke—looking as if he'd just materialized from the bottle. He waved us over. I was with a fellow French expatriate: a "diarist," by which I mean someone with enough money to be without profession but who vainly seeks to make his life interesting enough to publish. Michel was only too delighted by this glamorous turn of events, having read the article on Robin in *Face*.

We finished off their second bottle of Lafite Rothschild and ordered a third, a '74 Pauillac. Dresden may have been a bastard, but he possessed excellent taste in wine. For the time being, the other men acted as buffers between us. But I was determined to outlast them.

Robin had a subtle way of controlling the conversation that I wouldn't have noticed had I not sought a point upon which to criticize him—and thus I spent a good portion of the afternoon feigning interest in Kant's transcendental dialectic.

I'm drawn to the discussion of ideas, certainly, but philosophy has always seemed to me the frantic chasing after many unfurling rolls of toilet paper at once. This particular roll concerned the notion that there is a reality beyond that which can be detected by our senses—that is, beyond the realm of the mind that perceives it. The others, whom I suspected were also not up on their Kant, benefited from my blatant ignorance. "*Eh bien*," I said, "as we're limited to the minds we have, what matters what reality lies beyond them?"

Robin laughed. "Well, yes. Kant would agree. But the Pythagorean theorem was true before Pythagoras. Perception isn't static. And perception is reality. So isn't it rather a matter of expanding perception?"

"To what end?"

He shrugged. "To an infinite end. The notion of an end is always illusory."

Robin claimed, a bit like the surrealists, that art had a transcendental source; one channeled the impulses rather than created them. It was a constant dance of perception and that which there is to perceive. The infinite. Fine-tuning one's senses was the most elementary step. The second, he claimed, was the recognition that everything we touch, taste, and see is a limitation—a parenthesis in the larger sentence. Finally, by entering the illusion and learning to manipulate perception, we could "tug aside the curtain and see what's going on backstage."

"And you have done this?" my friend, Michel, inquired dryly.

"Many times."

"Simply by painting?"

"No, no. I try to channel it when I'm painting, but I engage it by out-witting my conscious mind." Robin shrugged. "Meditation is the sim-plest method and the hardest to practice. It's nothing new, of course, freeing the mind of distraction, focusing on nothingness. Nothingness is the misnomer. In light it would be white. In pigment black. In noth-ing lies everything."

"*Mais oui*," conceded Michel grudgingly.

"One can access it easily in others through hypnosis, by overload-ing the part of the mind that processes surface information. Essentially distracting the watchdog." In the dim room, Dresden's eyes appeared almost black and his smile was a little wicked. And there *was* something hypnotic in everything about him: his voice, his posture, his ease, and his certainty. "In meditation and in hypnosis," he said, "one is in dia-logue with something quite distinct and perceived as separate from the self. Something omniscient."

Michel shook his head, determined to hold up the atheist end. "Ah. I do not believe in God."

Robin shrugged. "Call it something else, then."

"How can I believe in something I've never experienced?"

"If you're alive, you've experienced it. You just don't know it. The mind is full of elaborate response systems designed to keep us safe and igno-rant. Reinforced by pain and fear, they lead to societal systems imbued with the same: religion, law. But if one has the will to override those reflexes, an entire unexplored landscape is open to him." He smiled his odd smile. Here and gone. "Those who fear are lost."

Michel, who was rather too pampered to interest himself in the over-riding of pleasant reflexes, let the subject drop. Robin ordered another bottle of wine, and I abandoned the notion of outdrinking him and began to play juvenile word games in my head (Kant can't). His companions rose to leave, citing appointments uptown, and Michel joined them. He has never paid full fare in his life, and his interest had shifted from Dresden to one of his friends, whose sexual proclivities were better suited to his own.

"Excellent," Dresden said when they had left us, with a remarkably self-effacing smile. "I rather hoped to lose them with that. You wish to speak to me about Gisèle, I think."

Now that the opportunity was here, I was oddly hesitant. "*Oui*," I said at last. "I wish to know if you did more than sketch her. If you . . . if you intend to try something more. I cannot let you do that, you see." The alcohol made me brave. And careless. "Gisèle belongs to me."

"Indeed?" And in his voice was a contemptible blend of amusement and pity.

"*Oui*."

Robin scratched his head. "Shall we play chess while we talk?"

And so we played: the match made manifest, however clichéd. Another drink and I'd have raised a pleasant suggestion of a duel. But you may have caught on by now to the fact that anything I could do, he could do better. I say this without rancor. The traits I admire most in myself I saw in him concentrated. I was not short (certainly not by French standards), yet he was quite tall. I was refined, of good appearance, well educated. He was as refined, of better appearance, and something beyond well educated. His bandying of philosophical ideas and linguistic skill was more than showing off, more than an interior Rolodex of anecdotes and theories; it had the exciting feeling of discovery to it, of happening upon the rusted keys to hidden doors.

And, too, there was the feeling that he was playing all the while. That life and death, winning and losing, love and loss—all the things that make up the human comedy every one of us muddles through with dreadful seriousness—were to him no more than a game of chess. His brilliance startled me. And yet I fancied us kindred. The reason, I imagined, for both my interest and my distrust of him.

Happily, I know enough of chess to get through the first three moves intact, and so we settled in. I brought up his visit to my apartment, his communications with Gisèle, the sketches. I told him he had quite captured her—and if he ever sketched her again, I would kill him.

He chose his words carefully. "I've only sketched her, Tristan. I didn't paint her."

"I don't see how that makes a bit of difference."

"Hmm."

"'Hmm' what?"

"Charcoal and marble are the only media fit to capture the human form as it can be perceived with the eye. To paint is to climb inside; it's not to study a thing but to possess it." A shrug. "I didn't paint her."

"Is that a fancy way of saying you didn't sleep with her? But I know that." I cleared my throat, unable to admit to the indignity of having spied on them. "I would know if you had. I know her."

"Ah."

"I simply want to hear your intentions." But, in spite of me, curiosity won out. "What exactly would you have painted that you didn't sketch?"

"Do you really want to know?"

"Yes."

"I'd have her part her legs for me and paint her magnified and fragmented—an abstract in flesh and rose that people would comment on when they came to dinner. Only the two of us would know what it was: that the core of her hung four foot by five on my wall." A shrug. "For a start."

"You're an odd man."

He gave a cursory glance at the board and moved. "The point is, the sketches were for you. From her. I'm incidental in the transaction, surely."

I was not so sure. "Why did you question her about California?"

"Because it interested me. People do, for the most part. People with ambiguous origins." An unassuming smile. "It is my hobby."

I made my move absently, scarcely dropping my eyes to the board. "Why do you suppose she came to New York?"

"Don't you know?"

"I'm asking."

"I'd say a misguided ambition of some kind: singing, dancing—"

"Why is that?"

"Because these are the reasons young girls from California come to New York."

I noticed he did not confront me outright with what he knew: that I had met Gisèle in California and, by implication, had engineered her escape. "Yes," I agreed simply. "Yes."

"And now her ambitions are limited to you."

I opened my mouth to protest, but it was true. Her former goals, the dreams born and nurtured in the tiny dark bedroom in San Francisco, were neglected now. She never spoke of writing anymore, though she read avidly and wrote eloquently of the books she read. (I was privy to her essays.) She was happy, I think, to make me her dream. "That's hardly fair. She's too young to worry about such things."

"It wasn't meant to disparage her."

No. Not her, but me.

I gazed at the board. He was offering an exchange of queens. I hate to lose my queen. I didn't take it. I also chose not to take the bait. "What is it you want with us, Robin? Gisèle is everything to me—"

"And you are everything to her, by default. You're smothering her, Tristan."

And I saw then—too late—that he could put me in checkmate; he saw that I saw. He pushed the board away. "I've had too much wine, I think." A lie; he was as clearheaded as ever. He didn't want to win, nor to offend me by letting me do so.

I am not a master chess player, but I know enough of the game to know when I am losing. "I don't mean to smother her. I mean to protect her. And you're trying to take her from me."

"That implies she's a thing to give or take."

I blundered on under the influence of jealousy and too much wine. "You've created a secret relationship with her. You call her. When do you call her?"

"I don't. She calls me, Tristan. She told me she wasn't able to take phone calls or to sit for her next sketch. You wouldn't 'let' her. And you were always there." He held my eyes. "And so I told her I'd leave her a camera—that she was to, in essence, sketch herself. I left it outside your door at a time she claimed was 'safe.' I believe this was while you were in the shower. Likewise, a few days later, she left it there for me. It was all very clandestine, and therefore all the more appealing to her." A pause. "You have nothing to worry about from me, Tristan. I respect another's obsessions. But if you keep this up, you will lose her. Control is . . . well, it's rather like chess. One doesn't win so much as allow another to lose. One doesn't take control so much as allow another to relinquish it."

I cursed in French. The impertinence of it all. He was ten years my junior. How dare he advise me?

He laughed at this, as if he'd read my thoughts. "What are you so afraid of, Tristan? I wouldn't try to spirit her away. She simply needs a friend, you must see that. She needs more than you."

And this time, with effort, I took it in.

"For myself, I have few friends," Robin went on amiably, offering me a cigarette as he took one for himself. "Many hangers-on, but few friends. I suspect it is the same with you." I was cynical enough to wonder if the suspicion prompted the admission, but I was beyond caring. He smiled, a real smile without irony, and held out his hand. "Shall we declare a truce?"

In spite of all the wordplay and intellectual games, he possessed a disarming honesty. The wine was good, the Turkish cigarette. I felt suddenly quite well. In spite of myself, I had to admit that I liked him. That I would miss him were he to disappear back into his bottle.

That afternoon was the seal of our friendship. As we parted company, he invited us to dinner at the weekend, and I pretended to need the address of his loft. It was the last of my pretenses with him, and a rare pleasure to shed it. But I will forever remember the long walk home. Lost to the sounds of the city around me, my mind was silent and still. I studied the cracks in the pavement, and I saw myself there suddenly, an impotent, envious creature, and I could not be that. I had to be impervious to that creature. I had to be stronger than it.

The next morning Gisèle found me naked, shaving before the mirror. In the past her eyes would roll away, or she'd speak and look only at my eyes, never letting her gaze travel over my body. But that day she sat on the edge of the tub and drank in my nakedness. I could see her in the mirror, peeking over the rim of her coffee cup with new curiosity. With pleasure.

It aroused me keenly, however invisible my arousal, a heightening of the senses merely. Yet it filled me with a frustration so sharp I felt as if

I were flayed open there, reflected. She only smiled naughtily. I smiled back and tried to see what she saw. In the abstract my reflection pleased me: broad-shouldered and narrow-hipped. I was perhaps a bit too thin, but it is better to err on that side. The hair on my chest was neither too much nor too little. The occasional wisp of gray, I thought, lent character. And I had always been proud of my—what is the inoffensive term for it? It doesn't work. I can think of nothing less offensive than that to the censors—*ma bite*, as we say in French. *Ma bite* was more bark than . . .

But Gisèle's eyes darted up and down, lingering there curiously.

Daily she grew more confident. She began to tease me. She wore dresses without panties, parting her legs for me when no one else could see. She invited me in while she showered, so that I was often unable to resist joining her. On Henri's day off, she strolled around the apartment in nothing but panties and one of my shirts, until at last I would rip them off to taste her, to touch her. But that was all.

Soon her puzzlement turned to irritation. Hurt. "Tristan," she'd murmur. "Don't you want to?"

At last it was impossible not to tell her. There were other things we could do, I explained. Things we could buy. Things I'd already bought. Different ways I could satisfy her.

"But I can't satisfy *you*." She stared at me as though I'd betrayed her.

"But you do, *ma petite*."

Her eyes filled with tears. "All this time you made me think it was me, when you *knew*?"

"Would you rather I were 'normal,' Gisèle? That I took advantage of you? Raped you? Surely—"

But at the moment, in her fickle feminine way, she had forgotten all the past. I saw only hunger and disappointment where the fearful little girl used to be and was filled with distaste at the transformation. "I want to give to *you*, Tristan, not just take. I want to experience everything normal people experience. Not just physical things. But love. Real love. You told me we would experience everything, remember?" Her mouth was small and cruel. Her eyes cold. "You can't spend all your life pleasing me. I don't want to spend my whole life being pleased."

I was dazed by this new, unforeseen variant of my inadequacy. "Whyever not?"

"Because I want to *share*." And the ice in her eyes melted into tears. "I want to share. I want to have your . . . your children, Tristan; I want us to be normal."

And I couldn't bear the word. "Fuck normal." How I hated the word. "Fuck normal, Gisèle." My voice was foreign; I saw the whole picture of my life quaking before me, splintering.

She tried to pull away from me then, and I was filled with violence.

I pressed my mouth against hers and dragged her to the floor, pinning her down with my weight. "Do you want normal?" Taking pleasure in her wide, startled eyes, I ripped the buttons off her linen blouse, savoring the popping sound as they burst one after the other and hit the wooden floor. I relished the cinematic connotations of this, the romance-hero illusion. It was me. It could be me. I would make it so. "Is this what you want?"

I slid up her skirt; she squirmed under me but was already wet beneath my fingers. I forced her thighs further apart and after a cursory caress plunged my middle finger into her; she gasped, in pleasure or in pain, I wasn't sure. For a moment I did not care. I only wanted to make her feel. She gasped something unintelligible. I worked deeper in and out, two fingers, three. She stiffened, and tears welled in her eyes. I rolled her over, my fingers still inside her, and then she was half moaning, half crying.

I told her to wait. She lay on the floor. I'd purchased something for this occasion, though I had never been quite able to envision using the crude latex thing on her. I did it slowly, was less brutal, more precise. I felt Gisèle stiffen all over with pain. But she never let out a cry, and after a moment I saw her fists relax, her fingers grasp at the carpet. She spread her legs wider, rising up on her elbows and knees. I was more excited than I had ever been in my life, with any woman I'd been with in my youth. I was beside her, behind her, taking her. At last she gasped, "Oh, Tristan . . ." with a kind of despair. There was a sudden stirring in my groin, that is all, and deep release. I was, for an instant, replete.

And she? I was afraid to ask. Her response had been ambiguous at best. I knew it had not been passion in her voice. I gathered her to me. On her face was a fragile, broken smile, and tears glistened in her eyes. Fool that I am, I took them for joy.

XIV

READING THE PART

NICOLA'S MORNING STARTED OUT the same as always. She walked into class like a lone soldier advancing on an army of enemies, her face stoic and her stomach full of knots.

The boys had warmed up to her because it turned out she was good at sports. But with the girls she was still *persona non grata*. Kelly Henshaw was the top of the sixth-grade food chain, and she'd decided Nicola was out. She never picked her for teams in PE; she made a game of *not* picking her, and all her friends followed suit. They called her sickly (because she made a point of being absent whenever possible) and taunted her with endless cries of "Ri-co-la!"

And why did it hurt so much to be likened to a cough drop anyway?

She'd managed to make one new friend. Meghan Phillips was new to Prescott, too, and sat next to her in homeroom. She said Kelly was just jealous of Nicola. But this morning Nicola discovered that Meghan had changed seats. She avoided eye contact and sat smirking and giggling in the corner with Kelly. She'd been enlisted.

Nicola went to her seat and lifted the top of her desk to place her books inside. It was filled with bags of Ricolas. With a clang she dropped it shut. Tears stung her eyes. She heard giggling behind her.

Don't cry. Stop it. Who cares about them?

But she did care. And all through first period, she tried to swallow the lump in her throat. She focused hard on three o'clock, when her grandfather would be there to pick her up. But when Mrs. Perkins called on her to spell "ostracized," three o'clock seemed a lifetime away. School, she decided, wasn't about learning at all. It was more like a chess game. And the key to chess, Robin had told her, was to anticipate. To stay three or four moves ahead. Only Nicola couldn't seem to anticipate anything but disaster, and this made disastrous things happen. It seemed she had forgotten how to expect good things.

At recess she complained of a stomachache, which wasn't really a lie, and at the office she asked the secretary to call her grandfather's private line. *Please come. Please come. . . .*

He came. With a keen glance, she could see he knew that her problem wasn't medical. Still, he frowned with convincing concern and lamented the flu that was going around; he actually managed to wipe the snooty expression off the secretary's face as he signed her out. And when they got into the car, he glanced at Nicola, a twinkle in his eyes and his expression affectionate. "Well, shall we go for ice cream, *mon chaton*? I understand it's good for stomachaches."

He winked at her, and for the first time that day she managed a smile.

"Can we stop at the college after, Grand-père? We could see Robin, and I'd like to go to the library."

"*Mais oui.* You will need some good reading material if you intend to make it a long illness."

Nicola had read practically everything in the children's library in town, but the truth was that she was too young for most everything in the college library. She liked to try the fiction and particularly loved the oversize art books. There was a whole section on fashion design. But mostly she went there to see Robin—or, as he put it, so he could see a bit more of her.

They usually found him in the art room of the stone tower on campus. His uncle had been one of the founders of the school and donated the land with the provision that the historic tower remain. Robin had refurbished the exterior to its original state and converted the interior into a sort of dormitory and dining hall for his students, with an art room at the top. In truth, it was an understatement to call it a "room": the space was the height of two floors, with an open gallery above. Light flooded in from long lancet windows that encircled it. Nicola thought of her grand-

father on the railroad trestle and realized now why he never went up to
the gallery. There was a wrought-iron railing, but it wasn't high, and it
was a long drop to the wooden floor below, where a hodgepodge of tabletops were scattered with art supplies and easels held works in progress.

Apparently Robin had no fear of heights; they usually found him
working on something high above them and not even visible at first.
Recognizing their step, he would call out a greeting. *Well, salut, Tristan.
Nico, how are you, darling?* But there was no such greeting today.

As they moved farther into the vast room, Nicola could see a figure
upstairs silhouetted against the light. It wasn't Robin. After a moment
Marc Kreicek turned; he went to the railing and called down. "Ah, a surprise. Good afternoon, Tristan. Nicola, my sweet. I'm afraid Robin's out
today. Gone to lunch with Luke."

Nicola felt her grandfather stiffen beside her. She could tell he wasn't
happy to see Marc, and she wondered why. He said icily, "Well, that can
mean only one thing."

"Yes, yes." Marc descended the stairs like a cat, barely making a
sound. "The exhibition's back on, it seems. The paintings are too good
to go unseen."

How could Marc be so cavalier about her mother's death? He spoke of
the paintings as if they were just paintings—not pieces of her. Nicola had
come to hate the idea of strangers ogling her mother at an exhibition.
She knew that her grandfather felt as she did, though he said nothing
at all. He busied himself in the way people do when they desire a distraction, picking in an unfocused way at the clutter on one of the tables,
where Marc must have mixed his paints.

"What are you painting, Marc?" Nicola asked him, to break the awkward silence.

"As it happens, Robin's asked me to work on something for the exhibition. A complementary piece." He cast a sidelong glance at Tristan.
"A surprise."

"Can we see?" Nicola asked.

Marc clucked his tongue in disapproval. "Then it wouldn't be a surprise, would it?"

"But I won't be at the exhibition. I can't go. It would just be too . . .
weird."

"Well, I'm afraid it's not ready to be seen yet, *malý květina*. I've barely begun."

Grand-père turned from his private musings. "And what's inspired all this creativity?"

"Gisèle's the inspiration, of course." Marc replied, as if she'd posed for him that very afternoon. "Must there be another?" A pause. "Since you're here, Tristan . . . Have you come to a decision about the business deal we discussed? You were to give me your answer today."

Her grandfather shifted his weight. The skin around his lips tightened, and his eyes touched Nicola and traveled away. He was going to get rid of her, she knew, so he could talk to Marc. "*Mon chaton*, why don't you run along to the library? I'll meet you there in a little while."

Something about his tone and Marc's smugness bothered her. When Nicola passed, Marc winked at her as if at a private joke, smiling his self-satisfied Cheshire-cat grin.

༄

Amanda was in the Devon College library, playing the part of visiting grad student. Tristan had threatened to drop in to see her one afternoon, and she'd worried about the prospect since. It was important, she'd decided, to at least be true to one's lies.

Anyway, it was an inspirational setting for duplicity. An ivy-covered sandstone dome, the library was three stories tall and as wide in circumference. Inside, parquet floors gleamed and the shelving was of mahogany. A delicate staircase zigzagged up from the center of the room. Plants and paintings hung on any wall devoid of books, and a quote from Socrates was gilded over the doors: *There is only one good, knowledge, and one evil, ignorance.* Soft lighting shone on high-backed cushioned chairs of leather pulled to tables of the same mahogany as the shelves and polished to a high reflective sheen. All it lacked was drippy candles and a picturesque smattering of dust on the books.

Ah, the joys of private funding, Amanda thought.

Beneath the opulence the library was more than functional. The computer system was the latest in technology and the collection vast for a college of its size. Amanda had selected a few fat psych texts and spread them on the table before her. Should Tristan arrive, she could hardly confess that her psychological "research" consisted entirely of conversations with him.

Two dates in as many days. Since her return, Tristan Mourault had monopolized her, and yet he remained a perfect gentleman—witty, worldly, and seemingly after no more than her company.

And whatever else he may or may not have been, Tristan was good company. He told her stories of his childhood, beautifully re-creating Paris and the countryside as well as his eccentric mother and father; he amused her with comic scenarios of his travels and his education and his early ill-fated marriage. But as soon as she attempted to bring up Gisèle, he'd do a perfect conversational pirouette and somehow the topic would turn to Amanda. She'd told him all the details of her sister's disappearance, and he'd had the usual sympathetic reaction. He gave away nothing. Tristan's evasiveness and her confessions quickly became the norm. She called him a frustrated priest. He merely laughed; he said she didn't know how true that was. When she was with Tristan, it was hard to believe that *any* of it was true.

When she offered condolences at the loss of his "daughter," she had never witnessed a more genuine display of grief. It showed through his polished façade like a morbid glimpse of the skull beneath the skin.

He'd dropped his eyes and toyed with the tiny handle of his espresso cup. "I'm not dealing with the loss gracefully, I'm afraid. The best of me left with her." He focused on Amanda again, and she felt it like a touch, not refined but raw. His voice was hoarse when he spoke again. "You see, we've a great deal in common, *chérie*. I, too, have lost my parents, and now my Gisèle. So much that I have loved is gone. It is my name. Our name is our destiny, and I was born *triste*." A poignant smile. "My sadness is fated. But I have hope yet for you."

Amanda almost felt she was exploiting *him*. It was absurd. And she could hardly consume four-course dinners and live in Robin's quaint little world-class inn forever. She stared blindly at a journal article and replayed their dinner conversation of the night before.

"Having a male friend is fairly new to me, too," she'd said. "But it's nice. I don't seem to do all that well with the other."

"Lovers?" It was so frank and old-fashioned. Such a queer combination of both. No American can say "lovers" with a straight face, but the French? It rolled off Tristan's tongue.

She'd managed not to laugh and simply nodded.

"What was his name?"

"Whose name?"

"The name you'd like to forget. The one who's here with us." The only name Amanda could think of was "Karen." *Karen is here with us.* Gisèle. But of course his interest was more prosaic. "Do not look so stricken, *chérie.* It doesn't become you. Of course there will be someone. Back in Seattle? It's none of my business, I know, but friends share confidences." Tristan placed no quotes around "friends," but each time he used the word, she felt them there.

"Well, the last 'someone' was called Luke. Luke Halvorson."

Tristan lifted his brows. Something crossed his face. Jealousy? Distaste. "Luke. How biblical." Luke, Amanda recalled, was also the name of Gisèle's husband.

"Yes," she said dryly. "He was a saint. It was all a huge mistake, but hardly the first, and it's over now. I'm not quite sure how it began, really. He was sort of flyaway and lost. I guess I was going to put him back together again. There's a psychological term for that, I think." She plunged her fork rather fiercely into a crouton. "Stupidity."

Tristan laughed.

"He had a habit of making himself disappear and reappear like magic. Anyone but me would have known from the start he was married."

"Perhaps you did."

"I don't make a practice of—"

"Unconsciously, *chérie.* Of course."

And what could she say? "Maybe," she admitted. "Maybe I can feel things only when they're doomed to end. Desire things I can't have. Lovely character traits, huh? The relationship before Luke was with my adviser. He was 'separated' from his wife. Turns out he meant that technically—while he was with me, he wasn't with her. "

"Ah." A slight, poignant smile, sympathy in his eyes. "And what did you do?"

"I was a sophomore. He was the handsome psych professor. Brilliant. Misunderstood. I saw him off and on for years." She met his eyes. "Does that shock you?"

"*Chérie,* I am not American."

Amanda laughed. "Oh, that's right. I can't possibly shock you, can I?"
He merely smiled.

"Well, the truth is, I have terrible taste in men. They're not all married, of course, but there's always something: a secret drug habit or a perverse fetish. Something."

Tristan clucked his tongue. "You're drawn to perversity? How very refreshing."

Amanda laughed, a little uneasily. "Not really."

"It seems to me you're attracted to men you will eventually have to leave, or who will eventually leave you. A psychologist would say it's because you were left as a child."

"Psychologists are a pain."

"I find them quite enchanting." A practiced smile. "Especially those with derisory taste in boyfriends."

At least he hadn't said "lovers."

"May I ask you something, Amanda?" And before she could say no, he'd said, "The death of your sister seems to affect you more than the death of your parents. Why is that?"

Amanda chewed without tasting; the Caesar salad might have been made of Styrofoam. "You say it like an accusation." He hadn't, of course—that was the way she'd felt it. "The one left behind always feels guilty for surviving, Tristan. It's as if you can't mourn enough. Who did I love most? I don't know. Yes, it was Karen, I guess. She's the one who stayed with me. They never found her body, and I can't get over the idea that she's alive and out there somewhere." His face gave away nothing; he looked sorry for her. "She was my best friend. My mom supported us for the most part, but she wasn't around much. She was unhappy. My father was a drunk and the reason for her unhappiness. I guess I blamed them both."

"For your sister's running away?"

Her fork dropped, clanging discordantly on the china. "I never said she ran away."

"She didn't arrive at school, you said, and was found at the pier. I assumed . . ."

"Karen wasn't found at all. Her things were. Why would you assume she'd run away? She just skipped school."

"She wouldn't have left you."

Were they baiting each other, speaking in subtext? "I don't know how she could have. We were always close. All we had was each other." How could he regard her so clear-eyed and calm? "She was the only one I could count on. With Karen I wasn't a problem, I was . . ." Amanda choked on the words. She blinked away the sudden tears, embarrassed. "Damn," she murmured. "Damn. I don't suppose I'm used to good wine."

"You're not used to feeling, I think."

She'd stared at him.

And then he'd reached for her hand. He did nothing but cover hers tightly, as if to brace her, yet a chill ran down her spine like a trickle of ice. "Is it not enough to know she loved you?" he'd asked gently.

"No, it's not."

"Because," he said softly, "if she could love you and also leave you, so will everyone else?"

Amanda drew her hand away. "Any more pop psychology clichés in your arsenal?"

"Clichés are clichés because they're common truths, Amanda." He spoke kindly. "I'm no psychologist, but the serpent is drawn to his own tail, I know. You feel abandoned, and so you seek abandonment. The unfulfilled duck fulfillment." *Yes.* "So much of what we do is beyond our conscious control. Can we change our prophecies, I wonder?" He held her eyes. "Even if we wish to?"

Someone somewhere dropped a book. The report echoed through the quiet of the library, jolting Amanda back to reality, or rather the reassuring unreality of academia. She let out a breath she didn't realize she'd been holding and tilted her head back to rest her neck. It was a dizzying view up to the domed ceiling. There was a beautiful mural there, surrounded by delicately scalloped wood: a Chaucerian figure sat at a crude table, writing on rags with a quill in candlelight. A figure from the Dark Ages. Had his feelings seemed elusive abstractions to him, puzzles to be solved? She thought not. Suddenly he seemed the more enlightened.

"Lovely, isn't it?" It was the head librarian, whom she'd gotten to know in recent days.

Amanda smiled. "Hi, Elizabeth. Yes, it is. I ought to look up more often."

"A student named Daniel Ekland painted it. A prodigy. He came to us when he was only sixteen. I expect great things of him."

"A student painted that? You're kidding." Amanda glanced around her and frowned. "They're not *all* like that here, are they?"

Elizabeth smiled. "Oh, no, dear. Dr. Dresden's students are unique. On the whole the geniuses are in short supply. I find it rather reassuring."

So he was one of Robin's. Just then Amanda saw a young girl come through the double doors and stop a moment, gazing around the library apprehensively. A music prodigy? "Is she one of his, too?"

Elizabeth turned. "Funny you should say that. She is, in a way. Pretty little thing, isn't she? Not a student, of course. That's his goddaughter, Nicola."

His goddaughter? *The beautiful, lonely little girl whose entire world is built on lies . . .* Of whom Amanda had hardly allowed herself to think. Nicola. Gisèle's daughter. Her *niece?*

⁊

Nicola didn't know how long she had; she'd have to be quick.

Why did she feel so nervous? It wasn't as if she were doing anything wrong. She just wanted to find out about Karen and Amanda Miller. She'd followed Marc's advice and hadn't asked her grandfather. But that didn't mean she couldn't seek the answers on her own.

The library had numerous sources of information online: Elizabeth had explained the computer system to Nicola when Robin gave her a library card last year. It hadn't meant much to her then—a huge network of databases containing archived academic journals, articles, newspapers, and doctoral theses. It was a research resource for the students, but Elizabeth had made a big deal of having Nicola choose a log-in ID and a password. Now she was grateful. She selected a computer station in an isolated corner and maneuvered through the options to find LexisNexis. She double-clicked the left mouse button, entered her ID and the name of her beloved wirehaired terrier who had died, Brigadier, and instantly accessed newspaper archives from all over the country.

She cast a furtive glance over her shoulder. No sign of her grandfather, but Elizabeth was smiling at her and a student beside her was staring. Nicola managed a wave and the sort of smile meant to indicate she didn't want or need any help, then turned her attention back to the screen.

Quickly, she typed in her search entry and held her breath. The search for "Amanda Nicole Miller" retrieved only two results. Surprisingly, both were from nearby Seattle—one from the *Times*, the other from the *Post-Intelligencer*. The first dated back to 1986. It was a cast shot of a ballet company. No, a ballet school: *"Students from the Pacific Northwest Ballet School join the pros in a presentation of The Nutcracker."* Nicola scanned the names. Amanda Miller was third row center—a sugar fairy, from the look of it. The photo was black and white and grainy, taken ten years after her snapshot. Nicola peered forward. Was that a dimple in her left cheek? Yes. Just like the little girl beside her mother in the photograph. But here her hair was up and the chubby cheeks were gone. It was impossible to tell if it was the same person.

The second link proved to be a recent photo in color, a close-up. Amanda was very attractive, Nicola thought. Her hair was shiny and straight with honey highlights, like Nicola's own. Her eyes were soft brown with flecks of green. She wore a cap and gown and a grave expression. *"Amanda Nicole Miller, Salutatorian of UW-Seattle's Class of 1992."*

Could it *really* be her mother's Amanda?

Once again Nicola tapped the keys. *"Karen Miller"* garnered a long string of results: notices of marriages and births, **Karen Miller Named Miss Iowa.** No. **Young British Economist Lectures at Yale.** No. **Performance Artist Raises Hackles in Brooklyn?** They went on and on, and Nicola's stomach began to sink. This would take forever.

Then she realized she'd left out the middle name in her search and inserted *"Louise."* This brought up a series of linked stories and a wire photo.

It was her mother. Only not as Nicola had ever imagined her. It was a school photo—though "Gisèle" had never been to school. Her hair was feathered, and she wore a brown-and-gold collared sweater that was hopelessly out of style. And though she had the same wide eyes and clear fair skin, this girl was different from the triumphant young woman in the baby photo, or the elegant woman her mother had become. Her cheeks were fuller and her smile less certain, the makeup lighter and less artfully applied. Yet her secretive, melancholy expression was as familiar to Nicola as her own face.

The photo had run with several stories from the *San Francisco Chronicle,* cross-referenced with similar stories in the *Examiner.* They were all over fifteen years old.

April 16, 1979:

LOCAL GIRL MISSING SINCE FRIDAY

SAN FRANCISCO, CA—Karen Louise Miller, 15, of the Mission District was reported missing Friday by her parents: Patrick and Maureen Miller. . . .

April 23, 1979:

ABDUCTION SUSPECTED IN MILLER DISAPPEARANCE

Police investigators released new information regarding the April 13th disappearance of 15-year-old Karen Miller today. An employee of The Daily Grind, a coffee house frequented by Miller, contacted police yesterday to report that he had seen her in conversation with an attractive middle-aged man on two occasions prior to her disappearance. . . .

May 1, 1979:

MISSING GIRL BELIEVED DEAD, BLOODY BACKPACK FOUND ON PIER

There is a tragic development today in the search for Karen Miller. The backpack she purportedly carried the day of her disappearance has been discovered by Ted Hinley, a fisherman for Pacific Waters Co., who spotted it from the water. The pack was filled with the personal effects of Miller, 15, who has been missing since April 13.

Following the grisly discovery Police Chief Thomas Felder issued an angry warning to Miller's attacker: "The city of San Francisco wants you, and you will be found." He also made a promise to Miller's parents: "We will not give up the search for your daughter." Yet by all accounts, they search now not for a missing young woman but for her body and her murderer.

January 28, 1980:

ALCOHOL INVOLVED IN GOLDEN GATE CRASH

Patrick Miller, the driver responsible for the January 22 accident that also killed his wife, Maureen Miller, and truck driver Michael Ramsey, had a blood-alcohol level nearly three times the legal limit, San Francisco police said Wednesday.

"Mon chaton?"

Nicola gasped audibly and stood so abruptly she toppled the chair. She had no time to close out the program. She used her body to block the monitor and with trembling fingers pushed the power button off. As the screen went black, she turned. "Grand-père, you scared me—"

"I'm sorry, *ma chère.*" Her grandfather was setting her chair upright again. "You were lost in your own world. Are you looking for a book?"

Nicola nodded stiffly. Her mouth wouldn't form words.

Tristan merely raised a brow and mused, "No more card catalogs, eh? I must be getting old. Why don't you show me how the computer works?"

"Uh." She felt her cheeks flush and averted her eyes. "Can I show you next time, Grand-père? I've already found what I was looking for."

He was puzzled. "But you've written nothing down. Are call numbers also passé?"

With effort she met his eyes. "No . . . but I can remember them."

"My smart girl." He studied her a moment and then smiled, reaching out to touch her chin.

His touch was cool, the touch of a stranger, but Nicola made herself smile back.

She forced herself not to flinch or run or scream, not to cast so much as a glance over her shoulder as she walked blindly to the nearest shelf. She gazed at the book spines intently, as if she knew just what she was looking for. But once safely within the aisle, Nicola did look; she couldn't help it. She turned in time to see Tristan lean forward and press the monitor on.

෴

Luke had been unable to eat breakfast and so found the first vodka tonic going to his head, but Robin was buying, which meant they'd keep coming. It was Friday, and they were meeting to discuss marketing strategy—which meant Robin would strategize and Luke would listen. Lunch was at a restaurant called *From the Terrace*, and in spite of the gathering clouds they were seated outside, on the famed terrace, beneath the tree-tops and heat lamps. It offered a charming view of downtown and served overpriced tapas and drinks.

Beside Robin sat a girl Luke would not have believed real if she didn't breathe and talk and otherwise animate. Her dark hair fell in delicate waves, and her face was as he'd long pictured the heroines of roman-tic novels: bewitching forest green eyes and pouty lips, delicate cheek-bones that made her every expression both graceful and blithe. And her body was enough to give one religion, though she conjured up more pagan visions. Everything about her curved, and Luke was charmed by her company before she'd ever said a word. He recognized her at once, though they'd never spoken. She had been Robin's date at the ill-fated party.

Her name was Chelsea Delaney, and she was just twenty, though in looks and confidence she transcended her age. When introducing her, Robin said simply that she was "his actress." His students were all into different arts. Robin instructed them in art philosophy. And what was that? "All there is to be taught."

Weren't there laws against professors dating their students? The sub-ject was neatly avoided, as was Chelsea's underage drinking. Tonight was her opening night in *A Streetcar Named Desire*, Robin was explain-ing, and her presence here was due to a ritual of lunch and champagne before first nights. Luke's presence was due, of course, to the Gisèle

Paintings—and the two combined because Chelsea and the other students had recently been given a preview. Would Luke wish to hear her reaction? Luke would not particularly, but he displayed a dutiful enthusiasm. Chelsea was a good audience, Robin assured him, a natural aesthete and a "sensualist." He said this last as if it were a mundane quality, akin to being a pragmatist or a Methodist or a Virgo.

As a sensualist, Chelsea didn't surprise. She was over the moon about the paintings.

"They're heavenly," she gushed, biting her lovely lower lip. "But I'm so sorry about Gisèle."

To hear her name spoken out loud stung. But of course the Gisèle Paintings would soon put everyone on a first-name basis. "Thank you," said Luke. Is that what one said?

"But with the paintings you've made her live forever," Chelsea said with a touching naïveté that washed over him like spring rain. And then, with a twinge he thought of Amanda and the troubling juxtaposition of Robin Dresden paying her hotel bill.

Rob's quick, observant eyes were on him now, and while everything was very amiable, Luke had the distinct feeling that something unpleasant was swimming beneath the boat.

Robin ordered tapas in fluent Spanish and another round of more intelligible American drinks. Luke found himself grateful for Chelsea and her bountiful distractions. "You say the paintings were part of an assignment?" he asked. "It doesn't sound like typical homework."

Chelsea smiled at the word "homework." Wasn't it called that nowadays? She glanced uneasily at Robin, who dispatched the waiter and said simply, "It's all right, love. Go ahead."

But suddenly Luke doubted it *was* all right, from her expression.

"The assignment was to analyze the relationship of artist and subject."

Good luck there. Luke drained the last of his drink.

"Some of us were a little disturbed by all the minute focus on her body. . . ."

"Well," he said, "they're nudes."

"Of course, but Gisèle's no more than an object in many of them. Taken as a group, they seem obsessive. Ashleigh felt that the nudity was a contradiction, that it showed an uneasiness with her body and her sexuality, not the opposite." This girl had no unease with it clearly; she didn't even blink along with the word.

"Well, that's probably true. And who is Ashleigh?"

"My writer," Robin said.

His writer. "Ah, yes," Luke said dully.

"And Daniel agreed." Luke had heard of Daniel Ekland, a painter, who Robin had managed to say on several occasions with a perfectly straight face was "clairvoyant." Chelsea ducked this but said, "He's the most intuitive of all of us, and he was looking at it from the perspective of the artist. He said that the nature of the nudity . . . well, it's just not the way a husband would paint his wife."

Not the way a husband would paint his wife. Sweat broke out on Luke's brow. Mercifully, the waiter arrived with the fresh drinks, and several small steaming plates followed: crispy mussels, prawns, baked manchego cheese, and God-knows-what concealed under a blanket of bubbling tomato sauce. Luke reached for his vodka tonic. "Well, I don't understand why this . . . er, Daniel, would say a thing like that." As he said the words, yet another source of paranoia struck him: maybe the kid actually *was* psychic. "How the hell would he know? Has he ever been married?"

Chelsea tipped her head, a flicker of surprise in her eyes. "Well, I guess it's just that a husband could look at his wife all the time. He could simply touch her." Innocently, she twirled a strand of hair around her finger. "The paintings, or so Daniel's theory was, are a replacement for that." *Ouch.* She dipped an edge of bread delicately into her gazpacho. "But I think that's what makes them so good. Honestly. All the longing." So remote, an abstract assessment. "Rob tells me she didn't pose for them at all. You must have a really fabulous eye."

Luke glanced involuntarily at Robin. He was damnably cool, as if they sat discussing stock-market quotes, but there was an unhealthy flicker in his eyes. Chelsea fastened those guileless green eyes on him, and Luke felt for all the world as though he were being set up.

He bristled. "Well, art is a subjective thing, as I'm sure Robin's taught you. The artist is least equipped to explain his art." *What a load of crap.* "I don't know myself just how they came to be." That at least was true; encouraged, Luke went on, "Gisèle was a ghost. Not quite real. That's the truth of it; it was part of her beauty. I guess that's why the paintings are so focused on the physical. Gisèle's thoughts might have been written in Sanskrit. I suppose her body's the part of her I knew best." That was quite good. His father had always said he could lie like a rug.

"Oh." Chelsea brushed her hair behind her ear with her fingers—a gesture so quintessentially feminine it seemed Luke's heart stopped at the simple abstraction of it. "That's strange. Because she's so real in the paintings. I feel like I know her intensely through them. But then, I only met her once." Chelsea shrugged self-effacingly. "What do I know? It just seemed at the party as if she were acting out a role."

Which you would know all about.

Robin still sat strangely silent, his dark eyes attentive, calmly eating a prawn. They were supposed to focus on selling the paintings, not sit around dissecting the hell out of them. Chelsea's arm brushed against Robin's sleeve as she reached for her champagne. There was not a moment in the entire time Luke had spent in their company that they were not touching—lightly at the elbow or shoulder, a brush of the upper arm, Robin's hand at the small of her back. Luke had a sudden surreal vision of this "assignment" as a strange sort of foreplay for Dresden and his young protégées; he pictured them pawing over prints of nudes, a cerebral pornography.

Chelsea went on matter-of-factly, "Maybe you knew her better than you think."

Luke stared down at the ice puddles in his empty glass. "Maybe."

Robin finally broke his reticence. "You realize you must have been the last to see her, Luke."

"I'm sorry?"

"Oh." Chelsea glanced at Luke and flushed guiltily. "Well, it's just that I saw you that night."

Luke's heart ceased to beat; sirens whirred in his ears.

"I got up for a moment. It was about three-thirty, I guess. I thought you'd gone out there for the paintings. I didn't realize Gisèle was staying out there." A meaningful pause. "I didn't even mention it to Robin at the time. I didn't know it was important."

Luke downed half of his drink in a gulp. "It isn't."

Robin said, "Strange you failed to mention it."

Luke's mind raced. He hadn't expected this. Robin selected another prawn and waited patiently. Luke pinched the bridge of his nose hard between his fingers and steadied his thoughts. "I couldn't sleep. I remembered that the paintings were still set up out by the pool. I went to take down the easels. That's all." He'd felt compelled to look at the paintings again. Sweat trickled down the back of his neck. "I had no idea she'd be out there. She came out of the cabana—"

"Were the lights on?" Robin asked quietly.

"The lights? I don't— Well, yeah, I guess I must have turned them on. It was dark."

"But you were aware that the investigators placed her death earlier. Due to the lights."

"So what?"

"So," said Robin, as if explaining to a child, "the overhead lights weren't on the next morning. If the timed lights for the paintings went off at three and you saw her at three-thirty, we're to believe she went out to the pool later, stumbling in the dark?"

"Well, that's probably why she slipped."

"But why wouldn't she turn on the lights, Luke? Why would she go out to the pool at all?"

"Maybe she was sleepwalking, I don't know. I don't know *anything*. She scared the hell out of me, coming out of the cabana; she looked like she was expecting someone else. Maybe she was. It sure as hell wasn't me." Luke wiped his brow and looked up. "Damned heat lamps. Listen, it was nothing, really. She turned around and left as soon as she saw me. I turned and left when I saw her. Earlier, in her room, we argued. I didn't want to argue anymore."

Robin said mildly. "You failed to mention that as well."

"What?"

"The earlier argument."

"Come on," Luke pleaded. "You know ours wasn't a great romance. Hate to disappoint you, Chelsea."

She was frowning. Artists were always painfully in love with their models, husbands torturously besotted by their wives. She probably thought Robin was in love with her.

"I'm afraid your friends win the day. Gisèle was uncomfortable with nudity, with sexuality. With me, mostly." Luke made a hapless motion with his hands. "Hell, I loved her anyway." He couldn't seem to stop talking; he had to convince them that he'd tried. He'd done everything he could. *It wasn't my fault.* "Listen, she didn't kill herself over me, if that's what you think. She had her issues, to say the least, but she didn't kill herself over anyone. She'd never have left Nic. Sometimes I think that's the only thing I know about her, but I know that much. I have no delusions about her leaving me. She told me she planned to—"

At last the record wound down. Luke stared at the tablecloth and looked again at his empty glass. How had it gotten empty? He tipped it back anyway, the expressions of his interrogators made fractured and abstract by the melting ice.

❧

Nicola selected her books blindly, fat ones from the row in which she'd chosen to hide. When she had the courage to peek out again, she saw Grand-père at a table laughing with a student as though nothing was wrong. He came toward her as she watched, and she couldn't quiet the hammering of her heart. Maybe the computer program had miraculously ended somehow, timed out. Maybe he hadn't seen anything.

He smiled down at her affectionately, his manner the same as always. He wanted to introduce her to someone, he said. They'd met at his wine club. ". . . Amanda Miller."

"Amanda *Miller*?" Nicola repeated, aghast. "What do you mean?"

"Mean? Nothing at all. Only that I should like you to meet her, *mon chaton.*"

"She lives *here*? And you . . . you're *dating* her?"

He smiled, teasing, "You mustn't worry, Nicola. You will always have my heart."

"But Grand-père—"

He had already turned. She followed him to a table. It was the same table where he'd been laughing earlier, and where Elizabeth had been standing with the pretty student who had been staring at her. The pretty student was Amanda Miller. Now Nicola stared. The graduate in the photograph had materialized as if by some dark magic. Her mother's sister. Her aunt?

Amanda couldn't possibly know the truth, but knowledge was coming to Nicola in waves; a terrible picture formed. She realized that the kiss in the garden was exactly what she'd thought it was. Not fatherly. Not fatherly at all. Her mother's father had died in a car crash.

Nicola gazed up at Tristan miserably. *You're not my grandfather. Who are you?*

☙

"Amanda, *chérie*. May I introduce my granddaughter, Nicola? Nicola, this is my friend Amanda."

She should have been more prepared, but until now her niece hadn't been tangible. Nothing could have prepared her for meeting her sister's daughter. The girl's very existence seemed an utter impossibility. Amanda had the urge to reach out and touch her to make sure she was real. To hug her. "Hello, Nicola."

Nicola was a beautiful child. Almost disturbingly so. Her face was lovely and utterly unaware of its loveliness, vulnerable. Her eyes were oddly adult, an unusually deep shade of blue, framed by long lashes and, against the pale skin, appearing deep and unfathomable, like little oceans. Little oceans that were sizing Amanda up. "Hi, Amanda," she murmured. "It's nice to meet you."

"You, too." If Amanda had met her on the street, would she see traces of Karen in her? Probably not, but they were there, vanishing and returning like the flashing lights in an eye exam—right here before her, then in the periphery, back again, gone. There was something in her bone structure, the resolute set to her jaw that Karen sometimes had, and a cagey quality to her posture as if she expected to be squashed at any moment by an unseen tennis shoe but wasn't going to be an easy bug to crack. She was at the awkward age Amanda remembered far too well, all arms and legs, her bones too sharp at that time when baby fat was still in vogue. She crept into Amanda's heart instantly and it overwhelmed her. At last, Amanda said, a little too brightly, "Which books did you choose?"

Nicola carried four very fat volumes and set them on the table gratefully: *The Complete Works of Edgar Allan Poe,* a volume of Proust, Plutarch's *Parallel Lives,* and a lit-crit text that must have weighed nearly as much as she, *De-Crying Lot 49: Deconstructing Pynchon.*

Amanda's eyes widened. "My goodness. No light reading for you."

Nicola reddened slightly, but Tristan smiled. "She's read everything in the children's library in town. We can't keep up with her."

Amanda raised a brow and smiled. "When I was your age, I was reading Ellen Conford."

"Really? I love her, too." The girl's face was radiant when she smiled and momentarily relieved the fragile quality. I've read them all. My favorite one's called *And This Is Laura*."

"Oh, yeah. Isn't that about the psychic girl? There's another one, at summer camp. . . ."

"*Hail, Hail Camp Timberwood*."

"That's it!" Amanda knew more about children's books than was healthy; they had been her best friends for a long, long time. "How about *Dear Lovey Hart, I Am Desperate*."

Nicola nodded. "*We Interrupt This Semester for an Important Bulletin*?"

They laughed simultaneously.

"How about Lois Duncan?" Amanda asked.

"Oh, I *love* her."

Tristan gazed at them, a little lost. "You two seem to have a great deal in common."

An inscrutable expression crossed Nicola's face, and she lowered her eyes. She must simply be painfully shy, Amanda decided, uncomfortable with eye contact.

She asked gently, "Have you read much Madeleine L'Engle?"

"*A Wrinkle in Time*?"

"Yeah, but she's written a lot of others, too," Amanda said. "My favorite character was Vicky Austin. She's in a whole series. I still think of her as a friend."

The radiant smile reappeared. "I do that, too. I haven't read those, but I will."

Tristan scooped up her weighty present selection. "Well, these ought to keep you occupied for a few days. We'd better be on our way, *mon chaton*."

Nicola only nodded. She seemed as reluctant as Amanda to say good-bye.

He went on, "We'll stop distracting you from your studies, Amanda."

"Oh no, that's all right. I hope we'll get to talk again soon, Nicola."

"Me, too." Her eyelashes fluttered, and she seemed poised to say something more, but Tristan transferred the heavy stack of books to one arm and put his other around her shoulders. Amanda watched goose bumps appear where he touched Nicola's upper arm.

"Bye," she said.

"Until tomorrow night, *chérie*," said Tristan, and Amanda remembered she'd agreed to go with him to the ballet on Saturday. Was it Friday already? She watched as Tristan guided his granddaughter to the checkout desk near the door. The librarian scanned her books. *What was up with Plutarch, Pynchon, and Poe?* Nicola couldn't possibly be that advanced.

The girl cast an apprehensive glance over her shoulder as they exited through the double doors. Amanda smiled, waving, but it was disturbingly clear that Nicola was terribly frightened of *something*. And was it only Amanda's imagination, or was that something her grandfather?

❧

The beautiful Chelsea Delaney had played her part and exited the stage.

Robin asked Luke if he'd like another drink, and he gave a nod, though what he'd really have liked was to get the hell away from Robin.

"You were quite frank with Chelsea. I'm surprised," Robin said to Luke.

"Well, she was quite frank with me."

"It's a very small taste of what the press will be. Don't expect many of the questions to be concerned with technique." A meaningful pause. "You won't want to be quite so frank with them."

"Is that what this was? A test?"

"I hope it wasn't too uncomfortable." Yet Robin's mild tone implied no hope of the kind. He was at his most dangerous when mild. "Anything else you've left out about that night?"

That was theatrical. "No. What the hell do you think I've left out?"

"Well, now I recall it, Luke, you seemed quite upset as the party was winding down. You've admitted that Elle planned to leave you. And now you've been placed at the scene of the crime—"

Luke's heart thudded. A trickle of sweat rolled down the small of his back. "What crime?"

"Let me think." Robin spread manchego calmly on a slice of baguette. "Oh, yes. Murder. You see, I don't believe that Gisèle's death was an accident, and I don't believe for a moment it was suicide. That rather narrows the field."

"I don't give a *damn* what you believe."

"Calm down, Luke. Have a prawn."

Absurdly, Luke did. He chewed. He swallowed. "I *am* calm. But I—" He broke off, reaching rapidly for his goblet of water. "It's fucking . . . hot. . . ." he choked.

"Is it? I should have warned you. Do you know that spicy food actually produces a rush of adrenaline, similar to battle? I rather enjoy it. It's like fencing with a worthy opponent."

Luke preferred not to fence with his food. Or with Robin. His eyes began to water.

"Try sugar," Robin suggested, opening a pack amiably. "I'm afraid water makes it rather a lot worse."

Luke dumped the sugar into his mouth and chased it with vodka tonic.

Slowly, the effects began to wane. He met Robin's eyes warily and spoke in low tones. "Robin, if you're trying to tell me I'm a suspect in Gisèle's *murder*, the whole notion's crazy."

"I assure you, my reasoning's entirely rational. It seems to me there are two possibilities. The first is the *crime passionel*—a moment's madness, a shove into the pool. That's how I envisage you doing it. On the other hand, it may have been far more calculated. There is some evidence to that end. Someone may have drugged her with sleeping pills and drowned her." He frowned. "That doesn't seem your style. But Nicola mentioned the traces of water in the tub. Someone could even have drugged her and drowned her in her bath. They would then have had to transport her to the pool without being seen."

"A neat trick. If you're trying to say—"

A shrug. "The evidence raises certain questions. We cannot limit ourselves to the pool because she was discovered there. There was no chlorine found in her lungs, but chlorine dissipates very rapidly. So. Why would she take a bath, down a great lot of sleeping pills, and then decide to leave her cozy room for the cabana? It's a riddle. Did she happen to explain it to *you*?"

"No, she didn't. I told you, we hardly talked."

"Yes. You hardly talked because you'd argued earlier. And she was going to leave you."

"Wait a minute."

"I'll be honest with you, Luke. I think you're a prick in many ways, some of which I'll detail in a moment, and I'm absolutely partial to you as a suspect."

Luke gaped at him, unable to believe his ears.

"But I'll grant you, it's not wholly impossible that someone else did it. If the crime was premeditated, I have to consider the possibility that it was Tristan. He's a premeditated sort of person, very patient, whereas you're rather blundering and impetuous. I think you know he was unhealthily attached to Gisèle, but I have no evidence of a rift between them. Do you?" Robin rapped his long fingers on the table and fixed his eyes on a point beyond Luke. "Maybe I'm looking at it all from the wrong angle. . . . Maybe it was for the paintings."

Luke spoke carefully. "You mean someone may have tried to steal them, and she—"

"No, no. I mean that someone had already stolen them. Perhaps I'm underestimating your ability to premeditate. Did she threaten to come out with the truth?" After a horrible silence, Robin waved a dismissive hand. "Oh, for Christ's sake, you can drop the charade with me. Do you think for a second I ever believed you capable of painting them? I'd place better odds on pigs taking to the sky." Robin's eyes were very dark, his voice emotionless and cold. "Let's abandon the tiresome pretense, shall we?"

In a paranoid blur, Luke glanced around him. Now he understood why Robin had chosen a public place—the murmur of sophisticated voices, punctuated by careless laughter and the clink of glasses. There would be no scenes. It would be civilized.

Luke said quietly, "I didn't kill her, Robin. I wouldn't have hurt Ella for the world."

"Ah, but you did, I think." Robin traced his index finger along the chilled rim of his martini glass. "Tell me about the paintings first."

The paintings. How Luke wished he'd never laid eyes on the damned things.

He spoke quickly, like a kid caught in a lie. "Listen, I didn't want to claim them. Ella practically forced me to. What was I going to do? Force her to admit that Tristan, her own *father*, had painted them? I thought . . . well, I *hoped* he'd done them without her knowing, somehow. It sounds nuts, but I convinced myself that's how it was. I thought I'd sell the paintings and get her away from there. That's all I wanted, Rob, honest to God. But then, that night . . . I saw her kiss him in the garden. *She* kissed *him*, you understand? And it made me so sick to think that all this time—" And yet now Luke could only feel utter grief and sorrow. Remorse. It overwhelmed him and tears stung his eyes. Embarrassed, he sat there, blinking them away.

"It's all right, Luke. You were sickened. Of course you were."

He felt a hot rush of anger. "Don't be so goddamned patronizing. You must have known the truth about them all along."

"You should be careful with words like 'truth,' Luke. You may not know the truths you think you know. Shall I tell you how I think it happened?"

"I think you had goddamned better."

"Well, I wonder. Was seeing Gisèle with Tristan an aphrodisiac for you?"

"I— Hell, *no*. What do you mean by that?" But he knew exactly what Robin meant.

The waiter appeared to clear their plates as Robin calmly fished around in his jacket pocket. He pulled out a cigarette case and extracted one, tapping it on the marble tabletop. The waiter made his exit. "You know as well as I do that Gisèle's autopsy results showed signs of recent sexual activity. You confirmed this, as I recall. It was one of the reasons the investigators decided against suicide." He lit his cigarette; Luke watched the tip glow red. "By all accounts the night was a joyous celebration of the paintings—the artist and the model, husband and wife. All terribly romantic." The words dripped sarcasm. "Things culminate in the usual way, and afterward the wife takes a late-night stroll to look at the adoring husband's paintings once more. She's so moved by them she intends to sleep there in the cabana, to be near them. Add too much champagne and sleeping pills to an impetuous choice and you have a neat, tragic accident." He took a long drag off the cigarette and exhaled.

His eyes were pitiless. "But let's put the thing into context. In light of new information—affairs and incest and such—suddenly it doesn't seem like the most romantic of nights. To what extremes did your moral outrage carry you?"

"I don't know what you—"

"I think you raped her, Luke."

"You're out of your—"

"Yes, I know. Husbands don't think they can rape their wives; the ones who do it don't like to think so. But I'm guessing it wasn't quite consensual. Did she take a bath afterward? Did you realize you could never really possess her? Did you keep thinking of all the things she might have done willingly with Tristan?"

Luke swallowed bile. His head was dizzy, vertiginous, and his stomach was a washing machine on spin cycle, churning prawns and gazpacho and vodka. "If you really thought that, you wouldn't be here. You wouldn't be doing the exhibition. You have no proof of anything."

"Then why are you so rattled, Luke? If you're innocent, you have nothing to fear. We're just having a conversation."

Luke started to rise.

"You're leaving before we even discuss the exhibition?"

"You really are debauched, aren't you?"

There was a poignant pause. And, slowly, Luke sat down again. He spoke quietly. "Why would you go on with it if you believe all this?"

Robin narrowed his eyes; he exhaled a ribbon of white. "In the beginning I agreed to an exhibition for Gisèle's sake. Everything I'm doing is for her sake and Nicola's. Let's put it this way, Luke, you may not be the fish I'm after, but your lies have caught you in the net. And that doesn't trouble me much. To my mind, Gisèle was murdered, and I intend to prove it. You've said Gisèle was expecting someone out there. If that someone actually exists, you may just be a bloody bastard and not a killer. And in this you have three points in your favor. One: My instincts are troubled by an easy answer, and the truth is, you're too damned obvious. I simply can't believe you're so stupid as to parade yourself through a well-lit glass corridor after disposing of your wife's body. Nor to confess to me an argument that culminated in murder. Two: I insisted that the gallery cut go to Gisèle for any sale, and she agreed. In the past she's always refused money from me. That means she had a reason for wanting it. For the first time, she had both need and desire for financial independence from Tristan."

Luke felt a leap of hope. A small redemption. "And what's the third?"

He frowned. "The third is that a very good reason for her to desire independence from Tristan has recently fallen into my lap."

"But you're not sharing?"

"I'm afraid not."

"And you really believe your good friend Tristan capable of murder?"

Robin hesitated. "Under the right circumstances, we're all capable."

"And suicide isn't a possibility?"

"Not if I knew Gisèle. And I did."

"If you knew about her and Tristan, why didn't you stop it?"

He contemplated Luke. "There was nothing to stop." But there was an uncertain note in his voice that Luke had never heard before.

"Is that what you tell yourself in order to sleep nights?"

There was a long silence. "I mostly don't sleep nights."

"What exactly does the exhibition have to do with any of this, Robin?"

"Exhibition. A telling term. Tristan has asked me not to show the paintings, but they are going to be shown. And he will be there. Likewise you must play your part, and Gisèle will be there *en force*. It will be revelatory, I think. This show is going to put pressure on all the right people, and one of them is going to snap." Robin's gaze was withering. "No man escapes himself, wouldn't you agree?"

And Luke did agree. "I didn't kill her, Robin."

"Glad to hear it. I'll be in touch. In the meantime I don't think I would do any interviews if I were you. You're bereaved, after all."

"Right." Luke rose, nearly toppling his chair. He turned from the table to find that the lunchtime crowd had thinned; he strode across the terrace in a daze. Clouds overhead threatened rain, and the lake from here was a roiling gunmetal gray. It struck him only then. All this and Robin still hadn't said a word about Amanda. Was she yet another weapon in his arsenal? *What was he saving her for?*

He cast a glance over his shoulder at Robin, who still sat in the shadows, a profile in black unhurriedly smoking, and Luke didn't have the nerve to go back. *What part had he played in all of this?* Luke had never quite known. And it was as if Robin had already forgotten him, lost in his thoughts, the lit end of his cigarette hovering in the air like a firefly.

XV

BUTTERFLIES AND POPPIES

It was a typical morning in the autumn of '81 when life as I knew it came to an end.

I rummaged through the day's mail to be met once again with the empty left-hand corner and my address set in distinctive typeface. Lulled into complacency, I'd come to think my anonymous correspondent benign, or even a co-conspirator. Patience seemed an unlikely virtue among blackmailers. . . . There had been no threats or demands or implied moral outrage. He'd chronicled me, that is all. And so I was dealt the death blow while glancing the other way.

The envelope contained photocopied newspaper clippings from the *San Francisco Chronicle* and the *Examiner*. There was Gisèle's "Missing" photo. And then a recent photo of us exiting a restaurant. She stared at the sidewalk, clutching my hand as if for protection.

There was meant to be reproach in this, I knew. And yet it was very clear she was looking to *me* for protection. Like a blossoming flower after a frost, Gisèle closed up and withdrew. She made me promise never again to touch her "inside." There was no further mention of my impotence. She was grateful for it, I think, as in a small, ugly region of my mind I was grateful for her past, however terrible. I need no longer fear the Robin Dresdens of the world; I need not battle normalcy and marriage and babies. She was ruined for everyone but me—just as I was ruined but for her. Together we were, in some strange way, whole.

But how could one explain this to an outsider? An opportunist too cowardly to show his face? Who was he to judge me? He was no moralist. For at last his motives were made clear. A single folded slip of paper was composed of three lines, with three sets of figures.

$3,000,000.
Sparbuch #9830479296 "Ueberbringer"
12-21-81.

Naturally, I had heard of the Sparbuch account of Austria. The harbor of choice for drug smugglers and tax evaders, it was not merely secret but truly anonymous. The account required no ID or address to open and need not be opened by the account holder at all. Such accounts are rarely held in the account holder's name, but under an alias or, as in this case, *Ueberbringer*, "passbook holder."

I didn't have a Sparbuch. Nor did I have $3 million. Secret or otherwise.

Now that the threat had materialized, I scarcely felt any anger. Emotion and conscience did not enter into the matter—all that remained was to act. But how? I could hardly consult a lawyer—what was blackmail to kidnapping? I needed more than legal advice. I needed the advice of a friend. And in a strange about-face, I found I had only one whom I trusted.

I found Dresden painting to a collection of the Beatles. The ballads. "Yesterday" and "Norwegian Wood" and "Eleanor Rigby." Rain drummed on the roof as accompaniment. He greeted me not with hello but, "I'm sick of the city, Tristan. I'm leaving at the weekend. "

It took me aback. "But you've just returned from London—"

"Yes." He had gone to visit his son and "the mother of his son," Eve Duvalier, whom I'd known as a girl. Their relationship was "complicated," according to him. Like mine, perhaps, only legal.

"It did not go well?"

"It didn't go at all well." Robin sighed, staring out a window, where the rivulets of rain had blurred the world beyond. "I'm not a terribly good person, Tristan. It doesn't typically trouble me, notions of goodness.

Except with him." His pressed his hands together and looked reverently heavenward. "My son, Joshua. Such a fellow you've never . . . Do you know he plays piano? I mean, really plays. Not 'Chopsticks'—Chopin." And then he frowned. "He despises me already."

"Was it inevitable?"

"Yes. No . . . I don't know. He's like his mother. Bloody high-strung, sensitive. I liked that in her in the beginning." A sheepish grin. "It's such a bore to be given an easy time, isn't it?"

It was nice to hear his failings rather than mine. "Divorce is difficult."

His expression clouded. "We're not divorced."

"Ah. More difficult still."

"She's Catholic. Absolutely refuses. She wants a 'traditional' life."

Again, "Ah." This rather explained it all.

"The thing is, she's ill. Her heart, ever since she was a child. Dancing's not an ideal profession for those with heart disease, but she won't stop. Naturally, everyone around her blames me. They've taken the term 'heartbroken' rather literally." His eyes raked over the room without seeing. "Maybe it's true."

"She was quite shy as a girl, with the flashes of radiance one finds only in the timid."

Robin gazed at me, and with his focus I felt myself materialize. "Yes, that's a good description," he said and gave a slight smile. "She *is* radiant, when she forgets herself. But it didn't suit me. Married life. Christ, I was twenty. And now I don't know what suits me. Nothing does. That's why I'm going."

"For the weekend, you say. Where?"

"Across the country. Not for the weekend, *at* the weekend. Indefinitely."

I truly was shocked. "You're not giving up the loft?"

"No, no," said Robin. "SoHo's the best investment in the city right now. Anyway, I don't intend to abandon New York. One can't, of course."

"But you won't be coming back to stay?"

"I think not."

How can I explain it? The sense of hollowness growing inside me? By all accounts I should have been glad to dispose of my rival, and yet he had by then proved himself to be so much more. He was the only close

friend of my adult life. A thing typical of me: I recognized its value only
when it was in jeopardy. I scratched my head, frowning. Everything was
fleeing, it seemed—finances, friends.

"I'd like you and Elle to come with me."

Like a bird in a cage too long, I found the idea of escape startling.
Could I simply go? "Where?"

"Middle of fucking nowhere." A smile and a motion of his hands as
if he could make the place appear and disappear by magic. "The home of
my more adventurous ancestors. It's just a village on a lake in the mountains, but so beautiful it'll knock you on your arse. Makes me think of the
Alps, but smaller, more controllable, you know? Ownable." Abstracted,
he stepped back, gazing critically at the canvas before him. "An uncle's
just left me the lot."

"Left you the town?" I asked, incredulous.

"Well, a good many of the leases and some undeveloped property on
the lake. Think of it, Tristan." He turned to me with a spark in his eyes
and a flash of his half smile. "What better challenge for an artist than to
create a world?"

He returned to his canvas, and it was silent. I had so much to tell him
I couldn't seem to begin. What if he too should condemn me?

"You really must come, Tristan. I want to populate it with interesting people, you see."

I said carefully, "You're not disturbed by the idea of harboring a
criminal?"

"We're all criminals, aren't we? We all have our crimes." But he
glanced at me sideways and focused, assessing everything in an instant.
He frowned. "Something has happened, Tristan. Tell me."

And so I did. I trusted him with it all. I handed him the blackmail
envelopes and walked to the window. The view down is still etched in my
mind: the vertiginous drop to the slick, reflective street below. The perpetual horns and the roar of the city quieted, the melodic lamentations of
the Beatles receded; there was nothing but the arched gray window and
the rain. I pictured him sifting through the photos one by one, reading
each photocopied news article. I watched the rain pit the puddles, bounce
off the curb, shoot from the tires of a speeding cab and spray an unwary
tourist, arms full of candy-striped shopping bags. I stood perfectly still,

blinking away my terror. And when he didn't speak, at last I did. Facing the window, I told him everything I had promised Gisèle I would tell no one. I told him of her father and the incest; I made myself the hero.

"*C'est foutu*, Tristan." It was not an exclamation, but resigned: It's fucked.

"I know."

"As for her history, I suspected something of the kind; it was in her body language when I sketched her. In her eyes. The bastard. But you mean to tell me her whole family is dead?" It was rhetorical; he'd just read as much in the newspaper reports. I simply failed to correct him.

Eventually he shook his head and sighed. "And I thought my life was crap."

"I know. I don't know how I shall ever pay—"

"Not your life, Tristan. Hers. Hers has been crap, wouldn't you say? You and I have been fortunate."

"*Oui.*" I felt a moment's embarrassment. A faux pas. "*Oui, bien sur . . .*" But as I'd hoped, her horrors consumed him to such a degree that he shrugged away my own crimes.

In the end he said only that our "dysfunctions" had been "rather well suited." But then that's what most relationships were. A strong note of fatalism, a minor note of censure. That was all. And then, "Surely you don't intend to pay it, Tristan."

"I . . ." stumbling like a schoolboy. "What else can I do? He may send these photographs to the papers, to the police—"

Robin said nothing. His painting, a mass of writhing shapes and shadows, was forgotten. He poured us each a double scotch. "Can you come up with that kind of money?"

I shook my head. "I live off a generous trust, but I'm allowed only three percent of the principal per year. I typically don't touch it. I live off the interest. It would take years to raise such a sum. Clearly, I can't go to the police. I can't even go back to France." I paced, my heart squirming in my chest. I quieted it with scotch, breathing deeply. How I hated this sensation—so foreign—of being at another's mercy.

"You *could*," said Robin. "France has antiextradition laws."

"And leave her?"

He studied me. "No. I thought not."

"But three million dollars, within a month's time? It's insane. It would be difficult to close a sale on the brownstone in that time. And then where will we live? What will we live on?"

"I could lend you the money." Robin didn't bat an eye, and I suppose I realized only then how very wealthy he was. Not even wealthy, really, but silly rich. I suppose one has to be wealthy to inherit a town.

"I couldn't possibly. How would I ever repay you?"

"Then we'll make it a gift." And in his slapdash way, he told me he had a Matisse. He had a Matisse he would sell.

"A real one?"

This amused him. "Of course it's real, Tristan. *The Window*, it's called."

"Fauvist?"

"No, rather past the Fauves—1916. Between 1909 and 1917, Matisse is considered to have painted his masterpieces. The piece has some unique features. Though for my part I always liked the Fauves."

"You're joking."

"I wouldn't joke about such a thing. The great orgy of color—"

"Not the period, Robin." I sighed. "The 'gift.' I cannot possibly allow you to . . ."

His response was predictable. "No one allows me to do things, Tristan. I simply do them. I have my own legacy of sorts. A little like yours. If it troubles you, we'll work out some means of repayment." He shrugged in a vague way. "It will at least put an end to this nonsense."

I was so touched at the offer that tears stung my eyes. Why should he do such a thing for me? "But it's folly. If I pay, this *cul* will only come back for more."

"Do you really have no idea who it could be?"

"None at all." I did not mention that when we met, I'd been certain it was him. The idea seemed ludicrous to me now. "I know of no one who would follow me to San Francisco, and no one knew me there. It was my first visit to the city. Only Nora and Henri even knew I was going—"

Robin raised a cynical brow.

"*Non, non.* She doesn't speak the language, and he's been with me since I was a boy."

"Yet he suspected nothing amiss in your returning with daughter in tow?" Robin scoffed. "He'd have to be deaf, dumb, and blind not to—"

"He knows that all is not as it seems," I admitted. "But he would never address such a thing explicitly. While I was in San Francisco, he was *here*, Robin, looking after the house; I spoke to him by phone. He lacks both the means and the foresight to have followed me all across the country. Or to have me followed. No one could possibly have known my intent; I . . . well, I did not know it."

"Perhaps they weren't following you but her."

The idea had never occurred to me. Who would have followed her and not saved her from my designs? Who would wait so long to act? "*Non.* It isn't possible. Even if her father had taken to stalking her after school, he'd hardly stand back and . . ." Watch her be seduced by another man. I straightened.

"He's dead now, in any case." I felt Robin's sharp gaze. "But she may have had other admirers."

"She was just a child—"

It was the first time I'd admitted it, even to myself. And from Robin's expression, I could see now that the photos had shocked him. He'd rationalized for me; he knew from his conversation with her that it hadn't been sexual, not then. And yet. I glanced quickly away, returning to my window.

"She wouldn't be involved in something of this kind, would she?"

"Gisèle?" I turned, gaping at him. I laughed. "Are you mad?"

"Stranger things have happened, Tristan. When the world shits on you, you reply in kind. If she desired her freedom badly enough, perhaps it was *she* who seduced you. You're a wealthy man; you have all the appearances of wealth. She has a girlfriend take the photos, and now—"

"*Non.*" It was vehement, final. I waved a dismissive hand in the air, as if to erase his words.

"You're right." He stroked his jaw. "She'd hardly wait so long for the payoff. And a Sparbuch is certainly out of her reach. . . ."

The logic of this flooded me with such relief that I knew the wicked idea had wormed its way into my mind in spite of me.

"I don't suppose you'll ever know who it is. But you can't get blood from a rock. Three million is a damned arrogant request. Perhaps he's thinking of your collection—"

"But it is known that I cannot sell any part of it."

"Well, perhaps our ambitious friend is banking on insurance fraud."

"*Pardon?*"

"Come now, Tristan. Use your imagination. The collection is insured, of course. So. A short in the wires, a fire. Poof. Millions. Millions and millions." He swept the roguish lock of hair from his brow.

"You're not seriously suggesting—"

Robin looked as stricken as if I'd suggested a modern-day bonfire of the vanities. "My friend, I wouldn't dream of destroying a piece of it. Not any *genuine* piece of it, that is." His eyes sparked wickedly. "But what if copies were destroyed? Very fine copies that had been carefully swapped out for the originals."

"Have you turned forger?"

He laughed. "No, no. I'm no good at copying. But I know of someone."

"*Oui.* Well, you would. But I can hardly set fire to my family home," I protested.

"Of course not. Your blackmailer may have had something of the kind in mind, but you needn't accommodate him. As I've said, the Matisse is yours." With a shrewd expression he added, "But why should the paintings sit in Paris gathering dust? Why should you be separated from your collection by the simple obstacles of an ocean and a trust?"

And I was reminded of his vague "some means of repayment . . ."

In truth, the waste of it had often troubled me: I'd not even visited Paris for nearly three years now, while a splendid salmagundi of the best artists and works of the age sat entombed in an empty estate. "Who is this forger?"

"A childhood friend of mine from Prague. He copies only the impressionists, and there are none better. Marc Josef Kreicek. We call him 'K,' after the Kafka novel." He poured us each another finger of scotch. "I've just come back from Prague, as it happens. I went there after London— for his father's funeral. I had a sort of father figure in him. The only father I recognize." His pause held both reverence and sorrow. Something in the determined set of his mouth revealed how much the man had meant to him, more than if he had cried. "Stefan Kreicek was a brilliant man—the most brilliant psychiatrist of his time, though most in the West wouldn't even know his name. A real-life Svengali, he was.

He taught me everything of value that I know." A smile flared brightly and rapidly dimmed. "He came up dead two weeks ago. He was murdered, more or less government-sanctioned. Marc studied psychology as well as art in Paris, but it doesn't pay to be either a shrink or an artist in Czechoslovakia now. He left the country without a cent and began to use his talents elsewhere." A glance away. "Do you know he could not reenter for his own father's funeral? We're practically brothers, but K's at loose ends. I worry about him. A project like this would be medicinal, I think. He has a few very negative tendencies I'm afraid will get the better of him one day."

"The tendency toward art fraud?"

Robin only laughed. "No, that is nothing. He's spry on his feet, old aristocracy like you, my friend." And not him? I'd always assumed Robin's father a lord or an earl or something of the kind. "No, K's rather troubled by the notion that he doesn't fit in. He can't bear rejection. And in his mind it's everywhere. Everyone's against him. I think that is the greatest vulnerability one can have. Far better not to fit in and not to give a damn, don't you think?"

He didn't appear to expect an answer. I imagine he knew the one I'd give. It was what we had in common.

"I quite like Prague," he said idly, as if to change the subject. "Of course it's a fucking sham, politically. But it's more Kafka than Kafka. The lovely old palaces and gaslights and narrow cobblestone streets. Everything is very gray. One loses one's ordinary signposts."

"How do you mean?"

A shrug. "Theoretically, the Iron Curtain forces one to function more creatively. Underground."

"Oppression feeds the artist?"

He shrugged. "Obstacles feed the man. One becomes lost in the crowd but finds oneself in an empty room. A child without toys will invent them with his imagination."

"Or invent ways to attain the toys of others?"

Robin laughed heartily. "Yes, that's infinitely more fun. But make no mistake, K's a world-class forger, Tristan. His copies are undetectable with the known methods; he uses aged canvases, nonfluorescing paint, and masking varnishes to defeat the black-light test. He's studied the mounting techniques and the signatures, perfected the brush strokes and style of Renoir, Degas, Monet, Manet, Pissarro—"

I knew that forgeries had been made so well as to go undetected for years. It was always a race between the forgers and the collectors: to take and not to be taken. Who knew how many fakes of impeccable provenance graced the walls of the Louvre, the Met, or the Musée d'Orsay? And no one had need to scrutinize my collection. A copy could remain on my family walls for my lifetime. In the meantime, as Robin claimed, we would have the originals.

I soon grew enamored of the idea. It was the first and only time I saw Robin desire something openly, as close as I would ever see him to admitting that anything lay beyond his reach. And with his envy, my collection grew infinitely dearer to me. I realized then that the primary joy of collecting lies in denying another one's treasures. A petty, potent power. And so you see that his willingness to part with his Matisse, on my behalf, moved me deeply.

"It's not without risk, my plan, but then nothing without risk is worthwhile, wouldn't you agree? What do you say we cheat your black-mailer *and* your trustees?" He grinned like a mischievous boy.

And what a comfort, this "we." And so at last I nodded. "What exactly do you suggest?"

"Don't wire the money until the deadline: the twenty-first, December. And then not the full amount. Your leech will have to be satisfied with a little less blood. Half, I think. I imagine the brownstone will fetch that, at least." I hesitate to ponder what it would fetch now; this was 1981. "In the meantime I know of a buyer for the Matisse. It's worth four million, but on the black market I can guarantee at least three quickly, and it'll avoid the publicity of auction. I'll handle it all, and our friendly neighborhood blackmailer will have no way of knowing about it. On the other hand, he *will* note the sale of the house." Robin paused, thinking this over. "I say you deliver the sales price. It's a lovely old place, with a lovely address—one point eighty-five or thereabouts? It'll seem desperate. And it will be adequate. He'll take it and be damned."

"And Gisèle and I leave New York for your rustic American 'Alps'?"

Robin laughed. "The town's called Devon. It's less rustic than you might think. Robert Hughes once wrote, 'With enough conviction, art can form its own republic of pleasure, a parenthesis within the real world—a paradise.' There is the idea of art as arena, in which all manner of unexpected things might happen. Why not extend that arena beyond the canvas? At Oxford I wrote my thesis on just such an idea. Life as it might exist under such rules. I called it 'Art Philosophy.' That's the life I envision in Devon. It shan't be dull, I promise you."

I squinted at him. With anyone else I might have been dubious. A republic of pleasure?

Robin went on in an offhand manner, "In any case, it'll be more difficult for this parasite to follow you. And by all appearances, you'll be stripped of your assets." He took a swallow of scotch. "In the meantime you make a few solicitous visits to your family home and lighten up security. K becomes a frequent houseguest. And we begin to move your assets across the pond, where they might be better enjoyed."

"But what of customs—"

Robin waved a hand, a gesture so dismissive and confident that I understood this was hardly the first time he and "K" had worked together. And that much of his money had probably arrived through less-than-legal channels. As you can imagine, the knowledge came to me as a comfort, not a point of critique.

"It's the best way, Tristan. And a change will be good for Elle, I think."

I nodded. Yes, my Gisèle. A change *would* be good for her. Very good.

And so I drank a great deal more of Robin's scotch, and the hours passed as he painted, the rain ceasing and starting again, gray light slanting long through the windows. I wavered on my fulcrum, finding a delicate drunken balance there. I was something of an anarchist, as Robin was. Arcadian and hedonistic. I took pleasure in the idea of sharing his unique lawlessness, co-writing his strange *Paradiso*.

He exhausted his painting at last, stepping back from the canvas. It is inaccurate to call his work "abstract," as he continually breaks the one rule of the abstract and gives form a meaning beyond form. I could see he'd painted my refuge—my gray window, from which I'd been staring all afternoon—and captured all the emotion there: fear and desperation, guilt, and all the mad pleasures of chaos. It was the rain, ephemeral

and fleeting, subject to any number of dangers—evaporation, condensa-
tion. I felt myself tense with the drops, as if it were I who fought to cling
to glass.

And it was.

Robin saw it, too. He wasn't the painting but the painter; he could
cross between worlds and step back from chaos unscathed. But I could
not. I felt my future then, with a fatalism I rarely acknowledge. There
would be no crossroads for me, I knew, merely the path I had already
chosen. And even as he offered to save me with art and forgery and uto-
pian fantasies, a deep misgiving slipped in with my gratitude. The scales
between us were forever tipped. And it was a dangerous thing, I couldn't
help but feel, to be in Robin Dresden's debt.

XVI

AT THE WRITING DESK

NICOLA WAS SICK, and it wasn't even a school day. She'd been sick twice. Maggie fussed over her and insisted she spend the Saturday in bed. Her grandfather came to see her before he left for his date with Amanda that evening. Nicola tried to pretend it was the flu.

"I should have taken you straight home yesterday, *mon chaton*. I've grown too accustomed to you crying wolf. Perhaps we should have a doctor in. You look so pale." Tristan sat beside her on the quilted bedspread. Peering down, his clear blue eyes narrowed in concern. "I miss your smile, Nicola. I see it so rarely these days."

She could not force one to appear for him. "It's nothing, Grand-père. Just my stomach."

He ran a hand through his salty blond hair, and the hollow place appeared in his cheek that meant he was thinking thoughts he couldn't share. She'd seen it yesterday afternoon, when they'd spoken to Marc at the college. That seemed a lifetime ago, now. Nicola wondered if her own cheeks looked hollow, sucked in by the force of all the words she couldn't say.

Tristan put his hand to her forehead. "You feel feverish," he murmured.

She fought the urge to shrink from his touch and simply stared at him, searching for some way to explain what he'd become overnight. This frightening stranger. She shivered.

"Do you have chills?" A frown. "Perhaps I should cancel my plans—"
What were his plans for Amanda? "Where are you taking her?"

"The ballet."

That's why he was so dressed up. She gazed at him. "Because she's a
dancer?"

He searched her face. Nicola wanted him to simply say it. *I saw the
newspaper articles; I know what you read.* Because if he didn't say it, it was
just possible she really was going crazy.

But he merely echoed, "A dancer? *Non,* I don't think so, Nicola. You
must be confused."

"She looks like one." And she met his eyes. "She looks like Mom."

"I suppose she does, a bit." Tristan rose. "You must rest now, *mon
chaton.* Rest is the best thing." He kissed her forehead tenderly. "Sweet
dreams."

But she could not rest. Mrs. Pengilly made her homemade chicken
soup, and finally Maggie gave her medicine to help her sleep. Her father
came in with strawberry Jell-O and magazines. *Did he know the truth?*
Somehow she could not ask. If he knew, he wouldn't refer to Tristan
as his father-in-law; he wouldn't have called her mother "Gisèle." *What
would he do if he found out it was all a lie?*

"Feel up to a game of checkers, Nic?"

"I don't think so," she murmured. "Maggie gave me some medicine. . . ." Her eyelids were mercifully heavy, her words slurred. "Will
you just stay with me till I go to sleep, Dad? Please."

"Sure I will, sweetheart." Luke sat down a little awkwardly in the
rocking chair beside her bed. "You'll feel better tomorrow." But he didn't
sound convinced. He pulled her blanket in tight around her, fumbling
with it, and gently smoothed her hair. Then he began to rock, and the
soothing creak at last drowned out all the bad thoughts.

Nicola woke with a cry. It took her a moment to realize she wasn't really
drowning, only mummified in blankets and twisted pajamas. The lamp
beside her bed had been switched off, and she could no longer hear the
comforting rasp of the rocking chair. The clock on the bedside table read
10:33. It was early still; she had the whole night ahead of her.

Nicola concentrated on the blank slate of the shadowed ceiling high above her. She tried to focus on nothingness, but it was shockingly difficult to do this. As soon as she let her guard down, the same questions swarmed her mind. Why was Amanda Miller in Devon? Had her mother *known* she was here? Why had Nicola never met her? Why had her mother left her sister and her whole family behind? What did all of it have to do with her death?

Wide awake and seized by a sudden compulsion, Nicola slipped out of her room and crept down the wide hall, walking on the balls of her feet so as not to make a sound. Inside her mother's room, she went to the writing desk and pulled open the drawer that held her stationery, removing only the top sheets.

She'd seen it in an Alfred Hitchcock movie, *North by Northwest*. Cary Grant follows Eva Marie Saint to an address he uncovers from depressions on a writing pad. But did it really work?

Back at her own desk, Nicola selected a soft-leaded pencil from her pen holder. Applying very light pressure, she shaded the stationery so the impressions showed white in relief. Mostly there were unintelligible squiggles, pieces of letters and words. People must write very hard in spy movies, she thought. But there were many lone words she recognized: her own name appeared several times. And once: *sister*. Did that mean Gisèle *had* known Amanda was here?

In the end her mother had left behind only a few deeply imprinted words. But they were enough. It was the first line that chilled her most: *Please meet me . . . cabana*. And farther down the page: *get away from here*. And farther still, a final plea: *Please come*. And: *I'm afraid*.

Nicola's heart thrashed against her rib cage like a trapped bird. With a few simple words, her worst nightmares materialized. But who had her mother written that night? *Who had come?*

☙

Tristan was taking Amanda to see *Giselle*.

Was he toying with her? Or was she toying with him? She could no longer tell. They were players in a masquerade. She prepared for her role, putting on the new dress and shoes she'd charged to her credit card. She wore her hair up in a chignon. His eyes held her as she opened the door of her cottage.

"You are . . . beautiful."

And it was a beautiful night, chill and bright with stars. Dinner was at a lovely bistro; they walked to the theater afterward. The venue was posh, if small, the ballet company even smaller. The story line—what there was of it—was the ethereal stuff of ballet. Giselle, a young peasant girl, falls in love with Count Albrecht. He disguises himself as a villager to woo her but is betrothed to another woman. When his duplicity is revealed, poor Giselle goes rather predictably mad. In death she becomes one of the Wilis, the ghosts of young girls betrayed by love, who torment their lovers by making them dance to death. This was a fate more likely to befall the dancers than their fictive spirits, Amanda knew, but Albrecht is rescued from his ordeal. Giselle's love for him transcends deceit, death, and aching calluses.

For Amanda the magical transcendence of dance was long gone. She'd chosen college instead—a sensible major, the certainty of right answers and job security—only to find herself with no security and no answers, in the grip of the very things she'd tried so hard to escape. And sitting beside the keeper of her secrets.

Tristan felt her unease. "Amanda, *ma chère*," he murmured. "Are you all right?"

"I'm fine. It's lovely."

At last the lights came up and the applause died; the dancers and the dream diffused. All was right in fantasyland, and Amanda felt the old, almost forgotten panic of being utterly alone.

The crowd rippled around her, and Tristan slipped his arm inside hers to guide her through the throng. "You love the ballet," he said simply.

Is this what love was? "Hmm," she murmured noncommittally.

A gust of cold wind met them at the door. Tristan gazed down. "Mycroft's for a drink?"

Amanda had never had so much to drink in her life as she had in recent days—cocktails before dinner, wine with, and nightcaps after; she felt as though she'd entered a Thin Man movie. She'd always been afraid to drink much, since her father's life had been a virtual paean to alcohol. But nothing sounded better to her at that moment than a sedative. She didn't want to go back to her hotel alone, and she was determined to get something out of the evening beyond the empty farce of polite conversation. "Yes," she said. "A drink would be nice."

Mycroft's had an Old World English air, with leather club chairs and marble cocktail tables grouped before fireplaces and paired along the windows. The atmosphere was a smoky haze, the music from another era. Tristan smoked foreign cigarettes from a gold cigarette case, and Amanda found she didn't mind the smell of his smoke either. It was less exotic than Robin's had been, yet there was no pungent edge to it, and it suited him somehow. She'd once been told that all Europeans smoked. So far she was two for two.

They sat close together.

"You used to dance," Tristan said in his unexpected way.

"I still manage passably."

He frowned. "*Non, chérie.* You were, I think, a dancer. You studied ballet?"

"For a long time, yes. How did you know?"

"The way you felt the music, the little unconscious movements of your body. It is like watching a pianist listen to Chopin. He listens actively."

"You're very perceptive."

"Also, you were lost to me the entire night." A small smile.

Amanda laughed. "Oh." He was right; she'd hardly said two words together. "I'm sorry."

"Don't be sorry." The drinks came. "Why did you give it up?"

"It gave me up." She was able to speak of it detachedly now; the emotions that played out on the stage in the theater were safely packed away. The death of old dreams. The death of everything. But Tristan puffed on his cigarette broodingly, as if her failures or losses were his. And maybe they were.

"You stopped believing in it?" he asked.

"Dance belonged to my childhood, and, like most childhood things, it was a glorified bit of self-delusion. The illusion of dance is carefully cultivated. In truth, Giselle is probably a bulimic narcissist who cheats on her boyfriend."

His eyes widened—not at the sentiment, Amanda felt, rather at the casual use of Gisèle's name. It didn't last long. "But the illusion is for the audience, Amanda."

"It doesn't last long enough."

"Beauty never does."

The drinks appeared. Amanda took a sip of her cocktail and felt the alcohol soothe her raw senses like a salve. "May I try a puff of your cigarette, Tristan? I've never smoked."

Tristan's eyes were clear and reflective, impenetrable; she saw the flicker of firelight there. He placed his cigarette between her lips. "It will burn a bit, *chérie.* Try not to cough, and it will pass."

It did burn. She didn't cough. It passed. She tried another and felt a bit light-headed. She gazed at Tristan through the smoke and half laughed, half coughed.

He rubbed his jaw; his eyes traveled over her. "It's bad for you, they say."

She laughed. "Is that still in debate among the French?"

"*Mais oui,* the French debate everything." But then he frowned. "You are reckless tonight. It saddens me to hear you speak of your childhood in such a way, Amanda. It is a precious thing, the innocence of children."

"I suppose it can be." She swallowed. "Meeting Nicola yesterday brought a lot of it back. She's very lonely, Tristan. I understand what it's like to lose your mother. . . . I'd like to help her."

He reached out to smooth a stray tendril of her hair. "I would like to help you both."

"She's at the more critical stage, I think."

"Is she?" Tristan put his cigarette to his lips and then to hers.

Had he invented evasion? Amanda inhaled slowly, then exhaled. It was true. She did it not for itself but for the recklessness in it. "Is she close to her father?"

"Not particularly. He's always been rather awkward in the role."

"That's a shame. So was mine. . . ." She plunged on. "But the two of you are close?"

"She is the center of my universe. Especially now." Tristan swirled his bourbon, gazing into the tawny liquid. "Tell me about your father, Amanda. You've never told me about him."

"For some reason I've been thinking of him tonight." She glanced at the legs of whiskey clinging to Tristan's snifter and laughed ruefully. "It must be your whiskey. The scent reminds me of him."

"I see." Tristan let the silence linger; he studied her and frowned. It was a tactic to make her say more than she wanted to, this frown. She'd begun to recognize it. "He drank. And you were frightened of him?"

"Terrified." She gazed into the fireplace, at the flames as they licked the wood in the iron grate. "I thought that was what fathers were for."

He offered her his cigarette; she inhaled. "He was . . . abusive?"

"Not beyond the norm. At least not to me."

"But to Karen?" The way he said her name. As if it were familiar to him.

"I don't know. I've . . . I've always wondered." Amanda stared down at her own drink; she felt a little dizzy. Just a moment before, she'd longed to be altered, to be numb. How quickly the balance tipped. Abstractedly, she realized this is what her father had done. Over and over. The balance tipping a bit more each time. Or maybe that was just an attempt to excuse him. Maybe he'd never had any balance to lose. "Whatever Karen felt, she dealt with it by taking it out on herself, not him."

Tristan was rapt, as always when she spoke of Karen, a thing evident by his posture, his stillness, and the tone that didn't quite convince in its neutrality. "How do you mean?"

"Listen, Tristan, I know we're playing true confessions, but—"

"We're not playing anything, *chérie*. Are we?"

"Well, our conversations are very one-sided. I'm always doing the confessing."

"That is because you need to talk to me." So certain he was of this.

"And what about you? Who do you talk to?"

He did not reply. He fingered the cuff of his dress shirt. But she was not to be dissuaded. Was it that she had seen her niece? She'd seen Nicola. . . . She was losing her patience for games.

"I'll tell you about my father, Tristan, but only if you tell me something in return."

"Of course." His tone was light.

She held his eyes. "Anything I ask?"

"*Oui.*"

"All right. Well, I've told you that Karen was terrified of the water?"

"I don't think so."

She knew she had told him. "She was phobic about it. Something from childhood. I'm not even sure she remembered fully. We were six years apart. It happened before I was born. But she wouldn't go near the water. And my father was crazy for it. One year he bought a boat. It was an extravagance, since we could barely afford rent on the house, but his father had died and left him a little money. Anyway, as soon as we got it, he insisted we have swimming lessons. I was dying to learn. I was six or so, Karen about twelve." Amanda felt jumpy. To reenter that time was like stepping into a black hole in her soul. It still filled her with fear. "She refused to even go in the shallow end. Simply flat-out refused. It wasn't stubbornness. She just . . . *couldn't*. The instructor finally gave up on her, but my mom didn't tell my father. Karen came to the lessons with me and knelt on the side, watching me the whole time, sure I'd drown. Afterward you could see the imprint of the concrete on her knees. . . ." Amanda swallowed. "So eventually Dad took us out in the new boat. It was the one thing he did well—he'd lived on the water as a kid and was in the navy during the war—so he kept teasing her, trying to get her into the water. She said she didn't want to go in, you see, not that she couldn't. It grated on him. He thought she'd had lessons, and he was a bully. He threw her in." Amanda swallowed again, hard. "She hardly even splashed, Tristan. She just . . . sank."

Tristan's eyes narrowed. She could see anger there, protectiveness. Natural things.

"I tried to tell him she couldn't really swim, but he just stood there, waiting for her to come up, not listening." Sudden tears stung her eyes. She remembered the helplessness. "I jumped into the water and tried to dive for her, which was useless. I'd only ever been in a swimming pool. I couldn't see, and the current was pulling at me. My mother began to scream and plead with him. Finally my father jumped in and dragged her up. I thought she was dead. I was crying. . . . But then she started to spit up water." A pause. "I knew something was wrong then, between her and my father. Something deeper. She looked at him. . . . I'll never forget the way she looked at him—the whites of her eyes—as if she were sorry to be breathing again."

Tristan sat cloaked in his smoke. "What happened then?"

"Dad was furious with her. After that he made it his mission in life to get Karen out on the water. He'd take her out alone." She hesitated. "I don't know what happened out there. But she never did learn to swim." Amanda felt like one of her hapless psych subjects, waiting for the next slide. "There was something not right with her, Tristan. She changed. There were a lot of disturbing things. Well, disturbing to a psychologist. . . . Back then I thought everyone was like us. Karen lost her friends. She stopped laughing. She fell at school once, bloodied her knees and kept picking the scabs. My father said he . . . he didn't want her to scar, and he started to bind her hands at night. 'For her own good.'" She flinched. "I'd see him coming out of her room."

Tristan's jaw tightened. He murmured something in French. "Your mother did not see?"

"I don't think she wanted to. But when Karen disappeared, something snapped in Mom. She actually filed for divorce from my father. But the night she died, she went to meet him one last time. She kept hugging me, reassuring me it was going to be all right. But there was something in her face. . . . It wasn't all right." Amanda arched her foot toward the fire. "I was terrified she was going back to him. She told me she never would. And then she looked into my eyes and asked if he'd ever touched me. I thought she meant had he hit me. . . . He hadn't. He didn't hit us. Now, of course, I wonder if she meant something else." Her voice broke. "I never wanted to believe it. But it would explain a lot. Why Karen left home. Why she would want to escape. It would be like her stories."

"Her stories?"

"Karen used to make up stories for me . . . for as long as I can remember. I'd rather listen to her than watch television. In the beginning they were just fun adventure stories and mysteries, big families that had mishaps but laughed a lot. Toward the end they were all about escape." Amanda held his eyes. "In one, the world had flooded and the only escape was an underwater city in a bubble. Karen drew it for me. It was so intricate and beautiful I thought it really existed. Her heroines always got away." She added softly, "I like to think Karen did, too."

Tristan's hand stiffened on hers. But he stared at her as if mesmerized.

Amanda said quietly, "She did get away, Tristan, didn't she?"

For a long moment, he didn't speak. She thought she saw the glint of tears in his reflective eyes. Turning, he reached for his coat on the arm of the overstuffed chair, retrieved his handkerchief, and rose. "Forgive me." Uncharacteristically flustered. "I'll be . . . just a—"

And he walked abruptly away. Amanda's heart beat hard and fast. She felt ill. *What now?*

"Excuse me, Amanda?"

Startled, she jumped half out of her chair. Marc Kreicek? He looked like a model in one of the edgier ads of *GQ*, with his high, sharp cheekbones and empty eyes, gazing at her with his usual expression— half solicitous, half lascivious. Jay had mentioned he lived in Devon. Still, it was odd to see him here. Two worlds colliding. Her thoughts were too jumbled to order, but she managed to murmur some form of greeting.

"What a surprise to see you here, my dear. What brings you to Devon?"

"Oh . . . just taking in the sights. I'd forgotten you lived here." She didn't want to engage him and glanced rather pointedly down the hall after Tristan.

"I see you have company. I won't keep you. It's just that something dropped from your friend's coat pocket a moment ago. I noticed it from the bar." From his expression it was clear he'd noticed *it*, because he had been noticing them. Marc knelt beside Tristan's chair and rose with a white envelope, which he handed to Amanda, purposefully brushing her fingers as he did so. "He is much too old for you, you know." A close-lipped smile.

"Yes, Marc, thanks," she said. "I know."

"You are staying in town?"

"Yes." She wasn't going to tell him where.

"Well, then. I am sure we'll run into each other again."

"Nice to see you." To avoid further conversation or eye contact, her eyes dropped to the envelope in her hands. She felt a wave of déjà vu that was tactile. There was nothing but a single scribbled initial on the front: an *R* or a *K*. But her fingers recognized the envelope.

Inside was a folded sheet of stationery. Shivers snaked down her spine. Both the stationery and the handwriting were familiar. Amanda read only the first line. Blinded by panic, she hurriedly folded it again, stood, and walked quickly to the door. Oblivious to Marc's curious gaze, she hastened down the narrow stairs and into the sobering night air.

❧

Luke saw her scurrying along the cobblestone street like a hallucination, a trick of the mist. "Amanda?"

The rapid clicking of her heels halted, but she turned unwillingly. When her eyes landed on him, they widened; her mouth dropped open in stunned surprise and unmistakable distaste. "*Luke?* What on earth are you doing here?"

At the sight of her, his heart had leaped. Now a sharp tug of guilt reined it in. "I was going to ask you the same thing." Marc had phoned Luke to meet him in the bar upstairs for a drink. Had Amanda been up there? It was just the kind of trouble Marc loved to stir up. A discreet inquiry at the Dorrington had produced no forwarding address. Luke had assumed she'd left Devon. "I live here, Amanda. But you know that."

She shuddered, whether from the cold or the unwanted company, Luke couldn't tell. "I don't think I know anything about you." She cast a nervous glance up the street. "If you'll excuse me."

"Amanda . . ." Luke jogged to catch up to her.

She cast another glance behind her and ducked into a side street, tugging him after her. The storefronts were still lit, though it was long after business hours. They halted before a jewelry-shop window where the neck busts stood eerily bare. "What is it you want?"

"What the hell are you so jittery about?" he demanded.

"You don't get to interrogate me," she replied angrily. "Obviously, you changed your mind, remember? And obviously I've changed mine."

"I'm sorry about that, Amanda. I never meant it. Honest to God. If you only—"

"You're in the clear, all right? Off you go. Don't lose sleep over it. Go back to your wife and kids." Again she turned away.

And for a moment Luke could not follow. *Wife and kids? Did she not know? But then what had she been doing at the gallery? What had she been doing with Robin Dresden?* "I don't get it," he called. "Why did you come here looking for me?"

She turned. "You've got to be kidding me. I wasn't looking for you."

"Come *on*. I saw Robin Dresden at your hotel—"

"How did you . . . ? Have you been *following* me?" Her hazel eyes flashed, and the dimple in her left cheek was almost as prominent when she was angry as when she smiled. Luke found himself charmed by it either way. "It's a pretty big leap from disappearing act to stalker, Luke. Cut it out."

"I'm not stalking you," he said quietly. "I thought you were stalking me."

"Don't flatter yourself."

"I know I've been an ass. You have every reason to hate me, Amanda, but there's something more going on here. I think you're being used, somehow, to get to me."

"You're an egomaniacal sociopath."

"Just tell me one thing. Why did Robin ask you up here?"

She squinted in confusion. "Robin didn't ask me. I came on my own, for reasons that have nothing to do with you. What is your connection to him, anyway?" But then she shook her head abruptly. "I don't even want to know." With a warning glance, "Don't follow me, Luke. I mean it. Just leave me alone."

"But you left a message for me—"

She didn't turn. "You have me confused with one of your other girl-friends." And then she turned onto the street and vanished, leaving Luke to stare down the murky alleyway after her.

As fantastic as it seemed, Amanda apparently had no idea that Luke Halvorson and Luke Farrell were one and the same.

❧

Amanda reached the Chaucer Inn at last and opened her door to a ringing telephone.

It couldn't possibly be Luke. She'd given several paranoid glances over her shoulder on the walk here. *What a small world it was. Too small.* But no, this would be Tristan. The idea sent a shiver of fear down her spine. Amanda moved toward the phone but did not pick up. She felt it had eyes somehow and could see her there, listening.

Mercifully, the ringing stopped. The message light remained dark.

Exhaling in relief, Amanda kicked off her torturous shoes and climbed onto the bed. She opened the envelope carefully, noting again the hastily scribbled addressee: it must be an *R*. She read.

> *Please meet me tonight at the cabana. It will be safe to talk there. I know it's late, but you barely sleep, and I have to see you.*
>
> *Nicky saw me in the garden with Tristan tonight. He had sensed something was wrong—he always can. I kissed him only to keep him from knowing I detest him.*
>
> *What a criminal fool I've been. This afternoon I discovered he'd taken something of Nicola's, a teddy bear. I found it hidden in his closet. He took a piece of her and put it with something of mine. To see the two things together, kept in secret, all at once I knew. Her teddy bear alongside an old stuffed bear of mine, a thing I'd thrown away weeks before I even met Tristan. But he must have been watching me, following me. He must have fished it out of the garbage. Imagine it. Our meeting wasn't serendipitous—he wasn't my savior. He was stalking me, and I was a child. Only now do I realize, looking at my own child. . . . I was just a child.*
>
> *All I want now is to take Nicola and go to my sister. But I'm afraid Tristan will follow us wherever we go.*
>
> *Please get this tonight. Please come. I've tried to sleep, but it's no use. Even the sleeping pills aren't working. I want to confront Tristan, but I don't think he can be confronted with himself. He'll smash the mirror.*
>
> *You're the only one I can turn to. You gave me the only true moments of joy I've ever known. I love you . . . And I know you'll help me now, if anyone can.*

> *~Elle*

Amanda read and reread the letter. Tears ran down her cheeks. For the first time, Gisèle . . . Elle . . . was real to her. She was Karen.

She reached for the phone and began to dial Robin's private line. It rang. And rang again. At last his reassuring, resonant voice filled her ear. *"I'm afraid you haven't reached me. There's still time to change your mind. Otherwise you'll be called upon to speak at the unimaginative tonal prompt."* *There's still time to change your mind.* And abruptly she did. Amanda hung up the phone. In the space of a second, doubts had swarmed in like bees to a hive. Could she really trust Robin? Her sister had; she'd asked him to meet her that night. Had that been her last mistake?

But surely he'd never received the letter. If he had, how had it ended up in Tristan's pocket? And yet why *had* it been there? Was it a trophy of some kind? Justification for his crime? A thing he couldn't discard and thus kept with him wherever he went, so it would not be discovered?

On the surface everything pointed to Tristan. He was in possession of the letter, therefore he'd discovered Gisèle writing the letter and killed her. But the case didn't quite hold up. She'd drowned in the *pool.* Robin had been staying in the main house. Clearly her sister had planned to slip the envelope under his door before going out to the cabana. If the letter was never delivered to him, why had Gisèle still gone to the pool house?

A needling inner voice reminded Amanda that she didn't really know Robin at all. She'd trusted him, and yet how often had she been misled by trust? Could the note have been forged, or planted on Tristan somehow? She pressed cool fingers to her throbbing temples.

Damn . . . damn . . . damn. If the letter was valid, there was no getting around its accusations. Amanda wasn't sure if possession of a stuffed animal was tantamount to child molestation, but when combined with the troubling evidence of Tristan's having taken a similar item of Karen's, it was damning. The horrible implications of this rippled through her consciousness like the concentric rings made by a stone dropped into a pond. Tristan had not met Karen in New York but in San Francisco, and *not* by accident; he must have even helped to engineer her "murder." Amanda thought of her sister's bloody backpack, ripped and left on the pier to do just what it had done—deceive.

What made her think he wasn't equally capable of preying on Nicola now? Shuddering, Amanda pictured her niece's face, that precocious beauty so like her mother's. Who was Tristan, *really?*

Amanda took a deep breath. Her sister had trusted Robin in her last hours. And Amanda still trusted her sister. She reached for the phone just as it rang and nearly jumped out of her skin.

Once, twice, three times. Its eyes bored into her. Finally she snatched it up. "Hello?"

"Amanda, *chérie*. Thank God I've reached you. Are you all right?"

No. "I . . . yes. Yes, Tristan, I'm all right now. I'm afraid I got sick from the cigarette."

His soft, urbane voice was full of concern. "I thought it was something of the sort. Do not feel bad. It took me several tries to carry it off properly." A pause. "I shouldn't have brought up such difficult topics for you. I'm sorry."

In truth, *she* had brought them up. Deliberately.

"Don't be. I'm sorry I left."

"I'm simply relieved to find you safe."

"Well, it's late." She steeled herself. "But I . . . I'll see you tomorrow, Tristan, at the wine club. And it was your turn for true confessions, remember?"

There was a brief silence, and then, coolly, Tristan replied, "I doubt I will have anything revelatory to confess, *chérie*, but I will make an effort. Shall I pick you up?"

"Yes . . . yes, Tristan. That would be nice."

"Good. *Bonne nuit*, Amanda."

She hung up and without hesitation dialed Robin's number. At the unimaginative tonal prompt, she said, "It's me. Amanda. I know it's late, but I understand you barely sleep. Please call me as soon as you can. I think I have something that belongs to you. . . ."

❧

Nicola's fever had disappeared by Sunday morning. Her father had an appointment in town that afternoon, so she asked him to drop her off at the college library. She'd been unable to reach Robin on either his private line, his home number, or at the gallery and didn't know how to call the tower. But he had to be there. He had to be. She had only an hour, so she walked quickly to the center of campus, came to the familiar wrought-iron gate, and pressed the buzzer.

When the gate swung open, she wasn't met by the usual familiar face of Hanna, who was the cook and housemother for Robin's students. Instead this must be one of the students themselves—of whom Nicola had heard much but never met, apart from Josh. They were usually in class when she came. Tall and quite thin, the girl was dressed in ragged jeans and a man's white dress shirt that was too big for her. Her complexion was like china, very fair and almost poreless, her features even and fine. Her eyes were a surprise: darkly intelligent, they were a bruised blue like Lake Devon on a stormy day.

"Hello." She ran a hand through long blond hair. It was faintly tangled and damp as if she'd just come from the shower, though at nearly two o'clock it seemed an odd hour. She shouldn't walk around with her hair damp, Nicola thought, unless she was trying to get out of school, too. Yet the girl had so sharply sentient an air that Nicola couldn't imagine giving her any advice.

"Er, hi. Is Robin here?"

"I'm sorry, he's not. But I'll be seeing him later. I'm happy to give him a message for you."

Nicola's heart sank. It wasn't unusual for her godfather to be unreachable, but lately it had been different. And she needed badly to reach him. He wasn't part of the inner workings of Falconer's Point—her father and Tristan, Maggie, Mrs. Pengilly, and Henri—all collaborating to ensure that things functioned as they always had, that nothing changed. Robin was a part of her world, but also apart. He'd be able to see things clearly.

The older girl studied her sympathetically. "It must be important." Her direct gaze reminded her of Robin's and gave Nicola the same sense of having been glimpsed beneath the skin.

"Kind of," she said at last. "I'm his goddaughter, Nicola."

"Of course you are. That's why I recognize you." She broke into a warm smile. "I've seen pictures of you at his house, but you're older now. It's nice to meet you, Nicola. You know, I halfway believed he'd made up a godchild. . . . Somehow I can't quite picture him at a christening."

Nicola smiled. She liked the strange girl.

"Well, listen. Unfortunately, he can't be reached where he is, so why don't you come in and leave a note for him?" She opened the gate and motioned Nicola in. "Maybe he'll show up while you're here. If not, I promise not to read it, okay? I'm Ashleigh, by the way."

"Oh . . . Robin's mentioned you before. You're a writer." And trailing after her, Nicola felt she was entering the pages of a book: Mary Lennox, maybe, in the secret garden. The tower had always felt separate from the rest of the college, cloistered by the gate and the gardens, the towering pines and evergreens. A path curved along a carpet of grass on which a discarded game of croquet had been left in midplay, mallets discarded and spread in disarray. The perfume of roses mingled with the sharp scent of mint and anise in the air, and everything was frosted over with heavy mist that had drifted up from the lake.

"Do you mind helping me collect the mallets before we go in?" Ashleigh asked. "All the moisture in the air's rotten for them."

"Sure." It was nice to have something to distract her. "It's a cold day to play."

"I guess so. The cold doesn't bother me much anymore. It used to, when I first came to Devon." They moved around the damp lawn. "Anyway, these are from yesterday. If I didn't pick them up, they'd still be out here next week, nice and mildewed. Where are you visiting from?"

Why did the question surprise her? Because Nicola couldn't imagine living anywhere but Devon; she'd never *been* anywhere else. "I live here. I was born here. We live across the lake."

"You're kidding." Ashleigh pushed a pale strand of hair behind her ear. "Robin's kept you such a secret."

"Not really. I mean, I'm here a lot," Nicola said. "I have a card for the library and usually come to see Robin on Thursdays with my . . . my grandfather. You're in class then, I guess. I've never even seen Josh here." But saying his name felt like entrance into a private club.

"Hmm. Well, Rob seems to compartmentalize his life like a cafeteria tray." Glancing at Nicola sideways, Ashleigh said mischievously, "I say we turn the tables on him. Tell me all about yourself." She took the last of the mallets from Nicola and slid them into the croquet rack. "Who are your parents? How does he know them?"

"Actually, he knew Grand-père. Oh, sorry. I call him that because he's French and it's French for—"

"Grandfather." Ashleigh smiled. "That's cool."

The kids at school had made fun of her for it. Nicola wished she could go to school here. "His real name's Tristan Mourault." She swallowed. "My mother's name was Gisèle—"

Ashleigh stopped short and stared at her. "Gisèle Mourault?"

No. Her name was Karen Miller. But Nicola only nodded. "Yes."

"Oh, God, I'm sorry." But Ashleigh didn't avert her eyes; they were full of sympathy.

"Did Robin tell you about her?"

"Yes. We saw the paintings."

"Oh."

"She was a very special person, wasn't she?" Ashleigh gazed at Nicola a moment. "You look a bit like her, you know—your skin and hair and . . ." She touched her own cheekbones lightly. "But not through the eyes. You must take after . . ." And then she frowned and with effort broke her gaze. "Poor thing, you're turning blue. Let's get you inside, okay?"

Ashleigh led Nicola through the familiar heavy door with the old-fashioned lion's-head knocker. Nicola heard the piano as soon as the door opened, and her heart began to thud. It was Josh. She could tell by the way he played and the haunting melody. They stepped into the familiar foyer with the iron coatrack and the oval mirror, and Nicola ran a self-conscious hand through her hair.

They didn't go up the stairs as she always did but turned to the right and continued down a hall, past a kitchen and into a vast sitting room. The sound was thunderous as they entered. Josh sat at the piano, his fingers cascading over the keys. She'd heard him play many times before but was still seized by a sense of disbelief at the sight. His hands flew over the keys so quickly, ambidextrously, and the notes were full one moment and the next so delicate and fragile that they did not seem to belong to the ponytailed, rough-looking kid who'd moved here because he had a habit of beating people up and smoking pot at his previous schools.

His back was to her, and so Nicola looked around the room. She thought it the most beautiful thing she'd ever seen. A marvelous mishmash of styles, it had a kind of magic to it. There were finely woven tapestries on the walls, of forests and streams and castles, and Victorian couches and chairs. Otherwise the space was appealingly cluttered with paintings and sculpture, lamps with silk shades and one of the tall stained-glass type: Tiffany. Beside it was a game table with a marble chessboard inlaid in its burled-wood top. There was also a standing globe and a curvaceous grandfather clock that chimed the hour as if in accompaniment for Josh's piano, candlesticks with drippy candles and incense burners that gave off a musty, pungent sandalwood scent that stung her nose. The fragrance of herbs and flowers mingled with it, overflowing from delicate pots on the windowsills.

An elaborately detailed Persian rug hid much of the antique floorboards and revealed a variety of anachronisms: a book bag with several battered notebooks, car keys, a fat textbook, and a dog-eared paperback. Beside it on the floor lay a stack of CDs, with open packs of chewing gum and cigarettes on top. A concert posting for a club in the village wafted to her feet, carried on a gust of wind that blew through a cracked window.

As Nicola stooped to pick it up, the piano stopped abruptly and Josh spun around, "Hey there, kiddo. What're you doing here?" Nicola met his lazy smile and the eyes that were always shifting color. He rose, pulling her into a hug, and she felt her cheeks flush.

"You doing okay?" he murmured, too low for Ashleigh to hear. Nicola, pleased by this show of genuine affection from him, managed a nod. He tousled her hair. Josh wore a string of brown leather around his neck, and the knot had worked forward so that it peeked from beneath his ponytail. His eyes looked a little glassy, and his breath smelled like alcohol, and she was overwhelmed, as always, by this potent mixture of attractively foreign things, masculinity and vice. But she knew that Josh would never look at her the way he looked past her, at Ashleigh. Slowly, his gaze returned to Nicola. "What brings you around?"

"I just came to talk to Robin about something."

Josh shrugged. "Well, he was here last night, looking for a book. Found it, I guess." He indicated a corner table with a dismissive wave of his hand. "Then he took off again."

"Where's he now?"

"Out at the castle." Then, noting her puzzlement. "It's not a castle, really. It's a wreck. To be honest, so's he. He's been a shit since the funeral. I'd avoid him if I were you."

"Charming advice." Ashleigh grabbed his arm less than politely, and he dropped amiably back onto the piano bench. "I told her she could leave a note for him."

Josh scratched his head indifferently, reaching for a glass from a table beside the piano. Nicola could see the doorway reflected in the polished black surface of the angled top door. Ashleigh disappeared through it, returning with a notepad and pen for Nicola. Then she left her to her own devices, sliding onto the piano bench beside Josh and taking a sip of his drink. He reached an arm around her waist and tickled her; she elbowed him, and Nicola felt a twinge of envy and curiosity.

Josh began to play again. Nicola turned and went to the table in the corner where Robin had discarded his book. It wasn't a real book, but a student's published thesis from the library: *Building Magic*, it was called, *The Vision of Bryan Prescott*. That was Robin's uncle's name, the architect. She picked up the volume and thumbed through it. The architectural plans of several buildings downtown were discussed in detail, and a few pages had been dog-eared. They belonged to a chapter titled "The Modern Secret Passage: Eccentricity or Historical Homage?"

To Nicola's surprise, she found she was looking at the plans to her own home. The folded-down pages all discussed Falconer's Point and had been marked extensively with a highlighter. It was strange to sort the two-dimensional squares into rooms, but she soon got the hang of it. The layout of the house was as familiar to her as the back of her hand. So, too, were the highlighted portions. It seemed her "secret" passageways weren't so secret after all.

There was the entry, the great hall, and the receiving room with its long passage in the wall. Another, smaller passage was concealed in the butler's pantry. There was the space beneath the stairwell and a few of the window seats, the hollow tenth stair, and many more. But a few were enticingly new to Nicola. There was a trapdoor on the ground floor and something odd along the second story: a long passage that extended the length of the wall.

Squinting down at the plans, she saw that the entry point appeared to be the closet of a bedroom. It was her mother's bedroom.

⤝⤞

"Hello, Mr. Farrell," Preston Murphy greeted Luke. "Thanks for coming. Your DNA results arrived on Friday. I apologize for the delay, but I just got in from Seattle this morning."

Luke's heart was pounding. "No problem. Thank you for coming in on a Sunday." But was he really thankful? He'd just dropped his daughter off at the library. Did he really want to know she wasn't his? Luke waited. His nails sank painfully into his palm.

"Well, I'm afraid your suspicions were correct. B is not related to A. That is, A is not your biological daughter, Mr. Farrell. Your testing result was exclusionary. I'm sorry."

I'm sorry. "Well," Luke said stiffly. "And how about C?"

"Yes, C." Even Preston Murphy seemed to prefer the remote quantities A, B, and C, as euphemisms. "I told you on the phone there was both good and bad news." He shuffled through a set of papers on his desk. "Here we are, yes. The two are related, but C's percentage doesn't equate to paternity."

"Thank God." *Thank God . . . thank God.* "Are you sure?"

"Quite sure. Genetics is a complicated science, Mr. Farrell. But on the most simplistic level, every child has both a mother and a father, and parents always contribute fifty percent to the genetic code of their offspring." As he spoke, Murphy spread obscure-looking diagrams across the desk before him. "Elsewhere it grows more confusing, of course. Siblings, for instance, share about twenty-five percent of their genes on average, but it's theoretically possible to share none at all. This would be highly rare. Each child would have to inherit alternate halves of their parents, if you will. The percentage here indicates that C is an uncle, or perhaps a cousin."

Luke sighed, barely following the monologue. "I've told you he's her grandfather."

Preston tapped his pencil on his desk in an annoying *rat-a-tat-tat* that bored through Luke's head. "Well, as I've said I'm no expert, but the results show roughly twelve percent in common."

Luke said, as if to himself, "So where does that leave me?"

Murphy abruptly ceased his pencil solo. "If I may say so, the very fact that you suspected incest makes it clear there are some very troubled family dynamics at work."

"That's an understatement."

"Does your daughter have developmental problems?"

"No, no. She's perfect. Very bright, very pretty. She gets A's and hardly goes to school. She has emotional problems." He shifted in his chair. "Her mother's just died."

"Well, my professional advice to you is to be her father and let the matter of biology rest. Is someone questioning your paternity?"

"Only me. I've always questioned it." *If Nicola wasn't his, and she wasn't Tristan's, whose was she?* The question reverberated over and over in his head. Along with another: *Had he known Gisèle at all?*

"Well." Gently, "Your wife may have had a relationship she regretted. From the dates involved, it occurred prior to your marriage. It's a grave mistake to view fatherhood in purely genetic terms, Mr. Farrell. Emotionally, you've been the child's father for eleven years—"

"But she ought to know who her real father is, don't you think?"

"In my business, people often learn things they later wish they hadn't." Preston made a neat stack of the DNA results. "That said, I feel I must tell you that you failed to understand me earlier, Mr. Farrell. The man you feel is your daughter's grandfather cannot possibly be so. For grandparents, as well as parents, the percentage is invariable. If C is the grandfather of A, they would share twenty-five percent of their genetic code. As I've said, the percentage here is less than half that."

Luke stared. "But that would mean he wasn't my wife's father. That's impossible."

Preston shrugged. "Perhaps he was an uncle who took her in?"

"No. Shit . . . that's impossible."

The detective laughed. "I can assure you, it is perhaps the only objective element of your highly subjective situation. Unlike people, DNA doesn't lie. Whatever the case, my advice is to weigh the benefits of pursuing the truth against the possible costs. Do you really wish to turn your daughter's life upside down?" With a prescient air, he added, "We all make mistakes."

And Luke had made more than his share. Had he been wrong about *everything*? If Tristan was not Gisèle's father and not her lover, then what had Luke seen in the garden? He no longer knew. But there was more than A, B, and C to be considered. There was now D.

❧

Robin Dresden stood before the ruins of a great stone mansion. It still possessed a stately, imperial air, though its roof had long since fallen in.

In the west wing, the remainders of a vast staircase ascended to the sky, and the jagged walls were surrounded by rubble.

He wore a white shirt, loose and haphazardly buttoned, and faded jeans ragged at the knees. There were shadows beneath his eyes, and his beautiful dark hair was unkempt. Shading his eyes, he blinked at Amanda as if she might be the product of his feverish imagination.

Robin's rumpled appearance only increased the anxiety she'd felt all day. She found herself speaking in quick, staccato sentences. "Well, thank God I found you. I've called and looked everywhere. Rolf gave me the address of your home. What's with all the security anyway? Are you expecting armies to invade? I was finally able to talk my way past the sentry, and a very nice woman—your housekeeper, I guess—told me you'd be out here." Amanda caught her breath.

"The mobile doesn't work here. It's a vortex. . . . Wreaks havoc with the signal."

"It's also in the middle of nowhere."

"That, too."

"You spent the night out here?" she asked dubiously.

Robin gave a distracted nod. "The exterior doesn't do it justice; it's rather comfortable inside. I find it a good place to think."

"Hmm." It did possess an austere, isolated beauty, a strange air of mystery and trespass. A grove of oaks, unusual at this elevation, lay to her left; a stream meandered to her right. The remains of the great house sat in the shadow of the mammoth mountains above, and Robin stood in the sun, his own shadow a long silhouette stretching out to the rubble behind him.

"I'm glad you've come." The raw inflection in his voice unnerved her.

"What *is* this place?" Amanda asked. "It's haunting."

"Some would say haunt*ed*." Robin turned, regarding the rubble. "This was the home of Stephen Prescott: first heir to Devon. Rather a madman. Though, had we met, he'd probably have been my favorite of the lot. My students call it the castle. Charming, hmm?" He gazed back at her. "And rather apt, it turns out. My family tree's as twisted as the English monarchy, and it is certainly rotten at the core."

She met his eyes questioningly. What had happened to prompt this unflattering glimpse of his genealogy?

His expression was pained. "I think I may have been wrong, Amanda."

"Is that so unusual an event?"

"It is. Yes." He managed to say it without ego or rancor, and it shook her to see him falter so uncharacteristically. His dark eyes narrowed. "I don't want you to see Tristan anymore. I should never have suggested it. It may not be safe for you."

Amanda cleared her throat, feeling the weight of the letter in her pocket. "What's happened?"

He gazed at the ground. "I've worked out how he may have done it. I didn't want to see it. I still don't. Affection makes you blind."

"Well," she said uncertainly. "He's your friend. . . ."

Robin's searching gaze must have mirrored her own. Finally he fixed his eyes on a point beyond her. "I'm afraid he's a good deal more than my friend, Amanda. Tristan is my brother."

XVII

ON THE LAKE

Devon was all that Robin had promised, the sort of place in which nature conspires to make a show of man's insignificance. Gisèle and I flew in to Sea-Tac and from there chartered a plane. Below us we could see the chalky, whittled points of the northern Cascades left over from an ice age; ancient glaciers had slowly carved out the lush green valleys, and the two Devon lakes sparkled like glorious gems. The lower lake was more immense in size but shallower, with water the color of Gisèle's eyes; the upper, our destination, was the most intense shade of blue I have ever seen, almost indigo, and said to be so deep in places it could not be measured. The very idea of this made Gisèle, with her aquaphobia, shudder.

It was late spring when we arrived, and the hills were still carpeted with vivid fuchsia and fireweed; brilliant meadows of mustard and blue heather rippled in the wind. Mist curled through the thick evergreens and pines like smoke through the Oak Bar, and the mountains crouched over it all like a huddle in American football, giant ice creatures poised to pounce. I was awed by the primeval wildness of it. The experience held a profoundly exciting sense of discovery—the thrill and terror of trespass. We were Adam and Eve entering the Garden.

At last the plane touched down; Gisèle and I descended the narrow stair, inhaling our first breath of alpine air. Robin was there to meet us, and he enjoyed playing tour guide, whisking us away to our new home.

"Falconer's Point," it was called. The name had a rugged charm, and so did its remote locale, across the lake from the village, seated high atop a hill. A mansion in the sky. It had been the home of Robin's uncle, who was something of a recluse, but was now standing vacant. A death sentence for a house, Robin said. The idea was that Gisèle and I would decide if it suited us.

It suited, perfectly.

Robin was having his own house built, and it's an irony that he'd chosen French design; his towering gray stone château could not have been a better architectural manifestation of him had he tried. (And of course he had—designing much of it himself.) Set upon the cliffs on the very edge of the lake, it was as dramatic as he. And, for me, Falconer's Point—the eccentric manor house that was almost a pastiche of architectural styles—instantly felt like home. With its stolid Georgian edifice and gently sloping roofline, it was English in its initial reserve, surrounded by faintly neglected and rambling gardens, crisscrossed with paths. But there was a surprise inside: a cloistered inner courtyard built to preserve a magnificent canopied oak, hundreds of years old. It lent the interior the whimsical feel of an Italian villa. Within, there were more surprises still—the strange Mr. Prescott had riddled the house with hidden passageways and false doors.

Despite its quirky appeal, I found that Falconer's Point possessed also a subtle air of morbidity. Literally, the air felt heavier within than without, as if too much had been enclosed by those walls. And this, too, felt familiar. I'd grown up in a similar humidified atmosphere. In boyhood nightmares I'd made metaphor my father's mental illness, imagining him perched precariously on an ice peak, surrounded by dark chasms on all sides. In Devon I had come to land on a peak of my own, and I found that it no longer frightened me. It felt like home.

Gisèle's enthusiasm equaled mine. If she sensed the vague oppressiveness of the house, it did not appear to trouble her. To her it was a haven; she would come to cherish its walls and rarely leave them. The gardens were her particular paradise. For all her youth in San Francisco and her brief foray into the wilds of New York, Gisèle was not a city girl, I realized. She loved the untamed landscape and its appealing contradiction in the polished charm of Devon.

The feral beauty of the Pacific Northwest is not where one would expect to stumble upon such privilege and panache. Devon was a salve for my European longings. Galleries, fine dining, and theater abounded, and nature was our playground. I taught Gisèle to ski and to golf. She would not learn to swim but loved long walks along the lake and even acquiesced to occasional excursions in Robin's sailboat.

Why is it I picture her there so clearly? I can still see her face in the sunshine of that first sparkling spring, glistening with spray off the water. I see her knuckles clenched white where she grips the deck rail, but resolve in the set of her jaw, light in her eyes. She's not carefree, not exactly happy, but newly . . . alive.

It was on the water that Robin renewed Gisèle's love for art. How different these conversations were from our early talks in San Francisco. An ascetic to the aesthetic, art was literally Robin's God. For him the need for creativity was as strong as for food or drink—stronger—and the condition was contagious. We were all innately creative beings, he claimed. We were either actively creating or passively molded by the creative forces of others. I can hear him as if it were yesterday, "If you're not creating, Elle, you are being created. . . ."

He encouraged her to reawaken her early love of writing, to keep a journal. Writing was unique, he claimed. It forced one to travel an inner terrain. It was a mirror, but also a window. The two, in the end, were the same. Gisèle tipped her head and simply listened. Gone were her claims of not knowing enough, not having experienced enough to write. Gone, too, was her fascination with "the writer," which by now she knew was not me and never had been. Nor was it a magical cloak she might one day slip into. It had lost its childish mystique. Yet as she listened to Robin, it was like watching an animal sniff the air; she sniffed this new inner terrain and left us.

I was quietly annoyed. I'd flattered her with ideas of art and the artist but was quite happy when she abandoned them and turned those energies on me. We still enjoyed painting together—I could instruct what she should see—but I knew that her writing would take her from me.

And Robin, I knew, was helping her in his way. He never broached her past directly but instead offered her "therapy" in the only form he knew: art. A thing to make her own. For months afterward I made a habit of going over her room. I never found a journal but was convinced she had begun to keep one. I was sure she had secrets from me. There was a new distance in her, a self-sufficiency, a gulf I could not seem to cross.

Yet how is it that I did not resent this friendship with Robin? Was it gratitude? His magnanimity had saved me from ruin. (I'd followed his plan to the letter and delivered to my blackmailer the sales price of the brownstone. It worked. I was never to hear from him again. . . .) Robin had given me back my life, my leisure—and, in time, even my paintings. And the threat of his presence was an inconstant one. He was absent for months at a time in New York or Paris, London or Prague. His mountain hideaway did not rein him in.

I knew of at least some of his activities in Paris, and those of his infamous friend Marc Kreicek, who was now a frequent visitor to my residences here and abroad. It was necessary on occasion to meet them in Paris, though I was loath to leave Gisèle for even a few days and so returned from the whirlwind trips exhausted. For the most part, the operation went absurdly well: Marc lived up to his hype, Robin lived up to his promises, and I lived extremely well.

Even when Robin was in Devon, his visits were not so frequent that I did not welcome them. Our friendship wasn't the sort that required constant companionship; we always picked up as we were, and our conversations had never been the frivolous kind. His art consumed him and was met with increasing success. In his personal life, however, he suffered a string of losses.

Eve died of her heart disease, and little Joshua was a brilliant but very troubled child. He was moved from music school to music school, and there were ugly custody battles with Eve's relatives—who claimed that Robin had killed her with his neglect and never been a proper father to his son. I believe in his heart he agreed with them.

His son would not come to live with him until he was sixteen, and the relationship would always be a tumultuous one. It was not for lack of effort on Robin's part. At the local liberal-arts college, he agreed to mentor a small group of handpicked prodigies, including Josh. He constructed a major to incorporate their disparate artistic talents—in effect producing the only school in America that could tolerate his son. Robin never complained about the demands of this on his time. It was, he claimed, "a great experiment."

So was Devon. He took an active role in the town, denying anything in his power that did not suit his vision. I didn't envy him this; it is a difficult thing to create a world. For my part, I was happy with the one I had created with Gisèle. And it was this that ultimately dissipated my jealousy. Living so near Robin made it clear to me at last: he lived in his own world, with its own strange parameters. He possessed much but desired nothing. One day that summer, Gisèle herself told me this. And it was true. While she—a rare confession—"needed to be needed."

And so you see, I was for a time truly blissful. For the first time . . . content.

And she? Gisèle gave me her answer on an evening some four months after our arrival.

I was enjoying a glass of wine on the terrace. She'd gone in to shower and dress for dinner. The sun was setting brilliantly, and I came in for her, nearly stumbling over her body on the floor. She'd passed out in our bedroom. In her lax hand lay a bottle of sleeping pills. Empty.

I rushed her to the hospital; her stomach was pumped. It cannot have been a serious attempt, for she'd known she would be found—and still I nearly lost her. She'd taken a great many pills and didn't weigh much; her body had already begun to metabolize the poison.

When at last I could see her, she stared at me from the bed of that sterile white room, her eyes dark-ringed and hollow, her face shiny from perspiration, and her hair in damp ringlets. And I began to cry. I could not bear her explanations. I could not bear the reality of what she had done, for it showed *my* reality to be a lie.

I paced, murmuring lines from Rimbaud as a frightened child might recite nursery rhymes. They were lines I'd recited to her many, many times. A seduction poem—it had once been her favorite.

"She was barely dressed though, and the great indiscreet trees touched the glass with their leaves . . ." They were words that had pleased an innocent, naïve little girl. Now I used them to resurrect her in the dubious young woman. "In malice, quite close, quite close."

She pleaded with me as one pleads with a recalcitrant child. "Stop, Tristan. Please stop it."

Through my tears, I saw her as she was years ago. "Sitting in my deep chair, half-naked, hands clasped together. On the floor, little feet, so fine, so fine, shivered with pleasure—"

She covered her ears and her eyes were so feverish bright, they scared me. Dark-circled, savage . . . but brilliant with a light that wouldn't go out. There were no tears in them. And I fell silent, turning. I wiped my eyes.

They were just the frail lines of a poem. Not incantations.

Barely whispered words: "Do you want to leave me, Gisèle?"

I turned back to her, and she lowered her hands then. I will never be sure if she heard me. "I'm sorry, Tristan," she said. "I don't know why I did it." No tears. She dropped her eyes and reached for my hand. "I don't know why."

The doctors threatened her with counselors, with reports to the authorities. I found my usual way around such things. An accident, it was, in the end. Accidents happen every day. No one need ever know. I did not even tell Robin. I could not acknowledge my failure to him, nor even to myself.

XVIII

CONFIDENCES

AMANDA DOUBTED HER EARS. "I don't understand," she said at last. "Tristan speaks of you as a friend—"

"To the world that's what we are. Doesn't it mean more in the end? One chooses one's friends. Family's a crap shoot." Robin laughed, a harsh, rueful sound. "I was illegitimate, Amanda. Such romantic origins. His father wasn't mine; we were raised separately. As a child Tristan was led to believe that his brother was born dead. Truth be told, I prefer it that way."

Amanda gazed at him uncertainly. "May I ask why?"

"Years ago, when I first learned of Tristan, I wasn't quite so well adjusted as I am now." Robin's tone was self-mocking, bitingly acerbic. "He had the life I ought to have had, I thought. I was raised a Prescott, a long line of landed gentry and religious zealots. I was brought up in Wales. My mother was from Brittany. That was the only tie between her and the Prescotts—a Celtic birthplace, a loose skein of mutual friends. Sadly, my adoptive parents lacked true Celtic spirit. God-fearing folk, they were. Interested in the afterlife and blind to this one." Another irreverent, bitter smile. "Alas. They believed that the individual ought to bend to God's will. For me that meant being forcibly bent to theirs. Religion is only ever an exercise in power."

Amanda's eyes narrowed. "Do you mean they beat you?"

"They wouldn't see it that way. No, they were simply employing the time-honored method of saving my soul. Being sensible, from the age of five or six I took to running away." There was no emotion in his voice, and Amanda could see that being open was a thing he must detest. She wondered why he had decided to be open with her. "My real mother, Tristan's mother, was an unapologetic hedonist. An enigmatic force of a woman who kept my identity a secret from me until my twenty-fifth birthday. It was quite a birthday present."

"Did she explain why she'd given you up?"

"It wasn't the usual teenage-pregnancy tale. No, she was a respectable married woman. Aristocratic family. Mentally ill husband. I feel for her already, don't you? I was the product of an affair, it seems, the much-beloved bastard product of the passion of her life. My father had died, she wrote, and with him her raison d'être. She could not bring me into her small, insular world. I belonged to 'another world entirely and was destined for great things. . . .' That sort of rot." He went on in a brooding tone, "I do understand it in a way. We're all many people at once, leading many lives. It's damned awkward to run into your mistress while walking with your wife in the park. You may love them equally, but certainly differently. And the worlds shouldn't overlap." He seemed to remember Amanda again. "Human beings are capable of all manner of betrayal, but we must be true to our treacheries. . . . Whatever her reasons, she abandoned me to the care of strangers who remained strange to me all my life. I knew I wasn't one of them. While Tristan grew up in Paris with little supervision and a parade of impressionists on his walls, I was locked up—when they could get hold of me—and surrounded by vivid depictions of the Crucifixion, somber portraits of dead ancestors, and scenes of the hunt." He scratched his chin. "I think it was their aesthetic palette, or lack thereof, that chafed most."

She squinted at him. "I'm sorry. . . ."

He laughed heartily. "Don't be sorry for me, Amanda. There are worse things than not belonging. Belonging, for instance. And my Dickensian tale has a happy ending. Everyone around me seems prone to dying, and more often than not they leave their material residue to me. Things could be far worse."

"I can't imagine money makes up for a miserable childhood."

"Ah, well. Maybe not. But it does provide a nice contrast, and contrast is everything."

She hesitated. "Tristan doesn't have any contrast, does he? That's what's wrong with him."

He gazed at her thoughtfully. "It's true. When I met him, all my envy disappeared. You may find it hard to believe, but I actually felt protective toward him. It was like stumbling upon an orchid in the snow. He's completely unaware of it, of course, but he can survive only under very select conditions." His pause was reflective. "And I might have been the same. If I hadn't made my way in the world before that twenty-fifth birthday, I would have doubted it afterward."

"How do you mean?"

"Well, I've mentioned 'material residue.' My mother left me a great lot of it, Amanda. Art. Priceless works. Cézanne, Picasso, and Matisse. Kandinsky, Magritte. Rumored pieces no one had ever seen." His eyes sparkled. "Nirvana. If I'd been given them too early, I might have been a collector instead of an artist."

Did people actually *own* such things? "I doubt that, Robin. I've seen your paintings."

"Ah, well. I may never have been driven to create them. It was pain that drove me. Artistic expression is necessity or it's nothing. Art is a hunger; collecting is . . . gluttony. Just look at Tristan. It is easy to fall under the spell of beautiful things."

Yes, it is. "You have a foot in both worlds."

"Let's just say the things I own do not own me."

"But why not tell Tristan the truth? I'd think he would be happy to know he's not alone in the world."

He held her eyes. "We're all alone, Amanda. Most of us deny it; I prefer it. I don't do particularly well with expected relationships, expected forms."

And in spite of herself, Amanda understood this. It was perhaps the reason he'd told her the truth: the instant, odd camaraderie of solitary souls. Only she hadn't chosen her solitude.

"Would Tristan resent me? I rather fear he would. And what would we do differently? Everything. There would be obligation instead of choice. I'm afraid I was soured by my upbringing. I have a compulsive need to choose."

"But you chose to know your brother, to befriend him. How did that happen?"

"When I first learned of Tristan, I wasn't sure I wanted anything to do with him. But I'm a curious sod. I had a friend of mine get his story. He took time to locate, traveled a good deal. It was over a year before I decided to meet him, in SoHo at a party. He was there with the loveliest young girl, whom he seemed to think he could own like a painting. He was pampered, out of touch—the paranoid-obsessive quality was his primary appeal. I found him an oddly engaging fellow."

"Who may have killed the lovely young girl."

Robin glanced away. "The motive is still damned shaky, Amanda. But yes. I'll admit there were signs Gisèle was finally ready to leave him, and he was certainly obsessed with her."

"'Finally ready'? I would think she was ready when she married another man."

"Oh, that." Robin's sideways glance was evasive. "Well, that was just another façade, I'm afraid. She chose someone utterly malleable and not inclined to whisk her away."

"But *why*? And why would Tristan hang around for it?"

"Obsession isn't a gentleman. He rarely bows out gracefully. The truth is, she continued to live in Tristan's home and she wasn't in love with her husband."

No, Amanda thought. *She was in love with you.*

He continued, "The sleeping pills bother me, because they imply premeditation. If Luke killed her, I can't help feeling it would be in the passion of the moment. But Tristan's a planner. I knew this from the start. Yet why drug her? On the surface the rationale is a simple one: To transport her to the pool house and ensure her drowning. To further ensure that her death would be ruled an accident or suicide. But I simply couldn't see Tristan carting her body through the house in the dead of night, out to the pool, with a house full of people."

Robin shoved his hands into his pockets and began to walk aimlessly. She followed. "But?"

"But I've since discovered he had a way of getting to the pool house without being seen. My uncle built that house, Amanda. He had a penchant for secret compartments and passages, taking his cue from the great homes of Europe with their priest holes and such. I remember being shown them as a boy. Turns out Uncle Bryan left quite a few out of my tour. I've looked at the plans, and the house is riddled with them. One passageway extends the length of the second story along the eastern wall." He met her eyes. "It *connects* Elle's room to Tristan's."

She stared. "You mean they used it to reach each other without being seen. . . ."

"Yes. And here's the damning bit. The passage eventually drops to the cellar, which has an outdoor entrance." He drew in a sharp breath. "It'd still be bloody difficult to navigate the passage with a woman in your arms. I'm not saying Tristan killed her, only that it's logistically *possible*. If I'd ever truly believed him capable—" She watched his jaw tighten beneath the skin.

"What's the case against the husband, Luke Farrell? You seemed so certain he'd done it."

"I'm still certain." But Robin frowned as if to contradict this. "He was seen leaving the pool house at three-thirty that morning and failed to mention it. He's admitted they were arguing and that she planned to divorce him." He paused. "And there's another nasty little detail." Yet he hesitated, clearly gauging the wisdom of passing the nasty little detail on to her.

"Tell me, Robin."

Another frown. "The autopsy showed signs of sexual activity. Luke's sperm. He admitted it freely. Sounds fine on the surface of things. Moral, even. They were married. But I happen to know that Elle was done with him in that regard, so it was unlikely to have been consensual—"

Her mouth dropped open.

In Robin's sideways glance there was a chill, and his gray eyes were like ice. "Everyone wanted a piece of Gisèle." He turned, gazing across the meadow; the tall grass undulated beneath the wind.

Amanda swallowed hard. The more she learned of her sister's life, the more fragile it seemed. A house of cards collapsing. *Was Robin at the center?*

"Everyone wanted a piece of her," she echoed coolly. "But not you?"

Robin faced her again. He stepped forward, and the effect was both confrontational and sexual. She stepped backward instinctively. "Do you think I'd be satisfied with only a piece of anyone?"

"You knew the lie she was living. Weren't you just another part of it?"

"Perhaps. But it wasn't my lie."

"That's convenient."

Tension crackled in the air between them. When he spoke, his voice had a ragged edge to it. "Lies were her mortar and bricks, Amanda. Elle built a fortress to protect what little was left to her. I understood that. I understood her. And I loved her. But to love her was to climb inside those walls for a while. She wouldn't come out."

"Did you ask her to?"

Robin gave a hollow laugh. "It's only in books and theater that marriage solves every problem. You'll notice they all end with the wedding. Don't be naïve."

"No happily-ever-after fantasies for you."

His gaze was sharp. "Nor you, I suspect."

"But you slept with her?"

His reply was equally direct. "Many times."

"So you got what you wanted."

"As did she."

"I'm guessing she wanted more."

"So she should have settled for nothing?"

Amanda reached out blindly, let the tall grass brush her fingertips. "It's just perverse. . . . What a cozy little rectangle. My sister, her keeper, her lover, and her husband."

"It wasn't like that, Amanda. We were separate from that."

"Why?"

"Because I didn't want anything from her."

No, thought Amanda, *but she wanted something more from you.* And maybe all human relationships could be summed up so transactionally. One always wanted the other more. Suddenly, in that moment, she understood her sister better than she ever had before. Had Karen satisfied herself with loving Robin without strings, because that was the only way she could love him? Lived on crumbs and called it a feast? She would need Tristan's obsessive adoration as a supplement. Karen, like Amanda, would crave love. Endless supplies of it. Obsessively seeking to fill up an empty core. And she would deny this need— even to herself.

"As I say, I don't want you to see Tristan anymore. Let me handle things from here."

"I can't do that. I'm making headway, Robin. I—"

"I'm not letting anything happen to you." His voice was very firm, used to getting what it wanted.

Amanda moved away from him but could still feel his touch; it tingled on her skin, and the physical pull was almost unbearable. Again she felt the weight of the letter in her pocket. *Why don't I just give it to him and be done with it?* She'd wanted to be sure of him, but she wasn't sure of him at all. Worse still, she wasn't sure of herself.

"Robin—" Nothing else came out.

"Amanda?" His voice was very low, very gentle. He went to her, touched his fingers to her chin, forcing her to look at him.

Neither of them spoke. There were only the cries of birds overhead, wind whispering through the grasses. She gazed in an unfocused way to the edge of the meadow, where the leafless trees were gray skeletons amid the evergreens, returned to look up at him. She was afraid he would kiss her and that his kiss would taste like the air here, of pine and smoke and woodsy things. It would be as seductive as Devon itself. Her heart throbbed in her ears, and the air pulsed around her.

His fingertips traveled along her cheek, to her jaw and to her chin, over her lips, as if filling in an outline. She stiffened, but his touch was feather-light and firm at the same time, unspeakably gentle. All the while he held her in his eyes. That was what it felt like, as if she'd lost all resistance in her body and was simply suspended there. And if he were to look away, she would fall.

At last he gave a slight, sad smile. "Such lovely, conflicted eyes. Don't worry, Amanda, I won't do anything you'll regret. I have a few ethics. In spite of myself."

"I remind you of her," she murmured.

"Yes." He made no attempt at disguise. "And no."

She lifted her chin, swallowed. "How am I different?"

"All the intrinsic ways." Robin smiled, with both fondness and regret. "You cannot lie. It's a beautiful thing and utterly foreign to me. I'm much more at home with liars and thieves."

Amanda reached into her pocket and held the letter toward him with trembling fingers. "You were the reason she was out at the pool house, Robin. She was waiting for you." She swallowed. "It was in Tristan's coat pocket, but it's meant for you."

His expression was indecipherable; she caught a trace of disbelief and felt it in his fingers as he took the letter from here. Tension rose from his skin as he scanned the lines. When he reached the end, he simply stared, the page fluttering in his hand with the breeze that rolled through the valley. His left hand clenched into a fist and unclenched, clenched again, as he tried to garner control.

"Nicola, my little darling," he whispered. His voice almost didn't sound like his own, it was so filled with tenderness. Then, "If Tristan's laid a finger on her, I'll kill him."

❧

Nicola found herself alone at last.

Her grandfather had left for his wine club. Dinner was being prepared early, and the staff was still downstairs. Her father was on the phone. Still, she knew that time was short.

She closed the door and made a beeline for her mother's closet. It was a vast walk-in, paneled in cedar. Nicola had always loved the way it smelled, but the scent of it now stung her eyes. It was the smell of long, rainy afternoons playing dress-up, trying on her mother's dresses and hobbling in her mother's shoes. And all the time, it had been here. A secret passageway.

She would never have found it if not for the book. The removable panel was located at the rear of the closet, hidden behind a row of her mother's dresses that she had to push aside like drapes. Knocking on walls was the trick to finding passageways—her "grandfather" had taught her that—and after many dull thuds her knuckles were met with a promisingly hollow rejoinder. But where was the button? There was always a button. In the receiving room, it was hidden beneath the framework of one of the wall panels, but here there was no framework; the cedar planks reached from floor to ceiling and appeared to join seamlessly.

And then she saw that a knot of wood had popped out of one of the planks, leaving a hole. She slid her index finger inside, and there it was.

She pressed down hard, and a "door" three planks wide swung smoothly inward without so much as a creak of the invisible hinges.

Nicola poked her head into a narrow, rectangular corridor, a long shaft of darkness that extended far beyond the single patch of light from the closet. The shadowy blackness yawned at her, and this, too, was her mother. It was all the things Nicola had never known about her.

She crossed the threshold with a tentative foot, but as her eyes adjusted, she could see a string dangling from the ceiling of the narrow passage. When she gave it a tug, a lightbulb flared to life above her.

Farther down the corridor, she could see light filtering into the passage from windows on both sides. *How was it possible to have windows on both sides?* She moved toward them.

On Nicola's right, a window opened to the outdoors. Storm clouds intruded on the sunset, gathering over the familiar landscape; Lake Devon lay below, restless, shifting and gray. But when she looked through the "window" on her left, Nicola found herself staring at the top of her mother's vanity—her hairbrush close enough to reach, her makeup brushes fanned in their porcelain vase.

She could see her mother's sleigh bed to her right and the great armoire beyond it. Directly opposite was her mother's long cherrywood dresser with its wide mirror above. And yet the mirror reflected not Nicola but the empty triptych mirror over the vanity: the familiar mirror and oval-backed cushioned chair in which she'd so often seen her mother sit.

The mirror was a window.

❧

Amanda stood before the mirror, getting ready for her charade with Tristan. It would be her last. She had assured Robin she wouldn't go. He was wrong, it seemed—when necessary, she *could* lie. And it was necessary. She was close with Tristan, she knew. To lure him into the open would take finesse, and in Robin's current state of mind he possessed none.

She pictured him now, striding determinedly across the meadow as she'd jogged to keep up. "I'm going up to the house," he'd said. "I'm getting Nicola out of there—"

Relief had welled within her then, and she felt it again now. "Thank God," she'd said. "But can you do that? Just *take* her?"

"I'd like to see someone stop me, Amanda. All these years I've protected Tristan. Have I been so *fucking* blind? If he's done a thing to hurt her, I'll rip him apart with my bare hands."

And she believed he would.

She glanced at the clock. Tristan was always on time. Sure enough, as the hour turned to seven, she heard a rap at the door.

❧

Nicola struggled to take it all in. The letter proved that her mother had written to someone the night she died. She'd been afraid. . . . Someone had met her at the pool house, and that someone, Nicola believed, had killed her. Yet, for all her horror, it hadn't been real until now. Suddenly, as Nicola stood in the narrow, dark corridor, her mother's secret life became as tangible as the passage itself.

Someone had stood exactly where she did now and observed Gisèle as she'd woken up and dressed, gotten ready for the day and ready for bed, like a hapless goldfish swimming in circles in a bowl.

Nicola turned and was dizzy; she felt along the wall as she drew farther from the light of the window. She had to climb up a few stairs, cross a plateau, and descend again. What was there? In her mind she pictured the layout of her mother's room. Oh, yes. She'd just crossed the wide picture window with its deep window seat, where her mother had read to her when she was small.

Blindly, she walked on and reached it at last. She knew it would be there: another "doorway." A bit of light shone through a knot in the wood. From this side the button was clearly visible, as were the hinges. She pressed it, and the door sprang toward her. Her eyes were met with a staunch line of starched dress shirts. Parting them, she glimpsed neat rows of slacks and ties, suits of white linen, orderly rows of shoes. Here the scent of cedar was secondary, overwhelmed by the scent of Grand-père—pipe tobacco and citrus cologne, the faint residue of smoke and shoe polish. The familiar scent she'd always loved. His room was at the end of that hall, separated from her mother's by a study and a private sitting room. Her father's room wasn't on this hall. Though they all resided on the same floor, it seemed the four of them were divided by miles. Miles of walls and halls and passageways. And lies.

Nicola had no desire to linger here. She closed the paneled door. Wandering farther down the passage, she came to a dark opening at her feet. Deepening gradations of black gaped at her. Stairs.

She reached above her and brushed a string. A quick tug illuminated the way down. Nicola wasn't scared. It was strange. She wasn't anything. It was as if the pit of darkness inside her had crawled out into the open. What else was there to fear? She just kept going.

When she reached the landing, she found another square at her feet, outlined in light as if drawn on the floor. It was the trapdoor she'd seen in the house plans. On top of it, a ladder was folded compactly onto itself. Nicola reached down and released a latch. The trapdoor dropped and the ladder unhinged, unfolding under its own weight. It led the way down. Cold air wafted up like a calling card. It was the cellar.

And then she heard the footsteps behind her. . . . No, they were above.

"Nicola? Where are you?" The voice echoed down to her. "Are you in here?"

Her heart pounded erratically in her throat. She couldn't have spoken if she wanted to. For a moment she doubted what she'd heard, for it was not her grandfather's voice. It should have been his, if anyone's. It was his house, his passageway. But it was her father's voice. How did *he* know about the passageway?

Nicola scrambled down the ladder to the floor below, and all at once she understood. Adrenaline hit her like a blow, and her fear was like a flood, rising. The room was empty, but her nose told her where she was: it was her father's art studio. The scent of paint and turpentine still lingered, though the easels and all the canvases were gone and the stained worktable lay bare. He had painted here. He'd painted her *mother* here.

"Nicola? I know you're down there. We need to talk. You'll hurt yourself . . ."

Was it his passageway, then? Had he been the one to spy on her mother through the mirror? It didn't make sense.

Yet all the secret passages in Falconer's Point had been published in a book. It was possible he'd discovered it—without her mother or Tristan knowing a thing. Once down here he could access the rest of the house, and there were stairs that led outside. Nicola wanted desperately to get outside.

She ran out the door of the studio and stumbled across the cellar floor. Her mind spun. She felt as if she were strapped into an endless roller-coaster ride. Her world had turned upside down again. Blood beat in her ears, and the sound was like an ax striking a chopping block. *Chop, chop, chop.* It drowned out the pounding of her footsteps and those of her father, whom she imagined closing in behind her.

Nicola tore up the stairs, but something caught the corner of her eye. It was a streak of blood on the floor. Fighting her panic, she quickly retreated. It wasn't blood at all, but a strip of crimson cloth. She knew that it was silk before she touched it; she would never forget that color, nor the seal-like slickness of the cloth when wet. It was a piece of her mother's robe.

A horrifying scene played across her mind: Her mother, in a panic, with the same beating of blood in her ears, had fled through the passage and up these stairs. One of the long full sleeves of her robe had caught on the railing. Nicola ran her fingertips along the nearest metal fitting that attached the wooden handrail to the wall. The heads of the screws were rough, sharp to the touch. She could see the delicate silk hem catching and tearing, a strip of cloth fluttering down to the cement floor.

Proof had lain in this dark corner all the time.

A noise came from behind her. Nicola enfolded the strip of silk tightly in her hand and raced mindlessly up the stairs and through the door. It was dark out, but there were lights along the circular drive, the garden pathways, and the trunks of the trees. She was gazing across the grass, over the gentle hill, directly toward the pool house. Through the pounding in her ears, she heard her name, and it was the starting gun—like a frightened colt, she bolted, not knowing where. She didn't glance over her shoulder or even look around her; she tore across the grass, just as she had the day her mother died. And she felt the same footsteps trailing her.

"Nicola—" He caught her by the waist and lifted her; she screamed, twisting and kicking. But the voice wasn't her father's, and neither was the beloved familiar scent. It was Robin. And then she stopped struggling. She clung to him and began to cry.

Nicola couldn't speak, and Robin simply held her, allowing her breathing to slow and the sobs to quiet. "Robin," she murmured, but beyond that she couldn't say a word.

He smoothed her hair with his hand and whispered. "It's all right, Nico. It's going to be all right now, I promise you."

At last she pulled away, wiping her eyes.

His eyes narrowed in concern. "Tell what's happened."

"I went to the college to . . . to find you, and Josh said you were looking at a book. And I looked at it, too, and there *is* a passage from her room, Robin. I've been in it. It goes from Mom's room to Grand-père's. And her mirror isn't a mirror at all; someone used it to watch her. I think it was Dad. The passage leads to the art studio in the cellar, and he followed me—"

Robin was looking beyond her. "Yes. . . . Shh, darling. I see. It'll be all right."

"No it won't," she insisted, and pushed the strip of red silk toward him. "I found this in the cellar. It's from her robe. She must have been r-running away." New tears welled in her eyes.

Robin took the cloth carefully, rolling it between his fingers. His expression was not dubious; it was tortured. He hugged her hard. "You're a brave girl, Nicola. My brave girl. I am so . . . so very proud of you, and so sorry. I shouldn't have left you here alone. I—" He kept stumbling over his words; she'd never heard him stumble over his words before. "I want you to pack a bag and come stay with me. Your father is coming now. Let me handle things, all right?"

She nodded. She wanted nothing more than to let him handle things.

❧

"Nicola, there you are." Luke's voice came out uncertain. *What had she been saying to Robin?* Coolly, "I didn't know you were here, Rob."

Nicola's cheeks were tearstained. Luke knew exactly what she'd seen. *But what could it mean to her?* To an eleven-year-old girl who should be playing with Barbie dolls, not two-way mirrors . . . Robin set Nicola down but braced her with an arm around her shoulders. "Hello, Luke," he said smoothly. "I've just come from the gallery. The last of the paintings are being mounted tomorrow. Do you know there are still a few you haven't signed?"

Luke stared, hardly hearing. "Really?"

"So modest you are. Most artists feel their signature is the best part of the painting." There was nothing unusual in Robin's voice, but his eyes swept over Nicola restlessly before returning to light on Luke. "I've just come to pick up Nico. I think she's due for a bit of fun, don't you? She's going to sleep over at the school with my students, stay the next week or two with me, so you can focus on the show."

Nicola gazed up at Robin wide-eyed, and Luke could feel her relief; it emanated from her in tangible waves.

"Go on into the house and pack a bag, Nico—"

"There's no need for that, Robin. She's not in the way, and I have plenty of focus."

"I insist," said Robin mildly. "With any luck you'll be very busy in the coming weeks. Go ahead, sweetheart." He gave Nicola's shoulder a firm squeeze.

"Nic." Luke cleared his throat and gazed at her helplessly. "Do you *want* to go? I think we should talk about . . . things."

Nicola looked at him and then back to Robin. No, that made it sound an even exchange. She gazed up at him like a scared mouse confronted by a cat and turned to Robin as if he were her rescuer. And Luke knew in his heart whom she would choose. "I'd really like to go, Dad. If it's okay."

"Of course it is," Robin answered for him. "We'll be inside in a moment, love. Come downstairs when you're ready."

Nicola went eagerly, without looking back. Luke's stomach wrenched as the last remnant of his fabricated life tore away. His world shifted sideways as she ran. He blinked and it straightened, blinked again and it fell. He watched his daughter run across the grass, away from him.

Without turning, he said finally, "You're trying to take her from me."

There was no attempt at pretense. "Yes."

"Nicola's all I have."

"You were never much interested before."

"Neither were you."

"She was Gisèle's whole life, Luke. You were Gisèle's husband. I played a peripheral role. But make no mistake, I was always interested."

"You're her father," Luke said dully.

"Yes."

"There are things beyond paternity, you know. I could fight you for her."

"Shall we fight?"

Luke felt the first touch of anger. "I'm not a coward, whatever you think." He turned to Robin, and for a moment he wasn't a coward. He had no fear. He had nothing left to lose. But then the anger and recklessness dissipated into the sepia shadows, like so much else. Like every noble passion. He *was* a coward, he knew. "You think Tristan will stand by and watch you pluck Nicola from his life?"

"I'm rather counting on his doing the opposite." But Robin frowned then. "Know this. My only concern is Nicola. And she tells me you followed her through a passageway just now."

Luke shifted his weight. "Did you know about it?"

"I do now." With a meaningful glance, "Who told you?"

"No one told me. I never knew it existed before today, Robin, I swear. Do you think I knew? I found it looking for Nic." He paused. "For Christ's sake, there's a two-way *mirror* into Gisèle's bedroom. The bastard watched her all these years studying her like an insect under a microscope—"

"Nicola thinks it was you."

"What?"

"The passage leads to *your* art studio, remember?"

Luke's heart pounded fitfully. His lies were smothering him. "You know that's not true."

"I do, yes."

"Then *tell* her. Tell her I . . . I didn't watch her mother like an amoeba under glass. I didn't keep her trapped in that room." His voice broke; he swallowed cotton. "Gisèle must have known about it. She must have *let* herself be put under a microscope."

"Maybe," said Robin, frowning. "I don't know. But I do know the microscope's turning."

∞

Tristan and Amanda walked in silence. The outside air held an icy chill, and inside his vintage Jag it was no warmer. They sat in shadows, their silence newly uneasy. There was between them no longer the easy rapport of friends, however frail the foundation of the friendship. The engine rumbled to life and was welcome white noise. Tristan turned on the heat, but it came out cold, and Amanda pulled her coat tightly around her. Beyond the car window in the dark, she could just make out the swooping arms of the pines.

"The conversation last night upset you," Tristan said at last.

"Yes."

"Let us avoid the past tonight."

She tried to formulate an answer. "The past is always present, Tristan."

"Yes." He sighed, and something in the soft, sad sound was dangerous. Predatory.

Amanda had hoped the wine would relax him, lower his guard. It had the opposite effect on both of them. Yet they muddled on in search of tars and black currant on the palate, lingering finishes with delicate accents of vanilla or toffee or earthy spice. In the end she could not focus at all on the wine, on the light conversation. Her stomach trembled when she swallowed. Her thoughts were abstracted, her conversation stilted. She did not attempt to hide her unease. The game, for her, was up, and she wanted him to feel it.

Eventually they returned to the car. "I made reservations at a delightful—"

"I couldn't eat a bite, Tristan. My stomach's been upset all day."

"Yes. You are not yourself, *chérie*. I hope you're not coming down with something."

"I've been coming down with it for weeks. Ever since I got to Devon. I've been drinking the Kool-Aid and savoring the strawberry finish."

"Kool-Aid? I don't understand—"

"It's just an expression. I mean that I've been mesmerized by you. By this place."

"And I by you. You are so very lovely, Amanda."

One by one, cars filed away around them; sets of headlights flickered good-bye as they passed. Amanda wanted to escape from the emptying lot. She cleared her throat. "I haven't been sleeping well, Tristan. I ought to get to bed early."

And so he shifted the car into reverse and drove them through town, but even the gingerbread charm of Devon failed to touch her. Amanda had come to expect not only Hansel and Gretel but also the witch.

The silence stretched taut as he drove; he switched on music to fill it. Classical. Amanda focused on the clean, pure notes. "And so you promised, Tristan. True confessions. It's your turn. May I ask you a question?"

"Of course." However, he sounded, for the first time, uncertain. He didn't meet her eyes but gazed at the road ahead, shiny from the light rain and mirrorlike.

She inhaled sharply. "Gisèle Mourault was not your daughter, was she?"

"Ma chère fille, what a question. I have her birth certificate."

Of course he would. Robin had told her of his first marriage and of the child: Marie-Gisèle, who had died. The symphony dropped to whispering notes, diminished. "But that's not the daughter you just buried."

They pulled up to the brightly lit thatch-roofed inn. Tristan killed the engine, and the quiet engulfed them; darkness pressed against the windows.

Amanda swallowed. "You see, Karen wrote to me."

He frowned. "Your sister wrote you before she disappeared?"

She spoke quietly. "No. She wrote to me in August. Last August."

"But . . ." He faltered. Black pine needles fell silently onto the windshield, crisscrossing one another like a game of PickUp Sticks. "She wrote you after she is meant to have died?"

She had to admire his perseverance; he wasn't going to give up his denial without a fight. "The letter is *why* I came here, Tristan. The postmark was from Devon."

His brow furrowed. "I see now. You said the other night you hoped she had escaped—"

"Yes. But someone must have helped her." She swallowed. "It was you, Tristan."

"Merde." He scoffed. "If you could hear yourself, Amanda."

"At first I thought the letter was a hoax. Then I came across an art review of a series of paintings of a woman named Gisèle."

Tristan shifted in his seat.

"And she had Karen's face."

"You're seeking your sister in *every* face, and my Gisèle's face suits better than most. That's all this is. Otherwise, you would have given this letter to the police."

"I did."

A flicker of alarm appeared in his eyes but not his voice, which was utterly cold. "Well, it does not bode well that *you* are here, not *them*. They must not have given much credence to this theory of yours. Listen to me, Amanda. You're lying to yourself. Gisèle is mine, not yours."

Gisèle is mine. "She's not anyone's anymore, Tristan. She's dead. The handwriting in my letter is Gisèle's. I could have the body exhumed and DNA tests done—"

"*Non!*" The single syllable was wild and feral.

Amanda felt her fingers tingle, poised over the door handle. Outside, the paths were lit and the windows of the inn glowed warmly. *Nothing can happen to me here.*

"One doesn't disturb the dead based on handwriting."

"There is another letter. One she wrote the night she died."

Tristan turned; his expression frightened her. "A suicide letter?"

"Tristan, you know it's not. Listen to me. I'm not trying to paint you as a villain. You called her your daughter. Maybe that's what she was to you. Robin said—"

"'Robin said'?" His voice was brittle. "Tell me, what did Robin say?"

Her heart stopped. *What had she done?* She hadn't meant to mention him at all.

"Tell me, Amanda. What did Robin Dresden, my dear friend, say about me?"

"I just want to know the truth, Tristan. I've told you about my father. Maybe you were a sort of refuge for Karen. A kind of church that takes in lost souls, a sanctuary—"

"A church?" He laughed harshly. "How chaste, Amanda. Am I so inhuman to you?"

And a chill ran through her, because he was.

"Do you want to know the truth? Do you really? *Eh bien.* Then I will tell you."

She hardly breathed. So this was it. She relaxed her hold on the door handle. She wanted only to stay and listen. "What is it, Tristan?"

He said calmly, "The truth is, you're being used."

She let out her breath. *Did you really expect him to confess?* "Okay, right. By whom?"

But his answer astonished her. "Marc Kreicek."

"Marc *Kreicek*?" He was part of her Seattle life, a world away from here. Yet he was also of this world. Still, for a moment, she couldn't even conjure up his features. "I hardly know the man. I've only met him a few times. He's collaborating on a book with one of my professors."

Tristan laughed. "That was merely the easiest means of forming an acquaintance with you. There will be no book, I assure you."

She stared. *What does this have to do with anything?* "But his father's writings—"

"His father left all his writings and a good deal more to Robin."

"Robin Dresden?"

"Whom you seem to know rather better than you've let on." He continued, in an oddly detached voice, "Robin was a sort of spiritual son to Marc's father. It's because of their relationship that Robin puts up with Marc, the problem child. A rather incommodious spiritual 'younger brother.'" He scratched his head. "That is why I couldn't tell Robin when Marc began to pester me, you see. In the first place, I couldn't tell him why. He would not have understood. And in the second, what is a friend to a brother?"

She stared at him. The irony of it all left her dumb.

Since she'd come to Devon, the world had been shrinking; now it seemed it could fit on the head of a pin. She managed to say, "Pester you with what?"

"With you, Amanda. With you." Tristan tapped the steering wheel with his gloved fingers. "You know, when I saw you that first night at the wine club, I thought you'd come to do the same. To blackmail me in some form or fashion. What else could I think? But what a joy it has been to discover you." He appraised her with the pleasure of an art lover. A collector. "You're really very engaging, very principled, in your own fashion. But alas, the truth is not principled. And the truth is, I loved Gisèle in a way you'll never understand. It was not the ugly thing you imagine. I was devoted to her. I created her. She was my life, and I was hers. She remained with me by choice. Of course she did." A shrug. "She always had the freedom to leave. That was the beauty of it."

At last the admission. But there was no triumph in it. Amanda was sickened by his detachment, his incomprehension of what he'd done. He spoke of Karen like an object. *I created her.* "Where would she have gone, Tristan? She thought she had no one else."

"The newspapers made the mistake. They reported you in the car with your parents."

"But you capitalized on it. *You* knew the truth."

"*Oui.*" He gazed at her, and sympathy softened his sharp blue eyes. "And for that I am truly sorry, *chérie.* My actions, of necessity, have hurt you. I never intended that."

Of necessity. Her brain moved at half speed. For the moment she had no words. "What does Marc—"

"Marc Kreicek claims Gisèle told him the truth about her past. I don't believe it for a minute, though they did grow close for a time." Tristan shook his head as if to erase the memory of this. "He's a spy and a thief, false in every way. She could never love him. However he discovered her true identity, I'm certain it was devious. And then he discovered you. For years he's used the knowledge, and I've paid." He was angry, she could tell, furious—yet his voice did not rise a decibel. "Until he asked for something I could not pay. And I foolishly called his bluff."

"Well, I guess he *must* have been bluffing, because he never told me anything." Amanda gazed at him, openly dubious. Was this simply some sociopathic deflection of responsibility?

"*C'est vrai.* He did something much more cruel than that." Tristan shifted in his seat. "I'm going to give you something, Amanda, and then I want you to go. I will not see you again, I think. But I want you to know I've enjoyed our times together. I hate to end it this way."

Was this a threat? Instinctively, her hand pulled the handle, and the car door opened.

"Wait, wait. I've said I have something to give you." Tristan's urbane voice could not have been less menacing, but as he reached into the backseat for a leather valise and began to rummage through it, garish scenes from horror movies played across her mind. She could almost hear the audience screaming, *Run! Run!* Was he going to pull out a knife or a gun? Surely he wouldn't shoot her in the crowded parking lot of the inn. *Run . . . run!*

He was not even looking at her. "I want you to know that Gisèle married, but the marriage itself was meaningless. It was a cover story, nothing more. I was the only one she ever loved." Amanda listened, but contradicted him in her mind with Gisèle's own words in her letter. She felt almost sorry for Tristan. She had mentioned the letter to him; he must know she was aware of its contents—yet he spoke not only as if he hadn't missed the letter, but as if he hadn't even *read* it. It was unnerving.

While Tristan continued his rummaging, he said conversationally, "She wanted a baby, you see, and that was the one thing I couldn't give her. That's the reason she married. For Nicola."

Amanda stared. Was it possible he *hadn't* read the letter?

"The marriage was a sham, Amanda. Let that be a comfort to you."

"Why should that comfort *me*?" But all at once comprehension came in a horrible wave. Connections. Coincidence. Her sister had married a man named Luke. Marc Kreicek had introduced Amanda to a man named Luke . . . whom she'd run into "by chance," here in Devon.

Tristan had not answered her. He'd extracted not a gun but an envelope and a small pamphlet. He handed these to her and shrugged apologetically. "I know you'll find the contents of the envelope particularly painful, and so I've selected only a few photographs. Marc took them, of course—or had them taken. And it was Marc who gave them to Gisèle. Perhaps he hoped to win her back with proof of my little betrayals. He did it anonymously, of course, like the coward he is. A petty retribution for my refusal to indulge him in his schemes."

Amanda fought a rising tide of nausea. Forgetting her personal safety, she began to open the envelope.

"*Non, non.* Not here, *chérie.* I regret causing you such pain; I prefer not to witness it. Look at them alone. They disturbed Gisèle, of course, but not for the reasons you may think. They were proof you were alive and proof I had lied, quite selfishly, in order to bind her to me."

The dots were connecting so rapidly now that she couldn't follow. Marc Kreicek had taken pictures of Amanda and given them to Gisèle. *That's* why Gisèle had written to her last August. Last August. With a sickening certainty, Amanda knew she had not been alone in the photographs.

Tristan frowned. "She was angry with me at first, but it didn't last long. Gisèle understood human frailty. She knew I'd acted only out of love for her, and she forgave me."

Did she forgive me? "Too bad she's not here to say so herself."

But the thinly disguised accusation was lost on Tristan. His eyes were misty and unfocused. "*Oui, chérie.*" He gave a slight, sad smile. "She would have been proud of the woman you have become. But you must put it all to rest now, as I have."

Amanda felt at a loss for words and utterly defeated. She stepped from the car. It was hardly the confrontation she had planned. She would never get any satisfaction from these meetings; Tristan seemed incapable of understanding what he had done.

"*Bonne nuit,* Amanda." He met her eyes. "Remember, *ma chère fille*, there is no living without guilt. In the end we are all guilty. We must still find a way to live."

His words cloyed to her as she started down the path to her room. She unlocked the door with a shaking hand and entered, turning the dead bolt behind her. Amanda watched until she saw the headlights of Tristan's car shift and fade and he was swallowed up by darkness.

In the dim light of the window, she saw that the "brochure" was in fact a small glossy catalog. "The Gisèle Paintings," it read. "The Work of Luke Farrell." Her hand was still shaking. She hoped against hope. *Please don't let it be him.* On the inside cover was a professional photo of the artist: a handsome blond man in his mid-thirties. The air buzzed in her ears as if it were alive with mosquitoes. Blindly, Amanda dropped the program on the end table and tore open the envelope, spilling the photographs out. She saw her own face going through the library doors at UW, walking along the wharf, exiting theaters and restaurants in Luke's arms, holding Luke's hand. He was beside her in all of them. Her sister's husband. Kissing her. Laughing. Lighthearted and innocent and in love.

Amanda covered her eyes with her hands. From her lips came a small animal cry.

❧

Nicola dreamed she was drowning. The surface of the water was a shimmering ceiling above. She kicked and kicked, but the water tugged at her feet as if alive. She gasped for air and swallowed water, kept swallowing—

She sat up with a shrill cry. Slowly, the nightmare released its grip, leaving only quiet despair. It took her a moment to realize that this wasn't her room; she was in the tower. But everything had followed her here. This room wasn't any different. It was a trap like all the other rooms.

Robin said it was going to be okay now; she needed rest and they'd talk it all over in the morning. Things looked black at night, he'd said. And there was a time when she wouldn't have doubted a thing he said, but now Nicola doubted everything. Things always looked black to her, and no amount of sunlight could change the fact that the whole world had gone crazy and she was alone in it.

She stumbled into the bathroom and stood at the sink. Her eyes were those of a stranger, glassy and foreign. She took off her nightgown, hanging it on a hook beside her robe, and turned the faucets on the tub. She didn't step in; she touched the stream of running water. She didn't like the clear emptiness of it. She could see right through it to her fingers, and her fingers looked funny—thin, fleshy things that seemed separate from the rest of her. And her arm. What a strange thing her arm was. Her eyes traveled over the rest of her body. The light at night was harsh on her pale skin, the scattered moles and disparate freckles like ink dots she couldn't connect.

It was very quiet. She was afraid to turn; she imagined figures from her dream reaching out for her. At last she couldn't help it and glanced quickly over her shoulder. There was nothing there.

She tried to make her mind a blank page, but its edges were burned black and curly, consuming the safe, pristine white spot. Her mind shrank as it was devoured; she closed her eyes and saw brown-black shapes shifting. There were fat-bellied fish and girls with long, flowing hair pulled back with ribbons; they metamorphosed into monsters with fangs, shadowy demons with fingers, reaching, reaching, reaching. *If she could just sleep . . . without the shapes. If she could just sleep forever.* Nicola clenched her eyes shut very tightly, and the images vanished into a spectrum of dizzying colors. That was better. Her mind spun, trying to keep the colors from fading, the bad thoughts from coming. Any thoughts from coming at all.

She remembered the bath and opened her eyes, searching desperately for familiar things. Bath gel. It smelled like vanilla. Vanilla was her mother. Vanilla and honey and apricots. She poured it in and watched the clear bubbles erupt in the water. She stepped in but slipped on the slick porcelain. Reaching for the vanity, she struck a mirror perched on top, and it toppled in slow motion, tumbling, somersaulting to the floor, impossibly slow, the marble floor littered with shards of glass.

Nicola stared down at them, feeling only a calm abstraction. She stepped back out of the tub, dripping water on the floor. Everything she touched broke. It was just a fact. And it was as though she watched herself, a naked, pathetic figure kneeling. She watched the shard of glass as it rose in her hand, savored its sharp, clean edges, and she wanted to be there at the edge, sharp and clean: no more pain, no more demons, no more dreams. No more . . . *anything.*

How easy it would be, a simple cut up the arm, not across; she'd seen that in a crime show. If you want to be rescued, cut across the wrist, across the delicate tendons and green-blue veins. But if you want to die, you pull the blade from the wrist up lengthwise. You go into shock then, while you're bleeding. You don't feel a thing. But there is a lot of blood.

She couldn't clean away the traces; they would be there in the morning for Robin to find. She couldn't leave a mess behind for him to find. He was trying to help her. Maybe she shouldn't kill herself that way.

The water touched her toes; it had begun to seep over the side of the tub. Nicola rose mechanically, turning the knobs counterclockwise: first hot, then cold. The water stopped running. It was very still. Very quiet. She still held the shard of glass in her hand; her fingers closed tightly around it, and she felt it cut before she felt any pain.

And then she laughed, a foreign, dry, desperate sound. There was something in the sound. It hurt, and she could hear it. She could hear her breath coming fast, quick and shallow. *Please stop. Please, God, just make it stop.* Silently, she began to cry, pressing her eyes shut so no shapes could creep in. *Please make them stop—*

And then there was a tap on the door and Robin's voice, very gentle. "Nicola?"

Her heart thudded. "I . . . I was going to take a bath." He at least was still her godfather, wasn't he? He was still Robin. "I knocked something over. I'm sorry."

"Darling, that's all right. It's three in the morning. Did you have a nightmare?"

"Uh-huh. I didn't know you were still here." He'd asked if she wanted to stay at the tower or at his home, and she'd chosen the tower because it was cozier and more familiar, entwined with library days and now with Josh and Ashleigh and the rest of his students, who had all been very kind.

"Of course I'm here, darling. I told you I'd be here as long as you're here. I've been upstairs painting. But I . . . I should have had one of the girls stay with you."

"Oh, no. That's all right. I'm fine."

"I don't think so." He paused, and in the pause it was as if he knew everything. "You're not fine, Nicola, are you?"

No, I'm not fine. I'm not fine. It came out like a sob. "*No—*"

She heard his sharp inhale, plus something under his breath that she couldn't hear. And then, "Let me help you, sweetheart. Please, Nicola. Let me help."

She wrapped Kleenex around her palm where it was bleeding and pulled her bathrobe from the back of the door. She tied it around her and opened the door to him. And if Robin noticed the water on the floor and the broken mirror and all the mess she'd made, he did not let on. He took her hand and washed it gently under running water, took a bottle of alcohol and Band-Aids from beneath the sink and dressed the cut. Nicola couldn't talk. All the while he was a blur through her tears. And then he lifted her and took her out of there. He held her tight to him and carried her up the stairs.

"Robin, I'm going crazy."

"No, Nicola, you're not." His voice was very firm. "Listen to me. The benefit of having been to hell is that nothing can scare you after that. *Nothing.* I'm with you now, and I'm not going away. You're going to tell me all of it. Everything you suspect and everything you know, and then the worst will be over. After that, darling, there's only the trip back." His voice was very steady, very certain. "I know the way, and I'll help you."

The fullness in her throat choked her. "I love you."

He closed his eyes, and his voice was hoarse. "I love you, too, Nicola."

He had never said that to her before, but she knew it was true. She'd always known, and it hadn't changed. And over hot chocolate, on the wood floor, surrounded by shadowed easels and canvases and the black night, things began to lighten.

XIX

THE CAGE

Gisèle changed when she turned eighteen. And by this I mean "Karen's" birthday in February of 1982, not my Gisèle's in June. As much as I'd tried to blot her out, Karen lived still. I'd underestimated the effect of officially sanctioned adulthood upon her. I suppose Gisèle realized she might simply go then, if she wished. The corollary of this, of course, was that in staying with me she had chosen to do so—not as a lost child but as a free woman. And though she remained with me, I knew in that terrible moment in the hospital that she wasn't quite satisfied with what she'd chosen.

But a month went by without mishap. Two. She grew healthy again. Quite healthy. She blossomed. And then, out of the blue: "I want to have a baby, Tristan."

My mouth hung open. "Why?"

Her eyes were secretive, the blinds pulled down. "Why does anyone want a baby?"

"I don't know." I said honestly. But I knew why *she* did. She was back to playing house, playacting "normal."

"I want something of my own, Tristan." As if it were a doll she wanted. Didn't she know it would kick and scream and cry and throw up? And in the end . . . *grow* up? A baby would transform my Gisèle into something else. Someone else's. "I want to give myself to something and see it grow."

To my horror I could see she'd become quite fixated on the idea (she needed to be needed, I remembered bitterly), and I fell upon a sharp point on which I must balance or be run through. I reached blindly. "That is a creative urge. That's all this is, Gisèle. You've never had time to simply focus on your writing. Now you can—"

"I'm better suited to reading than writing, Tristan. A reader in a writer's world. Or, as you and Rob might say, a painting in a painter's world. I want something of my own."

"But you have so many things."

"No." She held my eyes. "*You* have so many things."

"I'll buy you whatever you want," I said weakly.

"I know you will." Sadly. "But what I want, you can't buy. I want a life. You must have known that someday—I mean, my God, I'm not a kid anymore. I want deeper things."

"But you don't want that," I insisted, searching wildly for the right words. "Babies don't come from the stork, Gisèle. And you don't like that. Don't you remember—"

She gave me a steady look then. Of course she remembered. And I felt graceless; the right words weren't there to find, but I blundered on.

"You don't want anything inside you. You don't want a man or a baby; you're not a vehicle to be used."

She winced, but in the set of her jaw was the same resolve I'd observed on Robin's sailboat. In this context I read it as stubbornness, a spoiled child in a toy store who wants the one toy she can't have. That was the only way I could understand it, categorize it, fix it. What I did not understand is that somehow, without me, she had fixed herself. "Gisèle, you have a life. You have me."

She gazed at me clear-eyed, blinking calmly. And my balance wavered. I felt a sharp stabbing in my heart. At last she turned so that I saw only her silhouette. She said, very softly, "You're not enough."

And the blade ran me through.

It happened early that summer. His name was Luke Farrell, and he was summering in Devon at the home of a wealthy aunt, a society type named Eleanor Halvorson. It was at a party thrown by this aunt, which I had foolishly attended, that Gisèle met him.

Her interest in one so ordinary stunned me. He had only one thing going for him, and that was his Swedish good looks; he rather reminded me of the popular tennis player of the time, Björn Borg. I had to make a concerted effort not to actually call him Björn long afterward. It was an apt nickname. He was better suited to sport than to intellect.

They left the party together, slipping through the French doors. I watched from inside but did not interrupt. Not even when he kissed her. I wanted to see if she would tell me about him. She did. At this stage of our relationship, I must say Gisèle was painfully honest. She told me he'd asked to see her again the next night and that she intended to go. She wasn't "in love" with him, she said. She could not be. She only wanted to have his baby.

I said not a word; I didn't trust myself to say anything. I left the room and drove, I suppose, because I found myself in the village. The world blurred around me, and I staggered through it as though drunk. There were the usual shoppers on the sidewalks carting bags from the boutiques, mannequins in windows, paintings—the window scenes distorted all around me like a cubist masterpiece. Paradise maimed.

In a narrow room—a pub, with brick-faced walls off a side street—I got very drunk indeed on Irish whiskey to blunt the contrast, to match my surroundings. I've never been able to find the place again, nor have I cared to. For in that cramped bar came a crippling realization that my reign had come to an end.

Up to then I'd run the show. All our decisions had been mine. But her suicide attempt had been a brutally effective usurpation. Now I'd always fear she'd try again. That she'd succeed. And I could deny her nothing. As it goes with all obsessions, I had sought to possess her, but in the end it was she who possessed me.

And so, before long, I learned the inevitable. Gisèle was pregnant.

She had not yet told the boorish Björn, but he wanted to marry her, she said. Of course, the cretin wished to marry her. I was desolate, disbelieving. In my heart I'd felt that her interest in him was a whim that would fade in time. I'd gradually habituated myself to her caprices: there was the ongoing crush on Robin, which she'd long tried to conceal from me, and also a troubling interest in Marc Kreicek, who'd taken to dropping in to Falconer's Point far more often than I liked.

Marc was a rather presumptuous, arrogant sort of person, yet she told me he was her other candidate for paternity of the child. I warned her against this, against any involvement with him. I had the distinct feeling that his attentions, once encouraged, would be difficult to shake. Fortunately, a brief, intense affair was all that seemed to come of it. He was, she said, "too rough." Every man, I hoped, would be.

But I had grown practical; I realized at last that I could not be everything to Gisèle. And so I gave her just enough rope to tie her to me and foster the illusion that she was free. Yet a fling was one thing—marriage quite another.

Why should she desire this? I demanded. It was the baby she wanted.

"Yes, but the baby will need a father, Tristan."

I'm sorry to say I broke things, I called her a whore and worse, things I can't quite translate from the French. I looked at her with hatred and even imagined ways to destroy the baby inside her that wasn't mine: a slight spill on the stairs, a nice clean abortion.

And then I noticed that she was indifferent to it all; she glowed. It is true what they say about pregnant women—her hair had a gentler wave, her skin a translucent clarity, her eyes a secret sparkle. And a startling thing happened: images of violence to the unborn child were suddenly inextricable from violence to her. I loved her and so loved . . . it.

I sank into a kitchen chair in a misery of defeat. "You will live here."

"Yes," she said quietly.

"Why *him, ma petite*?" Though of course what I meant was, why anyone?

She took my hand in her small, cool one, closed her fingers around it, and found my eyes. "Because I don't love him. Don't you see, Tristan? It will still be you and me." And then she described how she envisioned her married life to be. And in spite of myself, I felt a pang of pity for poor Björn.

Robin, when I told him, said, "It's over, then." Did I only imagine there was a note of relief in it? A shrugged responsibility. "I wondered how long it could last."

"Over?" I echoed. "By no means."

Robin was too jaded to be surprised, yet he was unable to comprehend this weakness of mine. "Then you will become your role, Tristan. Can't you see that? You'll end up the father after all. That's not what you want."

I smacked this away, as if swatting a stinging gnat. "I'm only her father to the outside world, and I care nothing for that world. Gisèle will know the truth. We've always had our separate truth."

He scoffed. "You're rearranging deck chairs on the *Titanic*. What about this Luke fellow? You think your truth is going to be his? What about the baby? You're mad to think you can do this your whole life, to even want to—" And in his words it did sound mad. "You realize the child is going to be, to all intents and purposes, your grandchild."

"What would you have me do?"

He said intently, "Let her go."

"She doesn't want me to—"

"She doesn't want to ask you to."

"*C'est la même chose.*"

"No, Tristan, it's not the same thing."

I shrugged. "She will have to leave me. I cannot leave her. I love her."

And he only sighed, but in his eyes I saw how very much he pitied me.

XX

CONVERSATION

AFTER A SLEEPLESS NIGHT, Amanda phoned Robin early and left a message asking to meet. In the karmic way of things, he phoned back while she was in the shower. She listened to the message as she dried off.

"Amanda, sorry to miss your call. It's been rather a rough night."

Tell me about it, she thought.

"Turns out Nicola's done some detective work of her own and knows nearly everything, including the fact of her aunt. She's been through hell. But I'm convinced Tristan hasn't laid a finger on her, whatever his intentions. She went to school today—needed the distraction, I think. I've cleared it at Prescott for you to pick her up at lunchtime. Er . . . that would be twelve-ten. Sign her out at the office first." A pause. *"She wants very much to know you, Amanda. Come to the gallery afterward, and we'll talk."*

For a moment the horrors of the previous night receded. Amanda stared at the phone in dismay. *". . . the fact of her aunt"?* Nicola *knew* her? *Nicola knew her.*

Truth be told, it horrified Amanda to be known. She was a case of nerves as she drove to Stephen R. Prescott Primary. Her heart pounded as she stopped into the office to sign Nicola out, and as she waited in the parking lot for the bell.

Rain fell in sheets. Nicola came down the steep cement staircase by herself, her face nearly eclipsed by a big, bright umbrella. Amanda watched it swivel as she scanned the cars in the lot. Amanda pulled up to the curb. Lowering the passenger window, she called, "Nicola!"

Nicola's uncertain expression transformed into an ebullient smile. She waved, casting a quick glance over her shoulder at a group of girls who stood at the top of the stairs. From the way she glanced, Amanda felt an instant dislike for the girls. One of them called out something Amanda couldn't hear. The others just peered at the car curiously. Nicola opened the door.

Amanda smiled. "Hi, there! Climb in, quick—it's pouring."

Nicola lowered her umbrella and ducked into the car. "It's really nice of you to come."

"I thought you'd like a break from cafeteria food," Amanda said. "And I brought you the books we talked about. Madeleine L'Engle—the Austin series?"

"Oh!" Nicola exclaimed in delight. She took the gift bag and extracted the books one by one. "Wow. Thanks, Amanda, you didn't have to," she said with a touching sincerity. She bit her lip. "You know, you're just the way I imagined my aunt."

"Am I?" Amanda was touched by the innocent straightforwardness of this. Nicola had made it easy for her.

"Yes. I've imagined everyone—aunts and uncles, cousins. But I never expected one to come to life."

Tears filled her eyes. She gave Nicola's hand a tight squeeze. "Neither did I."

They went to *André's* in the village: quaint and cozy, white tablecloths and delicate china. A fire crackled in a corner fireplace, and they were seated before it.

"Mom and I always came here," Nicola said. "We did pretty much everything together."

"She must have been a wonderful person."

"She was my best friend."

"She was mine, too. Once."

Nicola gazed at her, curious but silent. After a moment she reached for her purse. "I have something to show you." The bag was barely big enough to hold lip gloss, pocket change, and a snapshot. Nicola held the latter out to Amanda.

Amanda took it and gazed down. She and Karen looked impossibly young, a ragamuffin pair, shabbily dressed and severely stair-stepped, with sun-dappled faces and squinting eyes. They stood together on a patch of lawn before their grandparents' ramshackle old Craftsman in Geyserville. The paint was peeling and the wraparound porch sagged, but it had been charming once—a thing remembered in the blooming flowers and in their smiles. She and Karen had looked alike even then, in the eerie way sisters can—the symmetry of facial plane, shade of hair, and shape of eyes. A mop-headed Amanda mugged for the camera, chin up and a grin from ear to ear, the left cheek dimpling on a suspiciously sticky-looking face. Karen was twelve and wistful and already lovely, one arm clasping the elbow of the other and her left foot bent painfully inward at the ankle. She was looking down at Amanda, and her smile was for her.

Creases ran through the middle, and dog-eared corners had been carefully smoothed out, signs of its travels, a journey Amanda would never understand. Yet as she held it, she felt suddenly whole, perhaps the way amputees still feel the weight of lost limbs. Her grandfather had died a few months after this photograph was taken, and Karen began to change, but for this crystal moment they knew nothing of those things. They were innocent. "This was taken at our grandparents' house," she murmured. "Your great-grandparents."

"I know," Nicola said solemnly. "There's an inscription on the back."

Yes, in their mother's spidery hand: *Karen Louise and Amanda Nicole— Grandma and Grandpa Miller's: 1976.* Choking back emotion, she gazed up at her niece. "How did you find this?"

"It was hidden behind a picture of me and Mom. She named me for you, didn't she?"

Amanda found it hard to speak. She nodded.

"She loved you very much. I can tell by the way she's looking at you." Nicola leaned forward, her bright eyes earnest and concerned. And again Amanda was struck by it: Nicola was concerned about *her.* Suddenly she seemed far older than her eleven years.

Amanda took Nicola's hand and squeezed it tight. "I'm so glad you found it. Thank you for showing me. I . . . well, we have a lot of catching up to do." And she could imagine it now: rainy afternoons, sharing photographs and stories with her niece. Making new scrapbooks. As she handed the photograph back, all her nervousness fled. It was going to be all right.

⁊

The bar wasn't a fancy one, though in Devon that was a relative statement. The walls were rustic brick, and the bar top wasn't marble or copper or zinc or limestone, but good old-fashioned wood, nicked in places, the lighting dim and anonymous. A fire roared in a central clay fireplace and flickered invitingly over the narrow room. It was an Irish pub, the *Fortunate Fox*. The fox in question fortunate for having made it to Ireland, Luke supposed, beyond reach of the British hounds.

How Luke envied him at that moment.

The only other un-English thing about Devon was the food; it was well known for being edible. But every once in a while, Luke liked to imagine a world without basil-infusion oils and wine-reduction sauces and wandered into the *Fortunate Fox* for pub grub. He'd come to deep-fry and inebriate his troubles—and maybe shed new light on them. He was meeting Marc Kreicek here.

Luke was a bit early, so he took a seat at the bar and had just been served a pint when he heard a voice behind him. "Luke, *můj přítel*, is that you? Come, I've already taken a table."

Marc had taken it sometime ago, from the sound of his voice. Luke rose. Sure enough, there he was, tucked away cozily in a shadowed corner, rapidly emptying a pint glass.

"I have a start on you, I'm afraid. Sit, sit."

Luke sat. Beneath the tailored clothes, Marc had a perpetually gaunt look, as though he'd been undernourished in childhood and never quite been able to make up for it. Today the effect was enhanced, as his fastidious toilette had been let go. Luke could see dark whiskers rising from his jaw and smell the beer on his breath.

"What is all this urgency? Is it the show? Only days away, I hear." Marc's smile was brief and wicked.

Luke sighed. The show. Yes, the show. "Yeah. Why I felt the need to drink."

"One never requires a need to drink, *můj přítel*." Luke assumed this to mean "my friend," not because Marc often used it with him but because he typically used it with Robin. "We can't change the course of our destinies. Gisèle wouldn't have it so. This is your big chance! Rob's lining up press and potential . . . shall we call them investors? It's like shooting fish in a barrel."

Except that Luke feared he was one of the fish. He took a long sip from his pint.

"What is that you're drinking?"

"Spaten." In keeping with the anti-English theme.

Marc loudly proclaimed his disapproval. "Spaten? Ach. Czechs make the best beer. *Mám velice rád české pivo!* People think it's the Germans, but we showed all of Europe how to make beer." And, clearly, how to drink it. He waved to the waitress for two more of what he was having: the world's most unpronounceable pilsner. "Why so glum, my friend? Don't you realize how lucky you are to have the great Robin Dresden backing you?"

Luke assessed him. "You sound facetious. You two have a falling-out?"

"Facetious? No, no. Everything Robin touches turns to gold. He has everyone under his spell. Everyone, that is, but me."

"Oh, yeah? How'd you escape?"

Marc scoffed, a short bitter sound. "I've known him a very long time. So long as to make myself indispensable. Not so our French friend."

"Tristan? I doubt that. As far as Rob's concerned, he can do no wrong."

"Ah." Marc's eyes glittered, like those of a child with a secret too big for him. "Not anymore, I fear. Tristan's going back to Paris." He clucked his tongue. "Oh, yes, it was quite a scene."

Tristan, dearly deported? On one hand, nothing would make Luke happier. On the other, where would next month's money come from? The paintings were still a question mark. "What scene? Where?"

"At Robin's house, just before I arrived here. He suggested rather strongly that Tristan ought to leave." A shrug. "It only makes sense. If you were French, you could escape as well."

"Excuse me?"

As if explaining to a fool, "You could escape to France with its beautiful antiextradition laws, along with Tristan."

"So Robin's been feeding you his bullshit theories, too. Hate to disappoint, Marc, but I haven't broken any laws." He dropped his voice. "You really think Tristan *killed* Gisèle?"

"I think he may have, yes. But it will be difficult to prove without a confession."

"Damned difficult," Luke agreed. "So why would he leave Devon, then?"

"There are other crimes than murder," Marc replied enigmatically. "And he left a good deal behind in Paris." The pints came then, occupying him considerably more than was healthy at this stage. "I've been there, you know. Many times."

"Paris?"

"Of course Paris. I studied in Paris. No, I mean Tristan's place in Paris."

"What is it, the palace of Versailles or something?"

"Very posh. Full of art. Art *everywhere*. Sickening, really, the gluttony. Perhaps I really am a communist at heart." This brought a considerable laugh. "Of course, the art was the reason Rob struck up so deep and profound a friendship with Tristan."

Luke was sick of art. "To look at his paintings?"

Marc scoffed. "To steal them, more like. Oh, there were other reasons, but they wouldn't have mattered without the art."

"I doubt Robin needs to steal."

"That's because you don't understand art." A sheepish shrug. "Neither do I, really."

"What does any of this have to do with Gisèle?"

"Ah, Gisèle." Marc's eyes flashed with malice. "Yes, Robin was very fond of her." A pause. "In fact, I have quite a secret to tell you, Luke. I think you have a *right* to know." The righteous tone didn't suit him. "But you must promise not to tell Rob you heard it from me."

"What are we, in second grade?" Luke's glib tone was a blind. Inwardly, he braced himself. Marc seemed to have forgotten they were discussing his wife.

Marc set his unshaven jaw stubbornly. "Promise."

"I promise." *Cross my heart, hope to die.*

"It seems Robin is Nicola's father."

Luke took a long sip of beer. "I know that."

Marc was visibly deflated. "You know? How do you know? It was quite a shock to me."

"I had DNA tests done. They prove she's not mine."

"That doesn't mean she must be Robin's," Marc pointed out. "Do you know, for a time I thought she was mine." He held Luke's eyes, and his gaze belied his casual tone. "Gisèle and I were very close once, you know. That very same summer she met you. Did she never tell you?"

Luke didn't want to give Marc the satisfaction of boasting over his conquests—his favorite pastime. Especially this one. "Well, she's not exactly here to contradict you, is she?"

"Ah, but you have my word."

"Okay. Pull out a hair or spit in a cup and we'll enter you in the lottery."

Marc squinted skeptically at Luke. He fingered the medallion he habitually wore around his neck. "It doesn't bother you, the possibility?"

"It's beyond bothering me," he lied. "I thought she was frigid. Turns out she was just exhausted."

Marc laughed cruelly in commiseration. "Yes."

It was the commiseration that got him. "You and she never . . . not *after* we were married?"

For a moment Marc hesitated, but then he simply shook his head. "No, no. It was done by then. She did not suit me." Which was his way of saying he did not suit her.

Suddenly Luke felt a kind of camaraderie with him. "Listen, I've meant to ask you. How do you know Amanda? Remember, Amanda Miller, the girl you introduced me to in Seattle?"

It was as if Marc had slipped on a mask. All expression left his face, and his eyes actually focused.

"The reason I'm curious is, she's turned up here in Devon. She was at the gallery asking about Gisèle and the paintings. Only she didn't seem to know *I'd* painted them."

"Well, why didn't you tell her?"

"I tried. She wouldn't listen to me."

Marc shrugged. "I scarcely know her. She was involved with the other man at lunch, you know, the man from the university. The psychologist. I know her only through him."

"And so you introduced her to me? 'She's just your type, Luke,' you said."

"She was. She likes married guys."

Luke groaned audibly. "Let's just order."

Marc nodded. "Here's the waitress. Hello, darling." He smiled winningly. "My friend here would like to order some food." It seemed he intended to drink his lunch.

When the waitress departed, Luke said, "The DNA tests turned up something else."

"Oh, yes?" Marc's tone remained laissez-faire, but Luke could tell his interest was piqued.

"Seems Tristan wasn't really Gisèle's father. They don't have enough DNA in common for that. But they are related somehow." He squinted. "Do you know anything about that?"

"I'm afraid not." Offhandedly. Then he rubbed his eyes, which had regained their depraved gleam, and swallowed a long swig of beer. "I never thought they were related at all."

Marc leaned back, clearly enjoying Luke's shocked stare. His eyes wobbled. It struck Luke that they were rather a bastardized version of Gisèle's, a paler aqua and almost transparent, like a shard of a ship's bottle.

"You *knew*?"

"Of course." In a conspiratorial whisper, Marc said, "Do you really want the truth, Luke?"

"Love it." How ironic that it should come from someone like Marc.

"Robin sent me to *find* Tristan, years ago. He was interested in his art collection. I tracked him to San Francisco and reported back dutifully. Rob arranged a meeting sometime later at a party in New York. Tristan was living there with a girl he called his daughter. Only *his* daughter— Marie-Gisèle Ariane Mourault—died in Paris in 1967."

Luke's right hand froze in midair. He helped his pint along to his mouth with the other hand. "But then you *and* Rob knew all along she wasn't Tristan's daughter."

"Yes, yes."

His eyes widened. "Why didn't Robin ever say anything?"

"What was he to say? He's not the morals police." He laughed. "If he is, we're in trouble."

"But I don't understand. If she's Tristan's niece or something, why call her his daughter?"

"I don't know anything about that. As I say, I didn't think they were related at all." He paused. "But it's very interesting, that. He couldn't have a niece. Tristan's an only child. A distant cousin, maybe." He shrugged. "We thought she was a runaway."

"So you find him living with a girl he calls his daughter. How old was she?"

"Too young," said Marc simply. "Tristan may have gone to prison. America is so puritan still. Where I'm from, the age of consent is fifteen."

What a fucked-up country, Luke thought. "So you both just stood by while—"

"Here's the rub, *můj přítel.* Turns out our friend Tristan can't get it up." This amused Marc a great deal; his eyes flickered with merriment. Maybe it was just the beer. "Robin heard this through the nasty little grapevine, and so he's not much troubled by the thing. She seemed happy, and Tristan was sitting on all those lovely paintings. Better to use his eccentricities to our advantage, eh?"

Luke hadn't had enough beer to follow. "So it was *platonic?*"

Marc scoffed. "I doubt that, but it was more psychological than sexual, I think. Father, lover, prison keeper. He may have been all of them rolled into one. He brainwashed her, I think. Mere sex, my friend, is nothing to psychology. It's a fascinating phenomenon."

"I'm glad you're fascinated. But if she was psychologically dependent on Tristan and sleeping with Robin," Luke asked, almost desperately, "what the hell was *I* for?"

A sly tip of the head. "Well, you were there to make it look all right."

And it was true, of course. "You knew all this, the whole time?"

"Not all of it. I thought Rob and Gisèle were no more than friends. The whole time I thought Nicola was mine." The drunken merriment faded. "But here's another little fact for you. I happened upon some photographs of Gisèle in Robin's desk." He had the dead gaze of a shark before it strikes. "Recent photographs, some of them. Nudes. Lovely. So erotic—"

"Get on with it."

"They were very like the paintings. And I understood then. It had been him all along. He was why she was so damned hard to get."

Luke stared. So his first instinct had been correct? Robin himself had photographed Gisèle. The paintings were his.

"It's amazing what is right before our eyes that we fail to see, is it not?"

"What's he got planned for me, Marc?" Luke's voice sounded desperate to his own ears. "What the hell is he doing the exhibition *for*?"

Marc's posture grew cagey. "I don't really know. But there are traps laid for Tristan, just as there are for you. And I wouldn't like to be either of you right now, my friend."

"I thought Tristan was going to France."

"Not until after the exhibition."

"Well, what *traps*, then?" Luke asked savagely.

Marc merely held a wobblingly admonishing finger to his lips and gave a shrug.

"What traps, Marc?" Luke wanted to shake him. "You listen to me—"

The harried waitress arrived then, with a steaming plate of fish and chips. She frowned at Luke. "Can I ask you fellows to keep it down?"

Marc was the picture of innocence. "Quite right, Luke. Where are your manners?" When she disappeared, he spoke in a whisper, more to the plate of deep-fried cod than to Luke. "He holds you both responsible, that's all I'm saying. You'll both be gotten out of the way, and he'll have what he wants in the end. He always does. Little Nicola. The art. He always gets what he wants. And I'll still be here, because I'm his best, most trusted hired hand." Marc paused, and his face possessed a poignancy that Luke had never observed in him before, a lost, forlorn quality.

But Luke had scant pity for him. He'd never understood quite so well the impulse to kill the messenger. His insides spasmed. "Why should I stick around and be set up?"

"I agree. You should go."

Go where? Every instinct shouted at him to bow out, give up the paintings and the whole charade. *But without it I have nothing.* Without the paintings. Without Gisèle and Nicola—even Tristan—he had nothing. He was back to being no one. "It's been fun, Marc. Really." Luke rose. "You're a lot of fun when you're fucked up. But I've got to go."

"Now, now." Marc reached for his arm. "Don't go away mad."

"I'm not mad. I just want to go away."

"I hate to drink alone."

"Then stop drinking."

Marc gazed up at him; his eyes tried to focus. "Yes," he said, dismayed. "I am very drunk. I've said too much. We'll forget about this the next time we run into each other, won't we?"

"I'll forget it as soon as I walk out the door. And I'll run into you at the opening on Friday."

"Ah, that's the spirit! Just because Rob is using you doesn't necessarily mean you won't profit from it." He took a swig of beer. "God knows I have. . . ."

❧

For a moment Nicola was almost perfectly happy. She didn't have to go back to Falconer's Point after school. She didn't have to go back there ever again. "From now on, you don't have to do anything you don't want to do," Robin had said. He was sending a car to pick her up after school—no one else here had that—and at the college she had his students. And now she had Amanda, too. Aunt Amanda. For a moment she could almost forget.

But no sooner was she back in class than she received another pink slip, requesting her to come to the office. Kelly made a face at her and stuck her foot in the aisle with an insolent smile. Nicola moved toward the door, kicking Kelly's shoe hard in the process. "Oh, excuse me."

"Mrs. Perkins, Nicola kicked me."

But Mrs. Perkins knew Kelly. "Keep your foot out of the aisle, Kelly, and turn to page one sixty-two. . . ."

Nicola merely smiled.

But she could find no suitable smile when she opened the office door to find her grandfather standing there, eyes crinkling at the corners, sneaking a wink at her when his back was to the secretary. "Had you forgotten your dental appointment, *mon chaton?*"

"I didn't . . . I don't think I have one." Robin warned her that Tristan might come to pick her up after school. She wasn't to go with him. But now she found that it wasn't so easy not to go.

Tristan cast a knowing glance at the school secretary. "I make it a habit to forget mine, too, *n'est-ce pas?* Come now, Nicola. I've already signed you out."

Her eyes flew around the cramped office; there was no one there but the secretary, who was glaring down at her keyboard with pursed lips. And before she knew it, Tristan had taken her by the elbow and guided her through the door.

"You're a bit slow on the uptake today, *chérie.*"

"Well, what are you doing here? Are we going to the library?"

"There is more to life than the library, Nicola. What's happened to your sense of adventure? I just want to spend the afternoon with you."

She shot him a sideways glance and bit her lip apprehensively.

"I understand from your father that you're staying with Robin for a few days," Tristan continued conversationally. "But I'm leaving soon, and we must make the most of our time."

Nicola stopped short. "You're leaving? Where are you going?"

"Home, *mon chaton.* My home. France."

"But it's not August—"

"Come." He nudged Nicola along. "We'll discuss it in the car."

Tristan opened her door for her, and she slid across the leather seat of his antique Jaguar. How she used to love long drives in this car.

"I was surprised to hear of you staying at the college dormitory. That's unusual, isn't it?"

"I wanted to go."

He turned the key in the ignition. "Oh?" His voice was strange. "And why is that?"

"It's just hard being at home. I can't stop thinking of Mom and what happened."

"*Oui.*" He eased the car into reverse and pulled out of the lot. "But I think you're under a misapprehension as to what happened. You see, I saw the newspaper articles, Nicola. On the computer screen. I saw what you were researching at the library. I have been trying to see things from your perspective." He turned to her. "What is it you think I've done, *ma petite?*"

Ma petite. He'd only ever called her mother that.

In a gentler voice, he said, "I must ask you not to look at me that way, Nicola. I'm no different than I've ever been."

Her mouth had turned to cotton. She fought the urge to jump from the car. "You're not my grandfather."

"No. But I've loved you from the minute you were born. And I loved your mother dearly. Not as a daughter, that's true. It's no good to pretend with you. I know you saw us together in the garden." He inhaled sharply. "I loved her, Nicola. I loved her more than life. But that's all over."

Ice ran through Nicola's veins. "The newspapers said she was dead. Her backpack was soaked in blood."

Tristan waved an agitated hand. "*Non, non.* The newspapers say *Karen Miller's* backpack was soaked in blood. But that girl has nothing to do with my Gisèle. I want to know who's told you these lies." He glanced at her. "Is it Amanda? Did she get to you somehow? Or was it Robin?" Nicola was silent. "It is madness. A chance resemblance. Amanda believes Gisèle to be her sister, Karen. *C'est ridicule*, Nicola. The name Karen Miller means nothing to me."

Nicola watched his knuckles whiten as he gripped the steering wheel. They stood out beneath the skin like a row of tiny skulls.

"I have Gisèle's birth certificate. I named her. It is true that I *called* her my daughter, though she was not. I married her mother, Sabina, when she was already pregnant. She died a few years after the marriage, and Gisèle went to live with relatives. She returned to me a young woman." His Adam's apple bobbed as he swallowed. "You must try to understand, Nicola. I loved her, she loved me. It is that simple. We weren't related. It wasn't incestuous. I loved her mother, and I lost her. I loved Gisèle, and now I've lost *her.* You must believe me."

Only she didn't believe him. He had lost the power to make her believe. Nicola thought of Amanda and of the photograph in her purse. "Even if I believed you, that doesn't make it right."

"She loved me, *ma petite.* There is no greater right."

"But if she loved you that way, why did she marry Dad?"

Tristan scoffed. The rain had turned to snow, and he took a corner of the winding road too fast. The tires lost traction, slipping sideways across the centerline. An oncoming car honked, and Nicola put her hands on the dashboard to keep from slamming into it as Tristan braked, hard. It was like a scene from a movie she'd already seen. *I've already seen it. I know how it comes out. It comes out all right in the end.*

He corrected, shifting the car back into their lane. "*Merde!* Damn this weather."

It was early for snow, but in Devon one never knew what the weather would do. Tristan took a swooping turn up to a vista point overlooking the lake. It was desolate on a day like today.

"Remember all the good times we've had on the lake, *mon chaton?*"

And she did remember; that was the odd thing. Nicola remembered all the good times on Lake Devon and everywhere, as if they'd happened only yesterday.

"Its surface is like a mirror, is it not?"

It was a fogged-up, broken mirror today, a deep gray, marbled by the white that fell from the sky. Wind chopped up the surface.

"We'll just talk here awhile, *n'est-ce pas?* And then I'll take you home."

"No, I—" She swallowed. "No, I'd like to go back to the tower. Please."

"A slip of the tongue. Of course I'll take you to the college, if that's what you want."

She shifted in the seat. "It's all right. You can just drop me back at school." It was closer and suddenly seemed a haven of safety. "Robin's coming for me at three."

"I see." Tristan ground his jaw; she watched the bone working beneath his skin. "You think I've committed a crime, Nicola, don't you?"

After a moment she nodded.

"What is my crime?"

"Karen Miller. *Mom.* You hurt her somehow and took her away. Her backpack was—"

"But I've told you that Karen Miller has nothing to do with your mother. Amanda has nothing whatever to connect your mother to Karen, only mad allegations."

"But *I* have something to connect them," Nicola said softly. "*I* have proof."

And the way he stared at her then, as if she'd stabbed him in the back. Nicola felt her pulse throb in her temples and felt it in her wrists, beating like a trapped thing. Her mother used to say she couldn't bear "trapped things." She'd rescued spiders and even removed window screens to free moths from the room. Nicola understood now.

The air in the car was smothering, oppressive, and everything she didn't normally feel was tangible suddenly: the weight of the air, the pressure of the blood through her veins, the heaviness of her own body on the worn, smooth leather of the seats. It seemed she could even feel the cold in the glass of the windshield, as it was quietly colored in by snow one dot at a time, like the work of the pointillist who had come to the party.

"What 'proof,' Nicola?" Tristan didn't raise his voice, but he was angry. And she could not show him; she was afraid to. She didn't want him to touch it.

"It's a photograph," she said at last. "I don't have it with me, but I found it in Mom's room. It's of her and Amanda together—"

"Standing in front of an old white house with a wraparound porch? A porch that sags?"

Nicola stared at him, wide-eyed. "Yes."

"That wasn't your mother, Nicola. I've seen the photograph." He paused. "Amanda showed it to me."

"I don't understand. She couldn't have shown you. She took me to lunch today, and I showed it to her. It was in Mom's room." And then all at once the words spilled out of her. She told him about the photo and the passageway through her mother's closet and the mirror that was not a mirror at all. "The passage leads down to Dad's art studio. I even found a piece of Mom's robe on the stairs. She was down there the night she died."

It took him a moment to reply. "You say it leads to your father's art studio?"

Her lip trembled. "Yes."

"But surely you see what that means."

"Not—not really."

"Your father was having an affair. Gisèle had proof of this. He was having an affair with a woman in Seattle." Tristan gazed at her. Sympathy crept into his eyes, and something else. Something unpleasant. "You have met her."

"I have?"

Tristan reached across her, ignoring her frightened jump. From the glove compartment, he drew out a packet of photographs. Nicola didn't need to thumb through them. She stared at the very first one. Her father was laughing. He had his arms around *her*.

Disbelieving her eyes. "*Amanda?*"

"*Oui.* Whom you seem to trust so much, after only one lunch."

Nicola shook her head. "I don't believe you."

"She was having an affair with your father, Nicola. You have the proof in your hands. She may have come here following him. She told me she'd read of the paintings in a magazine and grown fixated with Gisèle's resemblance to her sister, Karen."

Nicola covered her ears, and tears stung her eyes. She wanted to play the child's trick of talking nonsense to avoid listening. *Blah . . . blah . . . blah. I'm not listening! I can't hear you . . .*

Tristan put an arm around her shoulder to comfort her. "You've been misled. It's all a lie. She's unbalanced, *ma petite.* I believe she wants your mother's life. You. She must have planted the photograph, don't you see? She must be meeting your father secretly."

Her father. Her father laughing and kissing Amanda. The proof was lying in her lap. He'd loved Amanda. And her mother had been crying in the garden. Her father knew about the passage . . . And someone had followed her mother to the pool house and killed her. Nicola let out a sharp, unconscious cry. "He did it, didn't he?" Tears ran down her cheeks. It hurt to breathe. She wanted to protest, except all the bizarre pieces connected. "But what about Robin? He believes Amanda, too."

"Amanda came to him a month ago with her photograph and this story. But—" Tristan broke off and frowned. All at once he seemed to sense her terror. She couldn't take it in. He reached over to dry her cheeks with his handkerchief.

"Listen to me. You were your mother's whole life. You are mine. You eclipsed the rest of it. I can't bear to think I've lost you, too." Tristan touched her chin, and his eyes shone; he ran his fingers gently over her hair to smooth it but lingered at her neck, the way he'd begun to do this summer. It made her uncomfortable. Had she been uncomfortable then? No. Not at the lake. In the sunshine. She'd been swimming; he'd dried her off. Now there was no sunshine, and the world was white around them, and her stomach was jumpy. She pulled away.

He let her go.

"Think about all I've said. I know you will believe it, because it is true. In time I will prove it to you." A pause. "Unfortunately, we haven't *much* time. I don't know why Amanda is making these claims and approaching you. But if I'm right about your father . . . well, I'm worried for your safety. Wouldn't you like to come with me, *mon chaton*? To see Paris?"

Nicola stared. "But—"

"There is no *time* for buts." Tristan pounded the steering wheel with his fist, and Nicola jumped. He repeated in a whisper, "There is no time. After the exhibition Friday, I'll be gone. That's why I needed to see you today. We need to rush your passport—I may not have another chance. I'm begging you with all my heart, my sweet Nicola. *Come with me.*"

Nicola's stomach churned. Snow swirled around them, colorless and empty. Even the great lake was blotted out. *I don't know what to believe.* But that wasn't what she said. The words that came from her mouth were, "I don't want you to leave."

And Tristan smiled. There were tears in his eyes, and he kissed the top of her head. "Bless you. I won't leave you. But you must do what I say." He started up the car. "We'll apply for your passport now. I'll come for you on Friday. I must make an appearance at the exhibition first. . . ."

She hardly heard. She thought of her godfather the night before and his reassuring words: *It's all right now, Nico. You don't have to do anything you don't want to do.* "I can't leave without telling Robin."

Tristan frowned. "Nicola, it is very important that you say *nothing* to anyone. Not a soul. Do you understand? We'll contact Robin from Paris. I want you to pack only a few things. I'll buy you whatever you need. It will be fun, you'll see." He paused, holding her eyes. "I do want you to bring the photograph we spoke of, *ma petite*. Do you have it still?"

Nicola nodded, but didn't release her grip on her purse. She watched as the windshield wipers trudged through the thin layer of snow, sluggishly and then with ease, and slowly the world came back into focus.

XXI

BEFORE THE MIRROR

In the end the introduction of a husband into my relationship with Gisèle was not altogether unpleasant. At first, of course, I felt all the things one might expect: loss, bitterness, the sharpest sorrow. If my pendulum had swung both ways, it might have been different, but alas I was as heterosexual as they come. I found nothing sensual in him; he was too common to touch her, too banal in his tastes—too . . . everything but what she ought to have had. He was not me.

I weighed my options: Ought I to implore her to divorce him? Formally compile a long list of his faults? (For, truly, there were a great many.) Or perhaps give the appearance of approval, yet privately sabotage his every move. . . .

I leaned heavily toward the last. But of course, no. Even the lay psychologist could predict that this would only strengthen her resolve to have him, foster an empathy where it might not otherwise grow. Worse still, it would create in her an animosity toward me.

Strangely, I didn't feel particularly jealous of him; I never felt the threat I'd so long felt from Robin. Luke, I knew, would never live inside her head. For distinctly in my favor was the fact that he was a hapless, malleable creature with no serious prospects and no backbone. He called himself an artist, because in Devon that was the thing to call oneself, but the only innate drive he possessed was a rapidly acquired taste for the finer things. And so I would buy him off, I decided. I would own him.

I threw her a grand wedding. I walked her down the aisle. I let myself
be congratulated on the "joyous" event of her marriage. I even went so far as
to call him *mon fils*. Better to think of him as my son than as her husband.

Privately, I saw him only as the undeserving receptacle of my own pleasure. And a very great pleasure there was to be had—for a time. Gisèle
appeared to be experiencing a sexual renaissance; she never appeared
happier than in that first year. I was at no time fooled into thinking it
had anything to do with him. It was the pregnancy, of course. Little Nicola. With Luke there was always a faintly glassy quality to Gisèle's eyes,
as if it were not him she was seeing. And I could see she had been true to
her word: she did not love him.

But did she, I wondered, still love me?

She was very careful of my feelings, and we found time alone. And
I waited patiently for the cracks in the façade of her new life to widen.
I watched the way she kissed Luke, noted every occasion in which he
touched her in my presence—her hand, her cheek, the curve of her hip,
the growing curve of her belly. I watched for an unconscious stiffening at
his touch. And before long it appeared.

But it had also appeared with mine.

And here it was: the final shift in our relationship. I was now to be relegated to voyeur. My earliest role returned to haunt me.

There was a passageway along the second story of the house, a long,
narrow corridor that stretched the whole of the eastern wall, with a stair
at one end that descended to the cellar. It was invisible from the outside.
Even Robin was unaware of it, though he'd shown us many other architectural peculiarities of the house—hidden doors, secret rooms, compartments built into the walls.

I made the discovery on my own, for I had Bryan Prescott's old room.
There was a secret door through the closet. Fate, I called it. Providence.
It seemed a godsend to me and quickly prompted a change of rooms for
Gisèle. There was a similar opening through her closet that allowed us
to bypass the halls—to bypass Luke and baby Nicola as she grew, Henri
and the increasing number of servants required for a household of this
size. She embraced the idea and often came to visit me to talk, to lie
beside me and be held. We were again free from prying eyes.

Yet these intimate moments were becoming fewer and further between. And I realized that the passageway held other possibilities. It might also offer me a unique way to watch them, to watch her, anytime day or night. I owned an antique triptych wall mirror, a prize from an auction long ago. I had the glass replaced with a two-way mirror and installed it so that it concealed the opening cut into her bedroom wall above her vanity. It was a window through which I could see and not be seen.

There are many pleasures to be found in the vicarious experience. How can I explain this, except to offer paler analogies? An anorexic who yet relishes the appetite of others, the smell of food and the texture, preparation, and presentation? Or perhaps the musician who can no longer play. Does he then abandon listening? For myself, I cultivated still further the art of voyeurism, that art for which I realize I am best suited.

The thrill of the voyeur comes only when the object is unaware she is observed. Gisèle didn't know that her mirror was my window, of course. It was of high quality and undetectable unless well lit from behind. When I was not in the passageway, a black covering concealed it. And so she behaved as one does when no one is watching, and I realized only then how much she put on for me. I'd never seen her quite so relaxed, so reflective. Nor ever so full of joy as she was with Nicola. And I have never been quite so grateful for her elaborate toilette, the lovely moments I was able to see her gazing intently at me in her preparations for the day, in her acts of dressing.

I also witnessed her and Luke together at night. And once I learned to focus my eyes so as not to see him, it became a very great pleasure for me to watch. My pleasure, I'm afraid, often exceeded hers; from experience I was able to gauge the veracity of her response, and his success was sporadic at best. As I'd predicted, she habitually shunned intercourse in favor of other activities, and I took no small gratification in faulting his technique therein.

At these times I liked to imagine she was performing for me. I fantasized that Gisèle had secretly discovered the mirror in the passage—despite my efforts at concealment—that she knew I was there, watching her. I imagined this so often I came to believe it. It was a beautiful thing, this fantasy, for the dance of voyeur and exhibitionist is the sex act made intangible, a ritual far more sacred, it seems to me, as it exists in the mind alone and transcends mere touch.

Here, too, I convinced myself, was proof of my hold over her. If anything, mine was increased by their marriage and his diminished. He was her stud, if you will, for Nicola, and her surrogate for me. But I was at the very core of her pleasure. I convinced myself of this. She loved me. And she loved how she looked to me. She was the reflection in my eyes.

And so it was that I was struck down unaware, knocked from the heights of ever more frail fantasies. It had taken many years to build them and many years to bring them to ruin. I thought myself the master of my house, of her, of my destiny. But, in truth, my reality had grown just as narrow as my passageway and my porthole view in, and it was shrinking all the time.

XXII

LYING NUDE

THE EXHIBITION WAS a resounding success.

The paintings were splendid beneath the spotlights, soft and erotic and so quintessentially Gisèle, many forms of the feminine changing like a chameleon with each canvas. It was like stepping into a kaleidoscope of sensory stimulation. Her skin was everywhere, her eyes followed Luke wherever he went. Collectors and critics and artists alike were abuzz with excitement.

Luke was on Valium and working on his third vodka tonic and still not at all "abuzz." He felt something less than moderately at ease. But Robin more than made up for him: the perfect patron, he worked the room with grace and élan, slipping Luke pills. Luke felt like a badly dilapidated La-Z-Boy to Dresden's Louis Quatorze fauteuil, and this went unnoticed by no one but unremarked upon by all. He was riding a wave, which meant that one's shortcomings were all at once a source of intrigue. Luke had merely to shake the occasional hand, smile, nod, and subsequently eavesdrop. Around him, like butterflies, voices drifted and hovered, flitted away.

He's a bit of a bore, isn't he?
Do you suppose she posed for all of them?
They were married, weren't they?
That's why I ask—

She's dead, you know . . . the poor man.
Hmm. Does that mean he's available?

In six months' time, they'll double in value. Death is helpful, but
*   suicide's a godsend.*
I really don't have the stomach for that sort of thing. How exactly
*   did she do it? Virginia Woolf style, rocks in the pockets?*
Don't think so. Just sleeping pills to dull the survival instinct.
But how does one drown oneself without floating to the top?
I thought you didn't have the stomach for this sort of thing . . .

The work's divine, but there's something a little off about him. *Has*
*   he both his ears, you think?*
Dresden's taken him under his wing, I shouldn't think so.

Luke swallowed a green olive without chewing it; it lodged uncomfortably in his throat. He coughed discreetly, as his mama had taught him, into his hand. The woman before him withdrew her ingratiating smile and bejeweled fingers. He turned. Where were the drink trays?

Technically, they're far from perfect. Without Robin Dresden's
*   name attached to his, I doubt they'd make a drop in the*
*   proverbial pond.*
But the pond's so stagnant these days. Is it so terrible to attempt
*   something beautiful?*

What a wonderful use of color.
He's clearly a fetishist. This is just a sampling; they say there are
*   several of her feet alone, of her legs and the nape of her neck,*
*   the small of her back and buttocks. Personally, I find the nudes*
*   refreshing—just to see how it all hangs together.*

Luke felt ill and restless. The drink hadn't set well with the goddamn pâté. Why don't they just call it liver? Duck *foie gras*, lamb *persillade*, olive tapenade. What did rich people have against pronounceable food? Where were the traps and the stunning revelations? Where was

Tristan? But when Robin drew near, Luke only asked him meekly for another Valium.

He nodded, disappearing. And then Tristan arrived.

Luke watched as he and Robin gravitated toward one another in the crowd like chess pieces moving across a board, Tristan in characteristic white linen, Dresden flawless in black Armani. Each held a glass of scotch rather than a weapon, but to Luke's delight they were soon engaged in a heated debate. Yet for all Marc's talk, there wasn't much chance of its getting out of hand. For them, conversation was sport. Already Dresden was distancing himself from the argument. With his long fingers, he drew Tristan's attention to another wall, to one of the strangest of the paintings: a fingerprint, magnified and precise down to the tiniest detail. The cops could probably run the thing. Luke's prints were all loops, but Gisèle's was a spiral. Illuminated, it resembled a spiderweb.

Tristan grew visibly agitated. What was so special about *that* painting? Luke wondered. Apart from the rather morbid quality of it. But then they were all morbid. He gazed around him, and even the most benign paintings seemed portentous now. In Gisèle's lovely face, he sensed a horrible knowledge, as if she'd guessed her fate.

Luke let his gaze return to Robin and Tristan, then back again to her; his eyes shifted back and forth, and a monomaniacal jealousy made the crowd disappear, except for the three of them. He had visions of perverse sexual triangles, illicit trysts and conspiracies behind his back, under his nose. Robin, Tristan, and, just behind them, Gisèle, glancing over her shoulder at Luke. It was one of the older ones, and her hair was longer then, the way he liked it, the curls dark and silken down her back, her eyes the color of a tropic sea. A nervous smile played on her lips; her eyes were hauntingly clear. *You're watching me again,* they said. *Why can't you stop?*

Tristan caught his accusatory stare and approached him. "Good evening, Luke."

"Hello, Tristan. It's damned awkward having you here."

"You don't think I would miss your opening? I've heard of nothing else for so long." His smile was acid; it faded as he gazed around him. "I had to see her one last time."

Had Marc been right about Paris? "Going somewhere?"

"Not at all. But I . . . well, I imagine they'll sell. That's the point, is it not? To sell her?"

"You think I enjoy this?" Mechanically, Luke lifted his glass to his lips and swallowed an ice cube; his mouth was dry, and he felt reckless. "I'd rather live on the street than kiss up to this crowd for another minute. But Robin's promised a stunning moment of truth, and I'm here for it."

Tristan echoed icily, "'Moment of truth?'"

Luke snorted. "He ought to know. It's his show." Under his breath, "Always has been."

"What do you mean by that?" And he looked so smug, so self-contained, that Luke couldn't help himself.

"Seems Gisèle had quite a juggling act going. Or didn't you know about her and Robin?"

Tristan's eyes were arctic, his features so chiseled that the thin smile looked as if it might bring the whole edifice of his face crumbling down. And Luke could see he had *not* known. "She and Robin?"

"Yes. They were damned good at keeping a secret. He's Nicola's father, you know."

"*Non*, I didn't know." Disbelieving. "How do you know this?"

"I had DNA tests done and I know you're not Gisèle's father, Tristan. The DNA proved that, too. I guess that makes what I saw in the garden better by a little, but not much. It's still incest."

Tristan narrowed his eyes to a squint, as if it hurt to focus. "How do you mean, incest?"

"What was she to you? A cousin? Was Gisèle even her name?"

"What a fool you are." His voice didn't rise; it was as refined as ever. But there was a dark chord running through it of something worse than anger. "You're talking nonsense."

Luke grabbed a fresh drink off a passing tray. Taking a cue from Preston Murphy, he said, "DNA doesn't lie, Tristan, people do. You have only twelve or so percent in common with Nicola. The experts say that doesn't make you her grandfather. But what the hell is biology anyway? I'm the only father she's ever known. I have more right to her than anyone."

Tristan's eyes narrowed still more. "These tests show I'm *related* to Nicola?"

"Of course they do. Just not as much as you've led us all to think—"

But Tristan merely pushed past him, his expression more bewildered than angry. It was hardly the reaction Luke had expected, and a bit of a letdown. He'd have preferred defeated to nonplussed.

Robin swept in and slipped a pill into Luke's hand, gazing at the top of Tristan's head as it bobbed through the crowd. "Take this and chew it. It'll work faster. And lay off the alcohol."

"Chew Valium?"

A slight nod. Yes.

As if by magic, a tray of water goblets appeared at his side, and Luke discarded his half-empty tumbler and chastely replaced it with water.

"Step outside," Robin said quietly. "Breathe. I've already received offers above the asking price of those we've put up for sale. It is going well. There's someone you should meet in half an hour. You'll have to say something afterward."

"Meet who . . . er, whom? And say what? I didn't know I'd have to say anything." He'd read somewhere that the general population feared public speaking more than death. For Luke the two were indistinguishable.

"A dealer from New York. How lovely it is to have such a turnout at your first showing." Robin's slight smile didn't touch his eyes, "You needn't be profound, but you should be cogent. A good deal rides on this for you."

"Uh-huh." And Luke knew it did. On the surface, it did. But he didn't trust surfaces anymore. "So when's your great revelation coming?"

"It's already come, my friend. It's all around you." And then he was gone.

"Your work is simply brilliant, Mr. Farrell." A strange face appeared before him.

"Oh. Uh, thank you." He still stared after Robin.

"What technique do you use to get the paint so thin without sacrificing color?"

Luke turned. He didn't know, and the comical quality of this struck him. He laughed, dejectedly, aloud. He fixed his attention on the wall beyond him, to Gisèle's left nipple and right thigh, all that was visible through the small crowd of admirers who stood before her.

"I'm sorry, was that a stupid question? I'm a novice when it comes to art."

"Aren't we all?"

The painting was, like the others, from a photograph Robin had taken. Marc had said as much. Tristan must have recognized this when he saw the paintings. *But then why was he so surprised to learn of their affair?* "I'm sorry, what was your question?"

"Oh . . . er . . . what technique do you use to get the paint so thin without sacrificing color?"

"I just thin it."

"And the color?"

Luke stared down at the young man before him. Too young for a collector, surely. Aspiring artist? Journalist? He wasn't inclined to ask. He said, "Well, *she* provided the color."

"That's good, I like that. Can I quote you?"

Journalist, then. They milled through the crowd. Luke saw his signature again and again in the lights. Half of them he couldn't even recall signing, but there it was, proudly scrawled: *L. Farrell.* Again and again Gisèle confronted him with that unflinching, pained gaze. And then his eyes landed on a canvas he knew he'd never seen, never signed. It wasn't one of the paintings at all; it could not be. It was real.

Gisèle was alive, on the bed. Just as she'd been that last night. *Please, Luke, stop—*

Apart from the one protest, she hadn't made a sound as he did it. It didn't matter. Her eyes had spoken for her. Her pale, drawn face. The scarlet robe still tied but twisted around her waist and open. And then, afterward, her horrible shudder.

"You're a genius." The kid was still there, expectant, beside him.

Sweat sprang out on Luke's brow. He blinked. His eyes were deceiving him. He couldn't have seen what he thought he'd seen. It was a trick of the light, the Valium. He was afraid to look again. His head spun; he tried to inhale.

"Are you all right, Mr. Farrell? It's a little tight in here. We could step outside."

"Yes . . . yes," he managed. "And for God's sake, call me Luke, will you? Yeah, I need air." It was only as they moved toward the door that Luke risked a glance over his shoulder.

Am I out of my mind? He was. For the painting had changed. It had never been there at all. *Of course it hadn't.*

The frigid night air felt merely cool on his skin, refreshing as a drink of ice water on a summer day. Luke looked down, and the young man's eager face came in and out of focus; he heard the brush of his suit jacket against his own, magnified out of all proportion; the voices from inside had fused into a single low, unintelligible frequency. Luke's fingertips tingled, and he felt a rush of heat spread over him. This time the drug was really hitting him.

He felt his pulse quicken along with the growing sense of paranoia, and then something kicked in just in time to save him from the free fall. Rob's little pill. He didn't think it was Valium. All at once Luke wanted to laugh as if a breeze had buffeted him up, up, up.

He was very warm. His palms began to sweat. There was a surge of nausea, and then it began to recede, and he felt suddenly, unspeakably, good.

"Do you have any more?" the journalist asked. "It's better if you do it with someone."

"Do what?"

"X."

Blankly.

"Ecstasy?"

Ecstasy? "I don't . . . it's not mine. Someone gave it to me."

"Well, you're rolling." The boy grinned. "Your pupils are huge."

Luke blinked, panicking. Dilated pupils? Everyone would notice; how could he hide it? But then all his fears receded as an endless swell of pleasure rolled through him. Is that why they called it that? Rolling? He was rolling. Who cared? He didn't care.

"Smoke?" The boy asked, pulling a pack from his jacket pocket.

The face grew clear before him, eager and young and something else. Close. Too close. Christ, it wasn't a story he was after. Luke felt the graze of fingertips on his trouser leg. The kid was coming on to him. "Naw, I don't touch them. Never have."

"Have you ever tried?" The double entendre. "It's better on X. You might like it."

"No." He held the other man's eyes to drive home the point, feeling a

little nauseous again. "No. Excuse me." But as he brushed past him and went through the gallery doors, it came again: wave after wave of ease and merciful pleasure.

There was no sign whatever of Tristan. He must have left. Luke's pleasure increased.

He squinted in the light, trying to avoid eye contact, but no one seemed to notice anything amiss. Suddenly the crowd around him seemed a wonderful, warm entity. What had he been so worried about? He began to meet smiles. All at once he felt very powerful. This was his night. He spotted Robin talking to a woman. He wanted to thank him for the X but decided not to interrupt. Whoever it was, she was pretty from behind, and that was a good start.

Robin seemed very interested in what she had to say. The charcoal eyes, dark as night, had a light in them; that's how you could tell. His interest was almost always an unhealthy one, but people basked in it. Luke laughed aloud, feeling very fond of Robin suddenly. He felt good, and it had been so long since he'd felt good. He felt better than good. He felt marvelously . . . free.

He gazed around at Gisèle, and all at once her eyes seemed forgiving. Her eyes told him she understood—anyone would understand, given what he'd been through. He felt such love for her then. Such a lot of love. He wanted to tell someone how he felt.

His eyes returned to Robin and the woman in the form-fitting gown. Was this the illustrious art dealer from New York? The dress was cut a little like Gisèle's gown at the party that last night. He caught her profile and with a shock of recognition realized it was no art dealer. Not unless that was what Amanda was playing today.

She was clearly playing something. She never wore dresses like that or her hair up like that, in a chignon. Luke's feet would not move. He watched as she vanished behind a portly man and a couple crossed before him. Robin moved to greet a prosperous-looking snobbish sort and gestured Luke over. Had it been half an hour already? Would he have to speak? Why hadn't Amanda spoken to him? *Pull yourself together. Pull yourself together or everyone will know you're high.* Suddenly this made him want to laugh. What were they going to do? Ground him?

Luke straightened, smoothed his suit jacket, and put on his most disarming smile. He knew all at once it would be fine. All at once he wanted nothing more than to speak.

He was on a podium.

The last remnants of paranoia had fled. It was comfortable up here. A sea of faces spread out pleasantly before him, and through it hers appeared. Amanda. Involuntarily, his fingertips pulsed with the memory of her. Tonight she looked more like Gisèle than ever. Only she wasn't Gisèle. How he longed to touch her, to tell her everything.

He blinked, as if she might vanish like the painting that hadn't been there earlier. He looked to the wall where he had hallucinated it, and . . . *it was back again.* His gasp was magnified by the microphone, sending up murmurs in the crowd. Gisèle lay on the bed, staring at him with eyes that would never forgive him. And there, moving to stand just before the canvas, was Amanda, gazing at him as though she knew everything. As though he were a stranger to her.

The paranoia returned in force. If the painting wasn't real, neither was she. For a moment he could not breathe.

"Luke," Robin prompted gently. "You had something to say. . . ."

"Yeah." Luke looked away from Amanda, but he was drawn to her as he'd been drawn to Gisèle, a sailor lured to the rocks. "Yes." The rest of the room faded. What did he want to say to *her*? He cleared his throat and began to speak. "There's a story behind these paintings, a . . . a million different stories. To look at them, you might not understand. You didn't know Gisèle, most of you. And if you did, you knew how impossible it was . . . to know her." The words came out on their own. "Tonight I've heard the paintings called erotic. And I understand that, because she was beautiful to look at. She really was. And I guess, even when she was alive, we were all just happy to look at her." He swallowed hard; he had to focus. "I . . . I don't want to talk about me, or about painting. I just want to talk to you all a minute about Gisèle."

The whole room listened to him. They didn't mind the faint Virginia twang that had grown less faint suddenly. They didn't see through him. Amanda listened especially. Her eyes glistened in the lights. The one who had gotten to him, met on a ruse and intended for a meaningless fling, young and forthright, not seeing the point of lies. She was the only thing real in the room.

"I loved Gisèle in the beginning. I was so in love with her that I kept calling it that right up to the end, but it was something else by then, a game I couldn't quit and I couldn't win." He gazed around him. "Gisèle's getting the last laugh, I think. Pieces of her all over the room. Surfaces. Objects. She still doesn't want us to know her. She was always so perfectly done, so perfect, like a piece of china. It's how she kept herself safe. When I was a kid, I was always breaking my mama's china. I didn't mean to, but I was clumsy." He could see that they didn't see. "You have to understand, I never meant to hurt her. I just wanted to hold her. I just wanted to touch her. We were *married,* for Christ's sake, and it should have been all right. But it was never all right." He wiped away tears, scarcely hearing the murmurs that ran through the refined, scandalized crowd. Amanda was utterly motionless, holding his eyes. "She didn't struggle, she didn't cry. Afterward she said I was an animal. And she said—I swear to God she said this, I swear on my mama's grave—she said, 'I've made you one, Luke. I'm sorry.' She apologized to *me.* That was . . . that was the thing about her." He sighed. "She climbed inside you and wouldn't leave. But if you think these are erotic paintings, they're not. They're just pieces of china, and I was living in a china closet, not allowed to touch."

Amanda had closed her eyes. Her cheeks glistened, and the crowd rippled. Luke swayed with it but didn't fall. "And now I have to tell you all the truth, because this . . . I can't do it anymore. All of this is part of the game, too. And I'm quitting it. I'm quitting." His eyes roamed the room, the canvases on the walls. Would Gisèle finally leave him if he told? Would he finally be free? He wasn't a bad person, not really. *I'm just no damned good at anything.* And that wasn't so very bad. "I'm no painter. I've been pretending. These paintings—they aren't mine."

He gazed at Amanda when he said it; she rushed at him and then receded. Someone passed in front of her, and it was like cutting a lifeline.

Robin helped him down from the platform. "Bravo, Luke," he said softly. "I knew you had it in you." He was a nice fellow, Robin. He'd given Luke this wonderful pill, and his mind was so open now. But he

had to find Amanda; that was all that mattered. Luke descended the
few steps from the podium, ignoring the stares of outraged patrons. He
turned, waving at Robin. Robin waved back.

The furor around him died as Robin took the microphone and began
to speak.

"Ladies and gentlemen, friends and colleagues: I'm sorry to have
deceived you. It was Gisèle's wish in life that the paintings not bear her
name. But in death she has found a voice. Luke Farrell is not the artist
we celebrate tonight, though I salute his bravery and hope you will, too.
It has not been an easy time for him." There was a pause. "But, you see,
the Gisèle paintings are Gisèle's. They're self-portraits."

Luke felt as though he'd been slapped. It threatened to cut through
the buffer offered up by his magic pill. *Self-portraits?* The crowd devoured
it greedily. How they wanted her. Every piece of her.

He was nudged discreetly at the elbow. "Mr. Farrell, a car is waiting.
Mr. Dresden felt it best."

Mr. Dresden was continuing, "Though I encouraged her to exhibit
them as her own, what you see a glimpse of here tonight is not merely
the work of an artist and a model but a private, personal odyssey of an
extraordinary individual who was in many ways a mystery to herself. She
has left us with unflinching windows on a journey cut tragically short."

Luke stared. No wonder he was being rushed outside, to a car.

"But it is my hope—no, my belief—that not only her paintings are
emancipated tonight but Gisèle herself. You are a part of that, each of
you. And I thank you."

In the car Luke laughed. Mirthlessly one moment, full of mirth the
next. Helplessly. It was a great joke, that. Gisèle had certainly put over a
great joke. Self-portraits. Pieces of herself. And then he thought, *Good
for you, Ella. At least something was yours.*

Luke gazed around him. The car was moving, the privacy barrier discreetly disguised with drapes. And it was so quiet. He didn't want to go
back to the gallery, but he wanted to go back to Amanda. He wanted to
laugh with her as he had in the photographs, to feel her skin beneath his
fingers. He wanted to tell her he loved her, and he wanted to leave here
for good.

But then, like a tiny pinprick in a great balloon, reality filtered past the pleasure centers of his brain and he knew she would not have him. That this illusion would dissipate along with the drug. And for once in his life, he was utterly alone.

XXIII

BEHIND THE BLINDS

They grew apart, Luke and Gisèle—of course they did. Gisèle wasted little time finding a suitable pretense for separate bedrooms, due to the baby, perhaps, or maybe she claimed he stole the covers or snored. By their third year of marriage, they were reduced to the rare conjugal visit.

Luke, for his part, must have loved her awfully—it was the one thing we shared—for he would not leave her. In any case, not for good. He took trips to Seattle for his extracurricular activities. I had suggested "refresher courses" at the University of Washington, and he regularly sought out art exhibits at the CoCA and the SAM. He had to use the larger museums for his excuses, because most of the private studios and galleries in Seattle paled next to local collections. People came to Devon for the art, but our Björn left for it.

Gisèle changed as the baby grew to walk and talk; Nicola animated her. She animated me, the house, everything she touched. Such a beautiful, enchanted child she was, walking and talking from a very early age and curious about everything. She had much of her mother in her, and mercifully nothing of Luke that I could detect. I found I enjoyed playing grandfather—we were partners in crime from the beginning— yet at times she could be eerily adult; I often had the sense that she saw through me. And yet little Nicola gave me something I had per-

haps never had: an unconditional love. How I adored her. She could do
no wrong in my eyes. And I could do no wrong in hers. As Gisèle once
was—she, too, was mine.

Gisèle was a loving, devoted mother; Nicola was her *raison d'être*.
It seemed she no longer needed me, or any man. She was utterly
self-contained. I continued to watch her, but increasingly there was
nothing to see. When Nicola was old enough to sleep through the night,
Gisèle found she herself no longer could. She took to a habit of popping sleeping pills and simply slept, in her dreams escaping me. Sometimes I crept into her room and lay beside her, as we'd done in the old
days. Sometimes I'd even slip her the sleeping pills so that I might slide
between the sheets and touch her, and pretend she had asked me to.

And so we were trapped in a stalemate—or, rather, in perpetual
check—unable to call a draw even when we wished to. Robin was right.
In a certain perverse way, we had become our roles. We were devoted to
each other still . . . but the romance of our early days had died. It was
then, sometime around then, that she must have begun to paint. Not
with me, as we'd once done, but alone.

I should say she grew obsessed with painting. For I recognize obsession—my eyes are well suited to it—and *her* eyes had a secret light. I
attributed it all to Nicola, never guessing that there was a private artistic source to it as well. Oh, there had been signs: the occasional scent of
turpentine, smudges of paint on a fingernail or a piece of her clothing.
I'd thought she was merely teaching Luke a thing or two, since she was a
better artist than he would ever be, for all his courses and seminars. She
was a better artist than I was. For nearly eight years, she painted secretly.
It was nearly eight years before I discovered that she'd used our corridor not so much to reach me but to travel down to the cellar and explore
herself.

I never went down there. Why should I? After my initial exploration
of the catacombs, what possible inducement could merit the indignity of
my traversing narrow, musty passages and descending precarious ladders
to a cellar I had no need to enter secretly? The passage existed to link me
to Gisèle, and nothing more. And yet when I was shown to her "studio,"
I recognized it, of course. I remembered the trapdoor that dropped to a

small room in the cellar. It had been empty when I'd last ventured there. When I saw it again, it was full of her secrets.

She must have been painting in the hours when Nicola took her lessons and I assumed Gisèle to be shopping or idling somewhere on the grounds. I'd like to think she'd painted herself for me, but even with my pronounced powers of self-deception I could not convince myself of that. The very instant I saw them, I knew what they were. The paintings spanned years, and through them I saw Gisèle change. My crippled little butterfly had committed the ultimate betrayal. Somehow she'd gotten well—secretly, privately, without me.

I recognized the pattern set long ago by those early sketches of Robin's, when he'd given her a camera and instructed her to pose herself—to essentially "sketch herself." That is just what she'd done. Here she was both artist and model; she was painting but also posing. And it was certainly not for Luke, nor for me. I could not help but feel it was in part—as it had been years before—for Robin. A private dialogue between them.

It explains his anger at her cavalier treatment of them. For Gisèle had somehow managed things so that Luke—of all people—claimed her paintings as his own.

In August of this year, Luke and Nicola discovered her makeshift studio in the cellar. I often wonder what would have happened had I not been in France at the time. Had I not had time to measure my reaction—had she not had time to measure hers. Had I been present, would she have dared to stage such a farce? I did *not* wonder how she accomplished it; I've already made note of Luke's unique pliability. I did, however, wonder *why*. I thought at first it was for fear of exposure. Yet she pushed for their exhibition. No, I think it was rather that the creator had outgrown her creation.

The paintings were all self-portraits, and in releasing them she released the self they portrayed. The works are nothing if not a prolonged, poignant searching. She had documented her surface like a road map, in an attempt to find meaning at the end. Part of her beauty had always been her inability to perceive it. I had not studied art for nothing. I could read the subtext quite clearly: I had objectified her; she mirrored this by objectifying herself. And in releasing the paintings—as objects—she effectively subverted me. If the paintings themselves were not a statement of liberation, her release of them was.

She gave them to Luke as a consolation prize. I knew she felt guilty for her treatment of him, a thing quite beyond me. He was, by then, in it only for the money each month. My money.

In this, he had company. Like a lone ship on a turbulent sea, I was caught in a violent vortex of cross-purposes. A few years into our forgery scheme, Marc Kreicek let me know he had discovered the truth of Gisèle's identity. It seemed it was not Robin who told him; he claimed to have learned it from Gisèle herself. I hesitated to ask her for confirmation of this, for he had also gleaned another fact: in researching her few remaining relatives—a threat to hold over me—he'd discovered not only the aunt and uncle in Seattle but the orphaned niece they'd taken in years before. Amanda Miller. Gisèle's sister. Who was very much alive.

And so I was quite beholden to him. I could not even turn to Robin for help this time, for he, too, believed Gisèle's sister to be dead. Were he to learn the truth, he would never agree to keep it a secret from Gisèle. Marc began to pester me for trifling things, petty indulgences. I know he did not need the money; he was paid very handsomely for his fakes. No, he had another object in mind.

And here I must say that Marc—or K, as Robin called him—had a rather exaggerated opinion of his gifts, in that he confused mimicry with true vision. He wanted the acclaim of the world and, short of that, the "success" of having hoodwinked it. He actually wished to sell his copies as originals on the black market, using my provenance.

It is true that K was a truly prodigious forger, yet I could hardly risk my freedom on his infallibility. In the art world, the technologies of forgery and its detection are constantly leapfrogging. I was convinced Kreicek had the edge on science, but for how long? From experience I know that no lie goes undetected forever. And so it is a final irony that it was he who wormed out mine.

He had no aptitude for true blackmail. As I say, K was not in it for the money; he preferred to torture me. For years I put up with his needling— his perpetual presence either at Falconer's Point or at my home in Paris, always present and always painting, taunting me with copy after ceaseless copy. Such an ego! He was not chasing perfection, he said. Perfection was a plaything; he could attain it again and again.

Things came to a head this summer, when I told him I was bringing our smuggling scheme to an end. I cannot fault him for his work ethic; he'd succeeded in replicating twenty-five priceless works in twelve years. But, out of rising financial pressures, I'd agreed to open my home in Paris to tours. It was to be a private art museum, and the renewed scrutiny had addled my already addled nerves.

Whether out of bitterness or boredom or merely a depraved sense of spite, K exacted his revenge on me. He told me quite casually in early June that he had made Amanda Miller's acquaintance.

I did not need to know why. I demanded to know how.

"We are all connected in a million different ways, Tristan. It might have been any number of things. But she is a psychology major, and I have some knowledge of psychology." In truth, he had a degree. "My father was rather a renowned figure in the field."

"So."

"So psychology professors have pestered me for years to do a book on my father. I approached her adviser, whose enthusiasm for the idea is really quite profound. Through him, I met her." A shrug and that galling smirk. "There are many types of provenance, Tristan. And invisible threads that link us all—like little nets, waiting to be tightened."

And so he tightened his. He'd not only met Amanda but took it upon himself to introduce her to Gisèle's husband. Luke's lechery did the rest. And on her twelfth anniversary, Gisèle was given an anonymous gift: photos of the two together.

It was so cruel and had required such careful machinations on his part that I wonder if his revenge was not also directed at her. K had always wanted Gisèle. And, as I'd predicted from the start, he was not the sort to take no for an answer. Perhaps he thought to eliminate both his rivals with a single blow, for here was evidence of Luke's betrayal and of mine.

In truth, Luke's infidelity meant little to Gisèle. To her, the seedy evidence of his affair was manna from heaven, a miracle. Here was her beloved Mandy again, alive and well. And I was damned by my own treachery.

Gisèle said nothing at first. She watched me. I was to be given no opportunity to explain away my lies with another lie. She had lost her ability to believe.

She showed me the photographs. "How could you, Tristan?"

I remained calm. "It was a shock when Marc told me. I didn't know what to do. I believed she was dead, just as you did. You saw the papers."

"And Marc told you the truth." She gazed at me. "Marc told *you*?"

"Well, yes. I was shocked, too. Somehow he'd found out about you. But he can do us no real harm."

"No *real* harm . . . ?"

"I only mean he has too many secrets of his own." I paused, adopting an injured tone. "Gisèle, do you think I knew she was alive? Do you think I would deliberately deceive you?"

I could see that she did think so, yes.

But I made my case: How could she reunite with her sister now, without destroying her daughter? Her sister had mourned her and built a life of her own. Wasn't it selfishness to intrude upon that now? I never placed myself in the equation. Part of me knew how that balance would swing. But Nicola, precious little Nicola. Gisèle could not bear to shatter her daughter's beautiful, illusory life.

And yet it was as if until that moment Gisèle did not realize how very illusory it was. From one lie we'd spun a great web of them. How long could the web hold?

Idly, at times I ponder happier endings, alternate realities. I like to think Luke would have gotten fed up and gone. Marc, too; he'd already done his worst. And Robin would remain, but as he had always been—a fantasy, not quite real. I could allow Gisèle her fantasies, as she allowed me mine. And it would have been just the three of us: *ma petite, mon chaton* and me. She and Nicola were all I wanted.

But it is all folly. My house of cards was collapsing, and I knew it. Though I'd once successfully convinced Gisèle to deny her sister—how I reveled in this final exercise of power—I feared it would not last. Gisèle was physically ill afterward, and I wondered if she would be able to see it through. Amanda was alive, and she lived in Gisèle. I could see her in her eyes. And she even haunted *me*. How much did she suspect? I half expected her to walk through my door.

The Gisèle Paintings took on a life of their own. They were making their way to the world in spite of me. And I knew that if they made it, so would Gisèle. It is fanciful, even mad, but I felt if I could prevent their exhibition, I could still salvage . . . everything.

I implored Robin to refuse to show them, to confront Luke with the whole audacious fraud, but he would not. I could not tell him how precarious things truly lay, for it would mean confessing Marc's blackmail and the truth of Gisèle's sister, the whole tangled mess. And this time he would not have helped me. He would have taken Gisèle's side. Perhaps he always had.

He told me the exhibition would go on. He'd urged Gisèle to claim the paintings openly. So far she had refused, but he held out hope of convincing her before the opening.

"But that's not what *I* want." Angrily, I told him I knew them for what they were: a dialogue from which I'd been excluded. Like the sketches long ago. "She painted them for you."

And he suggested, in the perceptive way I'd begun to detest, that if I believed that the paintings were "for" anyone but Gisèle, I'd missed the point of them entirely. "Whatever she's done, she's done for herself." Quietly, he informed me that he intended to emancipate the art and believed that the artist would follow.

I could see then that we had never been co-conspirators in our crimes. Robin Dresden had no loyalties. And at the end of the day, he would betray me, too.

XXIV

LOWERING THE CURTAIN

TRISTAN HAD COME FOR HER.

Nicola saw him enter before he spoke. She was hiding in the art room at the top of the tower, peering down from the gallery high above. She'd come up here so she wouldn't hear the bell for the gate if it rang; it would be easier to ignore if she didn't hear.

"*Mon chaton*," he called up to her in mild annoyance. "There you are. Why didn't you meet me outside, as we planned? I've just checked your room. You're not even packed."

"I know, Grand—" She swallowed. "I know." Somehow the man who had pretended to be her grandfather had gotten past Hanna, Robin's housekeeper for the dorm, who was meant to be looking after her. Robin was at the gallery for her father's exhibition. The students were all out. Most had gone to see Chelsea's play in the village. Hanna was downstairs, down a lot of stairs, in the drawing room. She'd never hear Nicola if she called. Why did she feel so scared? Tristan had never laid a finger on her.

"Well, come down now. We haven't much time."

"I like it up here." She knew he did not. Nicola gazed down through the wrought-iron rungs that were all that kept her from falling. She didn't suffer from vertigo; she liked the dizzy sensation. Her legs dangled over the edge. Easels were set up around her, and there were more on the floor below. Some were empty, while others held works in progress, canvases both large and small. They were the work of Robin's students—watercolors and oils, sketches in charcoal and pastels. Nicola had lost the chance to hide behind them. Anyway, it didn't do any good to hide from things. Not in the end.

"What's happened?" His annoyance was less mild. "Why are you acting so strangely?"

"Nothing's happened." She gazed up, away from him. Arched windows rose above her; the world outside was black. "I . . . I just can't go with you. I can't. I'm sorry."

"What's happened?" Tristan repeated, agitated. "What's happened since Monday? You wanted to go then. I have your passport. Come down here now. We have to hurry."

Nicola swung her legs restlessly back and forth and wound her fingers tighter around the rails. "I've been thinking."

He gave a strident sigh. Her thinking bothered him. "Yes?"

"Let's wait and say good-bye to Robin. He'll be back soon. I can't leave without saying good-bye." She knew that Robin wouldn't let her go.

"He's at the gallery, you know that. It's your father's opening. He'll be gone for hours."

Nicola bit her lip. "Well, why do we have to be in such a hurry?"

"Because I've chartered a plane. Come down here now. I get nervous seeing you up there."

"I can't fall."

He began to pace. "People make the mistake of underestimating children, Nicola. But I've never made that mistake before, have I? I've never talked down to you. Tell me the truth. Something's happened, hasn't it?" The tone of the sentences rose and fell with his pacing; it made Nicola even dizzier looking down from above: back and forth, back and forth. Up and down. At last he paused. "Did you tell anyone what we talked about?"

Her eyes filled with tears. "Please, just go. I don't want to talk anymore."

"Why do you think I'm *here* talking to you? No one talks to children this way. Everyone assumes they're not worth talking to."

"Robin doesn't. He talks to me."

She could tell from his face that this was the wrong thing to say.

"Robin?" Tristan scoffed and cursed in French. It was always easy to tell the epithets, even when the adults around her resorted to other languages to use them. All curse words sound the same. He continued to pace, the click of his shoes on the floor pounding his displeasure into her brain. "Robin is not who you think he is, Nicola. He was jealous of us. Gisèle and me." He spit out the words. "Robin's turned against me, and I see now he's tried to turn *you*."

"He just told me the truth, that's all."

"The truth? What truth? He doesn't believe in the word."

"He told me about the paintings. They're not Dad's. The studio wasn't his. *Mom* was the painter. She painted herself."

"Yes, yes. A ridiculous charade he helped promote. It has nothing to do with anything."

"Yes it does. It means the studio wasn't Dad's. He didn't use the passageway. He didn't look through that mirror at Mom." She swallowed. Her voice broke on the words. "It w-was you."

The silence stretched and stretched, so taut that it seemed the very air would snap.

"Well, there you are." He spoke very quietly. Nicola found she preferred his annoyance. "Your mother knew all about that passage. She often used it herself, to reach me."

"No!" Nicola cried, covering her ears. "Stop telling lies about her. She *closed* the mirror. She closed it, so you couldn't see in. I found a piece of her robe in the cellar. She was running away from you—"

"From me?"

There was another long silence. Nicola could only nod.

"You think I killed her." His voice was so sharp it sliced through her. "Is that what you think?"

Nicola couldn't answer out loud; she could only nod once more, yes.

"*Putain!*" Tristan kicked the leg of an easel, and a canvas clattered to the floor. The easel fell, too, splayed out awkwardly with its legs askew. "The answer is no, Nicola. No, no, *no*."

Nicola brushed the tears from her eyes, but her voice was a sob. "I don't believe you."

"The passageway that connects her room to mine, she used it as much as I. She might easily have changed rooms. She might have changed *houses*. Whatever lies you've been fed about your mother and me, nothing can change that simple truth. I saved her from a life of meaninglessness and mediocrity. Of abuse. I saved her. And she stayed with me. You must see I didn't force her to stay."

"You've lied about everything. You lied about Amanda. I believe her. I *like* her. I don't think she's crazy. She's the only one who really understands, because she's lost everyone, too."

"But you have not lost everyone, *ma petite*." Softly, "You have me."

He would not see.

"Come down now."

But her fingers were entwined around the rails stubbornly, as if they had a mind of their own. "Grand-père. I can't go with you. You can go. You don't need me."

Tristan ran his handkerchief across his forehead, wound it tightly in his fist, and stuffed it in his coat pocket. His voice was weak. "Yes I do. I do need you, Nicola. I won't go without you."

"But you're not my grandfather. Mom *was* Karen Miller. I recognized her in the photograph. It's her eyes and her smile. It's *her*. In the car I didn't know what to do. I was scared you would go, but I was scared of going with you, too. I love you. It's weird, but I still love you." Tears blurred him below. "It's just, there's something wrong with you. You scare me, and I don't want to go to Paris with you—or anywhere. I want to stay here with Robin."

Tristan lashed out angrily, "Don't you dare mention his name to me. Stop this! Stop it now." He inhaled sharply and smoothed his coat with his hands. It didn't need smoothing. "I'm going to Paris, Nicola. And you are coming with me, if I have to climb up there and bring you down. You needn't pack anything. I'll get you all you need."

Nicola's eyes swam with tears, and her courage faltered. He wasn't listening to her. He wasn't hearing. Softly, she said, "I told Robin you were coming."

He froze, staring up at her.

She stared back.

At last he walked slowly across the floor and disappeared beneath her. It was so silent; there was not even the sound of his footsteps or his breath. Nothing at all. And then she heard the dragging of a chair, a grating sound; she imagined scratches in the wood. A trail as he pulled it to the center of the room. "Then, where is he? Did he simply leave you here alone?"

"No. He . . . he's coming."

"*Bien.*" His accent was all at once nasal and coarse. "*Bien,* Nicola. We'll wait."

Her heart pounded. She'd lied, of course. Robin probably *wouldn't* be back for hours. How could she convince Tristan to go? He sat resolutely in his chair, one hand in his coat pocket, the other dangling to the floor. Only it wasn't dangling, she realized. It was resting. And then she saw the glint of the pearl handle between his fingers, the nose resting on the floor. It was a gun.

"No!" Nicola cried. "You can't hurt him. I won't let you." She rose. "I'll come down."

"No you won't, darling. Stay right where you are."

She blinked hard. Like a vision, Robin had materialized in the doorway. Her heart stopped, but he glanced up at her calmly, with a shake of his head and a motion of his hand that said, *Back . . . back. Move back from the railing.*

"Good evening, Tristan."

But it was as if Tristan didn't hear; he didn't take his eyes off Nicola. They bored through her, and all the affection turned to ice. "Ungrateful *connasse.* Like your mother. I've given you everything, and you have no soul. You have no heart."

"Nicola, cover your ears. Go away from the railing now, sweetheart. It's okay."

"Yes, go, go." Tristan shouted at her. "*GO!*"

Nicola jumped; her skin stung all over as if he'd struck her. His eyes were glazed with anger, and hers filled with fresh tears. She wondered if she'd ever known him at all. *Did anyone really know anyone else at all?* She backed slowly away from the railing, and he disappeared.

Tristan turned on Robin in a fury. "*Fils de putain*! How *dare* you turn her against me! You call yourself my friend. You're a liar and a cheat—"

"And she's my daughter."

Nicola started at the words. Something in Robin's voice was more frightening than all of Tristan's fury. And the words themselves, they resonated in her ears as if they had originated in her own head. Had she really heard them? "She's my *daughter*," Robin said again. And this time the words were meant for her, very gentle, filled with apprehension and regret. *You're my daughter, Nico.* And she remembered the day at the lake when she'd cut her foot and he'd carried her out, all the proud pinochle games and secret sips of brandy, all the visits since her mother had died, the dizzying bear hugs. *For magic and wishes . . . and when you need someone most.* He had been the only one left to trust, and he still was. A strange sensation rippled through her body. Was it possible? Robin, her *father?*

It was as if her whole family had played musical chairs. None of them were who they seemed to be. And yet this new knowledge fit comfortably; some invisible part of her slipped into place. It was in the way her mother had looked at him sometimes, with private understanding and luminosity in her eyes. It was in the way she looked at Nicola and at Amanda in the old photograph; it was the way she looked at what she loved.

Tristan's bitter words tore through her thoughts. "Ah, yes. Luke's told me all about that. He's told me a great deal more without knowing it. I ought to shoot you now, before you have a chance to escape with all your manipulations and lies. I know you so well. *À bon chat, bon rat.*" He laughed; Nicola didn't recognize his laugh. "I know who you *are*, Robin. I know who you are. Luke told me, you see. For once, *le bête*, he's done something intelligent. DNA tests for paternity of Nicola." Another laugh, short and derisive. "Do you know, he thought she might be mine? There would be no reason for *him*, if she could have been mine. Or so I thought. All this time, I thought . . ." Tristan's accent was the same, but the timbre was tinny, erratic, wrong. It was, Nicola thought, frightened. She inched toward the railing on her stomach. "Well, Luke has at last served a purpose. Twelve years of bullshit to serve a single purpose. He let me see you for what you are."

"And what am I?" Robin asked quietly.

"A bastard." Laughter. "Quite literally. You see, the DNA shows Nicola and I are related. Ah, yes, it took me a moment to see. I wasn't related to Gisèle, so how then could Nicola be related to *me*?" He choked on a sort of laugh. "Unless I was related to her father."

The silence was deadly. Robin made no move to break it.

"And then it all grew so clear. This is what rankles most. When I met you the first time, I *knew* you were no good." A laugh. "I knew it. It's why I liked you. All your parlor tricks and mind games, always a step ahead of everyone. But you were my friend. You were *my* friend." His voice broke in a strangled sob, and Nicola had never heard a more frightening, more pathetic sound. It was the sound of despair. "My brother. You knew it all along."

Robin still didn't say a word.

"What a fool I am. From the very beginning, in New York. Even the *blackmail*." Tristan laughed almost hysterically at this. "It was *you*. Only you would have the means and the motive to seek me in San Francisco. So clever. You blackmailed me and paid off your own blackmail. You lured me here to Devon, placing me in your debt so I could hardly refuse you the collection. And Marc, incessantly painting copy after copy. What is hanging on my walls, Robin? Where are my originals?" His voice was barbed. "To *never* tell me the truth. You cared nothing for me as a brother, as a friend. You care only for art. And in the guise of friendship, you've stolen my fortune and my life—my Gisèle, and now my Nicola. From the beginning you've betrayed me."

"Calm down, Tristan. Put down the goddamned gun. You're talking rubbish. I haven't betrayed you, I've fucking *protected* you for years. I wish I'd protected Gisèle as well."

"Ah, yes, protected her from me?" He laughed. "You don't understand. You never did."

"No, I didn't. And I'll live with that all my life."

"You'll die with it, I think."

"You're not going to shoot me, Tristan."

"Aren't I? Wouldn't it be terrible if the great Robin Dresden was wrong just this once?"

Nicola trembled all over. "Please, Grand-père—" As if the word might conjure the grandfather she'd grown up with and loved, and make this frightening stranger disappear like a character from one of her nightmares. "Please!"

"What's happening is your fault, *mon chaton*." The endearment held none of the old affection. "We might have been gone by now. I trusted you. I care for nothing now."

"Stay put, Nicola, do you hear me?" Robin's voice was sharp. "What the hell were you thinking, Tristan? That I'd let you disappear with her to *France?* Some little hole in the wall in America? There's no hole small enough for you. For Christ's sake, she's a *child.*"

"If I must end up in a hole, so will you."

Nicola had inched to the edge and choked at what she saw. Tristan and Robin, in their elegant long coats, were squared off as if in a duel. But it was a duel only Tristan could win. He had the gun. Its long nose was polished so that it shone in the light; it was pointed straight at Robin. Nicola had seen it before, she realized, at Falconer's Point in a glass cabinet full of antique French guns that seemed to have no purpose. They were just . . . art.

Robin stepped across the floor like a cat, and Tristan circled him. "Just stop, just stay *still.* Do you hear me?" There was a horrible clicking sound as he cocked the gun.

Robin stretched out his hand. "Think of what you're doing, Tristan. You don't want to do this. I've been more than a friend to you. Who else would have protected you for so long?"

The gun shook. "Someone should have protected me from *you.* Was it you who followed me in San Francisco? Tell me the truth."

"It was K."

A bitter laugh. "Ah, yes. Yes, of course."

"I wanted to know about you. Hell, I wanted to *know* you. I didn't learn who my mother was until I was twenty-five. You'd known her, I hadn't. You'd grown up loved, I hadn't. I don't know who my father is. As far as family goes, *mon ami*—as sad as it seems—you are it."

"All you wanted was my legacy, don't try to deny it. I'm not a fool, Robin, whatever else." Nicola watched as Tristan continued to circle him. "And you got it, *n'est-ce pas?* In trying to get the 'perfect' forgery, Marc has gotten several, and you have the originals."

"You can't tell the difference. You never noticed a thing. Don't pretend you ever cared for them—"

"You have no *right* to them," Tristan sputtered furiously. "You're not a Mourault. You're not my brother. You're a bastard, a mistake, a thing that shamed my mother so that she denied you."

"Yes," said Robin evenly.

The gun wobbled as Tristan spoke. "I remember the baby. I remember Maman carrying you. I remember her screams. They said you were stillborn." Tristan's voice made her nervous, with its staccato sentences, laboring for control. She didn't want to think of what would happen when the words stopped coming. "She was everything to me, and I felt I'd killed you with my jealousy. *I mourned you.*" His voice shook. "And you've destroyed me."

"You've destroyed yourself, Tristan. Just like you destroyed Gisèle."

"I didn't destroy Gisèle," he said, his tone abstracted and flat. "I simply put her to sleep. . . ."

It was so silent that Nicola could hear only a faint whistle of wind outside.

At last Robin spoke, in a calm, firm voice. "Put down the gun, Tristan. Put it down. Do you want to lose what little is left to you? Do you want to lose your freedom?"

"I'm not worried about my freedom, Robin. I'll follow you to hell."

"Fine, but let's not make it tonight."

He gestured with the gun. "Send Nicola down to me and I'll go."

"Like hell I will."

Nicola shook all over. Her eyes scanned the room below. There were storage closets full of paints and brushes and drop cloths, cluttered worktables and a bookcase full of art books. Up here there were only easels. Her heart pounded. A canvas would fit through the rails, but it wouldn't hit Tristan in the center of the circular room. It would startle him, but then he might shoot.

Tristan said, "Do bullets bounce off you, Robin? Like everything else?"

"I doubt it. But you'll be dead before you can pull the trigger. Do you think I'd leave Nicola here, alone and unguarded?"

Nicola's heart rose. Was she guarded? She peered into the shadows around her.

"And the police are already on their way. I asked Amanda to wait for them downstairs. I received word at the gallery that you were on the grounds." Robin paused. "I hoped I wouldn't get that call, Tristan. I gave you a chance. You might have gone back to Paris, slunk from sight, and lived out the rest of your days. But you came for her, you sick fucking bastard. . . ."

"Don't turn it into something dirty." He sniffed and said archly, "I don't expect you to understand that kind of love. *You* love no one. If someone is here to protect you, where is he?"

"It would be very foolish of K to betray his location."

"Ah, yes. Kreicek. He's your favorite henchman, isn't he?" Mockingly, "Do you hear me, K? If you're here, you're nothing but a puppet. That's all you've ever been." Tristan spun around, waving the gun wildly.

"I wouldn't do that, Tristan." And it was not Robin's voice this time, but Marc's.

Where had it come from? Nicola squinted down. Tristan spun again, but he turned before Robin could take the gun from him. "*Connard,* get back! Do you think I care if I die?"

"Stop it!" Nicola shouted. "Please stop, Grand-père. I'm sorry."

And the gun shook. He was crying. "I love you, *mon chaton.* I would never hurt you."

"I know that. I know you wouldn't really hurt anyone—"

Then Nicola heard the whine of sirens, and, turning, she could see the red and blue lights swirling through the black outside.

"Nicola!" It was Amanda's voice, reverberating from far away as if she were down a well. But Nicola's heart leaped at the sound of her; it was going to be okay now.

"*Non, non, non.*" Tristan murmured it over and over. "*Non. Non. Non.*"

Robin moved quickly for the gun, but it was too late. Nicola screamed, clenching her eyes shut and covering her ears as the shot rang out. Was it beside her? Below? It was a horrible hollow popping, and she was shattered by it, as if the bullet had struck her.

Her eyes flew to Robin, but his back was to her. Marc emerged from the shadows, and she watched as a dark wetness appeared and spread across the white of Tristan's dress shirt. As startled and uncomprehending as Nicola, he reached his hand to his stomach, crumpling where he stood. And Robin stepped forward to catch him.

❧

Amanda was at the door when Tristan fell. Robin sank to the floor with him, and for a moment no one moved at all. A freeze-frame of a surreal picture, it had a precarious timelessness, the chasm between illusion and reality in which the lines blur and they are the same. From the doorway she knew that Tristan was dying and yet she did not believe in death.

And then she heard herself gasp, as if she'd been holding her breath; her feet propelled her forward, and suddenly the picture started to move. Tristan's blood had seeped onto the floor and through the knees of Robin's trousers, smearing his arms as he held him. "God fucking *damn* it, Tristan," he murmured. *"God fucking damn it."* Tears were in his voice, though Amanda couldn't see his eyes; she stood behind him, staring down at her nemesis and feeling only pity.

How had this happened? This wasn't supposed to happen.

Tristan's voice was hoarse and barely audible. "I'll explain to Gisèle now."

Robin only replied, "Yes."

"She's already forgiven me, Robin. I feel it." He choked, and a pained grimace twisted his features. The puddle of blood spread beneath them. "Who knows? I may even forgive you."

His eyes caught Amanda then, and he murmured, "I'm sorry, *chérie.* It should never have happened. She used to let me touch her, you know. I didn't have to drug her tea. She loved me." He gave her a pitiful, ghostly smile. "But that was a long time ago."

Amanda shuddered and clenched her eyes shut to blot him out, to blot it all out.

In her mind she heard an echo of Tristan's voice, talking to her over dinner. *So much of what we do is beyond our conscious control, Amanda. Can we change our prophecies, I wonder? Even if we wish to?*

There were quick, heavy footsteps behind her; she was pushed aside as policemen and paramedics swarmed around Tristan. But it was too late. His eyes had gone very still, like pieces of glass. There was some attempt to breathe for him, a horrible gurgling sound, the sound of life draining away. In a daze, Robin had risen to make room for them, and Amanda did not try to speak to him. She felt mute.

The man who had shot Tristan stood beside her. He was all too familiar. Olive skin stretched over a bony frame and eyes of a hollow green, Marc Kreicek's cagey gaze was without emotion. It was this that had always struck her as most foreign about him. He ran his fingers over his pencil mustache, and a frown formed in his forehead—the sort of frown one expected in math class, not at a crime scene. He still held the gun in his hand, and he stared at Amanda and then down at it in dismay. He muttered something to Robin in a language she didn't understand.

Robin did not appear to hear.

But Marc approached him, continuing in English. He hadn't meant to abandon the plan; he'd intended to wound, not to kill—in the arm, not the back. But Tristan had been moving so erratically. "He would have killed you." He was less certain with Robin, his posture deferential and his face anxious. Soon he'd have to tell his story to the police. He had just killed a man.

Robin stooped to pick up Tristan's gun, forgotten on the floor. He opened the barrel and spun the chamber with his thumb; it was empty. His face showed no surprise. His sharp eyes were dull. He dropped the gun and walked on without a word. Marc simply stared.

Nicola.

Amanda's eyes darted around the room. *Nicola.* Where was Nicola? She was nowhere to be seen. But with the thought of her niece, feeling came rushing painfully back to Amanda. Her skin felt fragile and thin, both numb and hypersensitive, and she trembled inside like an egg about to crack. *Where was she? She must be upstairs, hiding.*

Bypassing the commotion, she raced to the stairs and up them. Nicola lay in a ball on the floor, covering her ears and burying her face in her knees.

Amanda knelt beside her. "Nicola . . ." she murmured, reaching out a hand to touch her hair. "Nicola, it's me."

And, like a caterpillar, she unfurled; she clung to Amanda and sobbed, and they rocked together, suspended in a timeless limbo, high above death and the world below.

XXV

THE FABLE

What happened that last night? Gisèle's last night . . .

It was destined to end in disaster, for it was born of disastrous beginnings: Gisèle's party for Luke, for the paintings Luke had not painted. Late September 1994—the culmination of all that came before. My searching must in the end come to this.

I retreated with her to the courtyard after a sampling of the paintings was paraded before our guests. A mist crept over the cobbled walls, slunk through the rosebushes and the statuary, curled round the pedestal of the stone fountain and toward us, beneath the broad English oak. I reached up my hand to smooth a loose tendril of her hair. "How can you bear it, *ma petite*? How can you bear to have them ogle you?"

Turning away. "Perhaps I'm used to it." She knew how to mollify me but did not do so. She had not, you see, for some time.

This angered me, more than the paintings. "It's beneath you. People misunderstand."

"Do they? Should I have added loincloths or perhaps fig leaves?"

"*Oui*. It's a start. If you were *barely* dressed, it would be better, a little less indiscreet—"

In a scathing tone, she recited, "'She was barely dressed, though, And the great indiscreet trees Touched the windows with their leaves . . .'" Catching my eyes. "'In malice, quite close.'"

"You're drunk."

"Yes." She laughed recklessly. "I should have taken it up sooner."

She'd been agitated—more than agitated, ill—since her meeting with Amanda. And she *had* been drinking too much tonight, an unusual thing for her, yet I knew she was less intoxicated than incensed. Gisèle's rage is the quiet kind, and thus easy to underestimate. It happens on the inside.

I drew her to me gently and kissed her forehead, cool as marble, and her hair that in Devon seemed always to smell of this garden—gone was the childish honey scent, she was rose vines and tart Oregon berry and mint. And she was utterly unmoved, stiff as a statue in my arms. "Tell me what's wrong, Gisèle."

"I have to go, Tristan. I have to explain to Mandy—to Nicola—somehow." Her voice broke on the words, and her eyes filled with tears and recriminations. "I have to try."

"Go?" The word bounced off of me as if off armor.

"Yes, go. Away from here."

Take Nicola away? It was beyond comprehension. "But go where? And live on what? This is the only home Nicola's ever known. Think of it, *ma petite*. You can't introduce your sister to your 'father.' How can you explain to Nicola that she has an aunt but no grandfather?"

"Stop it. I know all your arguments." And she began to cry then, helplessly.

"I will not let you go." I reached out to wipe the tears from her cheek. "I love you."

"Do you?" There was no joy there. No understanding. No invisible string for me to tug. "I don't know why. I've never known."

I grew irritated. "I don't need a why. I simply do. And you love me. That's not a lie, is it?" She shone in the moonlight. I thought of the way we had been, long ago . . . "You love me."

She sighed, gazing at the dirt beneath my feet. "Yes, I love you. Of course I do."

"And you will not leave?"

She arched up on tiptoe to kiss me, and I felt in her lips the duplicity.

It was then that we heard it: a shattering of glass that reverberated like a gunshot through the courtyard. Beyond her, on the terrace, Luke materialized as if on cue. But Gisèle had turned quickly, desperately, in the opposite direction. And when she turned back to me, her eyes were wide, horrified, the pupils dilating like black voids in a tropic sea. I felt the panic rise off her skin and stepped toward her, but she pushed me back. And then I knew what it was, the only thing that could make her look that way—it was my little Nicola. Behind the trunk of the tree, I could not see her. I thought in vain that she couldn't see me.

It all happened very quickly. Luke, his face full of shocked disbelief, turned like an automaton and retreated indoors. I heard Gisèle's voice, sharp and foreign, telling Nicola to go. There was a crunch of pebbles beneath her pattering feet on the path and the rustle of dogwood near the French doors as her nightdress brushed the branches.

I put my hands on Gisèle's arms to brace her, or to restrain her—I do not know which. But she made no move to follow her daughter, to offer explanations to Luke.

"She did not see me," I said without conviction.

Gisèle closed her eyes and bit her lip. "Who knows what she heard? She saw me *kiss* you." In a hollow, desolate voice. "She'll *know* it was you. She adores you." She said it like an accusation.

"A moment ago you wished to tell her."

"Not this way."

"You see, then, that I am right. She must not know. We'll think of a way to explain to her what she saw. Listen to me—"

"You mean we'll think of a way to lie to her. I'm done lying." Fiercely, "I'm done lying."

There was nothing to say. My hands dropped, or she turned away; I'm not sure who left whom first. But she walked away, and I watched her go. For the first time, I did not follow.

I went into a sitting room, to a sideboard and poured a cognac. I sat alone in the dark and calmly made plans.

I was tired of being trapped in this role of father and grandfather; I'd been a fool to let it go on so long. We'd leave the paintings to Luke. Let him sell them and make a false name for himself. I'd be glad to be rid of them. Even the threat of Amanda could not dim my new utopia. Will you believe I entertained notions of a tearful reunion? What had I been so afraid of? The statute of limitations on kidnapping must be up. Time erases all crimes.

I sat there for a long while wallowing in my delusions, growing cheerful on cognac, and asking God to bless me in this new endeavor. At some point we all pray, you see—no matter how unworthy our cause, no matter how poor our standing with God.

Gisèle, I knew, was in a fragile state. I needed to ensure she wouldn't say or do anything rash. I would, as I'd so often done, bring her tea and dope the tea with crushed sleeping pills. I went to the kitchen and prepared it. The hour had grown very late. The party had died. The house was calm and still; everyone was sleeping.

Except Gisèle. Her door was locked, but I saw light beneath it. Rather than knock, I went in the back way, traveling my familiar corridor with my mug of tea.

But as I approached the two-way mirror, something gave me pause. I had watched Gisèle and Nicola get ready for the party, but I saw now that I had not replaced its covering. How had I been so careless? And something was very, very wrong indeed; though the window was uncovered, I could not see in. It had been blackened from the other side. And it was only then that a finger of real alarm crept in. *She* must have covered it.

I let myself in through Gisèle's closet. I could hear her in the bath. Her bedcover was rumpled but not turned down. I straightened the folds idly, trying to rationalize the closed mirror. The panels were made to close; she may simply have closed them innocently. I would say nothing. I'd let her tell me.

She jumped when I entered, giving a startled cry so that I nearly spilled her tea. She moved as if to cover herself.

"*Qu'est-ce qu'il y a?* It's only me, *ma petite.* Everything's going to be fine, do you understand? I will make it fine. You must relax." I spoke soothingly, sitting beside her on the edge of the sunken tub. "Here. I've brought you tea."

She took it, and I saw that she was shaking. "I've just seen Luke." Her voice was hoarse, jumpy. "He thinks I'm in love with my father. As a result of that, he decided we ought to make love."

I frowned. "*Comment?*"

"That's how he will think of it."

I leaned toward her. "Has he hurt you?"

She sipped her tea and swallowed, sipped again. "Not as badly as I've hurt him." She sighed. "I've told him I'm leaving him. I can't bear to have him touch me again. I can't bear to do one more thing I don't want to do, Tristan. I couldn't bear it if it were Nicola. I couldn't bear for her to have so little respect for herself."

I frowned. "Yes, yes. Of course you must leave him. We'll tell Nicola the truth. We'll move someplace new and start again."

Quietly, she sipped her tea. Then, softly, "No, Tristan."

"*Pourquoi?* Because of Nicola? But I love Nicola; she loves me."

Gisèle tipped her head, and her expression was odd. She set her tea-cup on the ledge beside her, gave a slight shudder, and brought her arms once more to her chest.

"We can explain to her," I insisted, feeling panic rise. "She's getting older now. Old enough."

"Old enough?" Gisèle's gaze was very direct then, very dark. And then four simple words, but they told me everything. "Old enough for what?"

"But you can't mean—" I swallowed. "You think I would harm her?"

"I think you wouldn't think of it in that way, Tristan. You wouldn't mean to . . . exactly." She bit her lip, hard. "I don't think you would even know that it was happening. But I see the way you look at her sometimes. Since the start of the summer, I've seen it. I can't have you look at her that way." Gisèle closed her eyes, shaking her head. "I can't bear imag-ining it—if I *am* imagining it. I can't bear any of it anymore. Please, just go. Just go." She reached again for her tea, her fingers curled so tightly around the cup I thought she would crush it.

"You don't know what you're saying."

"I do." She gazed down at the warm liquid, mindlessly sipping. "Believe me, I do." There were tears in her eyes. "Even if you don't."

It was this . . . and seeing the vanity mirror so neatly shut—so neatly shut off to me—that filled me with rage. I went to open it but never in the end even touched it. For on the vanity lay an envelope, unsealed. Upon it a single initial had been scrawled: *"R."* And inside was a single piece of stationery.

*Please meet me tonight at the cabana. It will be safe to talk
there. I know it's late, but you barely sleep, and I have to see you.
Nicky saw me in the garden with Tristan tonight.*

I should have stopped there. If I had only stopped there, I might have
forgiven her. I might even have forgiven him for being her confidant. But
I did not stop. I read it all.

"Tristan."

I turned to face her and did not even try to conceal the letter in my hand.

And when we come to our tragic end, it is simply this: change had at last
intruded on the unchangeable. We had slipped in each other's hierarchy.
We knew each other.

"So you are staying the night in the cabana," I said coolly. "Shall I
pack your things?"

She said nothing; her eyes spoke volumes.

I turned from her, extracted a cosmetic case from her drawer and
began to fill it. I knocked a bottle of perfume from the vanity and did
not bother to pick it up. Perhaps it was true. I *was* drawn to Nicola. *Oui.*
Yes, I was, and this is what infuriated me. To be judged out of hand and
found guilty. Guilty of what? Loving her? The truth of it is truth enough.
Truth is beauty, beauty truth. She was growing up so very lovely. And I
knew I'd be drawn to drink again from the fount of innocence—a lech-
erous metaphor, but apt—from which Gisèle had fallen too far.

I gathered a nightdress from her lingerie chest.

You must understand, I didn't ask for this . . . I loved my Gisèle from
the instant I saw her. It happened she was at an age that raises eyebrows,
causes tongues to wag. I see now that the fact that I'd noticed her then
was no accident. She was at the beautiful, transcendent age people mistake for awkwardness: it is the colt before it learns to run. I turned now,
and it was as if Gisèle matured before my eyes. All at once she was used,
as Luke had never used her, aged as marriage and motherhood had not
aged her. But that she saw through me. That she had abandoned me and
loved another. That she had not ever been mine.

"You'll need a change of clothes," I said. "And shoes. Yes, shoes. They
would be noticed."

"'Noticed?'" She trailed after me, into the closet.

Clarity was never possible before; the haze of romantic daydreams had long protected me. I was not the real thing, but she had never felt worthy of the real thing. And I had allowed her to be less than whole. Her fall from grace was the simplest, most profound kind—the old, unoriginal kind—of knowledge. Self-knowledge. That is where the story goes wrong, you see. Knowledge is not without but within. And shame not the result but the thing that keeps us from it. I'd long exploited her shame, but all at once my innocent little darling, *ma petite* Gisèle was experienced. Aware. And with our guises fallen around our feet, she found only a dirty, perverse man and I found not the child I'd loved but a woman. Which of us hated the other more?

I clasped her overnight bag shut. "Shall we go?"

She ran from me. In her robe and bare feet, she ran through the closet passageway and down the stairs, familiar to her from those many trips to the cellar studio. I followed at a more sedate pace. When I reached the open air, I saw her disappearing across the grass. There was only the pool house in which to hide. The pool house where I never supposed she went, until I saw the paintings. In inclement weather she knew she could hide there, far from even my prying eyes. In her paintings I could see she'd gone there often, taking photographs before the long mirrors.

What, I wondered, had precipitated this sudden mad flight? Was it something in my expression? When I opened the door to the pool house and quietly closed it, I think she knew what I intended to do.

She murmured apologies. An appeasement. I knew this; it was like the kiss in the garden.

"Are you afraid of me, Gisèle?" I forced her toward the water. "Surely not of me."

Her eyes were hooded and heavy; she was weary. She shook her head no but said helplessly, "Yes."

"But why, *ma petite*?" I backed her toward the water, and it happened very quickly, very suddenly. I pushed her in. Her robe, knotted at the waist and crimson like blood, blossomed around her like a flower. She was lovely even then, in an abstract way. It was a very large pool, very deep at this end. Bryan Prescott had believed in the health benefits of swimming. Gisèle did not. She was floundering. I turned for the door and switched out the lights, so that we were plunged into blackness.

And she let out a cry then; it sounded like a cat fighting, deep-throated and terrified.

"Tristan!" she screamed, gurgling. "Help me!"

And you will have suspected this by now, I did not answer her.

I went to the cabana and closed the door. I unpacked her things, methodically.

I heard another shocked cry and more splashing, wild at first, gradually growing weaker. I didn't know it then, but she'd already taken her sleeping pills. I'd thus tripled the dose. She would be disoriented, in her muscles the deadened drugged ache through which even adrenaline cannot cut. All the time she knew I was listening. This pains me in retrospect. She still needed me, you see. But at the time it gave me only a queer satisfaction.

Then it was silent, and I knew she really had—at last—left me.

I felt very still inside. I left the cabana door ajar. Through the windows of the pool house, I could see a sickly, wan line on the horizon, and I made my way across the lawn, damp with dew.

It would seem she had gone out to the paintings and slipped. The next day it would seem so to me. I mourned; I raged. It was all a dreadful dream to me then, an imagining. Madness, you see, is not the oblivion it seemed to me as a child; it is . . . beguiling. And if I have learned nothing else, it is that we are but cogs in the wheel of our destinies and puppets to our illusions.

The fable comes to mind:

A scorpion and a frog meet on the bank of a wide stream. The scorpion asks the frog to carry him across on its back, and the frog asks, "But how do I know you won't sting me?"

The scorpion replies, quite rationally, "Because if I do, I will die, too."

This satisfies the frog, and they set out. But in midstream the scorpion stings him. With the onset of paralysis, the frog begins to sink. Knowing they both will drown, he has just enough time to gasp, "Why?"

Replies the scorpion, and I think—*non*, I know—it is with sadness and not a little bewilderment, "It is my nature."

EPILOGUE: ACADEMIC STUDY

THEY WERE IN ROBIN'S HOME. Situated on a spectacular mountain gorge, the great château was a stone masterpiece, which in spite of its numerous turrets and chimneys, arched windows and glorious porticoes, seemed to sprout organically from the rocky cliffs. Rimmed by the dark beauty of the woods and teetering on the brink of Lake Devon, it seemed not a presumptuous trespass on the wilds but a part of them.

Inside, the atmosphere was dry and cool. "For the art," he'd explained to Ashleigh on her first visit there. That seemed a lifetime ago now. It was hard to remember life before Robin. But how apt, she'd always thought, that Robin Dresden should inhabit rooms better suited to art than to people.

"You're jittery, Ashleigh love. What's wrong? Too much caffeine?"

She appraised him warily. "I'm not jittery, Robin. I feel guilty."

"How unusual."

"It's just that we're playing God, aren't we? You're used to that, I know, but it doesn't fit me so well."

"You only helped to write the ending to a story: a fiction, a work of art. You should be proud, love. I am proud of you."

"Only it's *not* a fiction." Her voice was flat. "And it's Tristan's story, not mine. I can't write the ending of another person's *life*."

"You did, I think."

"I thought it was for you. For 'closure.'"

"It *was* for closure."

"Not just for you, though."

His gaze was restless. "Listen to me, Ashleigh. Tristan wanted his story told—he *wanted* to confess. We didn't edit anything out. It's in his own words, verbatim, right up to the night he killed Gisèle. But he couldn't see that last entry through. How many of us, I wonder, have the vision to write the end of our own narratives?" An ill-tempered pause. "I felt an obligation to finish it."

"Well, I'm not sure that's what he had in mind when he made you executor of his estate." She gazed out the window without seeing, chewing the end of her pen. "And I can't help feeling we got it wrong. Something keeps bothering me."

"Your pronounced guilt complex." In spite of his tone, she could feel the weight of his regret, and after a moment he sighed. "For what it's worth, I understand what you're feeling. When I found his journal, I didn't want to read it. When I read it, I wanted to burn it. There was so much . . . so many . . ." His voice trailed off. "But in a strange way, it gave me peace. I understood him better than I ever had. Except for the *damned* last entry."

"'What happened that last night?'" Ashleigh quoted from memory. "'Gisèle's last night . . . It was destined to end in disaster, for it was born of disastrous beginnings.'"

"'Gisèle's party for Luke, for the paintings Luke had not painted. Late September 1994—'"

"'—The culmination of all that came before. My searching must in the end come to this.'"

Robin pounded the desk with his fist, sending the usual clutter flying. "Come to *what*?" A few papers wafted down to Ashleigh's feet. "Come to what?" he repeated, swiveling around in his chair. "After all she's been through, Amanda deserved more than that. My *daughter* deserves more than to fester over it her whole life, to play out that night again and again in her mind. Trying to fathom how the two people she'd loved most in the world came to *that* end."

She knew he was also talking about himself. "All right, agreed. But you really think it's going to help her to know the details?"

"It's not life's horrors that destroy you, Ashleigh. It's becoming *entrenched* in life's horrors. The human mind is a remarkably resilient thing; it's also prone to obsess over riddles. I don't want her mother's death to be a riddle to Nicola. I want her to grieve and move on."

"But I've written the end of his story, Robin, and never even met him. It doesn't seem fair."

"Do you think Tristan was innocent?"

"No." Ashleigh bit her lip. "No, I believe he killed her. At least he didn't save her." She fidgeted, toying with a rip in the knee of her jeans.

"All the evidence has been factored in. Gisèle's letter fell from Tristan's pocket. We have two witnesses to the scene in the garden. Nico saw traces of water in the tub. Lab tests give us the level of sleeping pills in Elle's system, as well as Luke's surreptitious DNA. The scrap of her robe on the stairs implies she was fleeing, and then there are Tristan's own dying admissions—" He broke off, but no one had interrupted him. It was silent.

"Maybe they argued and she slipped," Ashleigh said at last.

"Maybe. But then, as you say, he didn't save her."

"Well, why choose *me* to write the ending? You know how to write. It's hardly a typical assignment, even for you."

"Your experiences have given you a unique aptitude for this little morality tale. You have an understanding of Gisèle I can never hope to have." A sad, reflective tip of the head. "And you're a writer, in the true sense. With the ethics of a writer."

"Meaning none."

He smiled. "Meaning none beyond the story. The integrity of the story. You embraced Gisèle, became her. You embraced Tristan. For a time you became victim and perpetrator both. I believe you saw that last night as clearly as it could be seen." A pointed pause. "The End."

"'The notion of an end is always illusory,'" she replied.

"The very notion of a *story* is illusory, Ashleigh, but that doesn't negate its power. It's Tristan's story, he started it, and all stories must come to a finite end. That is their beauty."

Ashleigh sighed. She held his eyes. "I can't help thinking how different it would be if the letter had reached you. She'd be alive now. So would he."

Robin nodded but said nothing; his jaw tightened, and his long fingers drummed on the arm of his chair.

Ashleigh changed the subject. "What if Amanda decides to release Tristan's story to the public, or to the police? Splash it all over the cover of *People*? Who knows, she may actually disapprove of art fraud."

"What could she gain from its exposure? The publicity would be painful to her and worse for Nicola. She'd never want that. And quite frankly"—with a shrug—"no one would believe it. No one ever believes the truth."

"And the art fraud?"

"I don't think Amanda's going to fret about any crime against Tristan going unpunished."

Ashleigh gazed around her. This room was full of the spoils of war: Tristan's paintings. Originals, not copies. On one wall was van Gogh's *Butterflies and Poppies,* painted just before he shot himself. The blossoms were overlarge and overbright, too heavy to be supported by their frail stems. And the butterflies weren't the fragile, benign creatures one considers them to be, but rather carnivorously feeding. It was a good analogy for life, Ashleigh thought. Nothing's ever quite what it seems to be.

It seemed to her that all the paintings had assumed characteristics of the story, become the characters. Glowing in the lamplight was a sketch of a nude, her face turned away from her audience. An unwilling exhibitionist, she made one an unwilling voyeur. Gisèle. On the other walls, too: a young girl who reminded her of Nicola. Lovely. Smart. Questioning. It was a Renoir. And on another, Degas: a bearded man with rather dead eyes. *The Collector,* it was called. Tristan?

Ashleigh found Robin gazing at her and knew he'd read her thoughts. *How can you surround yourself with these paintings?* For they were not simply paintings, they were living things.

His face brightened, and he let out an exclamation of triumph, as if to distract her. "I think I've convinced Amanda to take the money at last."

"Tristan's blackmail?"

"Yes, the Sparbuch account, with interest. It will change her life. It must change, of course."

Because she's part of yours now. "She's still not speaking to Luke?"

"I wouldn't blame her, but no, I believe there are diplomatic talks in the works."

"They're not together—"

"Friends. A tenuous friendship, I understand. Naturally, he'd like it to be more."

"I almost feel sorry for him. He was duped by everyone." She toyed with her pen. "How did you know that painting of Marc's would break him down?"

"The rape scene, disappearing and reappearing like a ghost? A neat trick, that. A mechanism within the wall. Well, the truth is, I didn't know. But it's difficult to be confronted with yourself, and the guilty crave confession. It's a perverse quirk of nature."

"Speaking of which, I ought to be leaving the confessional now."

He gave her a slight smile. Very slight. That said she should not go.

"Is Luke going to fight for custody of Nicola?" she asked.

"I think not. He'll visit her, of course."

"And the paintings?"

"His signature came off with water."

"Leave it to you."

"They'll be exhibited as Gisèle wished, but not sold. Do you know Amanda's agreed to exhibit them as the Gisèle Paintings? She understood that on some level her sister needed to leave Karen behind."

"Well, the Karen Paintings doesn't quite have the same ring." Ashleigh paused. "But in releasing the paintings, wasn't she also releasing 'Gisèle'?"

Robin gazed at her thoughtfully, then nodded. "Yes."

"So who was she in the end?"

"I like to think she was herself. Just herself."

Ashleigh's expression was reflective. "She was always looking at herself through someone else's eyes. The paintings are searching for something she'd never had. Confidence. Comfort in her own skin. I think she looked at her surface and wondered what people saw in it."

"That's why you were the one to write her story," he said quietly. "You understand."

Ashleigh liked to be the only one to understand Robin, and he knew it too well. She dropped her gaze, moving on restively. "How is Nicola doing?"

"Better. Much better." His eyes shone with affection. "She's in Seattle now, for a time, with Amanda. And sleeping without the light on,

I understand." Robin gave her one of his rare smiles—the kind she'd grown to covet but in this case was happy to share.

"She's a very strong little girl."

"She is. Though, sadly, I think the little girl is gone. Too soon, as always. Awareness comes too soon. But if you want a different ending, look to her. It's still being written in her."

From where Ashleigh sat, there was no ground to be seen, only sky. No lake, or woods, or people. No real world at all. "Ending or no ending, Tristan will haunt her all her life."

"Of course he will. She loved him." He continued in a brooding tone, "But with time she'll strike an uneasy balance. She'll love Tristan and hate him, too. With Gisèle it was the same. And the same is true for me." A pause, careless. "Haven't you ever loved something you ought to hate?"

Ashleigh rested her chin on her fist and gazed at him. "Yes, I have."

Robin gave her a prescient glance, a signature half smile. "Ashleigh." He spoke gently. "Have we circled the point long enough? Tell me what's on your mind besides writerly ethics."

"All right. Here's what makes me jittery, Robin. Tristan had to die, didn't he? That's the inevitable end. The one *you* wrote."

He appraised his most precocious pupil. "Would you rather I died instead, darling? He brought the gun. That was his choice."

"It had no bullets in it. It was suicide."

"I gave him the chance to go to France, to live there and die. But he came for Nicola."

"You *knew* he would."

"I hoped not."

"But you knew he would. Gisèle knew it."

A silence. His voice faltered. "Yes."

"And so instead of getting Nicola out of there that night, you let him come—as you knew he would—and Marc was waiting with a gun loaded with real bullets."

"All right, yes." Sharply, "But he was supposed to shoot to wound, if necessary, not to kill. He had a gun only to keep Tristan from forcibly carting her off. How could I know he'd come there with a gun of his own? I wanted Tristan to *show* himself. I wanted to trap him. Is that what you want to hear? I wanted him to prove to me what he was, because in spite of everything, I didn't believe it. And yes. When I saw him there with Nicola, I wanted to kill him myself."

"Well, I don't . . . I really don't blame you for that."

"You seem awfully bloody determined to blame me for something."

"Fine. Here goes. I don't just *think* we got it wrong, Robin. I *know* we did."

"Did we?"

"We forgot Luke."

"I've certainly tried."

"No. We forgot that Luke went out there that night. Nicola saw him walking to the pool house at three-thirty, remember?" She watched him carefully. "I was asking Chelsea about the party, and she said she hadn't noticed anything unusual—only that afterward you had her pretend *she'd* seen Luke that night, to protect Nicola. And when you confronted him with it, he claimed he went there for the paintings. When Gisèle came out of the cabana, he turned and left again."

Robin stared up at the ceiling, spinning his signet ring in agitation. "My God. You're right, Ashleigh. I'd utterly forgotten him. . . ."

"Chelsea said she believed him. He was nervous about the implications, but sincere."

"I believe he was, yes."

She went on uncertainly, "But then that means he saw her out at the cabana *alive*."

"Which means she'd delivered her letter. And she wasn't running from Tristan, she was waiting for me." He held her eyes, and she managed to hold his. "Ashleigh. For Christ's sake. You think it was me."

"No," she said, too quickly. "I mean, not really." She swallowed. "It's just that Gisèle may have been ready to leave Tristan, but not you. And you have other . . . interests."

He laughed aloud, but his tone was admonishing, "I didn't want to be *rid* of her. And I never got her letter—"

"I have only your word for that," Ashleigh pointed out.

He laughed again, settling back in his chair. "All right. Then how did Amanda end up with it?"

"Marc gave it to her, remember? *He* claimed it had fallen from Tristan's pocket. And he works for you."

"I see." Robin's dark eyes sparked. "I have to say, I'm impressed with your courage in confronting me. While I'm on this mad killing spree, I could easily do away with you."

She flushed. "Just tell me you didn't do it, Robin. You didn't kill Gisèle, frame Tristan, and then kill *him*—or have him killed—when you had the chance."

He leaned across the desk and said intently, "I didn't do it, Ashleigh."

"Well." She shifted in her chair. "All right. But our ending still doesn't work now. If Luke saw her alive, it changes everything."

"So Luke didn't see her alive. He saw her, but she was already dead. Maybe he saw her floating in the pool and got the hell out of there. Coward that he is."

"I don't think he's cool enough to keep his head. I think he loved her. Fool that he is."

"Ashleigh." He was angry, she could tell. He paused a moment to defuse it. "I'm convinced Tristan killed Gisèle. The details are open to interpretation. We've created our perception of the truth. That's all reality ever is."

There was a cursory knock, and Marc Kreicek entered. He'd probably been listening at the door, Ashleigh thought. He had a habit of showing up at awkward moments, but on this occasion she was grateful. She'd made a complete fool of herself, not for the first time, and was happy for an excuse to leap from the wreckage.

Marc flashed an appreciative smile at her, and she tolerated it gracefully enough, bracing herself for the pretense of his kiss hello, a thing worsened by the European insistence on assailing both cheeks. The man made her skin crawl. She stiffened as he leaned down and the medallion he always wore swung forward, an eight-pointed starburst that played before her eyes in the sunlight. It was a valuable piece of jewelry, a symbol of some sort, a reminder of Prague. "The black star," he called it, though it was not black at all but platinum with a diamond center. As he straightened, it disappeared. Ashleigh made her excuses and got up to go.

"Ashleigh," said Robin, "we'll talk about this later, all right?" He gave her a meaningful glance, adding with affectionate exasperation, "I want to clear up any doubts you may still have."

She nodded but rolled her eyes, mumbling something incoherent that ended in ". . . let's just forget about it." Robin's eyes followed her as she left. The fact was, she was too smart for her own good. For the first time, he doubted the wisdom of what he had done.

It hadn't been entirely rational to write Tristan's last chapter for him. An artistic, idealistic urge—perhaps not even a kind one. A glue for all the lives left shattered? The truth, Robin knew, was never neat and rarely kind. And it had certainly been a risk to enlist the talents of his most exigent student to do it. But he liked to challenge her.

And she certainly liked to challenge him.

Could I have gotten it wrong? K slid a few papers across the desk to him, the last in an avalanche of paperwork to do with the settling of Tristan's estate. Robin picked up a pen to sign, giving the document a perfunctory reading, but all the while it nagged at him: *What if Luke wasn't lying? If Elle* was *alive out at the cabana, then her letter should have reached me . . .*

But the truth was, it couldn't possibly have.

A final tragic irony he had forgotten. His date that night had switched rooms on a whim; they'd stayed in the room intended for Marc and Elyse. Even if Gisèle had been able to slip the letter under his door, it would have reached not *him* but K. And what would it mean to him?

Now that doubt had been allowed in, a swarm of if-onlys and what-ifs descended like flies feasting on the last of the carcass. *What would the letter have meant to K?* A pleading letter in the middle of the night from the longtime object of his desire? He'd have welcomed it; he would have gone to her—only to find he was not who she expected at all.

But surely he'd know from the contents that the letter wasn't intended for him . . .

Wouldn't he? Robin's mind ran back over Gisèle's words, memorized now. They had kept their relationship a secret from everyone. It would have driven Marc as mad as Tristan, had he known. He'd pined for her for years. No one made a wine of rejection, but for K it was a particular poison. He felt that the world and everyone in it owed him something, and he wasn't going to give up till he collected.

Gisèle had confessed as much to Robin years ago. She'd chased after Marc to make Robin jealous and regretted it ever after. That was the summer she'd met Luke, the same summer she'd become pregnant with Nicola. Even Tristan had written of their "brief, intense affair." Luke's DNA tests *proved* Robin's paternity—but K may actually have believed Nicola was his. If he had received the letter that night, he would have read it as a declaration of Elle's love for *him*. Only to be rejected again.

"What's the matter?" K asked impatiently. "The bill of sale looks standard to me."

Robin shook his head abstractedly and in the process shook off his suspicions. "It's nothing." He'd known Marc all his life. He was petty, jealous, vain, and amoral, but he wasn't a murderer. Robin had always been able to rely on K. He had no qualms about anything.

Robin signed the paper before him, and stared dumbly at his own signature.

His pen had skipped on the first letter. The sweeping *R* was open at the top, just like the hurried scribble of Elle's *R* on the envelope of her letter. Her writing was so familiar to him he hadn't looked at it closely; they'd often addressed each other by initial in letters, and she always left her *R* slightly open at the top. But her *R*, he realized now, looked very much like a *K*.

No qualms about anything . . .

Could it be that Tristan was guilty of no more than he confessed: slipping Gisèle sleeping pills so that he might touch her? He'd have felt responsible for her death, though he had not drowned her. Now, conveniently, Tristan was gone. And Marc Kreicek had killed him. *Had he also killed Elle?*

Robin gazed up at his oldest friend, and he frowned.

CLEAR WATER SEALED OVER HER like the lid of a coffin. Blindly, Gisèle fought to reach the surface only to plummet again; there was no edge, nothing solid to cling to. She'd had a phobic aversion to water all her life, and now it came like a patient predator upon its prey, reaching for her, tugging her under. She swallowed, tasted chlorine, and rose again to the glassy surface, coughing and spitting, sucking in air.

Gisèle screamed into the blackness, dimly aware of a shadowy presence above. She knew he heard her, just as she knew that no one else would. In desperation she thought of Nicola . . . of Mandy. She screamed, "Help me!"

The drugged dullness in her brain spread through her body; pins and needles ran up and down her arms, and her heart thudded like a drum within the white noise of her own struggling. Slowly, the drum weakened, receding, and through the enveloping darkness she saw a small flash of light, an eight-pointed starburst radiating from a brilliant center. It played before her eyes . . .

Unconsciousness seeped over her like a salve. For a moment Gisèle had the irrational sense that she might linger there, underwater, in the chasm between dreams and reality.

Marc Kreicek knelt by the side of the pool, her letter still in his hand. "You shouldn't have toyed with me, Gisèle." He spoke to the water; it was tranquil now. "How you toyed with us all . . . Making us want you."

And then he rose and walked away without a backward glance. He did not like to look back. It was a shame to destroy such a beautiful thing.

ACKNOWLEDGMENTS

Like every novel this one has a story between the lines; I want to thank those who know it best and without whom the rest would not be possible.

I've had the great pleasure of working with Carole DeSanti, Editor Extraordinaire, whose belief in me and my world—and knowledge of how to make us both better—exceeded all my fabled notions of the editor/author relationship. Laura Tisdel: thank you for your tremendous insight, wit and energy for this project. You made it such fun! Many thanks to my copy editor, Maureen Sugden, for your sharp eyes and enlightening asides. Jaya Micelli, for the beautiful cover art and Nancy Resnick for interior design. Veronica Windholz for coordinating it all. Thanks, also, to Chris Russell and Brandon Kelley.

I am indebted to Elyse Cheney, for her belief in my work and savvy representation of it. Thanks also to Nicole Steen and Hannah Elnan.

I'm profoundly grateful to all those involved with ABNA, the bottle that released this genie and started all the magic for me. At Amazon: Kyle Sparks, Aaron Martin, and Jeff Belle. At Penguin: Molly Barton, Nancy Sheppard, and a very special thank you to Tim McCall—who gave me the two most exciting phone calls of my life. Thank you all for your belief in books and in writers. I'd also like to thank all those who shared the journey with me, voted and expressed their support. You changed my life.

Within my inner circle: My deepest thanks to Eric Ryder, whose personal leap of faith and generosity humbles me. This book would not have been possible without you. I'm overwhelmed by the support of my family, who never once suggested a sensible career choice. Your love transforms me . . . (A special mention to my Aunt Char, who has read every one of the *many* versions of this manuscript.) Many thanks to my favorite professor and dear friend, Rob Swigart, for being such a stubborn proponent of me and my writing. To my high school English teacher, Wayne deGennaro, who took liberties with the syllabus on my behalf. Nils Peterson, for your poetry and passion. Michael Neff, for your friendship and fabulous Algonkian Writer's Conference, which gave me confidence and camaraderie when I needed it most. Miek Coccia, for the !!! email, barhopping in the Village, and being my first ally in the world of publishing.

I am grateful for the support of so many friends, who tolerate my odd hours and strange dinner conversation and general quirkiness with such good humor! I particularly wish to mention Elizabeth Olcott, Bill Craig, Mel Crosby, Diane Matuszewski, and Laura Bowly, my oldest friend and sharer of childhood dreams. To the wonderful residents of Yountville—my home and the most charming place on the planet, outside of Devon—who have shown such support for this book. In particular, thanks to the crew at Bouchon. How could I manage to write without you, the late-night menu and my cocktail?

Lastly, by way of inspiration: the Impressionists and their lovely works, from which I took the chapter titles. A. S. Kline for his brilliant, bold translation of Rimbaud's "First Evening" and generous consent to let it appear here. Gisele's funeral poem is extracted from the beautiful "Death Is Nothing at All" by Canon Henry Scott-Holland (1847–1918). The version used here came to my attention through its use in the memorial service for the inimitable British actor Jeremy Brett. To Reed and to Murphy, my beloved muses. And finally, to all those who googled "Devon, Washington." It exists for us.